Praise for

A
Beautiful
WAY TO
DIE

'From movie star glamour to the rotten core of fame, I couldn't put this down. A beautiful way to spend your time.'
Louise Hare

'Dark and gripping... Eleni's compelling story may be set in the past but it is just as relevant today.'
Nikki Smith

'Hauntingly beautiful and meticulously researched... I was utterly gripped. I will now read every book this author writes.'
Lesley Kara

'Captivating and cruel. Unsettling. Both dazzling and devastating... Where Hollywood's golden age meets its darkest demons.'
Clare Whitfield

'Shocking, moving, furious and ultimately hopeful, it's a novel that will stay with me for a long time.'
Nicola Rayner

'A dark, evocative tale that is utterly addictive.'
Victoria Dowd

'Outstanding... A brilliant skewering of the Hollywood dream machine but also a compelling thriller with a beautiful twist to die for.'
Trevor Wood

'A totally addictive thriller set against the glitz of 1950s Hollywood.'
Frances Quinn

'Evocative, tense, seductive. Combines Hollywood razzmatazz with murder and deception in one compelling star package.'
Tammy Cohen

'A gorgeously dark slice of Hollywood noir... Perfection!'
Louise Mumford

'Intriguing, insightful and unforgettable.'
Emma Christie

'Immerse yourself in fifties Hollywood behind the silver screen in Eleni Kyriacou's immensely evocative and entertaining novel.'
Tom Benjamin

'A pacy, addictive noir thriller... The characters are complex and nuanced, the scene-setting is vivid, and the writing taut.'
Gill Paul

'Compelling, intriguing and full of heart.'
Penny Batchelor

'Beneath the glitz and glamour of 1950s Hollywood lay a dark underbelly, which Kyriacou exposes with panache in this intricately plotted mystery... The author's beautifully drawn and complex characters are so compelling, they felt utterly real.'
Louise Fein

'Dripping with glitz and glamour... It's packed with twists and turns and kept me guessing right up until the end.'
Nicola Gill

'A twisty, riveting read which starts as a mystery and turns into a tale of strong women who refuse to let their lives be dictated by the men in power – whatever the consequences.'
Caroline Bishop

'*A Beautiful Way to Die* manages to be both a page-turning, exciting, glamorous thriller and a clever commentary on the dark underbelly of Hollywood and its treatment of women. I loved every minute.'
Charlotte Levin

'A darkly elegant story from a master storyteller.'
Susan Allott

A
Beautiful
WAY TO
DIE

A
Beautiful
WAY TO
DIE

ELENI KYRIACOU

HEAD
of ZEUS

An Aries Book

First published in the UK in 2025 by Head of Zeus,
part of Bloomsbury Publishing Plc

9 7 5 3 1 2 4 6 8

A catalogue record for this book is available from the British Library.

ISBN (HB): 9781837930395; ISBN (XTPB): 9781837930401
ISBN (E): 9781837930371

Cover design: Simon Michele | Head of Zeus

Typeset by Siliconchips Services Ltd UK

Printed and bound in Great Britain by
CPI Group (UK) Ltd, Croydon, CRO 4YY

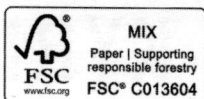

MIX
Paper | Supporting
responsible forestry
FSC
www.fsc.org   FSC® C013604

Bloomsbury Publishing Plc
50 Bedford Square, London, WC1B 3DP, UK
Bloomsbury Publishing Ireland Limited,
29 Earlsfort Terrace, Dublin 2, DO2 AY28, Ireland

HEAD OF ZEUS LTD
5–8 Hardwick Street
London, EC1R 4RG

To find out more about our authors and books
visit www.headofzeus.com

For product safety related questions contact productsafety@bloomsbury.com

*For Mia, when you're a lot older,
love from your yiayia x*

PROLOGUE

At night, when we're strapped to our beds, the lights have clicked off and the screams have settled into sleepy moans, that's when I see it. The Hollywood sign. I close my eyes and picture the towering white letters winking down at me through the violet-sore sky. That one word: H-O-L-L-Y-W-O-O-D. Promising so much, stealing everything.

And now here I am, in this place of wild women, where the rats grow fat as my hope wastes away. Where orderlies pinch and slap at whim, and if you retaliate you'll disappear for hours – days perhaps – and come back broken and spent. Disobedient women are punished here, just as they are out there. They dragged Jean away last week because she'd thrown a cup at Matron. I haven't seen her since.

I've stopped complaining about being tied down at night. There's one nurse who, when she's on duty, leaves my buckles a little loose. What does she want? Is it a trap? I don't know who's good or bad anymore, and yet I'm grateful for her flashes of kindness.

Today was Matron's birthday. I watched through the bars as an orderly pinned a large grey sheet to the wall of the nurses' station. Then a sound from my other life made me jump: the familiar clack of film rolling through a projector. Distorted music boomed and everyone rushed up behind me, pushing to see whatever they could.

As the picture sprang to life on the wall, the first words writ large, with an extravagant flourish, were his name – above the title, of course. His agent would've made sure of that. A few women started shouting and laughing, excited as they reeled off the cast of famous actors. I gripped the bars throughout, ignoring the shoves and pokes at my back, keeping my spot as the story unfurled. Every movement he made, every line he spoke, I drank it all in, mesmerised. That face, that smile, as devastating as the first day I saw him. A glance from him and you can come undone.

During a misjudged musical number, I turned to Nancy who was wedged next to me.

'I know him,' I whispered.

She looked at me and laughed. 'Of course you do.'

'No, I *know* him.'

'It's Max Whitman, you idiot – everyone knows him.'

I started to say something, but the whole cast began tap-dancing as if their lives depended on it. To hell with it. Who'd believe me anyway?

But the truth is I *do* know him. I know that he likes his martinis strong and his women weak. That he has a birthmark, the shape of a crescent, on the inside of his arm. That he owns the world yet is terrified of losing it all. And I know that when he yearns for something, nothing will stand in his way. He's destroyed people like this.

2

Up on the screen, I watched as he embraced his leading lady for their final kiss. As he tilted his head, I tilted mine and stared at his ridiculously straight nose, those elegant cheekbones, the perfectly dimpled chin. Then I remembered what he'd looked like, the last time I'd seen him, the night of the Oscars party. And the nausea rose in me again. The chaos, the screams, the blood.

During the dark hours when I cannot sleep, the memory of what happened that night prowls my bedside like a hungry tiger. I daren't move in case it pounces. Maybe this is what will drive me mad in the end, the fear that I will open the door to that night and lose myself forever.

But this can't be how my scene ends. No. My story isn't over yet. There are scores to be settled, secrets to be told, players to be destroyed. First, I need to get out.

CHAPTER ONE

Ealing Studios, London
July 1954

Stella Hope checked her watch and lit her third Lucky Strike of the morning. She'd brought twelve packs with her from Hollywood and was down to the last one. It was only half past seven but her shoulders were already tight and her temper rising. Johnny hadn't turned up. He'd promised he'd do her face this morning, said he'd cleared it with the union. Where was he?

She took a long drag of her cigarette, straightened her back in the make-up chair and glanced at the people rushing around her. How had it come to this? Back home, she'd had her own dressing room, an assistant and a little privacy. But not here. Here in London, they were all equal. Apparently. Even an Oscar-nominated actress like herself had to sit on display while she was primped and prodded.

'Excuse me… Stella?'

A hesitant, willowy woman in a red wrap-dress appeared by her side.

'Yes?' said Stella. 'I'm Miss Stella Hope.' Was nobody ever going to respectfully call her 'Miss Hope' again?

'Hello,' the woman said, holding out her hand. 'I'm Maggie. Johnny's not well – I'm covering for him.'

'*You're* a make-up artist?'

Maggie nodded, her hand left hanging in the air.

Stella finally accepted it, bestowing a half-hearted shake while she gave her a long up-down stare. Then she blew smoke into the air and said, 'Well, I'm glad to see they let women do the job here. At Star Studios, it was men-only for years.'

'Well, there's only me,' said Maggie, placing her sturdy vanity case on the trolley next to the makeshift dressing table. She flipped the clasp and pulled up the tan leather lid. 'I've been Johnny's assistant for ages, but they've just recently allowed me to run jobs by myself. The union finally agreed.'

'Well, good for you,' said Stella, as she watched three step-like tiers pop out of each side of Maggie's case. Brushes, sponges, eyeshadows, pencils, lipsticks – an Aladdin's cave of possibilities. 'Are you any good?' she asked, her soft Greek accent audible. It had more or less disappeared over the years, but re-emerged occasionally, especially when she was nervous or asserting herself.

Maggie laughed. 'Yes, I'm good. And I know it's a big day for you, and I promise the results will be wonderful.'

Stella nodded.

'I'm glad to hear it,' she said. 'Because I'm used to the best, you know.' She took another leisurely drag of her cigarette. 'You've heard of Dottie Ponedel?'

'Marlene Dietrich's make-up artist?' asked Maggie, unpacking some pots of cream.

'And Judy Garland's,' said Stella. 'Well, she did my face

once, too. I've had my pick of make-up artists, costume designers and even directors. Back in Hollywood.'

'Really?' said Maggie, with a smile.'Back in Hollywood...' She ran her finger along the eyeshadows and plucked a few compacts and brushes for that morning's work. Then she selected some panstick and lipstick.

Stella flicked her cigarette ash into a saucer. 'Yes,' she said, 'before they sent me to this godforsaken place. No offence.'

'None taken,' said Maggie. 'I'd choose Hollywood over Ealing any day. Shall we get the cold cream on?'

Stella nodded, left her ciggie burning in the saucer and leaned back.

'Oh, I almost forgot,' she said, sitting up again. She opened the cupboard under the dressing table mirror. 'Would you mind, darling?'

Maggie bent down to see what was inside and let out a delighted laugh. 'Champagne!'

'Why not?' said Stella, smiling for the first time that morning. 'And not just any champagne – Dom Pérignon. I ask Fortnum's to deliver a chilled one every now and then, on days I need a perk. There are glasses there, too. Would you be an angel and pour?'

Maggie took the ice bucket from the cupboard, held a small cloth over the cork and opened it with a gentle pop.

'Johnny sometimes has a drop too,' said Stella. 'So if you want a drop...'

'Oh, no thank you,' said Maggie, pouring her a glass.

'Let's get the cold cream on,' said Stella, 'then I'll have some.'

Maggie smeared a thick layer of cream over Stella's face

and watched as the actress leaned back in the make-up chair. With her eyes shut, she slowly reached out for her glass.

'Here you are,' said Maggie, laughing as she carefully handed her the drink. 'Your little pick-me-up, madam.'

'Well, I hope it's freshly brewed,' joked Stella, suddenly in a better mood.

Her hand was steady – it was her first performance of the day, sipping the bubbles without looking. She made quick work of it, and once she'd drained the glass, Maggie took it from her and placed it back on the tray.

Then she set to work. Using a soft, damp muslin cloth, she gently wiped the cream off Stella's face: from chin to cheek, the nose area, carefully around the eyes, then the forehead last. Upward sweeps, of course.

'You're much gentler than Johnny,' said Stella. 'I don't know how many times I've had to say *no downward strokes, Johnny – ever!* You'd think he'd know. It's not as if any of us are getting any younger. Men just don't understand.'

Maggie began to pat Stella's skin dry with a soft towel.

'You know what it's like,' continued Stella, 'trying to fight off the years. It's just what this business does to us. To women anyway.'

'Oh, I know,' said Maggie. 'I was forty-two last week.'

'Well, I'm not quite *that* age yet!'

'Oh, I didn't mean…'

Stella shifted in her chair. 'I'm not even forty, darling. Well, not for a while anyway.' She was actually forty-one, but nobody need know.

Maggie's face dropped and she stopped what she was doing, shaking her head.

'Oh dear, I've upset you now,' she said. 'I'm so sorry. The truth is, Stella... Miss Hope... I'm a bit nervous – I've been on tenterhooks all morning.'

Stella frowned. 'What do you mean?' she said impatiently. 'I thought you said you were good at this?'

'I am,' said Maggie. 'I'm one of the best. But... well, I'm also a fan.'

'Of *me*?'

Maggie nodded. 'A huge fan. I've seen every film you've made. I've loved you for years.'

Stella's face lit up.

'It's such an honour to be doing this today,' continued Maggie. 'But I think my nerves have made me speak out of turn. I'm sorry, Miss Hope. Truly.'

Stella smiled. 'Nonsense, nonsense, darling,' she said. 'And enough of this "Miss Hope". Call me Stella. Now, tell me. Which of my films is your favourite?'

And so they started chatting while Maggie prepared Stella's skin. It was lovely to talk about herself again. Ten minutes later, Stella glanced at her watch.

'Goodness – now let's discuss this screen test,' she said. 'We're due on set in an hour. Will we have time?'

'Don't worry,' said Maggie. 'I've been briefed. You're playing two roles – a mother and a daughter, that's right? For *My True Life*. The mother is early fifties, the daughter twenty-five.'

My True Life was one of Ealing's more serious social-realism films. If Stella pulled this off, it could be a way back for her. The producer and director had seemed less convinced, but after weeks of cajoling, she'd worn them down and they'd agreed to let her test for it.

'It was my idea, you know,' said Stella, smiling, 'to play both roles. I went into that meeting room full of men in suits to plead my case. I made them listen. They were all sitting around that famous round table, and Michael Balcon was there, too. It's never been done before. The English accents I can deal with – I've been doing American for years – but can I pass for twenty-five?'

'Of course,' said Maggie, not missing a beat. 'We'll do the daughter first. I've already pre-selected some shades for your approval, look.'

Stella glanced at the soft pastels.

'Wonderful!' she said. 'Johnny never prepares anything.'

She lifted her heart-shaped face to the large rectangular mirror in front of her, which was surrounded on each side by bright white light bulbs, examining her skin with a critical eye. Possibly softening just a little around that fine jawline, but with clever shading and the right lighting, Stella Hope was still a beauty. But *twenty-five*?

'Maggie, a dewy look, I think. What do you say?' she asked. 'Not too matte? And nothing harsh. I like the Pink Blush for nails and lips.'

'Exactly what I had in mind,' said Maggie, as she set to work. After a few minutes of silence between the two of them, she asked, 'Do you miss it? Hollywood?'

'Well, of course,' said Stella, letting out a weary sigh. 'Being a star in England just isn't the same. But in the end, it wasn't up to me.'

She held out her hand for the mirror to examine Maggie's work so far: a pale foundation, light enough to lift her skin a little, and Elizabeth Arden Eight Hour Cream on her cheekbones for a dewy look.

'Lovely,' she said leaning back into the chair again.

Maggie resumed her work.

'What the studio wants the studio gets,' Stella continued.

'I still don't see why you had to leave, though,' said Maggie, shaping Stella's eyebrows in a soft, warm shade of brown.

'The press blamed me for everything,' Stella said. 'Max's accident, his injuries.'

'But it wasn't your fault,' said Maggie, a note of injustice in her voice. 'I mean, you were in the car too, weren't you? And wasn't he the one driving?'

'Yes, but unlike him, I came away unscathed,' said Stella. 'His fans never forgave me. Now, had I died? Well, we would have cleaned up at the box office!'

Maggie gasped. 'Don't say that!'

'It's true.' She laughed. 'Then the studio was furious, because once he'd had plastic surgery for his broken jaw and fractured cheekbone, and recuperated, I said I still wanted a divorce. It was the final straw. They wanted a reunion – they said it could make us a fortune – but I was adamant. As soon as I'd finished my scenes on *Queen of Desire*, they made me leave. They didn't even let me see the final cut. By then, Ealing had expressed an interest, so Star Studios were happy to loan me out, and here I am. They can do what they want. You know what these contracts are like.'

She reached out her hand and pointed at the empty champagne glass.

'Just another small one, Maggie, to set me straight.'

Maggie poured a splash and handed it to her and she downed it in one.

'The funny thing is,' Stella continued, 'they were

convinced the crash and the divorce would finish off both of our careers. We *were* Hollywood's Golden Couple, after all. But the surgeons did a great job – he may no longer look perfect, but he has this brooding quality about him now – and he's reinvented himself as a "serious" actor, in earnest films.' She handed Maggie her glass. 'I, on the other hand, am stuck here... again, no offence intended.'

'None taken,' said Maggie. 'Nails, while your face sets?'

Stella put her hands out and Maggie pulled up a stool, sat and began to quickly, expertly paint Stella's nails with a first coat of Pink Blush polish.

'You know, Maggie,' said Stella. 'I have a good feeling about today. Will you run through my lines with me? I think we have time, and I just want to give it my absolute best shot. I mean, this could be—'

'Stella Hope?' It was Peter, the mail boy. 'Excuse me, are you Stella Hope?'

'Of course she is,' said Maggie, rolling her eyes.

'Your letters, miss.'

Stella waved her wet nails, so Maggie took the small bundle of envelopes.

'Anything interesting?' she asked.

Maggie rifled through them. 'All fan letters, I think,' she said. She pulled one out from the bottom. 'This one's got an American stamp. Hollywood postmark.'

'Really?' asked Stella. 'Open it, would you?'

Maggie took her metal hairdressing comb and slipped the sharp tail under the flap.

'Take it out,' said Stella, 'or you'll have to do my nails all over again.'

Opening the envelope, Maggie couldn't help but read it. She stared at the letter, then at Stella.

'Well? What is it?' asked Stella.

Slowly, Maggie handed it to her.

Stella took the single sheet of paper, read it, then twisted away from Maggie. She gasped as she leaned over the letter, clutching it so tightly her nails were now ruined.

After a few seconds she flattened it out on her lap and re-read it. The words, written in a heavy hand in blue pencil, lurched across the page.

$50,000 CASH
OR I SEND THESE PHOTOS TO THE PRESS
WAIT FOR INSTRUCTIONS

Stella turned the sheet over again and again, frantically searching for a hint as to who had written it. Nothing. She snatched the envelope from Maggie's hand to do the same, and a small grey square fell out onto the floor. Maggie bent down to retrieve it, had her hand on it, when Stella bolted forward, scrabbling at Maggie's feet.

'Give it to me!' Stella shouted, on her knees now.

She snatched it away, but Maggie had already seen it: a photo of a naked girl in a shocking pose. It had been taken years ago, and the flashlight had bleached out her features a little, but yes. It was her. It was Stella Hope.

Stella's face collapsed. 'How... I... I... what...'

Jessie, the wardrobe girl walked past slowly and stared at Stella, who was still kneeling, sticky pink nail polish all over her hands. Maggie turned her back to Jessie, shielding Stella in the process.

'Shall we go somewhere private?' Maggie whispered.

Stella stumbled back into her chair, photo in hand. 'Who'd do this?' Her eyes filled up. 'Who'd want to hurt me like this?'

Maggie didn't answer.

'I just don't understand,' Stella continued, in a hushed voice.

They were known as French photos, sold under the counter. The girls' faces were usually obscured or cropped out. The photographer had promised her. Stella sat, slack-mouthed, stunned, then became aware of Maggie gently but forcibly taking the letter and the photo from her hand.

'Let's put these away,' Maggie said, and placed them both in her vanity case, then quickly packed everything on top and clicked it shut. She shook Stella gently by the shoulder.

'Come on. We'll take a taxi to my flat. I'm not far.'

'The screen test,' said Stella, in a daze.

'We'll say you're not well. Perhaps you can do it tomorrow. I'll ask.'

She touched Stella's shoulder again, and Stella rose slowly. Maggie linked her arm through Stella's and, grabbing her case, pulled her at a smart pace through the make-up department and Stage Two to the gate. A cameraman stopped what he was doing and stared at Stella's ruined face and obvious distress. He began to come over, but Maggie shook her head to warn him off, Stella oblivious to it all.

After a few minutes, they finally reached the gate, and seconds later, they were in a black taxi, heading to Ealing Village. Maggie clasped Stella's sticky hand as they sat on the back seat. Stella turned and stared into her face, her mouth trembling.

'What will happen to me?' she whispered. 'I don't have that kind of money. If this gets out, it'll ruin me.' Her foundation was streaked with tears, her face wild with fear. 'I mean, I was young, everyone did it.'

'Shh...' said Maggie, stroking her arm, trying to calm her.

'No faces, they said. I was broke. What choice did I have?'

'I know,' said Maggie.

'*Who?*' asked Stella. 'Who'd do this? Who hates me so much that they'd want to see me ruined?'

Maggie didn't answer but held Stella's hand tight and stared out of the window.

It only took five minutes to get to Maggie's, and once upstairs, she sat Stella down on the worn red couch, took off her shoes and brought her a cup of tea.

'I've put three sugars in it,' said Maggie. 'For the shock.'

Stella reached out for the cup and saucer, but her hands wouldn't stop trembling.

'Here,' said Maggie, and drew up a stool to place them on.

'Let me have the letter again,' Stella said, and Maggie put her make-up box in front of them on the floor and snapped it open. She passed her the envelope and watched as Stella stared at the writing, turning it over in her hands.

Slipping her hand inside, Stella touched the contents but didn't pull them out.

'I can't,' she said, shaking her head. 'This will be the end of me, Maggie.' She lay down on the sofa, curled into a tight ball as protection against the world, and began to sob.

For the next hour, Maggie stroked her hair and shoulder,

shushing her and reassuring her that everything would be alright. Eventually, Stella fell asleep.

Later, when she woke, she had a knitted shawl draped over her shoulders and the curtains had been drawn. Two table lights were casting a soft yellow glow over the small, charming apartment. She watched as Maggie tidied away some magazines and rearranged some books on a shelf. *How wonderful to live so simply*, thought Stella. *No worries in the world, no terrible surprises around the corner.*

'Have I been sleeping long?' she asked.

Maggie nodded. 'All day. It's six now.'

'What about the screen test? Did they agree to see me another time?'

'I rang earlier and asked,' said Maggie. 'We just have to wait and see. You must be famished.' She walked out to the galley kitchen and returned with a bowl of soup on a tray and a piece of buttered toast. 'I just had some. It's only tinned, I'm afraid, but it's still hot.'

She placed the tray on Stella's lap. It was a curious orange colour and looked a bit greasy.

'It's Heinz tomato,' said Maggie. 'Give it a try.'

Stella dipped her spoon in and took a sip. It was surprisingly tasty, and she polished it off quickly.

'I'm not sure why you're being so kind to me,' said Stella, as she dabbed her mouth with the napkin. 'But it's lovely of you. We only met this morning, and look at us now.'

Maggie shrugged, blushing. 'It's nothing, really. How are you feeling?'

'A little better.'

'Shall I call you a taxi to take you home? Where do you live? Are you nearby?'

'I… er… well, Soho,' said Stella hesitantly.

There was a pause.

'You could stay here,' Maggie said, in a matter-of-fact tone. 'I mean, if you'd rather not be by yourself tonight?' She picked up the tray. 'You'd be very welcome.' She looked around her flat. 'I'm sure it's not what you're used to, but—'

'Oh, Maggie! Could I?' Stella asked, her face brightening immediately. 'That would be wonderful. Thank you. I'll just take the couch.'

'Nonsense,' said Maggie, carrying the things out. 'You're Stella Hope,' she called from the kitchen. 'You'll take my bed.' She walked back and gave her a smile. 'I changed the sheets just this morning. I'll take the couch. I hardly sleep anyway. Here.' She handed Stella an ice-cold flannel. 'Put this over your eyes for ten minutes. It'll stop them looking puffy tomorrow.'

Stella took the washcloth from her, sat back, closed her eyes and did as she was told. 'I think I've found my guardian angel,' she said, smiling.

CHAPTER TWO

Hollywood, Los Angeles
Nine months earlier
October 1953

It was common knowledge, among the girls in Ginny's apartment block, that young actresses were considered fair game by the men who ran Hollywood. They could touch you, threaten you, insist on sex and do what the hell they liked. You could protest, of course, but then you'd be labelled a troublemaker, find auditions thin on the ground or, worse, have your contract cancelled (if you were lucky enough to have one). The trick was to not get stuck alone with one of the bad guys. Of course, figuring out who the bad guys were was a whole other challenge.

'It's the ones you *don't* think would take advantage who are the worst,' said Sandy, the hip platinum blonde from upstairs, as they chatted on the landing. 'The ones who can't do enough for you.'

'So what about the others?' asked Ginny, leaning on the bannister. 'You know, the tough guys with power and money who you'd *expect* to take advantage. Are they usually okay?'

Sandy twirled the locket around her neck. 'Oh no,' she said, with a wry smile. 'They'll give it a shot too.'

Ginny laughed. 'Price of fame,' she said sarcastically, sounding bolder than she felt. They'd just been talking about a new girl who'd run out of her audition, crying, because she'd been asked to undress. Ginny had no idea what she'd do if that happened to her.

She offered Sandy a Chesterfield and lit one herself, and they both blew smoke into the air as they compared notes on which auditions were sought after that week.

That was all yesterday, and now Ginny stood in Stan Fisher's office, waiting for him to arrive, her mouth as parched as the California hills. She'd had a message that he wanted to see her, and she was both thrilled and petrified. This was it – her chance. He was Executive Manager at Star Studios, and his sprawling mahogany desk had a pile of scripts on one side, the racing newspapers on the other and a pot of expensive-looking fountain pens in the middle. Behind his squat leather chair, on the wall, was a framed Stars and Stripes flag. He oversaw the 'talent', as they called it here. She still hadn't got used to that. Talent.

There were lots of things about America she wasn't used to yet, and too many about London she missed. Best not to think about that.

She walked towards the row of three huge framed film posters on the wall. The most striking one was in the middle. Ginny stared at that heart-shaped faced, the perfectly coiffed dark hair with the distinctive gold streak right through the front, and those eyes – slightly hooded, a beautiful light green shade that glanced down at her as if to say, 'Yes, it's me, *the* Stella Hope.' She'd been a beauty in her day, still was. But the studio always needed fresh blood, younger girls who'd play opposite the much older men the fans never seemed to stop loving.

'Good!' The door burst open, making her jump. 'You're here. I like punctuality.'

Ginny smiled and held out her hand, feigning confidence. He was easily fifty, maybe older, tall, bulky even, with a bulbous nose, a well-worn look and a thatch of grey hair. If he were an actor he'd win character roles, never the leading man. The weary softness in Stan Fisher's face suggested a kindness that helped her feel at ease.

He reached his hand out. 'Hello…'

'Ginny,' she said.

'Ginny, yes.' He took her hand in both of his and gave it two shakes, then looked at her with a wide smile. 'Come sit down – no not there.' He ushered her away from the desk. 'Here,' he said, pointing to the couch. 'Let's be more comfortable. This is informal, after all.'

She sat down first, and when he dropped down heavily, his huge frame made the cushions bounce.

'I don't have much time,' he said, grabbing a sheaf of papers that were on the coffee table in front of him, 'but I wanted to meet you myself. You're the girl who won our beauty contest, right? In London?'

'That's right,' she replied, beaming.

'Well, that's some prize,' he said. 'A ticket to Hollywood and a screen test with Star Studios.'

She nodded. It was a one-way flight and no living expenses, but she wasn't about to complain. 'Yes, I feel very lucky, Mr Fisher. I'm so grateful.'

'Alright, Ginny, Ginny… let's see…' He flicked through the pages and she peered to see what he was reading.

Her height, her weight, colouring. Usual stuff. Plus a photo she'd had taken a year ago that she hated.

'Ginny Watkins,' he mumbled to himself, 'no contract yet, but you've had some small roles, in London?'

'That's right. And the last director said—'

'Can you sing?' he interrupted.

'Oh *yes*! And dance. I spent two years in London at—'

He put his hand out to stop her. 'I like the accent – sounds classy. Willing to change your look?'

'Excuse me?'

'Forgive me, sweetheart, but all that dark hair – it swamps you.'

She put her hand to her head.

'You'd make a stunning blonde, maybe white-blonde like Harlow and Monroe,' he continued. 'And your eyebrows, they're too thin. That shape's over now. You know, we have the best hair and make-up experts here at Star Studios. They can work wonders. And of course, your teeth.'

Her hand went to her mouth. 'What's the matter with them?' she said.

'Well, they need fixing. We can easily get rid of that gap.'

Her tongue immediately licked the small gap between her front teeth. She'd always been fond of it, had considered it charming even. It was what made her her. The shock must have shown on her face.

'Now don't get upset,' said Fisher. 'If you want to be a star, you need a perfect smile – Marilyn's had hers done, and you know Joan Crawford?'

Ginny nodded.

'Her teeth were rotten to the core,' said Stan. 'Extreme poverty as a kid will do that, but she has a beautiful smile now. Yours don't need much at all, but they do need *some* work. If you want to give this a shot, that is.'

The girls did whatever the studio suggested, but still, it was galling to have it put so bluntly.

'You're looking at two weeks of dentistry, tops,' he said. 'The studio pays for veneers, you get perfect teeth. So even if you don't get a contract at the end of it...'

She sat bolt upright. 'Wait – what do you mean?'

He raised his eyebrows at her indignant tone, but then his face softened and he looked amused.

'Excuse me, Mr Fisher,' she said, calmer now, 'but are you saying there's a chance I might not get a contract? Even if I change my hair, and my teeth, and my eyebrows and everything?'

He shrugged. 'Your prize was the flight and a screen test – that's it. So, yes, it could happen. Sometimes girls have everything done and it just doesn't work out.' He reached across to a silver case, offered her a cigarette but she refused. 'How much do you want this?' He gestured vaguely around him. 'Stardom, Hollywood, the whole deal?'

'I want it more than anything in the world. I have since I was a little girl.'

'Good, that's what I want to hear,' he said, lighting up. 'But let me tell you, Ginny, it's not just hard work that will get you there. You need to be amenable. I tell all our talent that, men and women. That way you'll get a lot further in this town.'

She nodded slowly and glanced at the poster of Stella Hope on the wall.

'Those stars up there,' he said, pointing at the glamorous trio. 'Ava, Stella and Jean. Each one of them sat where you are today. Each one of them did everything it took – and *more* – to get to where they are.'

It was the 'more' that worried her.

She hesitated and heard him let out a small, exasperated breath.

'Look, kid, can I be frank?' he asked. She nodded. 'It's not for everyone. Nobody's holding a gun to your head. You came, you saw Hollywood, you can go home. There are hundreds of Ginnys out there. If you don't want this, tell me now before we both put in the work – no hard feelings.'

Of course she wanted it. The velvet-black of the auditorium, her face on the big screen, the beautiful gowns, the parties, the wealth, the adoration. It's all she'd ever wanted. And anyway, she didn't have the money to return home. She had to stay.

'I absolutely want this, Mr Fisher,' she said, giving him her bright smile. 'I'm certain.'

'Good, good.' He got up and stretched. 'We'll send you to classes – acting, poise, ballet, the usual. They all take place here. And we'll get the hair and teeth sorted. Then you'll be camera-ready, and the rest will be up to you. Speak to Ida, my secretary.' He waved his hand in the air, some ash falling onto the expensive thick rug. 'She's been here for years – all the girls love her. She'll give you a list of places to be, times and so on. Oh – and your name?'

'Yes?'

'That's short for Virginia, right? It sounds classier. Let's call you Virginia... Virginia... Rose! How about that? We'll play up the English angle. Audiences will lap it up.'

'Oh, well, alright,' she said. He'd changed her name? Just like that?

'Good, good.' He shook her hand and walked to his desk. 'It's been good meeting you, Ginny,' he said, sitting down. 'I'll be in touch.'

She took her cue and walked to the door, a whorl of excitement twisting through her.

'Thank you, Mr Fisher,' she said.

'Please, just call me Stan.'

CHAPTER THREE

One month later, with hair a bright white, and eyebrows pencilled into a soft-brown angular arch, Virginia Rose made her way to Star Studios for her first screen test. Her head was held high, and she walked as she'd been instructed in her Elegance and Poise class: back straight, legs gliding as if she were on roller skates. She'd followed a strict diet that had a list of 'forbidden' foods much longer than those that were allowed, and each morning either had a 5 a.m. ballet class or Acting Theory at 6.30. She was exhausted and had barely socialised in the evenings. She'd lost a couple of inches off her waist and was constantly hungry. A few of the acting classes ran late, but despite her tiredness, she'd found the grit to get through them. If she won a contract at the end of this, it would have all been worthwhile. But what wouldn't she give for a fry-up at the New Piccadilly Café back home... and a weekend to sleep in as long as she liked?

She walked towards Stage C and ran her tongue over

her teeth, still surprised that the gap had gone. 'I'm Virginia Rose,' she whispered under her breath. 'And I'm ready for this.' Only her voice remained, and although she'd taken lessons in various accents, her elocution teacher had made it clear that her English accent would be in demand, too. In fact, she'd been asked to 'sound more upper-class'. Americans loved all that. The fact she'd been born adjacent to the slums of Camden Town in North London was neither here nor there. She knew that studios often changed the talent's backstories, as if they themselves were characters in a film. They cherry-picked what they wanted, rewrote your history and discarded the rest. Virginia Rose apparently came from nobility, and her family in England owned a small country estate somewhere remote.

All this preparation, and Ginny still didn't know what was expected of her today. She'd only been promised one screen test. If she screwed this up, then what? Would she be stuck as an extra, paid a terrible day rate, or could she try her luck at a different studio? She had so many questions but nobody to ask. She'd left a message with Ida, Mr Fisher's secretary, asking if there was a script for her, or any lines to learn, but had heard nothing.

'Name?' A flustered woman appeared next to her, clutching a clipboard. Her black hair was scraped into a bun and it was coming undone.

'Ginny Watkins. I'm doing a screen test.'

The woman ran her finger down the list.

'Sorry, Virginia Rose,' said Ginny.

'Yep, got you,' she said, ticked her off and gave instructions for her to stay put. After a few minutes, a side door opened, her name was called, and Ginny rushed in. A crumpled director stood in his shirtsleeves.

'At last! Come on,' he said, and motioned to the cameraman who was already set up. He gave Ginny the once over, a look of dismay on his face.

'Did they just give you that blonde hair?' he asked.

She nodded.

He looked exasperated. 'You're the third today,' he said. 'What happened to originality? Just do as I say, okay, kid?' He handed her a clapperboard with her new name chalked on it. 'Hold it in front of your face... and action!'

The camera whirred and she smiled.

'Did I tell you to smile?' he said. 'Drop the board. Now, walk towards me.' She did as instructed. 'Now walk away, that's it.'

She felt ridiculous. Was her whole future dependent on this one moment? She tried to focus.

'Be happy,' the director barked. She gave a huge smile, proud of her new teeth. 'Is that it? Okay, that's better. Now smile like you mean it, like you've seen someone across the street that you like. Good. I didn't tell you to wave, did I? Now laugh. No, not like a maniac, like a happy-go-lucky girl. Good. Now turn your back on me, and when you turn round, I want you to look shocked, then sad... really sad. Like a tragedy.'

She could barely keep up with the instructions but did her best.

'Sad, I said, not constipated. No, now you look like your dog died. Okay, okay, now go sit down.'

Ginny sat. She wanted to punch him and burst into tears

at the same time. No lines, no script, just bullying her, back and forth like a puppet.

'Okay, now let's hear your voice... What's your name, address and date of birth?'

She took a deep breath and calmed herself. 'My name's Virginia Rose,' she said, pausing to spin it out a little longer. 'I live at 220 Laurel Avenue, apartment 2c, Hollywood, Los Angeles. I was born on the tenth of January 1931, in—'

'Okay, I don't need your life story, that's it. You're done. Cut!'

The cameraman stopped rolling. Ginny got up.

'So, no lines, nothing else?' she asked. 'I can tap dance. Can I show you? And I can sing, too.'

Just then the door swung open. It was Stan. His huge frame blocked the light from coming in.

'Oh, Mr Fisher,' said Ginny. 'Hello.'

'Hey Ginny, let's go,' he said, motioning with his head for her to join him. 'We're doing photos now.'

Her heart leaped. 'For publicity?' she asked, but he didn't give a reply.

Everything was so rushed. She grabbed her pocketbook and followed him through the studio. He walked surprisingly fast for a man of his size, and she had to skip every now and then to keep up.

Trying to catch her breath, she tried again. 'Do you mean photos for the papers? Does that mean I'm getting a contract?'

He gave her a sidelong look and smiled, but didn't say anything. They took a sharp corner and were suddenly standing on a set where filming had finished. He called out

to a young lad who was sweating profusely under the lights
and carrying a camera and tripod, and he joined them.

'You're in luck,' Stan said. 'We just wrapped on *The
Silent Hero*. Come on, I'll introduce you to Max Whitman.'

Before she knew it, she'd been hurried into a seat next
to a bored Adonis, who was flicking through the pages of
Silver Screen magazine.

It was really him. Max Whitman, Star Studios' biggest
male star – in fact, arguably the most famous actor in
Hollywood. And, of course, husband to the enigmatic Stella
Hope. They were the ultimate Hollywood couple, on screen
and off. Ginny had watched several of his films, and now he
was within touching distance.

She stared. His face was perfect, his skin golden and
flawless. She had an urge to reach out and stroke his cheek.
She quickly closed her mouth, which had been hanging
slightly open, and fixed a smile on her face.

'Ginny, Max – Max, Ginny,' said Stan. 'New one,' he said
to Max. 'Stage name is Virginia Rose. We just need a few
quick welcoming shots. For the dailies.'

Max gave her a quick glance, winked, and said, in
that famous cowboy drawl that she'd heard in his films,
'Welcome on board the crazy train, kid. Watch how you go.'

He reached out a hand, and she nodded hello and
accepted. Instead of letting it go, he leaned down, gave it
a delicate, slow kiss, then carried on up her arm. Her heart
thumped, thumped, thumped. The photographer snapped,
snapped, snapped.

'Come on, Max,' said Stan with a sigh. 'You know we
can't use that. Your fans will riot!'

Max laughed, and she realised it had just been a joke, so she laughed too.

'Hello, Ginny,' he said, dropping the drawl now. 'Have we met before? You seem awful familiar.'

'No,' she said. 'I'd remember.'

He shrugged, then with a warm smile he shook her hand again, as if for the first time, and the photographer began to snap away.

'Let's get this done, shall we?' Max said.

He picked up a script, pointed to something, and Ginny realised she was meant to play along, so she leaned over and pretended to look fascinated. Snap. He pointed at the huge spotlights above them and she gazed at his hand, faking a startled, enraptured look at the nothing above their heads. Snap. He took the Stetson off the back of his chair and placed it on her head. She smiled, tilting her head for a great angle and making sure her new teeth showed. Snap.

A small table with a checked cloth was placed by their legs and two ice-cream sundaes arrived out of nowhere, with long spoons, cream and cherries on top. Ginny had seen a version of this picture in the movie magazines so many times she knew exactly what to do. She put a cherry in her mouth and leaned towards him as he grinned at her and dug into his dessert. Snap. And so it went on for a few minutes until Stan told them they had enough. As if someone had flicked a switch, Max Whitman dropped the smile, got up and stretched his arms up above his head.

'See you around, kid,' he said, taking the hat from her head and putting it on his, then giving it a goodbye tilt.

She felt hot, opened her mouth but couldn't get the words out. Had he been flirting? No, why would he? He was Max Whitman. He was married. She was just another young actress. A nobody, really. But she could have sworn there'd been a mischievous glint in his eye throughout the whole thing. He knew the effect he'd had on her. She felt dazed and excited and slightly ridiculous.

'Goodbye, Mr Whitman!' she called, but he'd already walked off.

At ten o'clock that evening, Ginny was just thinking about slipping into her pyjamas when there was a knock at her door. Hesitantly, she walked towards it.

'Yes?' she said. 'Who's there?'

'Open up, would you?' It was a man's voice.

She didn't have a peephole and didn't move.

'Ginny, it's Stan – Stan Fisher. Could you open up?'

What did he want, coming to her room? How did he know where she lived? Of course, he knew. She'd told them in the screen test, and anyway, Stan's reputation was that he knew everything.

She put on her cardigan, unsure why, and opened the door an inch.

'It's awfully late, Mr Fisher,' she said, peering outside. She could see Cynthia, who lived across the hall, peering out of her door. 'Is everything alright?' Ginny asked. 'Did the pictures not work out?' What a stupid question – he wouldn't come here this late for that.

'Fine, fine, just fine,' he said. 'There's nothing to worry about. May I?' He gestured indoors.

'Oh, of course.'

She opened the door and suddenly felt her neck flush.

Is this what the girls had warned her about? Being sloppy, letting yourself get caught alone with the wrong guy? But not Stan, surely. She just didn't know.

'Excuse the late hour,' he said, taking off his hat. 'And I hope I didn't alarm you. Or get you into trouble coming here. I noticed the signs about it being a female-only building.'

She didn't reply, just stared at him.

'I'm here as a messenger boy, really,' he continued, turning his hat in his hands. 'Mr Whitman wondered if you'd like to join him for dinner?'

She gave a surprised laugh. 'Oh – *really?*'

Max Whitman? Who was happily married to Stella Hope?

'At his hotel,' Stan continued. 'He's staying at the Sunset Tower. It's not far.'

'But I've eaten,' she replied, then realised how stupid that sounded. 'I mean, *now*? It's very kind of him, but it's awfully late and, well…' She didn't know how to say it, so she'd just say it. 'Won't Miss Hope mind?'

Stan gave a sad smile. 'Miss Hope resides at the Beverly Hills Hotel. They're on different schedules right now. Her film doesn't wrap for two days and Mr Whitman would appreciate the company. He'd like to celebrate the end of a tough shoot, you see, but finds himself alone.'

'Well, er…' She was flustered and wished she knew what to say.

Perhaps it *was* just dinner. She didn't want to look ungrateful, and maybe he could help her in her career? He was the highest-earning actor at the studio, after all. It could be completely innocent. Of course it could.

It probably wasn't.

Stan put his hands up. 'No obligation,' he said, 'but he's – how can I put this? – taken a genuine interest. Doesn't happen often. Said he could see you had potential, wanted to help you. He said—'

'Yes!' she blurted. 'Yes, thank you – that would be lovely.' Was she really going to do this? 'Can I have a few minutes to get ready? I'm…' She looked down at her faded-blue day dress and tired cardigan. 'What shall I wear?'

'Don't worry about that,' said Stan. 'I'll wait for you downstairs. Javier, Max's driver, is outside. He'll take you and bring you back.'

CHAPTER FOUR

Ginny stood inside the lift of the Sunset Tower as the bellboy pulled shut the metal lattice grille gate. He wore snow-white gloves, and she watched as his pristine finger punched the button for the top floor. He couldn't have been more than sixteen, but his whole demeanour was one of complete professionalism; he didn't look at her once, keeping his eyes firmly ahead. Discretion was everything at the Sunset. She'd heard of this hotel, because at fifteen-storeys high, it was one of the tallest in Hollywood. It was also a favourite haunt of movie stars.

It had all happened so quickly – Stan arriving, her getting changed and coming here – that now she was on her way up to Max Whitman's hotel room, her emotions were a wild rollercoaster of dizzying excitement and wary foreboding. As the lift made its slow creaking ascent, she glanced at the mirror to her left. The wrap she'd slipped on was too warm for this summer evening, but she hadn't wanted to turn up half-dressed. And yet, it was the black satin dress she wore underneath that worried her. It was all wrong – she'd lost a few pounds and it was now gaping slightly across her chest. She'd cinched it at the waist, trying to pull the fabric flat, but had only managed to crease it instead. This dress was the smartest thing she owned, and although Stan had said it didn't matter what she wore, she hadn't wanted to turn up too casual, as if this meeting meant nothing to her. It meant everything.

Of course, she didn't know what Max Whitman expected of her tonight. She'd tried not to think about it too much, had told herself, as she'd sat in the back of his chauffeured limousine, that it was just dinner, like she'd been led to believe. And if anything else happened, or if the situation got out of control, well she'd have to deal with it then and there. Not everything could be planned for, she told herself, however much she wished it could. She was smart, she could think on her feet. And anyway, there were worse things in the world than being propositioned by the studio's biggest star.

She heard her mother's voice – *trust your instincts, Ginny* – and she smiled to herself. Her instincts had said she should come tonight, so she'd accepted the invitation. She was twenty-two and was going to the hotel room of Star Studios' most famous actor. Devastatingly gorgeous, hugely talented, ridiculously rich. Very much married and easily twenty years older than her. Maybe her mother wouldn't approve of her instincts after all.

The lift jolted to a stop and the bellboy pulled the gates open with a clang.

'The penthouse floor, miss,' he said, eyes fixed on the corridor. 'Mr Whitman's suite is at the end.'

She straightened her shoulders and stepped out. *Breathe,*

breathe, breathe. She strode towards the shiny black door that seemed impossibly far away, her handbag swinging in her hand. The cherry-red carpet was lush and thick and conspired to trip her over. Just as she raised her hand to knock, the door swung open and she gave a small yelp.

'Sorry! Sorry!' Max said, laughing. 'Come in!'

'Oh, hello. Sorry... I...'

He put out his hand, and she fumbled as she swapped her bag over so she could shake it. He was wearing perfectly pressed cream trousers and a soft butter-yellow linen shirt, which set off his golden skin perfectly. She felt stupidly overdressed.

'They rang to say you were on your way up,' he said, leading her in, 'and I was coming to greet you at the elevator, but I guess I scared the life out of you instead.'

She laughed.

'I wasn't expecting it, that's all. Heavens...' She looked around the suite. It shone with chrome and mirrors and gleaming surfaces, as if she were caught in the heart of a diamond. 'It's beautiful.'

'Been to the Sunset before?' he asked, taking her wrap.

She shook her head.

'I'm spoiled with this view.' He pointed to the lights from the buildings that stretched out across the night sky below.

She peered out of the window, then put her bag on an armchair and walked to the imposing art-deco mirrored fireplace that reflected her image back to her several times.

'It's spectacular,' she said. 'Do you stay here much?'

He stood at the cocktail bar and started shaking a drink.

'Home from home,' he said. 'Martini okay for you?'

'Thank you.'

'They keep it for me so I can use it whenever I like. I pay them so it's always ready.'

Just that phrase said everything she needed to know about his wealth. He probably wasn't even boasting – this was just how it was for him.

She stared around and caught a glimpse of an open door and the corner of a bed in the next room. How many women had he brought up here, she wondered? Women like her, keen young actresses waiting for their break?

He poured the drink into a chilled glass, put an olive in it and brought it to her on a round silver tray, along with one for himself.

'Please,' he said, indicating she should sit.

There was a large navy velvet couch right next to her, where he sat in front of a chrome and glass coffee table, but she perched in the chocolate leather club chair instead, then immediately regretted it in case she appeared rude. She had to relax. She had to stop trying to second-guess every situation.

'It's not what you think, Ginny,' he said, leaning forward as he took his glass from the tray. He wet his lips and took a small sip, then glanced up at her. His lashes were ridiculously long.

'Sorry?'

'This place is a sanctuary, somewhere I can get away from everything. The studio, the press, the fans. I don't use it as a place to see women.'

'Oh no, I mean, I didn't...'

Was she really that transparent? She felt the blood rush to her face. He gave her a kind smile then looked away. How would she even get through the next few minutes without making a fool of herself, let alone the evening? He was impossibly beautiful.

'Let's eat, shall we?' he said, and he jumped up and grabbed a menu from the sideboard.

Yes, food. That was always a good idea.

'What would you like?' he asked. 'They'll make you anything.'

She suddenly felt hungry.

Thirty minutes and a second martini later, they were sitting at a small round table that had been carried in especially. It was covered with a damask white tablecloth and all the cutlery and plates gleamed in the warm yellow light. Two waiters stood, one next to each of them, and pulled the cloches off their plates simultaneously, revealing a bloody steak and fries on his and a toasted cheese sandwich on hers. It had been cut into triangles and the crusts were nowhere to be seen. Which was a shame because the crusts were the best bits. Max watched as the waiters exited the room, then he offered his glass for her to clink.

'So now you know I'm not about to pounce on you,' he said, nudging a pile of fries from his plate to hers, 'I can tell you why you're here.'

She took one, bit into it and leaned in. 'Yes?'

Was he going to offer her a part? Surely it wasn't that easy? That would be ridiculous.

'Well,' he started, 'I'm always looking for fresh talent – you know what Hollywood is like, right? Always searching for the next bright new thing.'

She nodded sagely as if she knew all about it. She'd been here all of three weeks.

'I like to know who's coming through – women, so I can see who'd work well for my movies, maybe discover some new talent. And men, so... well, to be honest,' he said, laughing, 'to check out the competition.'

'But you're Max Whitman,' she said. 'You're Star Studios' biggest name.'

'Even Max Whitman can be replaced,' he said with a wry smile. 'And I never assume otherwise.' His face softened, and for a moment a glimmer of vulnerability shone in his eyes.

This is not what she'd expected. Admittedly, she hadn't met any huge stars yet, but she'd assumed they all had egos the size of the Griffith Observatory.

'Anyway,' he continued, 'I think you have a very special look.'

'I *do*?'

'And that English accent is a delight. Don't let them make you drop it. I think we could have something here. Let me ask you, how hard are you willing to work?'

'I'll do anything to get ahead,' she said. 'Well, within reason, of course.'

He held up his hands. 'Of course. I mean, I'd never ask you to do anything untoward.'

She nodded. 'So, can I ask, what exactly you *are* asking? I mean, I'm ever so grateful that you've taken an interest. Please don't think I'm not. I realise how lucky I am, but I've done nothing here yet, and only a few films back home, with hardly any lines. You haven't even seen me act yet.'

He chewed his steak, wiped his mouth and put the napkin on the table.

'*London Calling*,' he said, putting up his thumb to start counting off on his hand. Then another finger went up. '*One for the Road.*' Then another. '*Special Agent Barbara.*'

'You've seen me act? But how? Those films were tiny – I can't believe it!'

'Only the first one,' he said, tapping more ketchup onto his fries. 'Stan's getting copies of the others for me.'

'But *when? London Calling* was such a small release. It came and went almost immediately.'

He laughed. 'The luck of good timing! A trip to London a year or so ago, a rainy afternoon. I snuck into the Rex in East Finchley and there it was.'

She grimaced. 'Well, it's not a very good film,' she said. 'I mean, that's why I'm here – to do something much better. Build a career. I know that film's no masterpiece.'

'You're right,' he said. 'It stinks.'

'Charmed!' she said, in mock outrage, though she knew he was right. It was the film she was least proud of, and she had such a tiny part, but still, she couldn't believe he'd seen her on the big screen.

'It was a terrible movie,' he said, 'and you were by far the best thing in it. Even with that awful script, you managed to come out unscathed.'

'You really think so?' she asked, thrilled.

'You shone. It was as if you were in a whole other film, a much better one. I waited for the credits at the end to find out your name.'

Was this really happening? Max Whitman thought she

shone in a terrible film. She took a huge bite of her grilled cheese sandwich.

'How did you get to Hollywood?' he asked.

She chewed and chewed, pointing to her mouth, then finally wiped it with a napkin. 'I won a beauty contest,' she said. 'First prize was a screen test in Hollywood, hence my studio visit today.'

He smiled. 'That's some prize,' he said. Then he leaned in. 'Tell me, Ginny, do you believe in serendipity?'

'You mean like fate?' she asked.

He nodded. 'Or that good things happen for a reason?'

'Not really,' she said. 'Don't we make our own luck? If it's just fate that makes things happen, then we're like chess pieces being shoved around and we can't change anything. I don't like that idea at all.'

He pushed his knife and fork to one side and stretched out.

'Well, serendipity or fate or whatever – something was going on when you came on set for those photos today. I mean, what kind of luck was that? I couldn't place you earlier, then it hit me. You were Ginny Watkins, the girl in that godawful film!'

'It's Rose now,' she said. 'Virginia Rose.'

'Yes, Stan told me – I called him straight away.'

She beamed. Stan turning up like that, her coming here, everything – it had all been above board after all. Max Whitman was genuinely interested in her talent.

'So,' she began, 'I don't want to sound pushy, but can I ask you something?'

'Fire away,' he said, taking another sip of his martini.

'What, exactly, are you proposing? You said you keep an eye on new talent for films...'

'Yes.'

'Well, I mean... and I don't want to be presumptuous, but I assume you didn't call me here just to have dinner with you because you're a sad, lonely film star, did you?'

He laughed out loud, a crazy almost bark-like laugh that was hilarious in itself, and tears came to his eyes. 'Well, kid – you don't mince your words, do you? Is that what you thought?' he asked, dabbing at his eyes with the napkin.

She laughed as well. 'Sorry, but I still don't know what I'm doing here. Stan didn't give anything away. He said you wanted company, and you'd seen something special in me, and well, I didn't know what to think.'

He shook his head. 'And yet you still came.'

She took a final bite of her sandwich. *I have morals*, she thought, *but I'm not stupid*.

'Of course,' she said. 'I'm not going to say no to Max Whitman.' He gave her a searching look, and suddenly the moment felt too intimate. Would he think she was coming on to him? Was she? 'So, is it for a part?' she asked brightly. 'On a new movie?'

He leaned forward, elbows on the table and clasped his hands in front of his mouth, like a child trying to keep a secret.

Then, in a quiet voice, he said, 'I want to drop the cowboy stuff. It's served me well, but I need to move on. I shot a musical last year, but I'm not sure I want to go that way, either. Did you see Brando in *A Streetcar Named Desire*?'

She nodded.

'I want more dramatic roles, like that. Something

meaningful, something urgent. And I've got my eye on a script that would be *amazing*. For both of us. Proper drama, sweeping story. Oscar-worthy.'

Her eyes widened.

'It's called *A Road to Nowhere*, not definite yet,' he continued. 'We're still getting rewrites, so you can't tell anyone. Not a soul, understood?'

'Of course.'

'Good. Nothing's confirmed yet, and I don't want to jinx it. I'll be able to tell you about it soon, I hope. The studio has to agree, but they usually do what I want. Well, for now anyway.' He smiled. 'While I still sell tickets at the box office.'

'I won't breathe a word,' she said, 'but, well, what kind of a part is it?'

'It's the kind of role that will change your life. A leading role most actresses would kill for.'

'Starring opposite *you*?'

He nodded.

'But...' Her mind buzzed with the possibilities. Famous leading actors usually wanted famous actresses starring opposite them, but sometimes a studio really got behind an ingenue and made her a star. Her mouth felt dry with excitement, and she wanted to ask a hundred questions but had to stop herself. Instead, she drained her martini.

'Promise you will keep this to yourself?' he said.

'Yes, yes, of course. Thank you so much.'

'I've got a really good feeling about this, Ginny. A really good feeling about you, too. Now come on.' He glanced at his watch. 'It's late and you've probably got some ridiculous ballet class at the crack of dawn, I bet?'

She pulled a face. 'Acting Theory at half-past six.'

'Sounds fun,' he said, getting up. 'I'll call down and get Javier to bring the car round.'

She stood, smoothed her dress and walked to the chair for her bag.

'Can I ask one last thing?' she said, once he'd hung up the phone.

'What's that?'

'What about, well...'

'What?'

'What about Miss Hope – Stella – your... wife?'

'I know who she is,' he said, smiling. And there he was again, teasing her. She quite liked it.

'Well, isn't *she* usually your leading lady? Won't she mind you having a new actress starring opposite you?' *And won't she want the part for herself?*

He ran a hand through his dark hair and a lock fell over his forehead. 'Again, strictly between us,' he said, 'I think our days are numbered.'

She didn't say anything.

'The papers call us Hollywood's Golden Couple,' he continued, 'but I don't know how long we can keep that charade going. We haven't starred together for a while now – we can barely be in the same room. Sure, we go to parties together and each other's premieres, for the sake of appearances, but it's only a matter of time.'

Ginny frowned. 'I'm sorry,' she said.

He shrugged then handed over her wrap as he walked her to the door.

'What can I tell you?' he said. 'She lost interest in Yours Truly a couple of years ago, when she was nominated for an Oscar. Thinks she can do better – that I'm holding her back.'

Ginny felt embarrassed for him, and surprised he was being so open.

'Seems she'd rather not work with me anymore,' Max continued. 'Doesn't want to share the screen with me, or anyone else. I, on the other hand, love having a leading lady, and need to find a new one.'

'But you might patch things up?' she asked tentatively.

He shook his head. 'Too many vicious arguments, too many terrible things said. We're going to divorce. Anyway, I'm at least twenty years too old for her taste these days.'

Ginny must have looked shocked.

'Sorry.' He flushed. 'That wasn't very gentlemanly, was it? I don't know why I'm telling you all this.'

'But...' she began. 'I mean... you always looked so in love.'

'We're actors. It's what we do. We put on a damned good show.' He opened the door. 'Enough of my sob story. I've said too much, and now you'll think I'm bitter and twisted, as well as sad and lonely.'

She smiled. 'I'm sorry for bringing it up,' she said. 'Thank you for inviting me tonight. I'm so pleased I came.'

'Remember,' he said, 'not a word, and I'll be in touch soon. We need to get your contract sorted quickly, and then I'll push on the script, and we'll wait for the green light.'

A wave of gratitude swept over her, and she felt flustered as he spoke because she was already wondering how to say goodbye. She'd never been good at goodbyes. What was the right thing to do? Should she lean in and kiss his cheek? Or just give him a cute wave and walk out? He decided it for her by taking her hand in both of his, shaking it warmly, like an old friend might, and suddenly she was in the corridor again.

The lift was waiting as she approached, the doors open, the same bellboy. She stepped inside and he closed the gates.

Max Whitman wanted to work with her. Could it be that easy? Her ticket to the top?

She'd come to Hollywood and thrown in all her chips on this turn of the roulette wheel. She *had* to make a success of it.

As the lift descended, the excitement of her evening tingled through her, but there was something else, too. She felt a faint whisper of disappointment. It had been wonderful, but if, as they'd said goodbye, he'd dipped his beautiful face towards hers, taken her chin in his hand and lifted it to kiss her on the mouth... well, then it would have been perfect. Just like a movie.

I wake on the floor, hands near my head, and I see the blood beneath my fingernails. It's a vile rust brown, and has embedded deep into my skin, surrounding each perfectly manicured pastel pink nail.

I sit up and stare at my palms, which are bloodstained too.

I try to make sense of where I am, but my pounding head and thrashing heart won't allow it. Exhaustion beckons and sleep pulls me down again, a seductive lover impossible to resist.

Later, when I open my eyes, I'm panting, struggling for breath, in a sea of dread that threatens to drown me. I try to swim away from the panic, frantically, my arms exhausted. The memories won't come fully formed and I am glad. Whatever happened to me is there, just over my shoulder, but I'm terrified to look.

I hold out my hands, fingers splayed, then turn them over and see the bloody smears of some tragedy or other racing up the insides of my arms. Frantically, I touch my face:

dried patches there, too. I trace the rough residue over my cheekbones, across my nose and up to my forehead: a tactile map of horrors. What happened to me? I touch my chest to check if I'm wounded, and that's when I see the grey canvas tunic. Someone has undressed me.

I peer down inside the wide neck of the rough fabric and look at my flesh. I'm naked beneath, my undergarments missing, too. There are no cuts, no sign that I've been hurt. I push at my ribs – nothing. My bare feet are blood-crusted, as if I've been dancing with death.

A nightmarish thought slides into my head and I frantically push my hand up between my legs. Is this where the blood is from? Has somebody hurt me there? My fingers press hard, searching for bruises at the tops of my thighs or worse, searching for proof that someone has wrecked me. Mercifully nothing. I lean against the wall and glance at the room for the first time: a thin mattress on the floor, no blankets, no pillow. And a bucket. Pale green tiles sweep up the entire walls to the ceiling. Beneath me, a cracked, filthy stone floor.

There's no window, but there is a door. It is made of metal and has no handle on the inside. The thumping in my head worsens and I clamp my hands over my ears, then jolt as I touch my matted hair. Tentatively, I put my hands there again: it is thick and stuck to my head, caked in something. Of everything, this is what upsets me the most and I begin to wail. I try to run my fingers through it, but it's no good. Instead, I use my nails to scrape at the residue. Then, still sobbing, I hold my fingers in front of my eyes to examine what it is. Now familiar rust-brown flakes cover my fingers; the blood has reached here, too.

My stomach turns and I dig my fingers through my hair, over my scalp, searching for a wound. I know I won't find anything. I have no injury. I haven't been hurt. This isn't my blood.

What have I done?

CHAPTER FIVE

Soho, London
July 1954

It had been one week since she'd received the blackmail letter. Stella poured a large jug of cold water over the bowl of ice cubes, took a deep breath and did the sign of the cross that her Cypriot *yiayia* had taught her. Then she plunged her face. She counted to ten, lifted her head, took another breath and plunged again. And again. The water sloshed everywhere, but never mind.

She reached out for the fluffy towel at her side, and very gently patted her face and neck dry, taking care not to rub. These ice plunges were no fun, but after a night of solid crying, her puffy eyes needed more than cold flannels.

The face baths had been Maggie's idea, and Stella now trusted her completely when it came to her beauty regime. She'd only known her a few days, but already felt close to her. Maggie had quickly proven herself a good friend. She'd taken care of everything, telling the studio Stella was unwell but would return soon. And had given up her bed when Stella had stayed for two days at her quirky flat in Ealing

Village before returning to her own apartment on Dean Street in Soho.

Before going home, they'd swapped numbers and Maggie had called from the communal phone in her hall and checked on her every day since. It was lovely being looked after again, and that's how Stella had come up with the idea. As well as being her make-up artist at the studio, she suggested that Maggie – for a reasonable fee – be her assistant too, dealing with Stella's everyday requests. Maggie had been thrilled with the proposal and readily accepted. Usually, Stella was at pains to maintain her Hollywood aura with anyone she knew, but Maggie had seen her at her absolute worst, and rather than feeling embarrassed about that, Stella had felt her guard fall away easily. She hoped they'd become great friends, even though, strictly speaking, Maggie was her employee.

She stood, adjusted her cream silk kimono and stared at herself in the mirror of her dressing table, lifting her face towards the sunlight that was pouring through the window. Her eyes definitely looked better now. After applying Pond's Cold Cream to her face and neck, she sat at her desk, took the key from its secret place and unlocked the drawer. Taking out the letter, she turned it over in her hands. She'd read the threat dozens of times, perhaps hundreds, since it had arrived, puzzling over who could have written it.

She'd always thought she was respected among her peers, but perhaps she'd been wrong. She'd been practically evicted from Hollywood months ago when she'd been loaned out to Ealing. How much further did her blackmailer want her to fall?

She opened the envelope, the words so familiar now. And yet, every time she looked at them a fresh fear sliced through her.

$50,000 CASH
OR I SEND THESE PHOTOS TO THE PRESS
WAIT FOR INSTRUCTIONS

Also in the envelope was the photo. She examined the black-and-white picture of her naked self. She was much younger here of course, only nineteen, and her hair darker and longer, but that distinctive heart-shaped face and cheekbones meant she was still definitely recognisable. Her blackmailer had to be someone who understood the shame she'd suffer if these photos ever appeared in the scandal sheets. Someone who knew that it would be the end of her.

At twenty, just before the studio teamed her up with Max, Stan Fisher had mentioned that most actresses had something in their past they'd rather forget, and if this was the case with her, she'd better tell him now so he could attend to it. So she did. She told him that these photos existed, and he'd paid off the photographer, but obviously not enough. And now, all these years later, when she was at her lowest ebb, they'd resurfaced. She pictured a bulging envelope of contact sheets depicting Stella Hope in all her vulnerability, shoved to the back of a drawer in some Hollywood dive, ready for the world's eyes.

But who would want to destroy her? It didn't make sense. Hollywood was cut-throat, yes, but she'd always been civil on her way up. Had she crossed another actress without realising it? Did she know someone who'd fallen on hard times and seen their opportunity? Who might consider her a rival? Of course, everyone was a rival, waiting to see if you'd tumble from a height, ready to scrabble for your spot.

She fleetingly wondered if the blackmailer could be one of Max's girlfriends, but then dismissed the idea. He was the wealthiest star at the studio, could give them anything they wanted. Why would they want her money, too?

The stamp on the envelope was American and the demand was in dollars, which was good, because it meant nobody here in London knew. But how on earth would she find her blackmailer when she was thousands of miles away? And she had to find them; she'd be damned if she was going to pay and let them get away with this.

The phone rang.

'Good news,' said Maggie excitedly. 'The director has agreed to let you screen test today.'

'Oh, Maggie!' gasped Stella. 'For *My True Life*?'

'Yes. They've done some tests, but haven't found anyone yet,' she said. 'I repeated what you told me to say, that you'd felt a little off-colour on Monday but were fighting fit now and it was unfair not to let you test.'

'Darling, well done!' Stella was thrilled. 'If they let me play both the daughter and the mother, this will be career-changing. It's the stuff of Oscars.'

'It's wonderful, but you do have to hurry, Stella. They said two o'clock sharp.'

Stella glanced at her watch.

'I was thinking,' Maggie continued, 'why don't you come here, to my flat? It's on the way, I have everything we need. We'll do the daughter first and get you to the studios so you can start, then I can set up and do the mother straight after.'

'Good idea. And I've just plunged my poor face into one of your ice baths and put on some cold cream.'

'Don't rub it off,' said Maggie. 'In fact, if you can bear to, spread on another thin layer before you leave and just jump in a cab.'

'I'll be there as soon as I can,' said Stella, and hung up.

This was it, her big chance. She called down to Samuel, the doorman, to hail a black cab to take her to Ealing Village. Then she quickly pulled on the casual day dress she'd bought in Petticoat Lane. Its thin cotton was the colour of vanilla ice cream and looked far more carefree than she felt. These paler colours suited her olive skin well – something else Maggie had been right about. She wrapped her waist with a wide black chiffon scarf, stepped into matching pumps and threw a short-waisted black jacket over her shoulders. She rarely wore her couture these days, although her wardrobe was stuffed with it. She donned her tortoiseshell Gucci sunglasses to hide her make-up-less face.

Stella hurried downstairs and stepped outside, just as her cab pulled up. Handing Samuel a few shillings as a tip, she jumped in and pulled the partition shut for privacy. There wasn't much traffic, and she watched the Soho streets quickly glide by and gradually turn leafier as they entered Ealing. It was going to be a hot July day. She took a handkerchief from her bag and dabbed at her temples. Even when her mood momentarily lifted, the blackmail letter still hung over her, a dark cloud obscuring the sun.

She recalled another scorching July afternoon, a lifetime ago, a hungry, worried girl of nineteen climbing the stairs to an airless attic studio with dirt-smeared windows on Fairfax Avenue. It was meant to be a one-hour shoot, but it lasted two, with the photographer saying he hadn't got a good shot yet, almost there, just one more. So many photos. His breath was rancid as he leaned over her, moving her into position, reassurances that her face would be cropped out. Then the fifty dollars at the end of it all, his offer to double it if she would let him bring his friend in, too. She'd refused but was so desperate she'd considered it for a moment.

The cab turned a sharp corner and she banged her shoulder on the window, cursing the fact she no longer had a driver at her disposal.

She would speak to Maggie and ask for her advice. She wanted to ignore the letter, but she couldn't just sit and wait for another to arrive. Perhaps she could go to the police, but what could they do? And she was worried it would get out somehow. Could she contact Star Studios and tell them what had happened? Would they even care? No, Maggie would know what to do. She was a great listener, and the only friend she had in this place. They'd only just met, but what difference did that make? She'd known Max for over twenty years now, and in the end, they'd become strangers to one another.

She straightened up and opened her silver compact mirror for a final check. 'So Christalla Petrakis,' she said in a whisper. She often called herself by her real name when she needed a touch of courage. 'Who wants to see your beautiful face in the gutter?'

CHAPTER SIX

Maggie sat on her balcony, a cup of strong tea in one hand and a half-smoked Woodbine in the other as she waited for Stella. She looked down on the perfectly manicured communal gardens of Ealing Village. This was home, for now. Who'd have thought all those years ago, living in her rundown council flat, that she'd end up in the well-to-do suburbs of Ealing?

When she'd first seen the art-deco apartments, with corrugated green tiles adorning the gabled roofs, she assumed the rent would be well beyond her reach. The whitewashed walls and brick-red balconies whispered wealth. The gated complex had, after all, been built for the stars of Ealing Studios. It even had an open-air swimming pool, tennis courts and clubhouse. But the big-name actors never came, and neither did the directors or producers.

No, they wanted the glamour and pace of London's West End, so the flats were offered at a much cheaper rate and filled up with technical staff and crew instead: cameramen, prop men, continuity girls, B-list actors and seamstresses.

And her. And if she was careful, and cut out her evening meal, she could make the rent without getting further into debt.

She pictured the dream she'd held on to for years: to establish her own make-up academy and teach young female artists coming through. But that all seemed so far away now, especially after everything that had happened.

Maggie sighed. She put out her ciggie and wound a piece of hair around her finger, the way she often did when she was thinking. She didn't mind cutting down on food, but was loathe to let go of her whisky. Her long evenings were filled with anxiety and terrible imaginings. Whisky numbed all that, if only for a while. She allowed herself one glass a night from the bottle of White Horse on her bedstand, but still, it was a generous glass – and it all cost. The extra money she was now earning as Stella's assistant could not have come at a better time.

A black taxi came to a stop downstairs and Maggie leaned over the balcony. Stella emerged, glanced up and waved.

Look at her, thought Maggie, *a beauty on the outside, a wreck on the inside.*

She waved back, flicked the ash off her skirt and carried her ashtray and cup to the kitchen. She'd risen early to tidy and had even got some of that fancy coffee Stella had mentioned from the Italian grocers, after she'd said how sick she was of tea.

In just a week Maggie had grown fond of Stella. She may have overstated the idea that she was a huge fan, but she did genuinely like the woman, despite her ego.

In the hall, Maggie looked in the mirror, adjusted her

headband – tucking in a lock of hair – reapplied a slick of Max Factor Clear Red – which she always kept in her pocket, because there was no excuse *ever* for faded lipstick – and waited for the knock.

Like most movie stars, Stella was self-obsessed and had asked no questions about her, which meant Maggie hadn't been forced to tell any more lies. And she was delighted at how quickly she'd managed to latch on to Miss Stella Hope, gaining her trust – the blackmail letter had proved the perfect opportunity – and now she was her assistant, too.

But she was still taken aback at how quickly Stella had spoken about her personal life with her ex-husband, Max. That's what loneliness did to a person, Maggie supposed.

Of course, Stella would find out what she was up to at some point, but not yet.

One hour later, Maggie had finished Stella's skin, brows and eyes and was about to paint on her lips.

'Tell me again about this party,' said Stella, the ice cubes clinking in her glass. Having announced it was too hot for coffee, she had wanted tea after all, but had ruined it by insisting on having it cold, American-style.

'Like I said,' began Maggie, testing the pale pink shade of lipstick on the back of her hand, 'it's a summer swim party downstairs on Saturday. Everyone's invited, and once the sun's down, it'll continue in the clubhouse. They're setting up a cocktail bar specially. Will you come?'

Stella waited for her to finish using the lip brush before speaking.

'I don't know,' she said. 'I mean, it could be excruciating, darling. If it's a party for the crew, will they really want me there? They hardly speak to me. And I haven't been to a party in ages. Not since that awful night after the Oscars.'

'All the more reason to come,' said Maggie. 'I mean, I won't abandon you if that's what you're worried about. We can stick together all night.' She smiled. 'It might do you good, you know – take your mind off things.' And she meant it. Stella looked so tightly wound, a carefree evening would be perfect right now. It would also give Maggie a chance to talk to her away from work, perhaps find out something useful.

She placed a tissue between Stella's lips and waited a few seconds for her to press them together. Stella then peeled it away and held it out as if not knowing what to do with it. Taking it, Maggie scrunched it and dropped it in the wastepaper basket at her feet. Stella had been famous for so many years, thought Maggie, it was as if she'd forgotten how to live like a normal person.

Well, there were no airs and graces for movie stars at Ealing Studios, as Stella was finding out for herself.

'Perhaps I will come!' said Stella brightly. 'I'll skip the pool party and just come to the clubhouse. I'm feeling a little heavy right now and would rather not be seen in a swimsuit.'

'Wonderful,' said Maggie, packing away her make-up and brushes, determined not to get into another conversation about Stella's weight. 'We need to get on. Let's jump in a taxi to the studios.'

Stella stood and slid her thumb inside the chiffon scarf she'd tied around her waist.

'Yes, I'm definitely a little heavier, and it won't do, Maggie. I wish I was blessed with your height.'

Maggie felt a pang of sympathy – the woman's insecurities were never-ending.

'You've got a wonderful figure,' she said, and meant it. 'Most women would kill to have your curves, me included.'

'Yes, I know, but is an hourglass still *fashionable*?' Stella asked, staring at herself in the full-length mirror, twisting this way and that. 'The young girls coming through are so thin these days. I blame this weather,' she continued. 'Hot one minute, chilly the next. I don't know *how* you stay slim in this godawful place. I just want to eat all the time. And this terrible blackmail situation is making me so anxious. I used to be so disciplined. Do you eat, Maggie? I never see you eat.'

Maggie laughed. 'Yes, I eat, of course I do. But I do sometimes forget, if I'm busy or running an errand. Come on or we'll be late.'

She grabbed the vanity case, her 'box of tricks' as Stella called it, and bustled her to the door.

'Make a note, Maggie,' said Stella, on the landing, 'on Monday I'll start a health regime. No more food from that studio canteen. Ask Rita in the kitchen to make us something special. Something light. We can eat together. It'll be fun!'

'Alright, I'll see what she can do,' said Maggie, knowing full well that Rita would be furious. 'And what about the champagne? The Dom Pérignon? Shall I cancel the order if you're on a health kick?'

'Good God, no! Whatever gave you that idea?'

CHAPTER SEVEN

Two hours later, Stella shook two aspirin from a bottle, took a swig of cold, weak tea and swallowed. The screen test had been a disaster.

Well, she was only halfway through it, and was about to play the role of the mother. But she knew. She'd lost her nerve playing someone so young, had given it no conviction. They'd refused a retake, saying it was fine, and now she had to see the whole thing through to the bitter end. And as if that wasn't depressing enough, Maggie had managed to age her for the mother character in a matter of minutes: a few extra lines here, a greying wig there, a brush of sallow powder on her cheeks and a slick of unflattering orange lipstick. Goodness, she looked a fright.

'It's as if I'm on my deathbed,' Stella complained, grimacing at herself in the mirror. It was a period piece, and the discomfort of the corseted gown was showing on her face.

'Nonsense,' replied Maggie, shading the space from Stella's nose to her mouth, giving her marionette lines. 'You have to convince them you can play both women.' She whipped off the cotton cape that had been protecting Stella's shoulders from a dusting of face powder and practically pushed her towards the set. 'Go on. You can do this, Stella.'

But Stella had been in this business long enough to know they'd already made up their minds. She took her mark, spreading her long, striped skirts as she sat in an unsightly, paisley-patterned armchair. She didn't mind having to do an English accent – she was quite good at it – but why did these Brits insist on such ugly costumes and monstrous furniture? Where was the glamour, the swoon, the joy?

The scene began. Her 'son', an actor called Frederick Stanley, had come to ask her for money after losing everything in a card game. After a lot of toing and froing, he finally sank on his knees, begging his mother for mercy. His face was in her lap as the camera closed in on her reaction. She did her best to show sympathy and then let it change to disdain followed by disgust, just as the director had instructed. *Almost there*, she thought. Just a couple more lines. Then she deserved a stiff martini and a long soak in the tub.

'Don't make a fool of yourself, boy,' she said coldly. She'd speak to the director, see if there was something else for her, a leading role that could stretch her but was perhaps more suitable. Frederick continued to wail, hamming it up, despite the fact this was *her* scene. Just as she was about to deliver her next line, she felt his hand go up, under her skirt and grab her thigh.

She jolted but continued – a decision made in a second. To stop now, mid-scene, would harm her more than him. They'd never let her reshoot, and he'd deny it anyway. He squeezed her flesh three times, his fingers digging in, but she didn't flinch and finished her line.

The director called, 'Cut!' and Stella jumped up and kicked the actor away. He fell back, laughing, and she kicked him again but this time he grabbed her foot, pulling off her silk pump. Everyone watched as she snatched it back and put it on.

'What the hell do you think you're doing?' she shouted. 'How dare you!'

Frederick stood up and grinned. 'You didn't stop,' he said with a leer. 'I was testing you. You just carried on like a trooper. I knew you would! It's true what they say about Hollywood actresses. You're real professionals.'

'I swear,' she said, trembling now. 'You do that again…'

A few of the crew had gathered near him, and there was a smatter of laughter.

'Or maybe…' he continued, 'maybe you liked it, and that's why you carried on?'

More laughter now.

She was trembling and lifted her arm to thump him, but Maggie was next to her in an instant, holding her back.

'Don't,' she said. 'Stella, don't.' She pulled her away and marched her off. 'He got a woman fired a few months ago because she complained about him. Someone in wardrobe.'

'I'm not putting up with this,' Stella said, seething, as Maggie led her back to the make-up chair.

'I know,' said Maggie.

She covered Stella's face in cleansing cream, using her fingertips to rub it in light circles, leaving it on while she attended to her wig.

'I mean,' continued Stella, close to tears, 'I'm here to do my job. Not to be groped by vermin like that.'

Maggie removed the wig tape, carefully put a hairband on Stella, and brushed out her hair.

'The thing is,' said Maggie, 'they think it's just a laugh. Just a perk of the job. You know what they're like, male leads. See it as their God-given right.'

Stella dabbed at her eyes and waved for a cigarette. Maggie passed her the box of Lucky Strikes from her handbag and her lighter.

'Perfect!' Stella exclaimed. 'I'm down to my last one.'

A couple of tears rolled down her face, and Maggie quickly swiped them away for her. Stella lit up and took a long drag.

'Don't let the bastards get to you,' said Maggie. 'Surely Hollywood's the same?'

Stella shrugged. 'Probably worse. They're like hungry wolves in Hollywood.' She tapped the ash into a saucer. 'But with Max at my side for years, well, I think I forgot how bad it was.' For a moment she missed him. Despite everything he'd done. 'I suppose he sort of protected me from all that. Nobody would dare.'

Using a warm flannel, Maggie wiped the cream off Stella's face.

'You're lucky,' she said. 'To have had that for a while, at least.' She applied some moisturiser and let it sink in before applying a light make-up look for the rest of the day.

'What I don't understand,' said Stella, 'and don't take this the wrong way…'

'What?'

'Well... I'm *Stella Hope*.' She paused. Maggie shook her head, not understanding. 'Doesn't that *mean* anything?' Stella continued. 'I've worked with the biggest and best, made the studio hundreds of thousands of dollars, been nominated for an Academy Award. I mean, you'd think they'd respect that?'

Maggie smiled. 'Everyone's fair game here,' she said. 'The leading actresses, script girls, Rita in the kitchen. As long as you have a pulse and breasts, they don't care. We're very egalitarian, you know!'

Stella gave a scornful laugh. 'Wonderful.'

'Frederick Stanley would probably see it as a badge of honour,' said Maggie, 'if he got you into bed.'

'Ugh, can you imagine?' Stella shuddered at the thought. As if today hadn't been bad enough, now this, a reminder of how far she'd fallen.

'Shall I tell you a secret?' said Maggie. She paused, looked around and then said, 'It'll cheer you up, no end.'

'What?'

Maggie leaned down and whispered in her ear: 'He wears a piece, Frederick Stanley. He wears a toupée.'

Stella raised her eyebrows, and Maggie pressed her lips together to stop herself smiling.

'You can do what you want with that information,' said Maggie, 'but you didn't hear it from me.'

'Oh, well, that *has* made me feel better.'

'You're still coming to the party at the weekend, aren't you?' asked Maggie.

Stella pictured facing the crew again after a day like today, but in a social setting. Would it be humiliating or would they admire her? And anyway, shouldn't she stay home and figure out what to do about that blackmail letter? The anxiety gnawed at her stomach.

'Come on,' said Maggie, 'it'll be fun, I promise.' She took Stella's own lipstick and applied it for her.

Stella looked at herself in the mirror. There she was again. Stella Hope. Why *should* she stop living? There would always be terrible men in the world, and hiding in her apartment wouldn't change that.

'You know,' she said. 'I think I will.'

CHAPTER EIGHT

Hollywood, Los Angeles
December 1953

It had been a month since she'd had dinner with Max Whitman, and still Ginny had heard nothing. Four weeks of excruciating Elegance and Poise lessons, painful ballet classes and tedious Acting Theory, and all with no prospect of a role. Four weeks of peering into her mail slot in her apartment block every morning, then pushing her hand inside, in case she'd missed a note from him: *Ginny – they said yes! We start tomorrow! Max.*

And while she waited and hoped, the small grain of doubt in her stomach grew and hardened into a pebble, pressing down with a persistence, telling her that he'd meant none of it. Worst of all was the anxious voice she heard inside her head during her most uncertain moments: that he'd seen her other films and had thought her mediocre after all. In a town that rewarded effervescence, mediocrity was the ultimate sin.

And now, here she was, at the crowded counter of Schwab's Pharmacy on Sunset Boulevard, nursing a sickly Coke ice-cream float, and looking up every time the bell on the door rang. The place was an institution and it had become a regular haunt for her. As well as a drugstore, it was where hopefuls rubbed shoulders with established stars, directors and producers. Some out-of-work actors contemplated a single cup of coffee for hours, despite the large sign stating: *30 minutes maximum.*

There were booths where you could get a cheap lunch, and a soda fountain too, where Ava Gardner had famously once made ice-cream sodas for everyone. A couple of gossip columnists were permanently set up in opposing booths on the other side of the store. Ginny loved the bustle here and, as it was close to her apartment, it was as good a place as any to loiter in the hope of bumping into Max. She knew he came here, because a couple of the girls in her block had mentioned seeing him.

She glanced along the counter and saw two other actresses staring around in awe, faces full of hope as they waited for someone to change their lives. Ah, she knew that feeling well.

Yesterday, as Ginny was coming out of the studio canteen, she'd caught sight of Max across the lot, walking briskly while a couple of people spoke to him. A woman – his secretary, maybe? – was holding a clipboard, and he was shaking his head in response to her questions. He'd obviously just finished filming a scene as he was still in costume: leather chaps, gun holster, checked shirt, the trademark cowboy hat. She thought of what he'd said about not wanting to make more cowboy films. An urge had swept through her to call out his name, but of course she didn't. And there was a split second when he looked over his shoulder, but he didn't see her. Or at least she didn't think he did.

She pushed the ball of vanilla ice-cream down in her glass with a long spoon and watched as it bobbed back up again. What was she doing? Did she think he'd walk in and throw down a contract in front of her? If she thought anything came that easily, she was wasting her time. If anyone was going to make this happen, it would have to be her. She'd never relied on a man to get her anywhere before, why now?

Oh, but how wonderful would it have been? Starring opposite Max Whitman. Going through scripts with him. Hearing his thoughts on her performance. Watching him, learning from him. Basking in the glow of his fame.

Pushing away her Coke, she picked up her handbag to leave. She'd speak to Stan Fisher tomorrow, that's what she'd do – if she could get past his secretary, Ida. She opened her Coty compact and checked her face. Stan had noticed her weeks ago, after all, and although he'd given no guarantees, she'd done everything he'd asked. She'd changed her hair, her teeth, and had starved herself. She touched the white-blonde curls near her cheek and gazed at her face critically. She had to admit, she looked better than she ever had. She ran her tongue over her front teeth. Even if she didn't quite feel herself anymore. She clicked the compact shut and dropped it into her bag.

Just then, the bell on the door rang and she turned to see Cynthia who lived across the hall in her block. Also an actress, she loved to chat, often with tales of jobs she'd been promised, or gossip about others. Ginny felt a bit mean turning away, hoping Cynthia wouldn't see her, but she just wasn't in the mood.

Her mind went back to Stan as she looked in her bag, pretending to be preoccupied with its contents. When she spoke to him, she wouldn't mention Max or what they'd discussed. She'd promised to keep it quiet, after all, and didn't know how much Stan knew about Max's plans. But she *could* ask Stan about a contract perhaps, about any roles coming up. Nobody got anywhere being shy. And she really wanted to work, to prove her worth.

Max had invited her to dinner on a whim and had then promptly forgotten all about her. She'd been gullible, and from now on, she'd toughen up. She slid off her stool. And there she was thinking he'd had designs on her. When, in fact, all she was to him was another girl trying to make it big. Another Cynthia. Another her. Everyone was probably interchangeable to him. Maybe he'd already found someone else? Hollywood was full of Ginnys and Cynthias. She paid her bill and turned to leave.

'Hey, Ginny!' Cynthia's hand was on her arm. 'Look!' She flicked a card in front of her face.

'Sorry? I'm in a bit of a rush...'

'An invitation!' Cynthia put the card on the counter and fiddled with a hairclip that kept her dark curls off her face, readjusting it. 'Look, an actual official invitation to a party on Saturday. From Star Studios.'

'*What?*'

Star Studios? *Max's* studio? Where Stan Fisher worked? Why hadn't she been invited?

'I mean, *how?*' Ginny asked.

There was a constant round of studio parties packed

with producers and stars and directors, but only the elite had entry.

'I was looking for you! Do you want to come?' Cynthia asked. 'It's a Christmas party. Tony said I can bring a friend.'

'*Really?* Well... yes! Of course I'll come! But Christmas is weeks away.'

Cynthia shrugged. 'Hollywood, darling!' she said, laughing. 'They make the rules.'

Ginny felt a momentary pang of guilt. She'd been trying to avoid her, and here she was, accepting Cynthia's invitation.

'Are you sure it's alright?' she asked. 'And who's Tony?'

'My cousin,' replied Cynthia. 'He's working the doors. He says nobody will notice if he sneaks in an extra guest or two, especially if we get there once the party's heated up. Say midnight.'

'They definitely won't throw us out?' Ginny asked. 'I mean that would be *awful*.'

'Are you kidding?' Cynthia laughed. 'You Brits are so proper! Trust me – all the security guys do it. It's at Gerry Sherman's place – you know, that big producer? Owns that mansion up in the Hollywood Hills? Last year, Tony says, they set up a circus in the entrance hall – it's *that* big! It's going to be the wildest party you've ever been to.'

Ginny burst out laughing. 'Oh my god, it sounds wonderful!'

'Come on,' said Cynthia, linking arms with her and leading her to the exit. 'We've only got two days to try and figure out what on earth we're going to wear.'

As the two of them walked down the road, Ginny's heart lifted. She'd see him. Max was bound to be there. Maybe he'd realise he'd been right all along and that she was the perfect person for his new secret project. And Stan would be there, too. Everyone knew it was Stan who made contracts happen. Get on the good side of Stan, they said, and you had it made. And he already liked her, didn't he? She just needed to place herself centre stage again. Remind them that just a few weeks ago, they'd considered her the next big thing.

This party was the perfect opportunity. Everything was riding on this.

CHAPTER NINE

Ginny leaned out of the taxi window as they snaked up the winding drive, the evening breeze tugging her hair. Head on arms, she watched, waiting for that first glimpse of the Sherman Mansion. There were so many wild stories about what went on behind the famous gates that it seemed nobody really knew what was true anymore. Just last year, a Christian group had held demonstrations outside, dubbing it the Palace of Depravity and insisting that the parties be banned. Yet despite the protests, nothing had happened. Everyone knew that Sherman was well-liked among the LA Police Department, namely because he often invited them along, too.

Finally, the elaborate wrought-iron gates loomed into view, encasing the mansion like a rare bird in a cage. Spotlights stood at either side of the gate and their beams shone diagonally onto the ornate golden G and S initials that were perched on the very top.

Cynthia nudged her. 'Well, we're in the right place,' she said, grinning, 'in case you were wondering.'

As their cab approached, the gates parted, and they drove in. The ribbon of dark asphalt wound this way and that, and each time they rounded a curve, they caught sight of the mansion itself, only for it to disappear again. Then the car took a final turn and there it was. Sherman Mansion.

'Wow,' said Ginny. 'Well, this is quite something.'

'Isn't it?' Cynthia laughed.

It had gone midnight and the house, covered in white fairy lights, twinkled in the blue-black sky. Gold flaming torches jutted from the brickwork, illuminating the dozens of flowers and woodland creatures that were intricately carved from stone. An immaculate lawn lay before the entrance, and Grecian statues were dotted around, arms aloft as if to welcome the guests. In front of the stairs stood a huge Christmas tree, decorated with exquisite gold and silver animals. Miniature boxes wrapped in shiny red paper hung from its branches, and as guests walked past, they occasionally plucked one off. They must have contained tiny gifts.

'What a riot!' Cynthia said, handing the driver some dollar bills. 'Imagine what it's like inside. Come on.'

At the door, a thickset man with a barrel for a chest waved at them.

'There's Tony!' Cynthia ran up and hugged him, her arms barely reaching round his front.

'This way, ladies,' he said, winking at Ginny. He swung the door open and let them in. Nobody checked their invitation, nobody asked any questions. It was that easy. Ginny was inside.

It soon became clear why. The party was at full throttle. The heat hit Ginny first, and she was glad she'd decided to wear an emerald-green halter-neck dress rather than anything with sleeves. She'd borrowed the floor-length outfit from one of the girls in her block, and had promised not to ruin it.

At the far end, a jazz band wearing paper party hats was furiously playing on a raised podium, shining with sweat as they sawed their trombones and blasted trumpets held high. The drummer was doing his own thing, whipping everyone into a frenzy with a frantic beat. Several crowds nearby were dancing and jumping to the beat, arms in the air, heads thrown back, men with shirts undone, women with cleavages bursting out. Any inhibitions had left the building a while ago. Ginny marvelled at it all, wondering if *she'd* ever feel this reckless and free. Maybe if she was rich and famous. You could get away with anything then.

She turned to say something to Cynthia but had lost her. Already? Never mind, she'd find her later.

A hand was on her shoulder, shaking her slightly.

'Klaus? Have you seen Klaus?' asked a woman in a German accent. She wore a spectacular headdress that was a burst of black shiny feathers around her pale powdered face, making her look like a giant crow. She had a long cigarette holder between her fingers, and the lit cigarillo was dangerously close to Ginny's hair.

'Sorry,' said Ginny, stepping back a little. 'I don't know who Klaus is.'

'I understand,' said the woman, tapping the side of her nose twice. 'He's lying low. You'd better too.' And she walked away. 'They'll come for us all in the end!'

Ginny shook her head and smiled. She took a coupe glass of champagne from a waiter who had magically appeared at her side and climbed the sweeping staircase to survey the scene better. She'd see everything from there. Max had to be here somewhere. He was the studio's biggest star, after all.

The balcony was full of cosy round tables, each bathed in its own warm, amber glow from the small, shaded lamp at its centre. The gold-rimmed side plates were piled with food at each setting. Caviar, which she recognised but had never eaten. Oysters, gloopy and unappealing. Tiny, intricately decorated pastries that someone had probably got up at 4 a.m. to make. All of it ignored.

At the tables sat couples having intimate conversations, some of them not speaking at all, just sipping their drinks and touching each other, kissing and stroking. Licking and laughing. A woman walking towards her, whose dress was around her waist, was draped in gold tinsel and laughing as she pulled a barely conscious man down the hall.

Ginny looked away and leaned over the gilt bannister, drinking in the chaos below. Is this what happened when you were famous, she wondered? You lost all modesty? While it was amusing because, well, they were all having such a good time, she had to admit she also found it somewhat shocking. Though of course she would never say that to anyone. After all, this was a party at Gerry Sherman's. If she didn't approve or didn't fit in here, then perhaps they'd think she wasn't cut out for Hollywood at all. No, she'd play the game and do her best.

Looking down on the scene below, she realised this wasn't just one party, but several. People had broken away into smaller groups, each celebrating in their own way.

In one corner, a group of men in their shirtsleeves were

playing cards at a small table, shouting and slamming glasses as the game progressed. They were surrounded by women, girlfriends, maybe mistresses, all of them egging them on, draping themselves over them, whispering into their ears. A haphazard pile of dollar bills was in the centre of the table – surely more than a year's rent for Ginny – and occasionally a couple of bills would fall unnoticed to the floor.

To her left, Ginny saw a sequinned acrobat dangling from the ceiling, spinning inside a hoop, while downstairs, a juggler in a similar sequin suit tossed lit torches under her. A woman circled the juggler. She wore a silver top hat, and her jewelled leotard depicted the Stars and Stripes. In her hands was a leash and at the end of it was a frantic chimpanzee. She paraded the poor animal on the short leash, stopping for guests to pet him.

Sipping her champagne, Ginny gazed at the partygoers, trying to make out faces. In one corner, leaning against a wall was a man in a day suit, someone who hadn't bothered to get changed because he either didn't realise he should or was powerful enough to wear whatever he pleased. She smiled as she recognised Stan's bulky figure, then gasped as he leaned forward and accepted a light from Max.

Max. He was immaculate in a black dinner suit with a white bow-tie, still tied, and his hair so shiny with brilliantine it could reflect the whole room. Stan said something and Max laughed. She couldn't hear them, but she remembered how much she'd liked that crazy laugh of his – uninhibited, real. How it had lit him up, and she'd felt a thrill pull tight right through her. She'd told herself she shouldn't think about him in that way, but the truth of it was, she couldn't help herself. His eyes, his skin, those eyelashes, the way he'd shaken her hand and smiled. She couldn't get him out of her mind.

She sighed and drained her champagne, then accepted another from a passing waiter, keeping her eyes on the scene below the whole time. She watched as Max reached out his arm and waved to a woman in a white fur stole who walked towards him. She kissed him on one cheek and then the other, continental-style. She kissed Stan too, and as she did, her stole fell off her shoulder. Max pulled it back on for her and kept his arm there, holding her, proprietorial.

Stella Hope wasn't just beautiful. She was exquisite.

Her face had a quality about it that Ginny had never seen before. Luminous, serene. A face that could elicit stares and make rooms fall silent. And she held herself with effortless poise, a kind of grace that was more common in ballet dancers than actors. A small crowd near the trio kept a respectful distance, till Stella said something and one of the women eagerly stepped closer and started chatting.

Ginny frowned. Whatever he'd told her about their relationship, Max didn't look like a man who'd stopped loving his wife. He was besotted – anyone could see that. Did Stella feel the same, she wondered? Not according to him. According to him, she had other lovers.

Stella turned her back to him as she continued her conversation, and he peeled off from the group and stood next to Stan, smoking, watching her the whole time.

There was a raucous cheer in one corner, and as it grew, Ginny saw that Ella Fitzgerald had arrived and was about to start singing. The band made space for her, and as the first notes struck up for 'Oh, Lady Be Good', everyone whooped with glee. Ginny couldn't believe Ella was actually there, in her beautiful pink chiffon lace dress and coiffed hair.

When the number ended to rapturous applause, Ginny turned to see what Max had thought, but she couldn't spot him. Stan had disappeared too, and Stella. After another drink, Cynthia found Ginny and made her come downstairs for a dance. A couple of older men joined them, but after one dance, Cynthia pulled her away from them and they danced together instead, faster, the two of them revelling in the chaotic beat.

An hour or so later and Ginny was hot, sticky and dead on her feet.

'I need the bathroom,' she shouted to Cynthia. 'Where is it?'

Cynthia shrugged. 'Upstairs, I guess. Ask a waiter.'

Ginny climbed the stairs, her feet pinching. She'd find the bathroom, have another quick look for Max and Stan and then head home. It was her turn to pay for the taxi, and Cynthia was bound to join her.

The waiters directed her down a corridor and she wandered through. The red carpet was littered with glasses and cigarette butts, and she wondered what Mr Sherman thought – it was his house, after all, though she didn't even know what he looked like, so who knew if he was even here? He'd probably hire someone to clean it all up as if it had never happened. All the craziness forgotten and everything back in its place by morning. But it was already morning. She glanced at her watch. Ten past three. Luckily, she could sleep in, as it was Sunday.

As she walked past a door it swung open, and inside she

saw someone bending over a silver serving dish. On it was a pile of white powder.

'You want some joy, honey?'

Ginny jumped at the voice behind her shoulder. The man was standing between her and the corridor.

'Sorry, I wasn't snooping, I was just trying to find the bathroom.'

He leaned across and pushed the door open wider.

'Joy powder for everyone,' he said. 'You can have as much as you want.'

Inside was a girl, maybe twenty at the most, with a metal tube in her hand about to lean over the plate.

'Are you in or out?' she said. 'We're not selling tickets.'

Another woman walked towards Ginny. She was stark naked. 'Come play,' she said, holding her hand out.

Ginny pulled back.

'In or out?' repeated the first woman.

'Out,' said Ginny, pushing past the man. 'Definitely out.' She knew lots of actors took cocaine, but she'd never seen platefuls of it.

'Come on, baby,' he called as she strode away. 'You won't regret it.'

She shook her head, rattled, and started to walk away.

'Here, Merry Christmas!' he called, and tossed her a small red box from his pocket. She caught it and saw it was one of the tiny gifts from the huge tree outside. She pulled back the paper and saw a little bag inside, stuffed with white powder. Crouching, she dropped it in the corner and carried on.

Finally, she came upon the bathroom and entered the lavatory, shuddering as she thought about what she'd just witnessed. She'd have to toughen up if she was going to make it here.

She stood at one of the basins and washed her hands, running the cold water over her wrists to cool down. Then she took a hand towel from the neatly folded pile that was on the side, and dabbed at her face, swiping away the smudged mascara. Opening her bag, she rummaged for her lipstick. She'd spruce up, see if she could find Max and then go. She'd had enough of this madhouse.

The door swung open and someone walked in just as she dropped her lipstick. 'Dammit!' She picked it up, opened it and looked at the damage, wondering if she could salvage anything.

'Here, have this.' The woman at the next basin handed her a new lipstick. 'Barely touched it – it'll suit you.'

'I... er...'

'Go on, take it, darling,' said Stella Hope.

Ginny took it and mumbled her thanks. She hadn't heard Stella's real voice before, and she could detect a soft accent behind the American drawl. It was enchanting.

'First time to one of these parties?' Stella asked.

Ginny nodded then applied the lipstick. 'Thank you, Miss Hope.'

Stella waved her hand. 'Keep it. I have hundreds.'

'Oh, are you sure?'

'Sure, I'm sure. I advertise them so I get them for nothing.' Stella gazed at Ginny in the mirror. 'You on contract?'

'Not yet – am hoping though.'

Stella nodded. 'English? That's a cute accent.'

'Thank you. If you don't mind me saying, I was just thinking how lovely your voice is, too.'

Stella smiled.

'I don't mind at all,' she said. 'Years ago, they decided that being Cypriot wouldn't work, and I had to drop the accent. But it still slips out occasionally. You should keep yours.'

'I'd like to,' Ginny replied. 'If they let me.'

'Sure, they'll let you,' said Stella. She leaned closer to the mirror, ran a finger over one eyebrow, seemed happy with what she saw and closed her bag. 'Tell them Stella Hope said it was charming.'

Ginny laughed. 'I will, Miss Hope, thank you.'

Stella turned to walk out. 'Good luck with the contract, darling,' she said. Then she winked at her. 'And watch out for the wolves.'

CHAPTER TEN

Ginny's face was hot again. She ran some water, splashed it a little and used another towel. Enough. She had to get out of here.

She left, making her way along the corridor and towards the staircase. If she didn't find Cynthia straight away, she'd get a taxi from outside and just head back.

A door opened to her left.

'*Ginny?*'

'Max!'

'What are you doing here?' he asked, incredulous.

He stepped out of the room and beamed that smile, genuinely happy to see her, and she felt herself light up inside. He looked left and right then motioned his head for her to step back inside with him. She didn't think twice. Once inside, he shut the door but didn't move. She could see there was an elaborate wooden sleigh bed behind him, piled with furs. He was standing so close.

'How come you're here?' he asked, his eyes searching her face then glancing down at her outfit. His gaze didn't linger – he was too much of a gentleman for that – but she was sure he was taking it all in: the shimmering satin dress, the daring neckline, the sweat on her skin.

She grinned. 'I got in with a friend. Her cousin is on the door,' she said. Then her face dropped. 'Oh! I'm not going to get him in trouble, am I?'

Max waved a hand dismissively. 'I'm not saying anything and nobody here cares.'

Then he paused and stared at her. She could hear him breathing. How many glasses of champagne had she drunk? And how many would it take for her to kiss him?

'I saw your wife,' she blurted.

Max stood back a little. 'Did you?' he asked. 'Well, I suppose that's not surprising. Everyone's here, that's why we're putting on our old show. The Golden Couple Extravaganza.'

'No,' said Ginny, sighing. 'I mean in the ladies. In the bathroom. I saw her. She was nice to me. We had a talk.' She saw the look on his face. 'Oh, I didn't say I knew you. She was just kind, you know. The way women are. Wished me luck. Said I shouldn't change my accent for anyone.' She was babbling like a fool now. 'That kind of thing.'

Max nodded, put his hands in his pockets and walked to the other side of the bed. He stared at it then looked up at her and gave a sad smile.

'I'm glad she was nice to you,' he said. 'Good to know she still has that in her. What did you talk about?'

Ginny shook her head. 'Nothing – really nothing. She gave me her lipstick. Mine broke. That's all. I don't even know why I mentioned it.'

She was kicking herself. She'd obviously upset him. 'I'm sorry, I shouldn't have said anything.'

He put his head on one side and looked at her properly now.

'Forget it,' he said, walking towards her again. 'I should be the one apologising. I've wanted to get back in touch for a while.' He was standing in front of her now, closer than before. 'To say I haven't forgotten you.' Pause. 'What I mean is I haven't forgotten what we spoke about.'

She didn't want to speak, didn't want to ruin it. So she just nodded.

'In fact, you've been on my mind a lot,' he said. A silence fell between them, and finally he shook his head and said, 'I can't do this.'

He put his hands behind his neck and sighed in exasperation. 'You look gorgeous and I've had too much to drink and I can't be trusted and you were right all along.'

She stood very still, then eventually she said, 'I was right about what?'

'I *am* a sad, lonely film star.'

She laughed and he did too.

'And I did want to have dinner with you. But that's not the only reason I asked you to my hotel room.' He took her hand now. 'I really *do* want to work with you. It's just going to take time, that's all. To deal with the divorce, and to make the studio see sense – that I need another female lead.'

'I can wait,' she said. Then she took a breath. 'But I want a contract. I need to work while I wait. I need to be doing something. And anything else, well...' What was she saying? The words came out before she'd had a chance to think. 'Anything else that might or might not happen, I can wait for that, too.'

'Of course, of course. I mean we can just wait for the script to be ready and the studio to see sense and, well... anything else that might happen between us, as you say.' He stared at her as if searching to see if they were on the same page. Then he moved an inch closer.

'We probably shouldn't do anything till I'm divorced anyway,' he said. 'I mean, maybe you don't want to do anything anyway? I have no idea how you feel about me? Why am I making such a hash of this?'

She stared at his mouth, opened her lips to say something but didn't. And that's when he took her face in his hands.

'I don't know what's happening,' he said, his breath hot on her face, 'but it feels like a craving. Do you feel the same?'

She gave a small nod, and in one quick move he reached behind her and locked the door.

She gave a short gasp.

'I mean, we *should* wait,' he said.

'But then again...' she added.

He put his hand behind her neck, pulled at the bow of her halter neck and untied it in one move. 'Nobody can know. Not yet.'

'Nobody,' she agreed.

At noon the next day, back at her apartment, Ginny was woken by a knock on the door. She clambered out of bed, her head thick as cotton wool. Then she remembered and grinned to herself.

'Who is it?' she called.

'Delivery!'

She opened the door. A courier stood on the threshold holding a huge bouquet of what must have been two, maybe three, dozen white roses.

'These are for you,' he said, shoving them towards her.

She'd never had flowers before.

'And this.' He balanced a large envelope on top. 'Sign here, please.'

After he'd gone, she put the flowers in the sink, wondering where she'd find a vase big enough. She opened the card that had come with them. It was typed and unsigned:

```
Let's always give in to our cravings.
                 Often.
     Can't wait to see you again.
```

She gave a squeal of delight. Then she picked up the envelope that was addressed to *Virginia Rose (Ginny Watkins)* and she ripped into it.

Inside was a contract for Star Studios.

*T*hey have come for me today. A woman in a white nurse's dress and cap pulls me off the mattress.

'You're disgusting,' she sneers. 'You need to wash before we take you to the ward.'

I start to protest: I don't belong in a hospital, why am I here? And where am I? But she drags me towards the open door, where two men stand guard, framed in the sickly light from the hallway. They wear grubby brown uniforms and look me up and down then pull faces at each other.

'She stinks,' says one. 'Is that blood?'

'What happened?' asks the other.

The nurse shrugs. 'That's how she came in. I don't ask questions.'

I stare at the first man's belt, where a huge metal ring hangs down. Dozens of keys dangle like fingers and then I see he's holding leather cuffs and some sort of chain. Am I in prison?

'I'm not sick!' I yell. 'I don't understand.'

In seconds he's buckled the cuffs on my wrists, and the

thick chain that runs between them means I can't move one hand without moving the other. The second man has dropped to the floor and done the same to my ankles. It has all happened so quickly.

'Hospital rules when we're moving you,' he explains. 'Make a fuss and the chain gets shorter.'

'But why?'

As I stumble along the corridor, I hear women's voices. One is crying, then I hear a moan, then a laugh. I twist my head to see where the noise is coming from but nothing. Are the women on the other side of the wall? Or have they long since disappeared? Hysterical ghosts who will return at night?

Now I'm pushed into a large white room. Along one wall are six deep baths, covered in sacking cloth. At the far end, a row of showers and hoses. They unchain me but the cuffs are kept on. As the men leave the room, an older nurse enters to help the first. In a matter of seconds, they've pulled off my tunic and I stand there naked, my hands darting to cover my shame.

'Nothing we ain't seen before,' cackles the second nurse. 'Go on – wash yourself.'

She tosses a yellow block of soap to the floor and I pick it up, then they shove me towards the showers.

I turn my back, reach for the tap and twist it. Nothing comes out. I look up at the shower head, waiting, twisting the tap this way and that. Still nothing. There's a giggle and suddenly a jet of water almost knocks me off my feet as I crash into the wall. They take it in turns to spray me down with the hose, whooping at the force of the water and my cries. Every time I drop the soap they spray it, making it *dance at my feet. My chest fills with hate. I will pay them back for this.*

I don't cry out anymore. I hold the soap tight and scrub at the bloodstains on my arms and legs, then I rub my hair over and over. The water pools around my feet and washes down the drain, first brown then finally clear. They turn off the hose and hand me a thin towel. As I dry my arms, I feel something. What's that? A soreness in the crook of my left elbow.

I examine it closely and see a red puncture mark surrounded by a purple bruise. Then a memory whispers in my ear. A man, injecting me while I'm on the floor. He's sobbing. Why is he crying? Someone is standing over him. What have they done to me? Did they poison me? Is this why I'm broken? My story comes to me in shards, a glass thrown to the floor.

My mind is fractured, but today I remember more than yesterday and tomorrow I will remember more. I rub myself dry and count the things I know for sure. Three things now:

1. *There was blood everywhere.*

2. *I was in a beautiful room.*

3. *There was a crying man.*

These are the memories that have stayed intact. These are the things I know to be true.

I wish I could remember my name.

CHAPTER ELEVEN

Ealing Village, London
July 1954

Maggie was treading water in the swimming pool at Ealing Village. It was the final day of July and the crew party was in full swing. The two long glasses of Pimm's that she'd already knocked back had taken the edge off her mood. She was exhausted: being Stella's assistant as well as her make-up artist was demanding work. Not that she was complaining – she was perfectly placed now to get what she needed – but the woman had so many neuroses and fears. Maggie was tired to the bone. And it wasn't as if she didn't have her own demons to battle.

She lifted her legs in front of her and wiggled her toes. She *had* felt sorry for Stella the other day, though. The way that awful Frederick Stanley had groped her on set. And the look on Stella's face. She'd been so shocked, as if something like that had never happened before. She had no idea how lucky she was.

Getting out, Maggie grabbed a towel, spread it on a lounger and lay down to wait for Stella. She'd quickly discovered there was a lot of waiting for Stella. There were a few stragglers hanging around, but most of the crew had already decamped to the clubhouse, and Maggie could hear strains of Cole Porter's 'Too Darn Hot' float towards her. Someone must have brought a gramophone from their room.

As the light began to fade and the evening surrendered to an inky blue, she heard her name.

'Hey, Maggie!'

It was Tom, standing in the pool by the lion's head fountain. He was one of the cameramen – funny, charming, always kind. They'd flirted a few times, but nothing had happened. He'd even asked her out once, but by then everything had turned sour and she couldn't contemplate it. Had things been different, had she'd been who she was a year ago, she wouldn't mind waking up next to him. Tom's mate, another cameraman called Bobby, was with him.

She waved and they waved back.

'Watch this,' shouted Tom. He looked at the lion as it squirted water from its mouth in an arc back into the pool. Tom dipped his head in the water and filled his mouth, and Bobby did the same. Then, with bulging cheeks, they turned and squirted water into each other's faces.

'You idiots,' she said, laughing.

A couple of people clapped and cheered, and they did it all over again.

Maggie heard the tip-tap of heels on the tiles behind her and turned to see Stella approaching. She was wearing a white and silver patterned silk kaftan that rippled in the evening breeze. Her hair was wrapped in a matching turban, with a sparkling brooch at its centre, above her forehead. She looked like she'd just stepped out of a harem.

'Hello, darling,' Stella said, bending down to give her a peck on each cheek. 'Is this alright?' Her arms gestured towards her outfit. 'I just didn't know what to wear.'

'Wonderful,' said Maggie.

It *was* wonderful, but ridiculous too, and something only Stella could pull off.

'Not too much?' Stella asked. 'I thought it was very Greta Garbo – you know, 1930s. Then I had misgivings, and I tried calling you to ask but there was no answer.'

'It's perfect, Stella, seriously,' said Maggie. Did she really have to help her get dressed now, too? 'I'm glad you came.'

Maggie grabbed her cotton kimono, tied it tight, pulled her lipstick from her pocket and applied it without looking. Then she ran her fingers through her hair and put her arm through Stella's.

'Come on, everyone's in the clubhouse now,' she said. 'Let's go and have a drink.'

The party was in full swing, with a makeshift bar at one end and dozens of people dancing in the middle of the room. The billiard table had been moved to one side, and a woman was lying on it – either fast asleep or passed out from too many cocktails.

Maggie grabbed a couple of drinks and pulled Stella away from the gramophone to a corner so they could talk.

'People are staring,' said Stella, a pink colour flushing her cheeks. 'I think they're talking about me.'

'Well, you look stunning, and Ealing stars rarely mix with the crew,' said Maggie. 'You'll be the talk of the studio tomorrow. It's a good thing, Stella. They'll love you for it, trust me.'

'I don't know,' said Stella, leaning into the corner and sipping her Pimm's. She pulled a face at the taste. 'I don't even know where I belong anymore. This is by far the worst kind of fame.'

'What do you mean?' Maggie laughed in disbelief.

Stella shrugged. 'Too famous to walk along the road and not be recognised,' she began, 'but not a big enough star here to get special treatment.' She reached in her bag and pulled out a pack of Piccadilly cigarettes, a new brand Maggie had bought for her to try. 'I sometimes think it would be nice to be unknown. Have an *ordinary* life, like you. You're lucky.'

Maggie bristled. 'Really?' she asked. 'Well, an "ordinary life", as you call it, isn't all it's cracked up to be.' She paused, intending to leave it there.

Sipping her drink, she looked around the room and thought of all the things Stella had that she didn't.

'I mean, yes,' Maggie began, 'this "ordinary life" is wonderful if you don't mind clocking in every morning and after lunch, and getting fined if you're a minute late.' Now she'd started, she gathered momentum, a train racing downhill with no brakes. 'If you don't mind having no say in what work you do, getting badly paid for it, having no prospects of ever earning more money or – heaven forbid! – a promotion, because all the men in your department are either threatened by you or are trying to get you into bed... or both. Living hand to mouth and seeing no chance of that really changing.' She took another long sip of her Pimm's. 'Well, yes, when you put it like that, I'm very lucky indeed.' She clinked her glass against Stella's. 'Chin-chin. Here's to being ordinary.'

Stella stared, her mouth slightly open. There was a long silence between them. A glass smashed on the dance floor and everyone cheered.

'Maggie,' she began, clutching Maggie's arm, cigarette still between her fingers. 'Darling, forgive me. I didn't know things were like that. You can always come to me if you need a little cash to tide you over.'

A fierce shame swept over Maggie and she felt terrible.

'But I'm so wound up with this letter, you see,' said Stella. 'I'm just not myself right now. And talking like that was very rude of me.'

Maggie shook her head and sighed. 'No,' she said, '*I'm* sorry. You must be frantic with worry. I didn't think. I'm just tired and I've had a few drinks. I didn't mean to sound ungrateful. I hardly know you and you've done so much for me, what with the extra cash and everything.'

And she meant it. The extra money had stopped her sinking further into debt, and at least she could manage her rent now.

Maggie leaned in and asked quietly, 'Have you heard anything else? From the blackmailer?'

Stella nodded and patted her bag.

'Today,' she said. 'Another letter.' Her eyes instantly glistened. She blinked back the tears and added, 'I'd really like to talk to you about it, but we can't discuss it here. I need to think about what to do next.'

'Let's go upstairs,' suggested Maggie. 'To my flat.'

'But the party?'

'This is more important,' said Maggie. 'Come on.'

CHAPTER TWELVE

M inutes later, they were on Maggie's balcony, drinking iced tea. Maggie leaned over to check if anyone else was sitting out, but she saw no one. Everyone must be at the party. Music floated up from below and an eerie calm washed over her.

She sat down as Stella took a sheet from an envelope and handed it to her. It was written in the same blue pencil, all drunken capitals stumbling across the page:

GET $50,000 CASH READY
YOU KNOW WHAT HAPPENS IF YOU DON'T
INSTRUCTIONS TO FOLLOW

'And another photo,' said Stella. She held it in her hand and Maggie leaned to see, but Stella shook her head. 'I can't,' she said. 'It's too awful.'

'What are you going to do?' said Maggie. 'Can you get the cash exchanged into dollars at short notice?'

Stella looked at her, shocked. 'I'm not *paying*!' she said. 'I don't have that kind of money.'

There was a pause as Maggie sipped her tea. Then she said, 'Don't you?'

Stella stared.

'I mean,' said Maggie, 'I'm not prying, Stella, your money's your business, but I thought you were the highest-paid actress in Hollywood last year?'

'Well, yes I was,' said Stella. 'I have been for a while.'

'And presumably you'll get some money from Max in the divorce? If you haven't got it already?'

'Yes, but that's not the point,' said Stella, putting her glass down with a thud. 'I mean, strictly speaking, *entre nous*, yes, I do have it – but why should I give it to some thug who's threatening me? And how do I know he won't ask for more once I've paid him? I've worked so hard for that money.'

Maggie nodded 'You're right, it's just…'

'What?'

'No, it doesn't matter.'

'No, go on.'

'Well,' said Maggie, 'the photographs.' She lit a cigarette and took a long drag. 'What I'm trying to say is you can always earn more money, but once those photographs are out…'

Stella started crying, and Maggie got up and brought her a handkerchief.

'I'm sorry, I didn't mean to upset you, Stella,' she said, sitting back down.

'But I thought you agreed that I shouldn't pay it?' said Stella. 'Now you're saying give him the money?'

'I just don't know,' said Maggie. 'I've been thinking, and it is so *risky* not to pay it. I mean *photographs*, Stella, printed *everywhere*. Because once one scandal sheet has them, you can bet that—'

Stella put her hand out to stop Maggie in her tracks. 'I know, you don't have to spell it out,' she said. 'But I'm damned if I do and damned if I don't. I can't just do nothing. I intend to find whoever it is. I thought of going to the police here, but I don't want to show them the photos, and I'd have to. I mean, I don't want *anyone* seeing them. In fact, you're the only person who's seen that first one.'

'And the blackmailer,' said Maggie.

'Well, yes of course.' She shifted in her chair and rearranged her kaftan.

'Anyway,' said Maggie, 'I agree, I don't think you should go to the police. I mean, how would they even begin to find this person if the letters are coming from America?'

'But what should I do? I refuse to sit back and do nothing. If I was there – in Hollywood – maybe there'd be a way of finding them. I could set someone on them. A private detective or something. But here, well. It all feels so hopeless.'

'What about the photographer?' asked Maggie. 'Do you remember his name? Where he lived? Could you get the police in Los Angeles to go there?'

'I remember his address, but it was years ago now. And do I really want LAPD involved? They're so corrupt.'

They both sat in silence for a while. The music downstairs had changed tempo and a slow, romantic song was being played. Maggie pictured the crew coupling off for the night, a last-ditch attempt to find someone to hold till the morning.

She wondered who Tom was dancing with right now, or if he was going home alone.

'There is someone,' said Stella, 'who might be able to help.'

'Really?' asked Maggie. 'Who?'

'Stan. One of the executives at the studio. He's always been good to me, like an uncle, really. He knows everyone. He paid off the photographer in the first place.'

'Okay,' said Maggie, brightening up. 'Well, that's good. Could this... what's his name?'

'Stan Fisher.'

'Could this Stan Fisher find the photographer, do you think? Put a stop to it? Maybe you can send him a telegram and ask?'

'No,' said Stella. 'I can't risk someone else seeing a telegram. I'll call him Monday. I'll try and catch him when it's morning over there. Though now I'm here, who knows if he'll still care.'

'You're on loan, Stella, but you're still a Star Studios actress. They have to care.'

Stella nodded. 'Yes, maybe.'

Maggie picked up the empty glasses and went into the kitchen. 'Do you want to go back down to the party again?' she called. 'I can fix your face in a jiffy.'

'No, actually there was something I wanted to ask you,' said Stella. 'Unrelated to all this.'

Maggie returned. 'What's that?' she asked, smiling.

'Something's been bothering me about that day we met, when you turned up to do my make-up.'

Maggie's neck went cold, but she held her nerve and forced a bright smile. 'Yes?'

Stella took a long drag of her cigarette and tilted her head a little as if really looking through her.

'Well, it's the funniest thing,' she began, 'but I bumped into Johnny the other day. Your boss?'

'Oh, yes?' said Maggie, starting to deadhead a few of the tiny roses that grew in the window box. 'Go on.' She turned back and picked up her cigarette from the saucer on the ground. She held it in one hand and squeezed the balcony ledge with the other. 'And?'

'Well...' Stella rearranged her kaftan then looked up at her. 'I thanked him for sending you in his place that day – the day we met. The day he was ill.' She paused, but Maggie said nothing. *Let her show her hand first.* 'I told him you were a godsend, and how you were my assistant now, too. And how lucky it was that we'd even met.'

Maggie stood very still.

'The funny thing is, he said you begged him.'

Maggie didn't respond.

'Those were his words,' Stella continued. 'He said you'd begged him to let you come and do my make-up that day. He hadn't been ill at all.'

Maggie flicked the ash from her cigarette, glanced down and took a deep breath. She nodded slowly and said, 'You've found me out.'

'What?'

'He's right,' she said, looking back at Stella. 'I told a white lie. I shouldn't have.'

'But why?'

Maggie shrugged. 'The truth is, I just wanted to be able to say I'd done your make-up,' she said. 'I knew he wouldn't let me do your face on a regular shoot, so I suggested the screen test. It was an early start, he didn't want to do it anyway – I suppose he didn't tell you that part, but he'd been complaining about it all week – so I said I'd do it.'

'I see.' Stella seemed sceptical.

'I mean, I couldn't really tell you he didn't want to do it, could I?' Maggie continued. 'He said… well, I'd better not say what he said…'

'No, go on,' said Stella, leaning forward now, frowning. 'Tell me.'

'Well, I don't want to upset you, Stella…'

Stella's voice went ice-cold. 'What else did he say?'

Maggie shook her head, pretending she didn't want to divulge. She'd probably gone too far now, but the lie had to be finished off with a bow. Something to convince Stella.

'Well…' Maggie sighed. 'He said… He said the whole thing was a waste of time, you testing for the part of the twenty-five-year-old daughter.' She hated herself for hurting Stella like this, but she couldn't tell her the truth. Not yet. 'I'm sorry, Stella, truly. Please don't say anything to him or complain to anyone. He has a vile temper. I'll lose my job.'

Stella let out a deep breath.

'I'm truly sorry I lied,' Maggie continued, 'but I just wanted to meet you. I've always been such a fan, and it seemed too good a chance to ignore.'

Maggie crouched down to Stella's seat, took her hands and looked her in the eyes.

'I'm so sorry I lied,' she said, 'but you know how difficult it is to get ahead here if you're a woman. You said it yourself. The make-up department is notorious for it – before you, I'd get all the awful jobs, and they'd get all the glory. And even if I had the chance to do something worthwhile, they'd get the credit. My name would never appear. I'm so sorry I lied.'

Stella stood up and pulled Maggie up with her.

'Darling,' she said, 'I have no issue with helping anyone get ahead, especially a smart woman like you. But don't lie to me again. I'll let this go, but please, I'm in a real predicament here and I need to be able to trust you.'

Maggie hung her head, because, yes, that's what Stella would have wanted her to do, but she did feel awful, too.

'You've done so much for me, Stella,' she said, 'and now this one thing, this little white lie has ruined it between us.'

'Oh, darling.' Stella spread her arms wide and took her in, enveloping her in a big kaftan hug, then giving her a peck on each cheek.

'You had the chance to meet me,' she said, holding her at arms' length, 'and you grabbed it with both hands. I admire it, really I do. But just don't tell fibs, okay? It's one thing I can't abide.'

Maggie nodded.

'Now – let's not speak of it again,' said Stella. 'In the big scheme of things, it hardly matters.'

Maggie gave her a smile but was furious with herself for not being more careful.

Later, as she stood alone on her balcony and contemplated how the evening had turned out, she felt sick to her stomach at how close she'd come to risking everything. And she hadn't even begun to get what she needed from Stella yet.

She was up to her neck in this now and it was high time she made progress. She had to push on.

CHAPTER THIRTEEN

Ealing Studios, London
August 1954

It was around eleven in the evening, a couple of days later, and the working day had ended hours ago. Everyone at Ealing Studios had long since gone home – except Maggie. She'd pretended to be busy as a deathly silence had gradually descended while she tried to kill time. So far, she'd emptied her make-up case, wiped everything inside, and had also washed and dried her brushes and sponges. The cleaner had been and gone, sweeping and mopping around her, and now finally, she'd been left all alone.

She checked her watch again: eleven fifteen. Wiping her clammy hands down her skirt, she told herself that, despite the risk of losing her job if caught, she had no choice. She had to make a transatlantic phone call, and the only private phone she knew of was in the meeting room, where the executives congregated. They could be seen all day, coming and going, one suited man after another.

She swallowed hard. The security guard was due to make his rounds soon, and by midnight, the whole place would be locked up. Walking to the room, she put her hand on the round doorknob and twisted. It was always left open because sometimes the top brass stayed late, but she'd kept an eye on it for hours now and knew it was empty.

The only phone at home was in the corridor and she'd already made the mistake of racking up a few bills when she used it. Also, she needed somewhere private.

The door opened and she quickly entered, gently closing it behind her. There was the famous heavy oak round table. So many careers had flourished or been destroyed in this room. And in the middle of the table sat the white phone.

She dug around in her bag and found the page she'd ripped from one of Stella's Hollywood magazines. It was an advert for a detective agency and it proclaimed: *No results? No charge!*

If only it was as simple as getting through straight away, but she'd have to wait to be connected. Lifting the receiver, she asked for the long-distance operator and gave the voice at the other end the number she wanted in Los Angeles. Then she replaced the phone and waited for the call that would tell her she was through. It would be three in the afternoon there. Hopefully, she'd find him in. She stood by the phone, waiting, praying the phone exchange wasn't too busy tonight – it could take several minutes but it felt wrong to sit, somehow.

After about ten minutes, the phone rang and she immediately picked it up, hoping the security guard was too far away to hear.

'Putting you through to JB Investigations,' said the operator. 'Please hold.'

A surge of energy flew through her. This was her chance. She had very little time and had to explain herself quickly.

'Hello, hello, is that Mr Brodsky?' Maggie asked, trying to keep her voice quiet.

There was a crackle at the other end, and just as she wondered if the operator had got the wrong number, a rough voice said, 'It is – this is Jim Brodsky speaking. Where are you calling from, ma'am? This line is terrible.'

'London – I don't have much time but you have to help me.' And with that she quickly unwrapped her story and spread it before him.

After a few minutes, she abruptly stopped. 'Are you still there?' she asked.

'I'm here,' he said. 'I've been making notes.'

'Will you take the case?' she asked. 'No results, no charge, like it says in the advert?'

There was silence at the other end.

'Mr Brodsky,' she said, 'I'm desperate.'

'I'll take it,' he replied. 'But… look, I don't want to upset you, but the chances of getting results. They're not that good.'

'I know, but please, will you try? I don't know anyone in Los Angeles.'

'I'll do my very best.'

There was a noise outside.

'I have to go,' she whispered. 'I'll call again in a few days.'

'Make it a week,' Brodsky said. 'Call any time. I work erratic hours, and I have an answering service if I miss you.'

She put down the phone gently, walked to the door and opened it a crack. The security guard was standing at the far end, his back to her, waving his torch down the corridor. Quietly, she crept out and left the building.

As she walked home in the damp night air, she felt

optimistic. She'd done it. She'd put it in motion. He'd said not to hold out much hope, but she refused to give up. Without hope, she had no reason to wake every day.

CHAPTER FOURTEEN

Star Studios, Hollywood, Los Angeles
January 1954

Ginny stood on set and pointed to her chest, where her breasts threatened to spill out.

'It's so tight,' she protested to Dolores, the wardrobe mistress. 'I mean, *look*.' She was trying on her costume, a red cotton dress with a low neckline and a tight waistband, from which a skirt flared, giving her an exaggerated hourglass figure. Dolores tugged and shifted the stiff fabric, then zipped her in tight.

'It's indecent, surely?' asked Ginny.

Dolores shrugged. 'That's the look they want,' she said. 'With the lace brassiere showing. You're the hoodlum's girlfriend.'

Ginny's throat tightened and she pressed her lips together, then felt Dolores' hand on her shoulder.

'Honey,' she said, 'they were very specific.'

Ginny gave a little nod. This was the third film she'd been cast in since she got her contract six weeks ago, and in each small role, she'd been what was euphemistically called a 'goodtime girl'. She stared at herself in the full-length mirror and sighed. Did all the big actresses start this way? Some had done worse to get ahead, she was sure.

'Okay,' she said. 'Let's give them what they want. At least I have some lines this time.'

'You do?' said Dolores. 'That's great.'

'Yes,' said Ginny. 'For ten seconds, the audience will be looking at my face, not my tits.'

Dolores laughed. 'Take it off,' she said, unzipping her. 'You're right, they don't need to see quite so much of them.'

'Really?'

'Let me see what I can do,' Dolores continued. 'Just a tiny adjustment can make a difference.' She looked at her watch. 'There's still time.'

Ginny quickly slipped out of the dress and grabbed her robe.

'Thanks, Dolores,' she said, giving her a peck on the cheek. 'You want a coffee?'

'No. And don't thank me yet,' she replied. 'Make sure you're back in ten, just in case it doesn't work and I have to change it again.'

Heading to the trestle table where the urns squatted like giant chrome beasts, Ginny wondered if she should mention all of this to Max. He knew she was working, of course, had said he was proud of her, but he'd taken little interest in exactly what she was doing. But he was busy, she understood that. Over the past few weeks, they'd fallen into a routine: he'd send a card and his driver, and she'd go to him. They'd have dinner in his suite then fall into bed, sometimes not bothering with dinner. Max always seemed tired, so she found herself keeping the conversation light. He had the weight of the studio on his shoulders, after all. And he hadn't mentioned their project for ages.

She placed a cup underneath the urn, turned the tap, and the boiling coffee spluttered out. She settled on a nearby stool. Come on, she told herself, she mustn't forget that this was what she'd wanted, a contract. And the timing had been perfect, as her savings had dwindled so quickly. Now she was earning $50 a week, she was more secure. She could never repay Max for pulling whatever strings he'd pulled, she knew that. But there was no denying that these films she'd been cast in were awful. Could he get her something better? Would she sound spoiled if she asked? Ungrateful even?

She lifted the cup to her mouth and blew on her coffee. What worried her was being typecast: if she continued to play these parts, perhaps she'd never be considered for anything decent? Once a goodtime girl, always a goodtime girl. She wanted something she could sink her teeth into, a role that required her to act, not just lean against a wall in a low-cut dress and watch as the men around her killed each other. And even if Max's project didn't come off – and of course she was still hoping it would – if they didn't end up acting opposite each other, she still wanted to make a name for herself.

'Careful!' shouted a prop man.

An ornate carriage, obviously made from lightweight balsa wood, clipped the side of the trestle table as it was carried by, making the cups and saucers clatter. A bored-looking woman dodged past in a regal cloak and crown, followed by six men in tights dressed as her courtiers. Ginny smiled. Just a few weeks ago she'd have been open-mouthed at the sight, but here she was in the middle of it all. Star Studios: her place of work.

She sipped her scalding coffee, put her hand into her pocket and pulled out a tiny pill box, flipping it open: blues, to stay awake. The pinks that helped her fall asleep she left at home. She popped a bluey in her mouth and swallowed. She no longer took them in secret since she'd seen others do it quite openly. After all, it was the studio doctor who handed them out. Even Max said he occasionally took them when he needed 'a little help'.

In the first week, she'd overslept, missed her elocution lesson, and was fined $10 for it. That's when her speech coach had mentioned the doctor. A call was arranged, where he asked general questions about her health, and before she knew it, she had a supply. She didn't even need an examination. Every month, another supply was automatically sent to her apartment. It was just another one of those things that everyone accepted but rarely talked about. Like how unfair the contracts were.

Her stomach grumbled as she stared at the pastries on the table. Better not. She still had the rest of the day to get through in that dress. She stood and gave a big stretch. It might be her imagination, but she felt the bluey starting to work already. She had a relentless morning schedule of classes that had to be squeezed in before her work on set even began, and it was all taking a toll. She was relying on those little pills every day now.

She began walking back to the set. Seven years: that's how long her contract was for. It was standard. But every six months, the studio could reconsider if they wanted to keep her on. She, on the other hand, wasn't allowed to walk away, but they could dismiss her just like that. Stan had explained it all when she'd delivered the signed contract. Well, he didn't spell it out, but everyone knew if you were 'difficult', got caught up in some scandal that hit the papers, or perhaps your face didn't fit anymore for whatever reason, then they could wave goodbye. You'd lose everything overnight.

She stared at the set and the men wearing their gangster costumes, bored and smoking before the next take. Could she do seven years of *this*? If she refused a role she didn't want, they could suspend her.

'My advice?' Stan had said. 'Stay amenable. Don't forget, if you're suspended, the studio still owns you – you don't get paid but you can't work for anyone else. And *that's* when the problems start.'

She'd heard about actresses who were forced to do all sorts to survive: nude photos, pornographic films, whatever it took. Some actors, too. Sex for rent and food money were commonplace, and there were plenty of powerful producers, directors and small-time gangsters who were only too ready to lend a helping hand in return for a favour.

It seemed the men in suits were good at sniffing out desperation. What was it Stella Hope had said? *Watch out for the wolves.* She couldn't let herself become one of those women – playing them in movies was bad enough.

Of course, she didn't mention any of this in her letters

home. Instead, she recounted the thrill of being on set, and the joy she felt to stand on the verge of what might be a glittering future. The dark side of this town though, the threatening shadows and precarious nature of it all, she kept to herself.

'Ginny, hurry up!'

It was Dolores, waving to her from the clothes rail. She had a smile on her face, which meant she'd managed to make the alteration. Ginny rushed over. There were lots of good people in Hollywood – people like Dolores and Max.

As she slipped into the dress and Dolores pulled the fabric around her, Ginny wondered what she should wear this evening. It was Wednesday, so he was bound to send a funny, cryptic note to say that Javier was waiting at the designated spot two streets away. She'd hurry, as she always did, and as the light faded from the sky and an indigo cloak was thrown over Hollywood, she'd slide onto the luxurious leather seat of his car and glide through the streets towards the Sunset Tower, where he'd be waiting.

She'd sleep over, then the wake-up call would rouse her, and Javier would bring her home around five the next morning. Before the rest of the world woke, she'd climb the stairs to her flat, let herself in and relive delicious moments from the night before. Of course it wasn't perfect. She was constantly shattered, he was still married, and although he said he was getting a divorce, they were still creeping around like thieves in the night because it was yet to be announced.

She knew it was wrong. If she thought about it too much, she despised herself. But then she remembered that

Stella had given up on him long ago. So why couldn't she go ahead and help herself? No harm could come of it, surely?

CHAPTER FIFTEEN

That evening, Ginny pushed her hand into her pigeonhole and pulled out a stiff envelope. She ran upstairs and closed the door, leaning against it as she ripped open the seal. Inside was the familiar plain, thick cream card with the elegant italic logo of the Sunset Tower Hotel in the corner, surrounded by an art-deco border.

As usual, the message had been typed:

```
I have a surprise for you -
        7 p.m. sharp!
Bring a coat, a headscarf and
        dark glasses.
```

She read it again, puzzled. They couldn't possibly be going out – they never went out. It was too risky. All it would take was one person to see them together and their story could be all over the papers. Or one quick snap from a photographer who was hanging around that café opposite the Sunset Tower, where the press liked to sit and chat and compare notes.

She looked at her watch: almost seven. They usually didn't meet till eight or nine, so it was lucky she'd come straight back. She slipped out of her pedal pushers and shirt and quickly pulled on her white sleeveless dress with the swing skirt. He'd seen it before, but no matter. It was smart, so wherever they went it would work. She smoothed down her hair in front of the mirror and used a lip brush for her Revlon Fire and Ice lipstick, building several layers before blotting. Now she was a white-blonde, she'd started wearing a strong red lip and it suited her. She smiled in the mirror to check she hadn't smudged it. It seemed that the little gap between her two front teeth had never existed, and she barely thought of it now, the way she barely thought of the old Ginny Watkins, that awkward girl who'd arrived four months ago. Look at her now. Virginia Rose.

She grabbed her shocking-pink wrap. She'd brought very few clothes with her from London and couldn't imagine ever needing a coat here. Why waste money on a coat when she could buy frocks? She opened her chest of drawers and pulled out a pretty headscarf the colour of raspberries, then checked her bag to make sure she had her sunglasses.

Javier, who'd only spoken to her once to introduce himself, was waiting outside the laundromat, as usual. The tinted windows of the limousine shone in the evening sun and the purr of the engine was so familiar now she immediately associated the sound with the heavenly evenings she spent with Max. Javier got out and opened the door.

She slid onto the back seat and jumped to see Max already inside.

'What are you doing here?' she said, laughing, as he leaned across and kissed her hello. He pressed a button and the glass that separated their domain from Javier's slid up.

'Like I said, it's a surprise.'

They'd never been anywhere outside his hotel room. Of course, they'd bumped into each other at the studio once or twice, but they'd just nodded hello, pretending they barely knew each other.

'We're going *out*?' she asked. He was wearing a beautiful camel cashmere coat and held a trilby in his hands. She turned towards him and stroked his lapels. Linen, silk, cashmere, skin – she found it impossible not to touch him. 'But how? I mean, where are we going? Is it safe? And aren't you hot in that?'

'It's chilly on the way up. Do you have your headscarf?' he asked. She nodded and pulled it from her pocket. 'And glasses?' She showed them to him.

'Well done,' he said, putting his arm around her. 'Tonight, madam, I'm taking you to the cinema.'

She laughed, incredulous.

'What? Really?'

He nodded.

'But how?'

How could two secret lovers go somewhere so public?

He leaned in close. 'Look at you,' he said, stroking her face. 'You're so excited.' He touched her lips with his fingertip and swooped in for a quick kiss. 'Don't you know I'm Max Whitman?' he asked jokingly. 'Anything is possible.' He winked. 'I know people who know people.' It was a line from one of his films and she groaned in recognition.

'Seriously, Max,' she said. 'I mean, you have so much to lose if anyone sees us.' And of course she did too, but she didn't say that. She couldn't risk wrecking her reputation by being seen with a married man, especially when he was one half of Hollywood's Golden Couple.

'I know, trust me,' he said. 'I've got it figured out. Anyway, I'm fed up of never being able to go anywhere with you.'

He looked out of the window.

'We're almost there,' he said, donning his trilby.

He motioned for her to get her headscarf on, then he slipped his hand into his coat pocket and pulled out a pair of dark glasses. She did the same.

'We look like a couple of spies,' she said. The car drove past a queue of people waiting outside the large movie theatre on Melrose Avenue, then swung down a small side road round the back.

Max pressed a button and the dividing window rolled down.

'Thank you, Javier,' he said. 'You'll be here as agreed, yes?'

'*Sí, señor* Whitman. I'll be waiting.'

Javier then got out and held the door open for them, and they slid out into the alley.

Directly in front of them was an old wooden door that had been painted several times. The blue paint had peeled, and under it was green, and under that grey. Max knocked on it twice and almost immediately a bolt scraped across and it creaked open. A wiry man wearing thick round glasses beckoned them in, and once he'd rebolted the door, he started climbing a winding metal staircase. They both took off their glasses and Ginny stared up. A breeze whipped around the staircase as if there was no roof at all, and Max looked down on her to make sure she was alright.

'Do you want my coat?' he asked.

'No, I'm fine, thank you.' She looked to one side and saw that the tall sash windows on the side of the building were all wide open. The wind rattled louder the higher they climbed.

Up and up they all went, spiralling to the top. On the other side of the wall, Ginny could hear the chatter of the audience as they came in for the show, the slam of the seats as they settled, the buzz of excitement in the air.

Just as she wondered how much further they had to go, the man stopped on a platform and they joined him. He pointed to what looked like a small attic space, to indicate that this was where he was going. They followed him and Ginny peered in at the window where a huge metal projector sat, already loaded with a fat reel of film. A high stool stood next to it. The man went inside.

'Are we sitting in *there*?' she asked.

'Of course not,' said Max, and pulled her by the hand. To the left of the projectionist's room, just outside, was a pool of soft light that illuminated two crimson velvet cinema seats. Just two, there all alone in the half-light, as if they'd been plucked right out of the auditorium below.

'Here?'

'Your seat, madam,' Max said, helping her out of her wrap and pushing her seat down for her.

Well, this was just the best.

'Oh, but it's perfect!' she said.

She looked around and spotted the railing and got up to

peer over at the crowds below. 'We're in the heavens. Movie heaven!'

Even if someone did look up, they'd never see them this high up, just the light from the projector beaming onto the screen. She sat down again.

'How do you know about this place?' she asked.

'I've been here a few times,' he replied, sliding out of his coat and folding it neatly on his lap. 'I like to come here to watch my movies.'

She gave him a look. 'You watch your own movies?'

'It's not as vain as it sounds,' he said. 'I want to watch them with an audience – you know, see what their reaction is. But I can't exactly buy a ticket and join them, so this is the next best thing. I have an arrangement with the projectionist. He lets me know when they're screening.'

'You watch your own movies,' she said again, trying not to laugh.

He nudged her. 'Stop teasing. I'll learn more from the audience down there than from any film critic.'

She had to ask: 'Are we watching one of your movies now?'

Max burst out laughing. 'Just how vain do you think I am?'

The lights dimmed, there was a swell of applause downstairs, and the music began.

Ginny leaned across to whisper. 'This is ingenious,' she said, putting her hand in his. 'A proper date.'

'Look,' he said, and lifted the arm rest that divided the two seats.

Now it felt like they were sitting on a couch and he pulled her close to him. She wondered if he'd ever been here with another girl. Or Stella, even.

A couple of hours later, they were sitting in the back of Max's car again, eating the burgers and fries that Javier had brought them. Ginny sucked on her chocolate milkshake and talked about how much she'd adored *Roman Holiday*.

'It had everything,' she said. 'It was funny, romantic, and that scenery – I'd love to go to Italy. Have you been?'

'I have, it's magical,' he said, as he chewed on his burger. 'Have you heard the rumour about the script?'

'What?'

'They say it's written by Dalton Trumbo,' he said, 'but they didn't credit him. You know, one of the Hollywood Ten?'

'The people accused of being communists?' she asked.

'Yep, it's like a witch hunt – so many people's lives changed overnight. Most of them jailed for contempt of court. He's banned from working, so they can't credit him.'

'That's awful,' said Ginny.

They carried on eating for a while, then he asked: 'What did you think of the lead, Gregory Peck?'

'Loved him, and she's wonderful, too – what's her name again?'

'Audrey Hepburn. They're saying she'll get an Academy Award. You don't think he's too old for her?' he asked, wiping some ketchup off her face with a napkin.

'Not at all, no,' said Ginny. 'I mean, it works. He's handsome and suave, she's fed up with being a princess and just wants adventure.'

'Movies, eh?' He laughed. 'They can make you believe anything.'

'Did you think she was too young?' Ginny asked. 'For him, I mean? Will he get bored of her?'

He gave a mock frown. 'Hmmm... who knows? Forbidden

love, great scenery, I don't think he'd get bored for quite some time.'

'No, but would he get bored of *her*? In real life? Because she's young?'

He reached out and stroked her hair. 'Are you asking if I think you're too young for me, by any chance?'

Her cheeks felt warm.

'Not at all,' she said, embarrassed she'd been so transparent. She looked down at the remnants of her food and picked up a French fry. He stopped it halfway to her mouth.

'I could never get bored of you,' he said. 'You're gorgeous and funny and smart and talented.'

She grinned. 'But not in that order I hope.'

'In whatever order you damn well like. How could you bore me when I can't get enough of you? I told you before. It's like a disease.'

'Well, that doesn't sound good at all!' she said. 'And I'm sure you called it a craving before, not a disease. I mean you can *die* of a disease.'

'Let's get back,' he said, sliding his hand up her dress. 'I think cravings are lethal too.'

At around four the next morning, as they were both tangled in the Sunset's cream silk sheets, Ginny decided to mention what had been on her mind.

'You awake, Max?'

'Mmmm.'

'Can I ask you something?'

He opened his eyes and leaned up on one elbow.

'Of course,' he said, stroking her shoulder. 'What is it?'

So she took a deep breath and told him about the roles she'd been getting and the misgivings she had. He sat up and swung his legs out of the bed, grabbing his robe as he walked around the room. She could tell from the stiffness of his back that he was cross. She shouldn't have said anything. He'd think her a brat. She'd screwed up.

'Look,' she began, 'I do know I'm very lucky, and I do appreciate everything you've done for me. I mean, I can never repay you for getting me a contract, I know I can't.

'You probably would have got one anyway,' he said, lighting a cigarette. 'I just helped speed things up.'

'Well, I don't know that for sure, but anyway, I don't want to seem ungrateful, I just want good work, you know?' There was a hint of pleading in her voice and she hated herself for it. Why couldn't she just say it without apologising? Without feeling bad for not wanting to play hookers and delinquents? 'I... I just want work I can feel proud of. And I know we all have to start somewhere, and I'm sure you did too, but I'm worried that this is it.'

He didn't say anything.

'This *isn't* it – is it, Max?'

He blew the smoke to one side and ran a hand through his hair, exasperated.

'Don't you trust me?' he asked. 'Didn't I say I'd get it sorted?' He leaned over and tapped the cigarette into the ashtray several times.

'Oh, no – of course I trust you,' she said, half up now. 'It's just, well, you haven't said anything about the project for a while and I just wondered, that's all. I mean, I didn't want to say anything but thought, well... I was worried and didn't want to *not* say anything either.'

He tilted his head to one side and gave her a stiff smile.

'Look, Ginny,' he said. 'These things take time. The truth is that Stella is being an absolute nightmare. One minute she wants a divorce, the next she's arguing and saying if I have any leading lady on a regular basis it should be her.'

'But I thought she wanted to branch out on her own?' said Ginny. 'And, well, she's seeing other men, isn't she? Younger men you said.'

'Exactly, but she wants to have her cake and eat it, too. Now I've finally agreed to a divorce she seems to be wavering. She seems worried about the impact it will have on her career. I think she's only just realised it's harder to be a film star in your forties if you're a woman. The movies she's done without me have flopped. And between you and me, she's not the studio's favourite person right now. Demanding more money, better billing. That woman wants everything.'

'But they'd never drop her, would they?' Ginny asked. 'I mean, Stella Hope *is* Star Studios.'

He shrugged. 'Stella Hope with Max Whitman is Star Studios. After that, who knows? When stars get difficult, they lose their shine. That's what Stan says.'

There was an awkward pause as if he wanted to say something else but stopped himself. Was this a warning to her? Was she being 'difficult'? She wanted to cry.

'I know I'm not a star, Max,' she said, her voice cracking a little. 'I'm nowhere near that. But I have to look out for myself, you know?'

He dropped his cigarette into the ashtray and rushed to her.

'Darling, I know, I know.' He kissed her on the forehead. 'I don't blame you for mentioning it. Forgive me for being abrupt with you, but there's so much at stake, and we need to do this right. I promise you it will happen – if not with this script, with something. I want you as my leading lady and that's that. But you just have to wait. A little bit longer.'

She was crying now and felt so foolish. Why couldn't she stay calm? Keep a hold of her emotions? She thought she'd toughened up in the few months she'd been here, but her feelings lived so near the surface that all it took was a little scratch and they poured out.

'I can wait,' she said, wiping her nose with her hand. He passed her a handkerchief and she had a good blow. 'Of course I can wait.'

'Good girl,' he said. 'And in the meantime, let me see what I can do. I'll speak to Stan.'

'You will?'

'Sure, let me see if there's anything he can do about the roles you're given. Maybe there's something with dialogue, or at least where you get to keep your clothes on.'

She smiled. 'Really?' she asked. 'You'd do that for me?'

'Of course,' he said, coming back to bed. 'I mean there's only one person in this town who should see what's under here and that's me.'

Later, when she was getting ready to leave, she asked if Stan knew about them.

'He's the only one who does,' he said. 'If you ever need anything and I'm not around, Stan is your man.'

'Good,' she said, pulling on her wrap. 'I like Stan.'

MATILDA MAYHEW'S CONFIDENTIAL

January 8, 1954

THE SEARCH IS ON FOR A NEW STAR

Well, it's all change in movie land!

The charmed life of rising star Rosie Moreau has taken an almighty dive. It seems the stunning bit-part blonde who, despite a series of humdrum performances, was tipped as the Next Big Thing after clinching her first leading role, won't be on our screens for quite some time.

When Love Comes to Town was due to start shooting this week, but apparently, she's exhausted before she's even begun. Stan Fisher, Executive Manager in charge of talent at Star Studios, says rumours that Moreau has succumbed to the excesses of Hollywood life are simply unfounded. 'She's a true professional and has just been working very hard,' he says. 'Rosie is under strict doctor's orders to take it easy. We look forward to seeing her back on the lot once she's rested.'

Moreau, who made fifteen films last year, including the well-received romantic comedy *My Biggest Mistake*, in which she had a rare speaking role, was unavailable for comment.

But Hollywood doesn't stop for anyone. Fisher confirmed that shooting for the big-budget romance, *When Love Comes to Town*, will go ahead without her. So the search is on for a new leading lady to star opposite rebel heartthrob Michael Pezzi.

Get in line, girls. No pushing!

Till next time, movie lovers.
Your friend,

Matilda

CHAPTER SIXTEEN

Cynthia was sitting at a booth in Schwab's poring over Matilda Mayhew's column.

'You're so lucky you're blonde,' she said to Ginny, who was opposite her. 'You can't even get a look in if you're a brunette.' She reached across and gave her arm a squeeze. 'Can you believe you got an audition? I'm so excited for you.'

'Thanks,' said Ginny. 'Now I've just got to remember my lines.' She tapped the pages in front of her. After badgering the director each day for a week, she'd finally got her name on tomorrow's audition list. Every young actress at the studio wanted this role, but why couldn't it be her? This was what she'd been waiting for: a prestigious part that would get her noticed.

'I know the test is only a few pages long,' said Ginny, 'but I'm so nervous.'

'You'll be great,' said Cynthia, stirring her third coffee. 'I think you're going to get it. I just have a feeling, you know? You deserve it.'

Ginny smiled at her. Cynthia had really grown on her

in the past few weeks. She was fun to be around, but more than that, she was generous and honest – not something you often came across here. The atmosphere among all the young actresses was so competitive that up to now Ginny had avoided getting too close to anyone.

'And you don't feel weird about it?' asked Ginny.

'Of course not.' Cynthia shrugged and sipped her coffee. 'I'm not blonde so I can't even try for it. And if anyone else is going to get it, I'd rather it was you.' She looked over her shoulder and whispered. 'Did you see Theresa's face when she heard she didn't stand a chance?'

Ginny tried to casually glance over at Theresa, the Italian girl nursing an ice-cream sundae at the bar. She was mortified to see her staring straight back.

'She knows we're talking about her,' she said, turning quickly.

'Who cares?' said Cynthia in a loud voice. 'I mean, she shouldn't have gone around boasting that it was hers. Reckoned she knew the director and he'd let her wear a wig. You got the audition fair and square, but she wanted it handed on a plate.' Cynthia motioned to the waitress. 'I fancy some pie. Want some pie?'

Ginny shook her head. She folded the script and put it away. She'd look at the lines again tonight.

The plate arrived and Cynthia attacked her cherry pie with gusto.

'I mean, it's hardly fair,' she said, between mouthfuls, 'that she should get anything just because she knows people. That makes me so cross.'

Shifting in her seat, Ginny wondered what she'd think if she knew about Max.

'I feel sorry for Rosie Moreau,' said Ginny. 'Can you imagine? You're about to get your big break opposite Michael Pezzi and you get ill.'

Cynthia pushed away half of the pie, grabbed a napkin and blotted her mouth then opened her bag and pulled out a compact mirror.

'She's not ill,' she said, checking her teeth before reapplying lipstick. 'I mean, they say she's overworked, but that's code.'

'For what?'

'Anything. We're all overworked, right? It usually means she's addicted to something – easily done. Everyone loves a buzz, but some girls take too much. Then they can't remember lines, start turning up late and everything falls apart.'

Ginny nodded and thought about the blue pills in her handbag. Perhaps she should stop taking them every day? Maybe every other day, instead? She was sure she wasn't that dependent on them. And yet, she loved the lift they gave her when she needed it, and how, when she craved sleep, the pink ones enveloped her in a comforting calm.

'They'll take her somewhere, to a sanatorium to detox. If she's lucky, her career will still be here when she gets back. Even Stella Hope had a "rest" years ago. Rumour was she had a breakdown and was in an institution. Of course, the official story was that she was exhausted.'

'Really?' asked Ginny. Max had never mentioned it.

'Oh yes, it happens the whole time,' said Cynthia. 'You know that actress years ago, Jasmine something – the one who was at the very top and then stopped altogether?'

'Jasmine Sheldon?' Ginny asked. 'What happened to her?'

Cynthia leaned across, put her hand up to her mouth and said in an exaggerated whisper, 'Overdose.'

'No!'

'Yes. Though of course the studio's story was that she'd been dieting too much and needed to rest. The gossip magazines, on the other hand, said she'd had a bad break-up with someone and couldn't handle it. Never saw her again.'

'Did she...' began Ginny. 'I mean... did she die? From the overdose?'

Cynthia shook her head. 'Worse,' she said solemnly. 'Her contract was ripped up and her career was shot to pieces. So, I mean, she may as well be dead.'

'You're terrible,' said Ginny, laughing from relief, despite herself.

It was a tightrope, this town, she thought. Just one huge balancing act. Keep going, one foot in front of the other, even if you're exhausted, no matter. Take these pills, don't look down, don't complain, look straight ahead. The alternative was not to try at all. And if you fell? There was no safety net, but at least you'd given it a shot. If you made it, the rewards were so high. And if you didn't... well, it was a beautiful way to die.

*M*y bed has metal bars, and the sides are pulled up at night, imprisoning me in a cell. I now sleep in a large dormitory, which I share with so many other forgotten women. There are dozens of us – row upon row, tossing and crying into the night, a symphony of pain. Only the ones who are having shock treatment are quiet. Electricity to the brain. They say it helps calm you if you're distressed, but I know it's used as punishment. They choose the violent ones, the ones who are the most disobedient, dispatching them to the first floor kicking and screaming. They return, silent, scooped out.

We have a few minutes between being sent to our beds and the lights going out, and each night I play a game with myself; I stand on my mattress and try to count the beds as quickly as I can before the nurses arrive. My mind flutters, and it's difficult to get to the end, but I think I'm getting better. Yesterday, I reached thirty-two before the numbers unravelled. If I could count them all, to the very last bed, *it would really be something. The pills they give us make me slow and stupid. I have to find a way to avoid taking them.*

While I'm counting, the woman on my left kneels and prays out loud, and the young girl on my right slides into her neighbour's bed to hug her tightly in silence. She doesn't seem to mind. And I stand and count. It calms me. It's important we're all accounted for, so I make sure to start with myself. I have slipped through the cracks before and it cannot happen again.

Once the nurses enter, I sink into bed and hope it will be the kind one tonight.

There she is! She approaches, her hair a halo of golden curls and my heart lifts a little. She pulls up the rails of my bed, constructing my prison, then gently takes each wrist and straps the leather cuffs to the metal bar. Then she does the same for each ankle.

'Sorry, but it has to be done,' she says every night. And when she buckles me to the bars, she does it with a smile and leaves it much looser than the others do.

I thank her, and tonight I find the courage to ask my question.

'Excuse me,' I whisper. 'But do you know my name?'

She nods. 'Of course I do – you're one of our special patients.'

'What is it? I get so confused. Please tell me.'

And so she does, but I start to cry because even that feels unfamiliar. I try to explain but even my voice sounds like it's not mine. Everything is changed now.

'Don't worry,' she says, 'it's the medication. It makes you

feel you're losing yourself, but you'll get used to it, you'll see. Soon you'll feel better, then everything will come back.'

I want to remember, I do, but I'm also frightened. There's a deep betrayal at the heart of why I'm here. I can feel it in my bones. If I stare it in the face perhaps it will end me. How can I be so frightened of something I can't name?

She smooths the covers and pats them.

'When you do remember, when your memories return, you'll have some wonderful stories to tell us, I'm sure,' she says. 'Who doesn't love a Hollywood tale?'

CHAPTER SEVENTEEN

Star Studios, Hollywood, Los Angeles
January 1954

It was the day of the audition and Ginny was trying to calm herself. She took a deep breath and let it out very gently, trying to slow the rapid drum of her heart. Dolores tugged at the back of her floor-length silver satin evening gown.

'Way too big,' she said, taking a couple of safety pins from her sewing kit and securing the waistband tighter.

Ginny motioned her head towards the two blondes who were standing a few feet away, blatantly staring.

'How did the others look in it?' she asked.

'Not as good as you, honey,' said Dolores. 'You've got the poise to carry it off.'

'Thanks, Dolores,' she said, grinning. 'Even if it's not true.'

'Well, it is,' Dolores replied, tying a wide piece of white chiffon around Ginny's waist, and finishing it with a perfect bow at the small of her back. 'Down to the last three on a Michael Pezzi movie,' she said. 'I bet you can't believe it?'

'It feels unreal,' Ginny said. 'Is he back yet? Mr Pezzi?'

'He'll turn up at the last minute,' said Dolores. 'That's

what he did with the others. It's a power thing – they all do it. Now stand still, we're almost done.'

As Dolores smoothed down the dress, the director called, 'Last looks!' and a hairstylist checked Ginny's chignon was still in place then gave her nose a final light brush of powder. As they fussed over her, making sure she was camera-ready, Ginny told herself she was doing one scene, that's all. She'd read for the director earlier and he'd obviously seen something he liked. It was down to her and the other two actresses who'd already had their screen tests and were watching.

She had to ignore them. Yes, her test was with Michael Pezzi, who was on the covers of both *Photoplay* and *Silver Screen* magazines right now, but she had to focus on the role. The part in *When Love Comes to Town* was perfect for her: that of a sassy girlfriend who was always getting into trouble. And she suspected she had a real talent for comedy if she could conquer her nerves.

After all, this is what it had all been for: the aching legs from 5 a.m. ballet, the dull Acting Theory where her head felt it would explode, the relentless speech lessons to perfect an array of American accents she may one day use or not. All that effort had been so she could shine *right now* in this instant. Because she knew that, if she didn't get this scene right the first time, she wouldn't get another shot.

She thought of her mother, as she often did when she was nervous. She could feel her hand in hers now, as they stood across the road from the big school in Camden on her first day, and she'd whispered in her ear: *Remember, you're as good as all of them, Ginny. Nobody can see what you're thinking, so show them what you want them to believe.*

A loud bell rang, the crowd cleared and a hush descended. She walked to her mark and Michael Pezzi strolled onto the set, immaculate in a beautiful tuxedo, hair shiny as wet tarmac. No getting ready behind a screen for him.

'Ginny, yes?' he asked.

She nodded.

'You ready?'

She nodded again, then realised she should speak.

'Absolutely, Mr Pezzi.'

'Well, great,' he said. 'Let's make this work, okay? And it's Michael.'

'Okay, Michael,' she said.

They ran through the scene once, without the cameras rolling, then did it for real. Only one take, as she suspected. As soon as the director called 'Cut!' Michael walked over to him. They stood in a huddle and talked for a few minutes then called over a man who'd been sitting on a stool watching everything. He had the swagger of wealth about him, so was probably the producer. They were a breed apart, these money men: always perfectly turned out, tie pin, handkerchief in breast pocket. Probably had weekly manicures. Ready for a day of telling others what to do, rather than a day's graft.

She stood to one side watching. Surely it was good that they were discussing her? After a few minutes, she wondered if she was meant to leave but nobody had said anything so she stayed where she was, still in costume. Finally, the director beckoned her over. She hurried towards him, then her heart sank when he called the other two actresses, too.

'We're watching the auditions after lunch,' he said to

the three of them. 'You'll hear by the end of today, so stick around. That's it for now, ladies. Thank you.'

And with that he went off.

Faced with the other actresses, Ginny gave an awkward smile and a shrug. The taller of the two let out an exasperated sigh, while the other stood perfectly still, staring her down. They all knew that, in a few hours, for one of them, something life-changing was about to happen. But for the others? They'd return to waiting: for the perfect opportunity, the right audition, the chance that would shift everything for them beyond recognition. Never once allowing themselves to consider 'what if?'

What if the waiting never ends? What if the break never comes? What if I'm not good enough, or worse, if I am but I just never get the chance to prove it? How do I live then?

CHAPTER EIGHTEEN

After getting changed, Ginny grabbed a coffee and found a stool out of everyone's way. Although the whole afternoon stretched before her, she was too nervous to go home. The smell of paint and plaster on the set was getting to her, and what she'd really like to do was step outside for some air. But she refused to leave till she knew the outcome.

She'd done well, she knew that. She'd delivered her lines with good timing and had even heard a ripple of laughter, but she couldn't assume anything. After all, she had no idea how the other actresses had performed.

She sipped her coffee, put it on the floor and picked up her canvas tote bag. Pulling out the script for *Kill Me Again* – a predictable gangster film with a small role for her – she sighed. She'd use this time to run through her scenes again.

They didn't bother sending her the entire script, just the scenes she was in. Months ago, when she'd started out, she'd mentioned to one of the director's assistants that there were pages missing from her script. He'd laughed at her: 'You don't need to understand it, just do it.'

In this film, as with most of them, she was learning when to move from one spot to another in the scenes: stand *here* to be grabbed, and *here* to be kissed, and *this* is where he slaps you and you fall to the ground. Could this be the last time she'd have to do this? She turned the pages, hoping she was right, fearful she was wrong. Max had promised things would change soon, but when? She couldn't bring herself to ask again.

Her stomach tightened and she realised she hadn't eaten anything. She lit a Chesterfield and glanced around the studio. Maybe she had time to buy a sandwich from Schwab's? Bring it back to eat? She wondered if those cute red pedal pushers had arrived in her size at The Boulevard Boutique yet. No, she had to stay put.

Leaving her script and jacket on the stool, she grabbed her bag and went to the ladies. She took her time fixing her hair, which was dry and stiff from all the lacquer that had been holding her chignon in place. She pushed it back behind her ears, tried to smooth it down and sighed. This was costing her a fortune. She'd need to get it washed and set again. What with the hair, the nails, the clothes, it was an expensive business trying to break into Hollywood. But she had no choice. It was an unwritten rule that you had to always look your best or you'd get reprimanded. She knew how some girls afforded it, but she wasn't that desperate. Well, not yet.

As she walked back on set, she could see someone standing by her stool, reading her script.

'Hey!' she called. 'That's mine.'

He turned. It was Michael Pezzi.

'Oh, Mr Pezzi! Sorry, I—'

'This is terrible,' he said, laughing and waving the script before he dropped it on the seat. 'What's it called?'

Her face felt hot. A couple of stagehands nearby were close enough to hear.

'*Kill Me Again.*'

He raised his eyebrows, amused. 'Really?'

'I know – shocking, isn't it?' she said. 'You die once reading it, then again when you have to act in it.' As the words came out of her mouth, she wondered if she'd gone too far.

But then Michael Pezzi laughed.

'Funny *and* talented,' he said. 'Tell them you can't do it. Tell them Michael Pezzi needs you for his new film.'

CHAPTER NINETEEN

Ealing, London
August 1954

Stella sashayed out of the gates of Ealing Studios, her navy and white Dior belted day dress swinging around her hips. She'd dressed for confidence today, and it had worked. She jumped into the cab that was waiting to take her to her flat in Soho and smiled. Yesterday she'd decided to start wearing her couture and felt so much better for it, like herself again. What was she keeping it for? The crew had stared when she'd arrived on set this morning, but she didn't care. She was Stella Hope, and it was her duty to look impeccable.

She gave the driver her address and sat back, a burst of optimism washing over her. Now that her day's work was done, she was going to do something about those dreadful letters. Or rather, she'd ask Stan to.

She glanced at her watch. Wonderful. She'd be home by four o'clock, so that was eight in the morning in LA – a perfect time to catch him before his day began.

The cab turned a corner as they trundled towards the West End. Shooting had just wrapped on a poignant low-budget film called *A Heart Like No Other*, in which she played the plucky landlady of a pub about to be demolished. Her character had real substance and, along with the intelligent script, she suspected it would be a hit, but she worried about starring in films where there was so little glamour. Where was the sparkle? The gowns? Would her fans accept her if she didn't still look like a star? Or perhaps she could do both? Now that would be something. Perhaps this was a way forward for her.

Thirty minutes later she was in her flat and had placed a call with the operator. Stan had always been there for her at every turn of her career. He'd help her now, wouldn't he? While she waited for the phone to ring with her connection, she pushed open a window and wondered if she had time to slip into her robe. It was a stifling August day, and yet yesterday she'd been cold. She just couldn't get a grip on the climate here, didn't know how to dress, what was expected of her. In LA, life was more straightforward; it was always warm.

The phone rang, making her jump, and the operator asked her to hold while she connected her.

The line crackled and then she heard a wonderfully familiar woman's voice. 'Good morning, Stan Fisher's office. This is Ida, how may I help you?'

'Ida?' asked Stella. 'Ida, is that you? It's Stella Hope calling from London.'

'Oh, Miss Hope. How lovely to hear your voice. Let me see if I can get him for you.'

There was a pause during which Stella pictured Stan sitting behind his huge desk, that ridiculous zebra-skin rug sprawled on the floor. She wondered if he still had her movie poster hanging on his wall.

'Well, well, Miss Stella Hope!' His voice boomed down the phone.

'Stan!' she said. 'Oh, I'm so glad you're there.'

'How are you, Stella?'

She suddenly missed him and felt a wave of nostalgia for the dozens of breakfasts they'd had over the years in the courtyard at Chateau Marmont, where they'd share a pitcher of mimosa and gossip.

'So how's London?' he asked.

'Oh Stan,' she began, 'well, London's fine, I suppose, but it's not Hollywood, that's for sure.' Her throat tightened and she reined in her self-pity. He hated whingeing, and she needed him on her side.

'I know, Stella, but for now London's the perfect place for you. I hear you're doing some fine work.'

She doubted he'd heard anything of the sort, but let it go.

'Your new one,' he continued, 'about the woman who owns a pub? That sounds interesting.'

'You heard about *A Heart Like No Other* already?' she asked, surprised. 'But it's only just wrapped.'

'Hey, it's me,' he joked. 'I hear everything!'

'Well, there's something you won't know,' she said. She lit a cigarette. 'I have a problem. And I need your help.'

'Go on,' he said, trepidation in his voice.

'It's... well, it's a delicate matter.'

'God, Stella – you're not pregnant, are you?'

'What? No, of course not!' she said, laughing.

'Because if you are,' he continued, 'you know that can be easily fixed.'

'I'm not pregnant, Stan, honestly. It would be a medical miracle if I were.'

'Good!' She could hear the relief down the phone. 'Well, everything is fixable, what is it?'

She took a deep breath.

'Well, darling,' she began. And then she told him. She told him about the letters and the photos and the money demands. She explained how they'd arrived, the American stamps, the writing. She opened her bag and took them out as she spoke about it. And the more she said, the more her voice wavered as she became upset all over again. By the end, her breath had become erratic, and she forced herself to extinguish her ciggie and calm down – she'd started with such composure, too, and now look at her.

She flicked away a single tear with her finger. 'I won't have it, Stan,' she said, her breath jagged now. 'Someone doing this – ruining everything I've worked so hard for. You must find him. You've got to make him stop.'

'But Stella, I don't understand,' said Stan. 'I destroyed those photos myself. And in exchange, I paid him off, to keep him quiet. Quite a lot, if I remember rightly.'

'Well,' she said. 'He was holding out on you, because I'm looking at two of these photos right now and they're definitely me.' She stared at the pictures intently. 'I mean you can *tell*, Stan. Anyone could tell. It's awful.'

She dropped the photos onto the table and immediately felt better for having told him. It was his problem now, too. Yes, she'd discussed it with Maggie, but here was someone who truly understood what was at stake. She waited but didn't say anything.

After a few moments, she asked quietly, 'You *can* help me, darling, can't you?' She could hear her Greek accent return, as it often did when she was anxious or passionate.

'Well, of course I will try,' he said. 'I'm livid at the thought that you're being subjected to this. But Stella – my dear – it was, what… twenty odd years ago that we went to him? I don't know where he is now. I mean, I probably have his name somewhere. I could try and find him but…'

'I remember his address, if that helps,' she said. 'That's something I won't forget.' She gave him the details of the place on Fairfax Avenue and heard him take them down. 'I'll never forget that place,' she continued. 'It's next to that grocery store that's been there forever, the one on the corner. I still do a detour if I'm nearby. I can't bear to walk past.'

'Okay, well, I'll look into it. I'll dig out his name, and now I have an address, that's a good start. But listen, you know the chances are slim, right? People move on. I doubt he'll be there after all these years.'

She let out an exasperated sigh and picked up her cigarette again.

'Do you think he sold the photos to someone else?' she asked. 'Because I can't understand why someone from years ago would suddenly want to harm me this way.'

'That's what I was thinking, but who?' asked Stan. 'You don't have any enemies, do you? Unless there's anything you haven't told me about?'

'Heavens no,' she said, lighting up again. 'The only person who dislikes me with a passion is Max, and he'd never do anything like this.' She paused. 'Would he?'

'No, don't be ridiculous,' said Stan. 'I know you've been at each other's throats for months, but Max will always love you, in his own way. And anyhow, he has more money than God. He doesn't need any more.'

'Exactly,' said Stella, tapping her ciggie into the chrome ashtray by her side. 'That's what I thought.'

'What about that crazy fan – remember him?' said Stan. 'The one who wouldn't leave you and Max alone? Even came to your home, I think?'

'Oh, yes! I'd forgotten all about him!' she said. 'But didn't you have him arrested?'

Stan laughed. 'Even I can't put someone away for that long,' he said. 'Look, Stella, leave it with me. Let me see if I can trace either of them and I'll be in touch, alright? I'll do my utmost and, in the meantime, try not to worry.'

'Alright.' She was about to say something about how scared she was that it would get into the papers and ask whether the studio would back her if it did. Or would they abandon her? She wanted to know, but she also didn't want to broach the subject.

'Sorry, but I have a meeting,' he said. 'I must go. Now look after yourself and I'll speak to you soon, okay?' And with that he hung up.

She looked at the phone in her hand. She was pleased she'd called. If anyone could fix this, Stan could.

A breeze whipped through the open window and the photos blew onto the floor.

CHAPTER TWENTY

Hollywood, Los Angeles
January 1954

Ginny and Cynthia sat at the bar of the Mocambo club on Sunset Boulevard, ready for a night of drinking and dancing. Ginny had never been here before, but Cynthia had promised her that this was *the* place to celebrate being cast in *When Love Comes to Town*.

Ginny leaned on the bar and stared at the glass cages on the wall that held live cockatoos and macaws. The décor was extraordinary: jewelled plaster figures surrounded them, including a cat in a top hat, and – when she looked up – an ornately painted little lamb balanced on a highwire above their heads.

Cynthia pulled the straw out of her orange cocktail, dropped it onto the bar and took a swig from the tall glass.

'I love a Zombie!' she shouted to Ginny, trying to be heard above the band. 'Try yours.'

Ginny put her lips to her straw and took a slow, deep sip from her drink. Her eyes opened wide.

'Wow! That's strong!'

'Great, huh?' Cynthia leaned towards her and started

counting off the ingredients on her fingers. 'Three kinds of rum, pineapple juice, orange juice, lime juice, apricot brandy and, of course – this.' She plucked the maraschino cherry from the top and popped it in her mouth. 'I can't believe you haven't had one before.'

'That's going to be one hell of a hangover,' said Ginny.

'What?'

'I said, the hangover!'

Cynthia gave her a friendly nudge. 'Oh, it'll be worth it. We had to celebrate in style! *You* and Michael Pezzi!'

'Shh!' said Ginny. 'It's not announced yet. I haven't even—'

She was about to say she hadn't even told Max. Tomorrow was Wednesday, so she'd see him and tell him then. Or she could go to the Sunset Tower tonight and surprise him, but she'd never turned up unannounced before. He might not be in. Of course, she could call his hotel to check – she'd spoken to him a few times on the phone, from the booth in Schwab's – but she didn't want to make a habit of it. He'd told her so many times how much he appreciated her discretion till his divorce came through. The last thing he needed was that gossip columnist Matilda Mayhew finding out. Ginny felt so close to him, but she hated not being able to contact him easily, hated that he called all the shots.

There was a cheer as the band struck up a fast samba beat. First it was the tambourines, then the maracas and finally the drums joined in.

'Come on!' Cynthia grabbed Ginny's arm and she happily allowed herself to be dragged to the tiny dance floor.

It was heaving with bodies, but that made it even wilder. For the next hour, they didn't stop. Ginny couldn't help but swing her hips to the music. As she laughed and danced with Cynthia, she spotted a few people she recognised: a couple of the waiters from Schwab's smoking and eyeing up the girls, some extras she'd worked with last week, and Jimmy, the prop boy, with Angie from the back office, draped over each other. There were even a few well-known faces, actors and actresses who'd get recognised in the street. Here, nobody asked for autographs, nobody introduced themselves or pushed for work. Everyone came for the same reason. To have the time of their lives.

As she surrendered herself to the music, a couple of men – at least twice her age – tried to insert themselves between her and Cynthia. The girls laughed and Cynthia shouted, 'Not today, thank you!' She pulled Ginny away from them and they danced by themselves, arms up, hips out, free of all inhibitions. Ginny hadn't felt so carefree in ages. To hell with the hangover.

A tall, blond man sidled next to her, holding his cigarette to one side as he started dancing with her. Ginny reached up, took the ciggie from his fingers, had a puff and passed it back.

He laughed and nudged his friend. She gave him a wink then turned her back and carried on. Tonight, she was invincible. She was going to be a star, a great star. It had finally happened, and right now, here in the Mocambo at 8588 Sunset Boulevard, West Hollywood, she was happier than she'd ever been.

'I need the bathroom,' shouted Cynthia, leaving her alone in the crowd. Ginny carried on dancing, arms up, eyes closed, face turned to the ceiling as if it was the sun above her, and she was basking on a hot summer's day, rather than the pulsating lights in the smoke-filled air.

'Hey, how about we go to a party?'

It was the blond man. She smiled.

'This *is* the party,' she replied. 'Why go anywhere else?'

'So we can get to know each other,' he said, talking loudly above the music, moving closer. 'I'd like to get to know you. I'm very agreeable, or so I've been told.'

He was handsome, in that outdoors, American kind of way. About her age, too. He put his hand on the small of her back, but she twisted to the side and he let it drop away. His friend who was standing behind him let out a guffaw.

'Okay, okay,' he said, hands up as if to say it had all been a mistake. 'You winked at me, I just thought you might want to...'

'I have a boyfriend,' she said loudly. 'Thank you, but I'll pass.'

'You alright?' It was Cynthia.

'I'm fine and dandy,' said Ginny. Then she turned to the man and called, 'Thanks for the offer, blondie.'

He grinned, and as his friend pulled him away, he called back, 'See you around, blondie.'

'What's wrong with you?' asked Cynthia, laughing. 'I leave you for five minutes and you're turning men away? Did you *see* what he looked like?'

'Not in the mood,' said Ginny, grabbing her arm. 'Come on, let's have another drink.'

Three hours later, Ginny left Cynthia at her apartment and crossed the hall to her own. She leaned against her door to steady herself. She'd only had two or three Zombies. Maybe four.

Struggling with her key, she shushed herself, giggled and finally managed to open up. Dropping her bag and shawl where she stood, she stumbled to the sink and poured herself a large glass of water. She downed it and did the same again. She couldn't be bothered to take off her make-up so wandered to her bed, ready to collapse. She'd sleep in her clothes, it didn't matter.

She was about to lie down when she saw a beam of light on the eiderdown. She looked up and realised the hallway light was pouring in; she'd left the front door wide open. Even in her woozy state, she knew she couldn't leave it like that. Hauling herself up she trudged to the door, groaning. She tried to close it gently, and her foot kicked something.

She looked down. A card – was it from Max? Had she missed him? He always had the cards sent to the lobby. This had been brought to her door. She crouched to pick it up and saw it was much thinner than the usual envelope from the Sunset Tower.

Her name was printed on the envelope. In the top left-hand corner, the Star Studios logo.

She ripped it open, her heart pounding even more now, her mouth completely dry.

    Ginny, come and see me first thing.
    There's been a change of plan. Stan

CHAPTER TWENTY-ONE

It was a night of twisted sheets and fitful sleep. The blond man had danced into Ginny's dreams, his hands firm on the small of her back. He swept his fingers along her bare shoulders and touched her face. She reached up and kissed him, and when she pulled away, he was Max.

When she woke, the note was still held tight in her hand. She sat up, smoothed it out and read it again.

```
Ginny, come and see me first thing.
There's been a change of plan. Stan
```

The alarm clock told her it was seven. If she was to catch him, she had to get up now.

He was rarely in his office, his days full of meetings or dropping in on various sets unexpectedly. She looked down at her crumpled dress, sighed and got up, trying not to move her head too much. She'd only had a few hours' sleep, but she couldn't bear to wait all day to find out what this was all about. The sooner she knew, the better.

Half an hour later, after a brutally cold quick shower, she was standing in Stan Fisher's office, waiting for him to arrive. Ida had let her in with no fuss, so she was expected. Not good.

In her hurry, Ginny had wet her hair and pushed it back with a polka dot headband – so far, it was behaving. Her blood pounded in her ears and she realised she had forgotten to take something for her hangover. And she felt nauseous. What if she threw up, right there, over Stan Fisher's expensive zebra-skin rug? Taking a deep breath, she wandered towards the gilt-framed movie posters on the wall. Stella Hope stared at her, fur slung over her bare shoulders, diamonds at her throat.

Ginny looked down on the pale blue day dress she'd pulled on that morning and her white pumps. She took her compact from her bag and, despite having no other make-up on, gave her lips a quick slick of her trademark Fire and Ice. The note was there in her bag, but she stopped herself reading it again.

For hours, the possibilities had somersaulted through her mind: perhaps Michael Pezzi was ill and they'd had to delay the filming? Or they'd finally cast her alongside Max? That was possible, wasn't it? And if so, they'd want her to start straight away. She sighed and wondered if she could ask Ida for a glass of water and some Alka-Seltzer.

Of course, there was the chance that the studio had made a mistake or changed their minds about her. The whorl of anxiety curled up through her stomach. But she had nothing to be afraid of, did she? She had a contract, she told herself. She had a role starring alongside one of Star Studios' most promising young actors. Everything would work out.

The door swung open and she turned around. Stan walked in, jacket slung over his arm, briefcase in hand.

'Ginny, Ginny – how are you?' he asked, as he dropped his belongings on his desk. 'I thought you might be here.'

'Er... fine – I'm good, thank you.'

He motioned for her to come to the couch and sit, then did the same, making the cushion rise with his bulk, like the first time they'd met. She remembered that Max had said Stan knew about the two of them. That would count for something, surely?

'So, look,' he began. 'I've heard good reports, and we're all very pleased with your progress and your attitude.' He gave her a smile. 'And while I do appreciate all your work, there's no easy way to say this.'

Ginny sat back a little.

'We need you back on *Kill Me Again*. Today,' he said.

'But... I mean, I can't, Stan. Michael Pezzi wants me for his new film. You know that.'

Stan didn't say anything.

'I've got the script. I'm replacing Rosie Moreau,' Ginny said. It sounded so ridiculous out loud.

'Well,' said Stan, leaning over to get a cigarette. He offered her one but she shook her head. 'I'm afraid there's been a change of plan.' He lit up. 'Pezzi got it wrong – the part has gone to someone else.'

'*What?*' Her throat tightened and she felt a weight pressing her down. She could feel her mouth tremble, the way it did when she was about to burst out crying. '*But why?* He said he wanted me.'

'I'm sorry, Ginny, but it wasn't his decision to make. It's

out of my hands. You still have the film you were on before.'
He stared at her, trying to gauge her reaction.

'But,' she began, her tears were flowing now, 'I need this
so badly. Did you see my audition? Everyone said I was by
far the best one.'

'It's simply not possible, sweetheart,' he said gently. 'We'll
get you something bigger soon, I promise. Just be patient
– something really good.' Then he leaned towards her and
said in a hushed voice, 'Perhaps even with Max.'

There was a look of such concern in his eyes, as if he
was genuinely sorry. He handed her a handkerchief, and in
that moment she felt like a child being placated. Were his
promises real? She rubbed at her face and tried to level her
voice.

'But Michael told me himself,' she said. 'He told me he
wanted me on his film. That was just yesterday.'

Stan pressed his lips together but didn't say anything.

'Stan?' she asked. 'Did I do something wrong? What
happened?'

He let out an impatient sigh. 'It's not your fault, Ginny.
But things constantly change in this business. You know
that, surely?'

He tapped his cigarette on the edge of the amber
glass ashtray that sat between them, and he looked directly
at her.

'Look, it's come from above. And to be frank, I don't
question these orders. It's not my place. And you shouldn't
either.'

Her leg began to tremble a little, and she pressed it down
with her hand so he wouldn't notice.

He'd noticed. 'I know it's a huge disappointment,' he

said, gentler now, 'but don't forget you're under contract. The studio doesn't need to explain itself.'

'I know,' she said, swiping the tears from her face again. 'And I'm grateful for the contract. And of course I want to work, Stan, I really do.'

'Good girl,' he said, shifting to get up.

'But can I try something new?' she blurted. 'I mean I've been getting the same kind of roles for months now. And with all of them I'm bursting out of my clothes and hardly have any lines. I don't want those parts anymore. I've got so much more in me. I can do something much better.'

There. She'd said it before she'd lost the courage.

He stood up.

'Those films you turn your nose up at?' he said. 'They sell out at the box office, week in week out. People queueing around the block to see them. And every time someone buys a ticket, they're seeing your face up there on the screen.'

'But I hardly speak,' she protested, 'and the outfits are... well... I don't think they'd remember my face, if you know what I mean.' She knew she should shut up, but it felt good to say it out loud.

His cheeks reddened and he put his hand out to stop her saying anything else.

'You're barely two months into a seven-year contract,' he said sternly. 'Don't be difficult. You don't want to be suspended, do you? Because if you don't work, you don't get paid. You know that.'

She clenched her jaw to stop herself responding.

He turned his back as he walked to his desk.

'Now get yourself to hair and make-up,' he said in a matter-of-fact voice. He sat in his huge leather chair and smiled at her. 'Go on, Ginny, they started shooting yesterday and you missed a whole day.'

She stayed frozen to the seat.

'Ginny?' he said. 'I like you, I like you a lot, but don't push back on this, okay? You're making it very difficult for me. You'll get a reputation, then *nobody* will want to work with you. Not even Max.'

She got up and rushed out of his office.

In the ladies, she knelt on the floor and retched into the toilet, bringing up everything from the night before: the cocktails, the music, the dancing, the flirting, the laughing with Cynthia. All of it meant nothing now. Perhaps it never had.

She stood and stumbled to the sink, where she rinsed her mouth, splashed her face and patted it dry with a rough green paper towel. She'd carry on with the same tired roles she'd been ploughing through for months. No-hope girlfriends of no-good men who were easy with their fists.

The door swung open and Ida walked in with her bag. 'You left this.'

'Thanks, Ida.' She took it from her.

Ida reached over and fixed Ginny's collar, which was sticking up.

'They think they're gods,' she said. 'Don't let them get to you.'

'But...' Ginny shook her head. 'That part was mine. I was the best person, they said so. And now I'm waiting again. It's all just so unfair.'

'I know,' said Ida. 'Fix your face.'

Ginny turned to the mirror, blew her nose and stared

at her red, blotchy cheeks. She opened her bag and took out her compact to try to even out her skin tone.

'Look,' said Ida, behind her in the mirror. 'I've worked for Star Studios for twenty-five years. Nothing in Hollywood makes sense.'

Ginny sighed as she dropped the powder in her bag again and pulled out her lipstick.

'There's only one thing I know for sure,' said Ida.

Ginny turned to look at her.

'What's that?'

Ida gave her a tight smile.

'That person there,' said Ida, pointing at Ginny's reflection in the mirror, 'that's the only person you can rely on. You.'

The man sitting behind the large wooden desk is bald. His greying beard and moustache are bushy and his sideburns unruly. He says he is called Dr Faulkner.

'The nurses have reported that you're frequently asking questions,' he says, tapping his pipe on the desk. 'They say you have issues settling in.'

I shift in my seat.

'I don't want to settle in,' I say. 'I don't belong here.'

His smile is full of contempt. 'Nobody thinks they belong here,' he says. 'But everyone does.'

I shake my head. 'No, I don't,' I say. 'I'm not unwell, not in the way you think.' I realise I'm twisting my hands in my lap and sit on them instead.

He opens a folder on his desk and I peer to see what lies they've written about me, but he pulls it away.

'All of our patients are sick up here.' He points to his head. 'In one way or another. There are so many ways you can lose your mind.'

'No.'

'Yes,' he insists.

'My mind is not sick, I'm not sick. I don't know why you think I am.'

'Look,' he says, exasperated. 'You're no different to anyone else here. I know you think you are, but the sooner you realise you're not, the better.'

I shake my head.

'You might be an actress out there,' he says, 'even a famous one for all I know. That fantasy world holds no interest for me. What I care about is this hospital, and inside these walls you're just another woman with psychiatric problems.' He tips his head to one side. 'Did you think you were special?'

His meanness burns through me. I haven't felt special for such a long time.

'You were brought here,' he continues, 'for your own good because you're hysterical.' He taps his folder. 'Out of control.' He taps again. 'Violent.' Tap. 'Unmanageable.'

In another life I reach across and smash his head down on the desk. But the punishment here for violence is more violence. They erase our minds with electricity. My mind is all I have left.

I breathe slow and deep and stare around the room to try and calm the pounding in my chest. There's a framed certificate that hangs crooked on one wall, and damp has erupted in the corner like an overblown rose.

I will try now. I have to try. I have nothing to lose and I don't know when I will be brought before him again.

'Doctor,' I start tentatively. 'I think I understand. I think I was hysterical when I came here because I saw something terrible. But I don't remember it clearly, the memory comes and goes.'

He doesn't speak.

'*Perhaps if I could stop the tablets,*' *I continue,* '*then my mind would come back, and I could accept whatever happened.*'

Still silence.

I try and peer at the folder again.

'*Does it say in my report what happened?*' *I ask, leaning forward.* '*I'm sure once I know, then I would get better and I could leave?*'

'*Leave?*' *He laughs.* '*This is a mental institution.*'

'*I know,*' *I say.*

'*But I don't think you understand,*' *he continues.* '*You're here because you've been committed by people who care for your welfare. People who want to help you. These people are paying your bills.*' *He knocks his pipe against the desk again.* '*I doubt you'll be leaving.*'

His words slam through me, and I'm pushed back into the chair.

Who has done this to me?

CHAPTER TWENTY-TWO

Hollywood, Los Angeles
February 1954

Although she'd had to show up every day, Ginny's scenes on *Kill Me Again* had been minimal. Today, she'd spent much of her time hanging around the set in an uncomfortable black satin playsuit, waiting to be called.

One of the other bit actors kept stroking her backside, standing right behind her, and it was all she could do not to burst out crying. The shorts on her outfit rode up, and she spent much of her day tugging them down so as not to reveal her knickers. And the outfit was too long in the body and gaped at her chest. Dolores, the wardrobe woman, was off sick and her assistant was no match for her skills.

Ginny imagined herself ripping off the stupid outfit and going home, burrowing under her eiderdown to forget the world. But she'd be fined if she walked out and, anyway, being on set was a distraction. Once she was in her apartment, she'd have to face the deluge of sadness lapping at her, threatening to knock her off her feet.

Hours later, after an exhausting day, she stood in her

living room and opened the thick, cream envelope that had arrived for her.

I heard what happened. Come to me.

Thank God for Max.

After her initial tears on seeing him, and her jumbled version of what had happened, they fell into bed. Later that night, as they both dozed, she started talking.

'I just don't understand,' she said, as he stroked her hair. 'I mean, one minute I had the role and the next I didn't.'

He sighed. 'That's the movie business for you,' he said. 'There's no figuring it out – it'll drive you crazy.'

'What do you mean?' she asked, sitting up and slipping on her robe.

He sat up too and, reaching for a Lucky Strike, offered her one. She accepted and he reached for his lighter, but it wouldn't ignite. 'Pass me the matches,' he said, pointing to the bedside drawer.

'It's a multi-million-dollar business,' he continued, as she rummaged around. In the drawer were press cuttings and a couple of pens. She reached into the back for a book of matches and her hand hit something hard. 'But so often,' he continued, 'the decisions are ruled by hearts and gut feelings – that's why there's no point trying to understand them, because they don't make sense.'

'Max?' She tentatively pulled out a gun. 'Is this a prop?'

He shook his head. 'I got it years ago – got one for Stella, too. We came back to the ranch one day and there was this man, just waiting on the porch. Said he was a fan. Spooked us both.'

She shook her head in disbelief, placed it back and gave him the matches.

'Stan said the order to drop me had come from above,' she said, as he offered her a light. 'What does that *mean*?'

'It means he can't do anything about it – it's probably gone to a girl some studio exec is bankrolling, because she makes him feel twenty-five again. Someone at the very top.'

'I don't know,' she said. 'I got the feeling Stan was holding out on me.' She flicked the ash from her cigarette into the ashtray between them. 'He got really defensive.'

'Stan?' he asked, laughing. 'He's doing everything he can for you, trust me. His hands are tied.' He shifted in the bed. 'And anyway,' he continued, 'I heard things aren't so great on that film. Between Pezzi and the director.'

She raised her eyebrows. 'Go on.'

'Well,' he said, 'rumour is they're fighting a lot, which can mean one of two things: the film will overrun and they'll get a new director, or it will wrap on time but will be a turkey. When a movie has issues at the start, it never ends well. You're probably better off not being involved.'

Although she'd barely smoked it, Ginny stubbed out her cigarette.

'Maybe,' she said, 'but I hate what I'm doing right now.' Her voice was starting to crack a little. 'And this was the best chance I've had so far.' The unjustness of it all cut her again, the way it had when she'd first heard the news. 'Maybe the best chance I'll ever get.'

'Come here!' Max swept the ashtray away and took her

hands. 'Don't say that. That *wasn't* the best chance you'll ever get.'

Her face was wet now. 'But... but how do you know?'

'Your best chance,' he said, gently wiping her tears with his thumb, 'is me. *I'm* your best chance.'

There was a pause and then she laughed, and he did too when he realised how vain it sounded.

'Seriously, though,' he continued, 'Michael Pezzi has promise, sure, but, well... can you keep a secret?'

She nodded.

'I have some news. Remember that film *The Silent Hero*? We'd just wrapped the day we met.'

'Yes?'

'The studio thinks there's a strong chance I'll win the Academy this year.'

She threw her arms around his neck. 'Max! That's wonderful!'

'And in the meantime,' he said, 'if a bigger role comes up that you want to audition for, just tell me first. I know all the producers and can dig around and find out if it's worth your time. You don't want to pin your hopes on something that's a washout.'

She nodded, but there was something that had been worrying her.

'Max,' she began, 'I don't want this to come out wrong, but...' She wanted to ask but didn't know how.

He looked at her. 'Hey, you can say anything to me.'

She took a deep breath and let it out. 'Okay,' she said. 'I was... well, I was just wondering why. I mean what do you get out of it? Us working together. You're a big star, I'm an unknown. Why are you doing this?'

He smiled and his face lit up. 'Are you kidding? I get *everything*. I mean, being with you has been... How can I put this?' He sighed contentedly. 'I feel new. I feel young again. I'm drinking less, I'm sleeping better, and frankly, I look *great*. Come on!'

She grinned and pulled the covers up for a glance at his glorious nakedness.

'You look okay,' she said.

He gave her a mock slap on the arm.

'And,' he continued, 'I get to introduce the world to an exciting young co-star. You know my solo films haven't done that well. I need a female co-star, someone to spark off. My fans love that. And who better than you?'

She didn't want this to stop.

'You're talented,' he said, kissing her. 'You work incredibly hard.' He kissed her again. 'You're a knockout and...' He stroked her face.

'And?'

He pulled her towards him. 'I'm besotted with you.'

He kissed her long and slow and, still holding her close, said, 'There's something I have to tell you. I thought it was a disaster but it's good news, really.'

She pulled away. 'What is it? What's wrong?'

'Well,' he said, sitting back a little. 'We were seen. By a photographer. The other day, getting in and out of the car at the movie theatre.'

'But how?' she asked. 'We were so careful.'

'I know, but I think he must have been following me – everyone knows I stay here at the Sunset. Perhaps he tailed me and just got lucky? He contacted Stan – showed him the photos and asked for an interview. Stan's had to give them your name, told them you're a promising young actress, but it's not a disaster,' he added. 'In fact, it's time we went public.'

He glanced at her as if testing out his words to see her reaction.

'What? You mean it?' He nodded. 'Really?' she asked, not quite believing she was going to be Max Whitman's official girlfriend. 'But what about Stella?'

'We'll announce the divorce first, then next week we'll mention that you're co-starring in A Road to Nowhere. I just got the rewrites through and it's so good now. We'll say you and I became friends at work, our friendship blossomed but it's early days – you know, the usual story.'

Ginny stared at him, amazed it had all been worked out without her. 'What about the photographer?' she asked.

'He'll hang on for an exclusive interview – he's agreed not to use the photos till then.' He paused. 'We'll be official at last. How does that sound to you?'

She moved closer to him and he put his arm around her.

'It sounds wonderful,' she said. 'No more creeping around.' She looked up at him. 'Can we go out dancing? And for dinner? And to film premieres together?'

'I'll take you out every night if you like,' he said.

That weekend, Max arranged for them to visit his cabin in the Hollywood Hills. It was in a secluded spot, and until they were public, they had to stay away from prying eyes. As they sat on the veranda, heavy crystal tumblers of Johnnie Walker whisky in hand, and a blanket thrown over their legs, he asked her how *Kill Me Again* was going. He rarely asked about her work, so she decided to be honest.

'Dreadful,' she said, taking a gulp.

'What?' He twisted around to look at her. 'Why?'

'One of the actors keeps whispering lewd suggestions in my ear, what he'd like to do to me, and so on. Yesterday he followed me around and kept touching my backside. He did it when we were rolling so I couldn't shout at him.'

Max carefully placed his glass on the tiny wooden table in front of them and pulled away from her, to see her better. His body was stiff with fury.

'He did *what*?'

'I must have slapped him away dozens of times,' she continued, 'but he wouldn't stop. And then he cornered me in the dressing room and, well, thank God for the make-up girl who came looking for me.'

Her cheeks felt hot as the shame and fury swept through her again, as if it had just happened.

'Did you speak to the director?' he asked.

She scoffed. 'He doesn't care – says I should be flattered. But it's like being on a battlefield sometimes, like you're constantly under siege,' she said. 'Always thinking ahead, trying not to get caught with the wrong person in the wrong place. All the girls feel the same.'

Max's face had hardened. 'Why didn't you tell me? Why didn't you say something?'

She shrugged. 'I wanted to, but it never seemed like the right time. And I didn't know how to even begin. It happens to all the women at the studio – actresses, crew members, writers – it doesn't matter who you are. Last week a cameraman put his hand down a secretary's blouse and she punched him, but then she was fired.'

'She punched him?' he gasped. 'Good for her!'

'Was it though? He lost a tooth, but she lost her job.'

'Stella told me it was bad,' he said, sighing, 'but I never knew it was like this.' He pulled her into his embrace and gazed out into the indigo dusk that was streaked with wisps of tangerine. 'What's his name? The actor who's bothering you?'

She shrugged. 'Sammy something. Jonson, Jones – I don't know for sure.'

'Does he have a big part?'

'No, he's in one scene, two maybe. Why?'

Max turned to her and nodded. 'Okay, he won't bother you again.'

She paused, then laughed when she realised he was serious.

'Just like that?' she asked.

'I'll make sure of it. What's the point of you being with me if I can't protect you from men like that?'

'Well, that would be *amazing*,' she said. 'I mean it's not the first time it's happened, but he's definitely been the worst.' Then she frowned. 'How?'

He lit a cigarette and one for her too. 'How what?' He passed it to her.

'How will you get him to stop?' she asked. 'We're still not officially together – people will guess if you kick up a fuss.'

'Don't worry about that,' he said. 'I'll talk to Stan. It'll come from him.'

She was relieved to know Sammy Jones or Jonson or

whatever his name was would never touch her again. But she was also quietly furious that it took a man to make this behaviour stop.

'You know,' he said, 'Stella used to say it was the best thing about being married to me. Protection from the wolves she called it.' He gave a sad smile. 'Sometimes I think that's all she wanted me for. That and the fame, glory and money, of course. Then as soon as she was famous enough, she abandoned me.'

She'd never heard him speak like this before. Self-pity didn't suit him.

'Hey,' she said, as she rubbed his arm. 'You're hardly abandoned, are you? You've got me, for a start. And thousands of fans adore you, *and* you're the biggest box office draw for Star Studios.'

'Maybe,' he said. 'But these young stars coming up...' He sighed. 'Ready to jump at any chance.' A flicker of fear darted across his face as if he could see into his future. He sat up a little.

He took a long draw on his cigarette, slinging an arm around her shoulders. 'I think Stella grew tired of me,' he said, blowing smoke into the chilly night air. He drew her in close. She wanted to look at him but he'd pulled her so tight, she couldn't.

'She wanted different roles, by herself,' he said. 'I reckon she thought she'd be a bigger star without me, but now look at us. We're not as good apart as we were together.'

He seemed to be thinking out loud now, rather than speaking to her. And he didn't sound like a man who was over his ex, let alone someone about to announce a new love to the world. Suddenly her neck felt cold and she managed to wriggle out from under his arm, tugging her shawl tighter.

'You miss her.' She wasn't asking him a question but stating a fact. *And you still love her*, she thought. It was clear as anything.

He shrugged. 'I did miss her, but not anymore. Now I just miss being part of a screen couple.'

Ginny nodded slowly, unsure if she believed him.

'And I know you think I still love her,' he said, 'but I don't. You can't love and despise someone at the same time, can you? Anyway, enough about her. I have you now, don't I?'

They sat in silence for a while, and she wondered if one day he'd speak about her this way.

'I'm cold,' she said. 'Let's go inside.'

CHAPTER TWENTY-THREE

Ealing Village, London
August 1954

Maggie had dreaded this moment all day. The moment when she put the key in her door and entered her flat. The anxiety that constantly gnawed at her stomach grew stronger in the evenings, when she was alone and had time to drink and think.

She kicked off her shoes, slipped out of her clothes and took off her make-up.

Then she slid into her dressing gown, put on her pink mule slippers and looked at the clock. It was only seven, and the prospect of the empty hours ahead made her stomach clench. Being alone was dangerous these days. It would usually start well, but then she'd begin to stew over her predicament, pondering all the worst-case scenarios as her panic cranked up a gear. Eventually, she'd be in the eye of the storm, in full-flow hysterics, trying to sob quietly into her hands so the neighbours wouldn't hear.

She was desperate to call Jim Brodsky again, the private detective in LA, but she needed to give him more time to dig around. He was really her only hope. Well, him and Stella.

Then there was the worry of how to make the call. She couldn't risk ringing from the studios again, could she? It was only a matter of time before she was caught.

She switched the radio on for company and the sound of Nat King Cole wafting through the room lifted her spirits a little. Peering into the larder, she grabbed the bread and a tin of beans, and made her dinner. After eating, she poured herself a shot of whisky and picked up her copy of *Vogue*, settling in on the sofa. *This is alright*, she thought. A perfectly pleasant night in. See – she could be by herself. She was fine.

An hour or so later, tiredness swept over her so she wandered to bed, hoping to fall asleep before her whirring mind could take control.

The dream came upon her by stealth, as it always did. At some point between losing consciousness and waking, the nightmare would enter her room, pull back the covers and creep into bed with her. It held her tight, and she slipped inside the horror of it all. She saw herself crying, pulling at her own hair, heard her terrible screams, her pleas, and while the detail of the scenario was always disjointed and muddled, on waking, her body was flooded with the familiarity of utter despair, powerlessness. And, above all, loss.

She carried these feelings with her every day: when she was sipping her coffee, fixing Stella's make-up, laughing at a joke one of the crew had made. The grief, in particular, was an invisible shroud, impossible to shrug off. But she carried on regardless, forcing herself to breathe deep, stand straight and pretend she was fine.

If she didn't, her heart would stop beating.

CHAPTER TWENTY-FOUR

Hollywood, Los Angeles
March 1954

It was the final day on *Kill Me Again* and in a last-minute rewrite, Ginny had been given two more lines to say as she leaned over her gangster boyfriend's body: *Oh, Frankie, they got you too. Sleep well, Frankie.*

She gave the words as much conviction as she could muster, despite a deep urge to roll her eyes. Well, it was better than nothing, she told herself. And it meant her name would appear higher on the final credits. But she couldn't wait for this fiasco to be over. What with all the grabbing and lewd remarks and the awful outfits, this film had worn her down – she just couldn't do this again.

Although it had only been a couple of days since she'd mentioned all of this to Max, he must have acted on it immediately because Sammy had kept his distance – hadn't touched her, hadn't even spoken to her. Stan must have warned him off. But Sammy stared constantly, as did the other men on the set. And they whispered as she walked past. She heard one of them refer to her as 'Stan's girl'. If only they knew the truth. Well, they would soon enough.

The director called for lunch, and she wandered to the trestle table, poring over the sad sandwiches already curling on the platter. She'd eat later. The last day on a film was usually upbeat, with everyone glad to be done and full of hope about what might come next. Sometimes, catering arranged for a celebration cake, but not today. There was a tetchiness in the air, and a sourness pervaded the set, as if everyone knew they'd been part of creating something quite dreadful. *Not for long*, thought Ginny, as she helped herself to a coffee from the huge chrome urn. The Academy Awards were just a few weeks away, and if Max won – as everyone predicted – there'd be nothing the studio wouldn't do for him. She wondered if he'd invite her to be his guest at the Oscars and felt a sudden jolt of excitement. Then she realised she'd have nothing to wear. She needed to stop this fantasising. Nobody even knew about them yet.

She took her bag from under the table, where she'd left it earlier, and was about to pop a blue pill into her mouth when she stopped herself. Did she really need it? She wasn't that tired. She could have it later, perhaps – though she had to be careful not to take it too late, or she'd need a pink one to sleep. She hadn't taken a pink one for days and pictured the bottle at home, crammed with a month's supply. They used to provide an easy comfort at night, but now they just left her groggy, and a couple of times she could have sworn she'd blacked out altogether. Anything could happen while you slept, especially in this town.

'Virginia Rose?' A short man with a pencil moustache was standing next to her, his hand outstretched ready to shake hers. She'd noticed him earlier, chain-smoking as he'd watched her scene. 'I'm Harry Carrillo,' he said. 'I'm shooting *Double Trouble* over on 3B.'

'Oh, hello.' She shook his hand and put down her cup to take the card he was passing her. She turned it over. Under his name in small capital letters, it read: *DIRECTOR*.

'It's about two female detectives,' he continued. 'We've got the brunette and we're still casting for the blonde. Doing run-throughs today with whoever is around.'

Her mouth opened. 'Really? It's a lead?' she asked. 'With lines?' This would be perfect.

He laughed. 'Well, I wouldn't say lead. But yes – with lines and everything.' He had a charming, well-worn face. 'The lead is their boss who runs the agency,' he continued. 'We've got Gary Stanning – you know him? Plays good guys, cops, lawyers and so on.'

'Of course,' she said, nodding. 'He's great.' Stanning was an older actor. He had class and was a cut above the rest. 'I watched *Witness Unknown* just last week.'

Harry Carrillo looked impressed. 'Well, an actual film buff working in Hollywood,' he said, smiling. 'Whatever next? So you'll come for an audition?'

'Of course!'

'We need someone by tomorrow. I hear you made some films in London as Ginny Watkins?'

'That's me,' she said.

He'd been talking to someone about her. Was all the hard work about to pay off? Someone had noticed her; someone who could change her life. She *needed* this. Gary Stanning was never in bad films. Harry Carrillo *had* to choose her.

'Great, 3B in an hour,' he said. 'Will you be done by then?'

'Definitely, Mr Carrillo. Thank you.'

He turned to walk away then looked back and called out, 'By the way, what did you think of *Witness Unknown*?'

'I loved it,' she shouted.

'Good to hear! It's one of mine.'

An hour and a half later, script in hand, Ginny crouched in a corner of Studio 3B trying to memorise her lines. She was surrounded by at least a dozen other blonde actresses doing exactly the same. Everyone was reading for the same part, the part she *had* to get. Unlike the set she'd just left, the energy here was electric as voices repeated lines out loud, either to themselves or to friends who they'd grabbed for help. People had come from other sets where they'd wrapped for the day to watch; it seemed this was the audition everyone was talking about.

Someone dropped to the ground next to her.

'Cynthia!' Ginny gasped. 'What are you doing here?'

'Everyone's here,' she said, laughing at Ginny's surprise. 'Do you need some help?' She took the script. 'I'll read Josie. You start.'

And for the next thirty minutes they ran the four pages repeatedly, till Ginny had got it down perfect. It wasn't easy, as the two characters were interrupting each other and finishing each other's sentences, so timing was everything. But there was real humour and heart in this script, and the dialogue sparkled like nothing she'd read for before.

A bell rang and everyone got up.

'It's the best script I've seen in ages,' said Ginny.

'I know, right?' agreed Cynthia.

A woman with a clipboard asked the actresses to line up in alphabetical order, according to first names, blonde on blonde. Harry Carrillo explained that they were running right through, and everyone would watch everyone else. There were twelve auditions and he wanted them to be as courteous to the last as the first. Nobody would leave till he said so. Gary Stanning walked on set and waved a quick hello to the line of actresses, then took a seat next to Harry.

Now Ginny was Virginia, she was last in line and she turned to grimace at Cynthia, but couldn't see her.

Then suddenly there she was, on her mark in front of the cameras.

'Everyone, this is Cynthia,' said Harry.

Cynthia?

'This morning, she got the part of Josie. So you'll read with her.'

This was just too perfect. And she hadn't said a word. Cynthia must have been the one to tell Harry about her.

Silence was called for, the cameras rolled, and Cynthia read the same lines with each actress. Every time one was finished, filming stopped, the actress joined the back of the queue and they all shifted up. Ginny watched the performances, her hands sweating.

Some actresses faltered with all the interruptions in the dialogue, others got the timing right but put no heart into it. But two or three of them were very good. And yet, she was good too, wasn't she? Maybe better. She took a few deep breaths as the conveyor belt of talent slid along. Finally, she was at the head of the line and it was her turn.

Her name was called, she walked to her mark and stood opposite her friend. Cynthia began the scene with Ginny, and their lines flowed perfectly. There was an undeniable chemistry between the two women, and as the words danced between them, their interruptions and pace fit perfectly, hand in glove.

Of course she got the part. She ran all the way home to see if there was a card from Max. Maybe he'd heard, maybe he'd ask her to visit him? In the apartment lobby, she pushed her hand into the pigeonhole. Nothing. She'd call him.

Filming started tomorrow, and in her bag was a script with the scenes she had to learn. She needed a good night's sleep. She didn't have a telephone in her room and didn't want to risk calling him from the hallway, so after a quick shower, she wandered to Schwab's and the enclosed phone booth in the corner.

She flicked through her small red address book and found the number for the Sunset Tower Hotel. She put her coins in and dialled.

'Sunset Tower,' said a woman's voice. 'This is the operator, can I help you?'

'Penthouse Suite, please.'

'Who shall I say is calling?'

'Wardrobe department,' she said. She'd used this before with him and he'd liked it – said it was apt because he was always taking his clothes off in front of her.

'One moment please,' said the operator, and the line clicked as she tried to connect them. Ginny waited. He might want her to come over, to celebrate. Perhaps just a quick visit? Then she'd have time to look at her script before bed and get up extra early to go over it again. She was lucky she learned lines easily.

Finally, she heard another click.

'Max? Max, it's me!'

'I'm sorry, madam,' said the operator. 'But the gentleman is indisposed.'

'Sorry?'

'The gentleman is indisposed.'

'Oh.' She felt a wave of disappointment. 'So, he's not...' she stuttered, 'he's not there or he just can't come to the phone?'

'He simply said to pass on a message that he's indisposed.'

'I see.' Perhaps he was having a business meeting in his suite. Yes, perhaps he couldn't speak in front of whoever was there. But it was seven in the evening now. Who would he be meeting at this time?

'Can I just ask,' Ginny said. 'Did you say it was the wardrobe department calling? When you rang through to his suite?'

There was a pause on the end of the line. 'I did, madam. Just like you asked.'

'Okay, thank you.'

She frowned, hung up and pulled the door of the booth open. He must be in a meeting. Oh well, she'd catch up with him tomorrow.

As she wandered back to her apartment, she pictured the script for *Double Trouble* at home, with her lines already marked. A whole script, not just a few pages. She thought about the weeks of fun she'd have playing opposite Cynthia, and Gary Stanning, no less. After this, surely, she'd be offered much better roles. She'd be ready to take on anything. To be Max Whitman's co-star.

Later that evening, before getting into bed, she rubbed Pond's Cold Cream onto her face and held up her hand mirror. It was an expensive, silver art-nouveau mirror that Max had given her. Around the handle twisted swirling leaves, and when she turned it over, there was a delicate dragonfly on the back, wings half open, ready to take off. Like her.

Why would he avoid her? He loved her, didn't he? Well, he'd told her he was besotted, which wasn't the same thing. But he'd been so keen to announce their relationship, to tell everyone about them becoming co-stars. Why didn't he take her call? His silence was deafening. It didn't make sense.

CHAPTER TWENTY-FIVE

Harry Carrillo was a taskmaster. He insisted that Ginny was in the make-up chair by five thirty every morning and ready to start working by seven. The same went for Cynthia. The schedule for *Double Trouble* was gruelling, with a tight budget and a shoot that was to be completed in three weeks. Ginny knew that during the silent era, actors churned out films in a matter of days, as if they were in a factory. But she'd never experienced this crazy pace herself because she'd never had a part that demanded much of her. Her roles had been small, her scenes few. At times she heard her mother's voice, pushing her on: *You can do this, Ginny, believe in yourself.* But it still felt overwhelming, with everyone relying on her stamina to make sure they stayed on schedule. And they still had two weeks left.

'It's how the big stars make so many films,' Carrillo had said. 'They work themselves to the bone.'

Ginny had looked aghast, and he laughed at her expression.

'You think Stella Hope got where she is by lying in bed?' he asked.

His charm had worn off since she'd got to know him. Thankfully, the ridiculous starts meant both she and Cynthia were excused from all classes. By early afternoon each day, Ginny was exhausted.

'Just take a bluey,' whispered Cynthia, when she caught her yawning during a five-minute break. 'I've had two today.'

'I was hoping to manage without them,' said Ginny. 'Or at least not take them every day.'

'Don't be silly. How else will you cope? You don't want to look like you're struggling.'

'I know, I know,' said Ginny, grabbing her bag and taking a pill from the small brown bottle inside. 'You're right.' She put it on her tongue and swallowed.

The two of them fell into a routine of having an early dinner at Ralph's Diner each evening. It was quieter than Schwab's and they could always get a booth. Sitting at the back, they'd discuss their day and what they had coming up. Cynthia was always keen to go over the next day's lines. To begin with, Ginny worried that by joining her she might miss a card from Max, but for days now nothing had arrived. And anyway, what kind of a friend would she be if she didn't do this? It was Cynthia, after all, who'd put her forward for the part. And Max often asked her to visit quite late, so even if he *did* want to see her, she could still make it.

Tonight, they'd eaten grilled cheese sandwiches, which had taken Ginny back to that first dinner she'd shared with Max, in his hotel room.

Scrunching up her paper napkin, Cynthia got up to leave.

'I'm going to stay a while,' said Ginny.

'You okay?' asked Cynthia.

'Yes, I just think I'll have another coffee and go through these lines again.'

Cynthia nodded. She left a few dollars on the table for her share of the bill.

'See you tomorrow.'

The bell on the door rang as she exited, and Ginny looked down at her script. His silence meant nothing. Perhaps he was busy filming on a tight schedule, like her? Maybe he was on location somewhere and had forgotten to tell her? But it had been well over a week now with no word from him. She could go and ask Stan; he'd know what Max was doing. No, that would be awful – she hated the idea of involving Stan, like some suspicious girlfriend.

There'd been no argument with Max, no falling out. In fact, the last time she'd seen him had been the weekend they'd spent at the cabin, and he'd been so affectionate, enamoured, obsessed almost. That's what puzzled her more than anything.

She stared at her lines and they started to blur. She grabbed a paper napkin from the holder and quickly dabbed her eyes. She had to keep her nerve. It was probably nothing. She'd find out soon enough, she was sure.

But it broke her heart that he hadn't been there to celebrate with her, to toast her with one of his lethal martinis, to make a fuss over her and congratulate her on her cleverness and talent. It had been such an important moment for her and she'd had nobody to share it with. Cynthia had been there, but it wasn't the same.

She wished she could confide in Cynthia and ask her

advice, spend hours dissecting her relationship with Max the way girlfriends did when it came to men. But of course, she couldn't breathe a word, and Cynthia was the only person she had, really. The only person she was close to in this town. Apart from Max.

Suddenly, she missed home. The waitress walked over and refilled her cup, and as Ginny blew on the scalding coffee, she felt an anxiety descend that was new for her, but already growing familiar. For days now, she'd sensed an inexplicable dread, like a shadow following her, its hand on her shoulder, breath heavy in her ear, whispering that her dreams were about to turn sour.

MATILDA MAYHEW'S CONFIDENTIAL

March 12, 1954

EXCLUSIVE * EXCLUSIVE * EXCLUSIVE
MAX WHITMAN'S NEW CO-STAR REVEALED!

You heard it here first, movie fans. Debonair heartthrob Max Whitman has told me exclusively that he has a new leading lady – and she's someone you've never heard of!

Over a cup of tea in his luxurious suite at the Sunset Tower Hotel, Whitman revealed that his new big-budget drama, *A Road to Nowhere*, will feature an actress who'll be sharing the screen with him for several projects.

Newcomer and 26-year-old blonde bombshell Diana di Lorenzo has signed up to star with Whitman for at least four films over the next two years.

'Diana has an urgent, exciting youthfulness,' said Whitman, looking at her as she sat by his side. 'I knew she'd be perfect for my movies. When I first spotted her in a chorus line, I had a gut feeling she was special. This is a project I've had in mind for months, but I needed to find the right actress. She's mesmerising.'

When asked what his wife, screen goddess Stella Hope, thought of the new arrangement, Whitman, 45, confirmed that their marriage is over. Hollywood's so-called Golden Couple haven't lived or worked together for months.

'I wish her well,' he said, ever the gentleman.

Another surprise is that the new films are a far cry from the sweeping melodramas and westerns he usually stars in. It seems Max is keen to try his hand at dramatic roles now, with serious themes. Perhaps he's been inspired by the success of young Marlon Brando, whose films are gaining record audiences.

'Times really are changing,' Whitman said, 'and now that television is in many homes, people want more from cinema, something new and exciting. *A Road to Nowhere* is a movie experience like no other. It has a powerful social message at its core and, of course, a passionate love story, too.'

Miss di Lorenzo sat close to Max Whitman throughout, beaming in adoration. When I asked her for a comment, she blushed and said, 'Well, I feel like the luckiest girl in the world, of course.'

Who knows if romance will blossom off-screen too? Either way, we're in for a treat.

Till next time, movie lovers.
Your friend,

Matilda

CHAPTER TWENTY-SIX

Furious and dishevelled, Ginny ran into the Sunset Tower Hotel, straight past reception and into the elevator.

'Penthouse Suite,' she said.

The bellboy stared, his hand still on the criss-cross gate, unsure what to do.

'Is... is he expecting you?'

She reached across and pulled the gate closed with determination.

'Just do it,' she said. 'Please.'

He didn't move, so she punched the button and the lift began its ascent.

'I'll... I'll get into trouble,' he said. His face had gone pale. 'I'm only supposed to take guests up if he says so. I don't want to lose my job, miss.'

She didn't reply as the lift chugged up and up.

'Miss?'

They jolted to a stop.

'Tell them I took the stairs,' she said. 'If they ask you, say you refused to let me in.'

She pulled the gate open, stepped out and hurried towards the black door at the end of the corridor. The clank of the metal told her the lift was returning to the lobby. Now all she could hear was her ragged breath. She made herself breathe slowly and, after a few moments, raised her hand, knocked twice and waited.

'It's open!' shouted Max. 'Leave it on the table.'

Inside, everything was as before. The sumptuous navy velvet sofa, the elegant chrome and glass coffee table resplendent in front of it. At the bar in the corner, a chrome cocktail shaker waited in readiness on a round silver tray, two martini glasses at its side. It all shone with wealth and privilege. Her eye went to the shimmering mirrored fireplace, in which she could see a fragmented version of her surroundings again and again.

'What the…?' Max stepped out of the bathroom, tussling his wet hair with a towel, barefoot, shirtless, wearing only his cream linen trousers.

A bolt of longing pierced Ginny's chest. *Still beautiful,* she thought.

'How did you get in?' he said. 'What do you want?'

'When were you going to tell me?' she asked, walking towards him. 'What happened? Why did you choose someone else?'

He didn't speak.

She had so many questions. How long had he known this woman? Why had he lied? Was it over between them? Did he love this other actress?

'Max, just a couple of weeks ago you told me you wanted to go public,' she said. 'I deserve an explanation.'

He dropped the towel to the floor.

'You don't deserve anything,' he said, sitting down on the sofa. 'And I can choose who I want as my co-star.'

His voice was as brittle as his surroundings, and she battled to take deep breaths.

'I owe you nothing,' he continued, 'it's the other way round. You owe *me*.'

He took a cigarette but didn't offer her one, then grabbed the heavy silver lighter from the table. It flared as he lit up, and he snapped it shut. Blowing smoke towards her, he stretched his arms out along the back of the sofa.

'I got you a contract,' he said. 'I looked after you, bought you things, treated you well, tried to give you advice – but you wouldn't listen, would you? You had to do things *your* way.'

She could feel the tears rising and she reached out for the club chair, leaning on the armrest. She sat heavily on the soft leather seat.

'What do you mean *my* way?' she asked, trying to control her voice despite the fact she was crying now.

'You could have had a great future with me,' he said, flicking his cigarette into the ashtray. 'I told you to wait. That I was sorting something, but you went right ahead and wrecked it all with your selfishness and ego. With your need to have everything you want right now.'

Her mouth trembled and she was shocked at the fierce surge of anger she felt, mixing now with the bitter injustice of it all. There was no coming back from this; it was clearly over between them. But she'd have her say.

'I didn't wreck anything,' she said violently, her voice breaking. 'What are you *talking* about?'

He pulled a face.

'Stop blubbing,' he said. 'You look ugly when you cry.'

She reached in her pocket and pulled out a handkerchief, then blew her nose.

'I'm talking about *Double Trouble*, with Harry Carrillo,' he said. 'I told you to run everything by me first. Why did you audition without asking me?'

'*Asking* you?' Her voice was a rasp now. 'Max, you're not in charge of me.'

There was a pause.

'Aren't I?' he replied.

A chill ran through her.

'I got you a contract,' he said, 'and that contract got you work. I can make it all go away too, you know.'

Her stomach tightened. Drying her eyes she raised her chin and looked directly at his beautiful, pampered face.

'Is that a threat?' she asked. 'What does that mean?'

He shrugged. 'Whatever you want it to,' he replied, putting out his half-smoked cigarette. 'Just remember, the only thing that matters in this town is money. And if you don't have enough, well. You know what happens to girls like you. Easy prey, shall we say?'

'*Girls like me?* Listen to yourself,' she said. 'You're just like this town, aren't you? Beautiful from a distance, but rotten up close. When did you become so cruel? Or were you always like this and everything else was just a big act? After all, you do it so well, don't you? Pretending to be other people.'

Neither of them spoke for a moment. The funny, caring, considerate Max was nowhere to be seen. She despised him right now but also knew that, when she returned to her apartment, she'd mourn the loss. She knew he could destroy everything she'd worked for, but would he really do that? What would become of her? She couldn't make an enemy of him. Her life was Hollywood: this *had* to work. And she had no money for the fare back to England, even if she wanted to go.

'Max, look,' she began, her tone conciliatory. 'It's not that I'm ungrateful, but Harry came on set, he'd watched my scene and he asked me to audition. My friend Cynthia had put him on to me. What was I supposed to say?'

'You could have said no,' he replied.

'But why would I? How would that have sounded? "No, Mr Carrillo, I can't audition for you because my secret boyfriend won't let me!"'

His face tightened and all the softness she'd known in him disappeared.

'Be reasonable,' she continued, trying to cajole. 'I have to take the jobs I can to survive. And you were full of promises, but nothing seemed certain. This film came along so of course I said yes.'

'You think you can do better than being with me?' he asked. 'Always looking for the next guy – Carrillo, Pezzi. You're just like her, you know.'

'What?'

'Stella,' he said. 'You're just like Stella. Never satisfied, impatient to go your own way, ruining everything because you want to call the shots like a man. She abandoned me and you were going to do the same thing. Every time I give my heart to someone, they break it apart.'

'Oh, please!' She laughed. 'I didn't *abandon* you. You're the one who promised me everything then found yourself a new co-star. And anyway, I mean'—she gesticulated at their surroundings—'look at all this. You're Max Whitman. You can have anything you want. They'll probably give you an Academy Award soon too, and there'll be no touching you.'

He shrugged, got up and walked to the window to peer at the lights of Hollywood from the fifteenth floor.

'All I know,' he said, 'is that I wanted it all with her. We had so much and we could've had even more. But no, I wasn't enough for her.' He turned and looked at her. 'And now, here you are, just the same. Going your own way before we've even begun. Looking at younger men like Pezzi because you think they're rising stars. Call it what you want, but you both betrayed me.'

There was a loud knock at the door.

'Leave it outside!' shouted Max.

There was a clatter of plates, then silence. He gave her a sidelong look then turned his back again, staring into the evening sky.

'You can go,' he said. 'I don't want to see you again. Stay out of my way and I'll leave you alone.'

She stood. A searing rage rushed through her, like a bolt of electricity from her head through her spine and right down to her hands and feet. Had the window been open there was no telling what she might have done.

'Go on – leave,' he said, still not looking at her. 'If you're lucky, I'll let you see out your contract.'

It was then that it became clear.

'It was you, wasn't it?' she said.

'What?'

'You got Stan to withdraw my part – in the film with Michael Pezzi. The decision hadn't come from someone higher up. It was you all along.'

He didn't deny it.

She walked to the door, opened it, and made a point of slamming it hard behind her.

On the carpet by her feet was a large tray, with plates, cutlery, napkins and a silver cloche, under which, no doubt, was his dinner. She gave the whole lot an almighty kick, then walked along the hallway. She heard him open his door and shout after her, but she carried on and didn't look back.

CHAPTER TWENTY-SEVEN

Soho, London
August 1954

It was going to be a wonderful evening because Stella Hope said so.

Maggie had spent an hour making her up and had even given in to Stella's whim to slick down her hair and create pin curls on her cheekbones, using egg white to keep them in place. It was a trick she'd learned from reading an interview with Josephine Baker.

Earlier that day, Stella had received a telegram from Stan, announcing that she'd been nominated for a Best Actress Academy Award for *Queen of Desire*, the last film she'd made in Hollywood before coming to London. And of course, they had to celebrate. But now Maggie stood in front of the mirror in Stella's Soho apartment, in a pale pink satin evening gown, and pulled a face at her own reflection.

'I look insipid,' she said, frowning.

'Nonsense,' said Stella. 'I know it's a little big on the waist,' she continued, tugging it from the back. 'But you can cinch it in.'

Maggie shook her head. All of Stella's couture outfits looked ridiculous on her.

'No, it's all wrong,' she said. 'I'll feel out of place at the Café de Paris. The colour is too pale and it's far too short.'

They both glanced down at the hem, which swung inches above her white ankles.

'Oh dear,' said Stella. 'You may be right. And you have no bosom to speak of, either, darling, so there's that issue too.'

Maggie smiled. Barely a day went by without Stella referring to what she called her 'attributes', as if she were the only woman in the world with an ample bust.

Stella sighed and said, 'You know, Carole Lombard used to shade her cleavage to make her bust appear larger – God rest her soul. Could that work?'

'Let me just try mine on,' Maggie said, grabbing her bag. 'You'll see, it's much better.'

'But you can't wear a drab dress to the Café de P,' said Stella.

Maggie ignored Stella's assumption that anything she owned would look awful, and pulled out a long, sleeveless black satin sheath dress that was a Givenchy rip-off. She'd bought it from a charity shop off Portobello Road. Quickly slipping out of Stella's dress, she wriggled into hers, getting Stella to zip her up. It fit her perfectly, snug on the top and falling gently from the waist down to the floor.

'Well, it looks like it was made for you,' admitted Stella, 'but it's so plain. And it's a special night. I so wanted to lend you some couture.'

'Perhaps I could borrow some accessories?' suggested Maggie.

Stella opened a large jewellery box and gestured for

Maggie to help herself. Gold, silver, rubies, emeralds. A handful would probably set her up for life. Maggie began picking through everything, lifting each layer to reveal another. She pulled out a simple string of plump, iridescent pearls.

'Are they real?' she asked, holding them.

Stella raised an eyebrow. 'Of course.'

'Oh, in that case...' Maggie went to put them back.

'Don't be silly, go ahead – wear them.'

They had a satisfying weight to them and were exquisite against her simple dress.

Opening a small drawer in her wardrobe, Stella then took out a pair of long black silk gloves, and Maggie pushed her hands into them.

'I might stretch these,' she said.

'I have so many pairs, you can keep them,' said Stella, waving away her worries.

Then she gave her a quick glance, head on side, thinking. Stella flung open her wardrobe doors, rifling through the sequins and velvets and furs that all jostled for space, and pulled out a shimmering white silk wrap.

Maggie put it on and stared in the mirror. *Now* she looked the part.

'You look wonderful,' said Stella, beaming. 'Shoes?'

Maggie pulled some plain black pointed evening shoes from her bag.

'Perfect!' said Stella, then peered at herself in the mirror. 'You've worked wonders on my make-up tonight, darling, thank you. You really should consider setting up that training school one day. You have so much you could teach.'

'One day,' said Maggie, knowing it was unlikely she'd ever find the money.

Half an hour later, Maggie stood next to Stella as they queued for the coat check at the Café de Paris. Stella was in a stunning red silk gypsy dress from Dior's new collection and looked every inch the star. The dark-haired woman behind the desk was dancing on the spot, rolling her shoulders to the music, as she handed tags to customers.

'Good to see someone enjoying their work,' Stella said, smiling, as she placed her fur wrap on the counter.

'Miss Hope!' The young woman flushed. 'I can't believe it's you. I love your films. I'm Cypriot, too.'

'*Yiasas*,' said Stella, greeting her in Greek.

The woman put her hand out and Stella shook it.

'I'm Eva,' she said. 'It's an honour.'

Stella dropped her a tip.

'That's nice,' said Maggie, as they walked away.

'Isn't it? The thrill never wears off.'

Maggie pulled her silk wrap around her; she hadn't wanted to hand it in at the coat check because she loved the confidence it bestowed. She'd never been to the Café de Paris before, and as they edged their way through, she was astounded by the display of wealth before her.

The women looked like leading ladies in their own films, shimmering in their sequins and silks and satins as they moved around, their diamonds and rubies and emeralds catching the light. The men, simply their supporting cast – elegant, impeccably dressed in understated dinner suits.

While Stella chatted to the maître d', who'd greeted her with kisses on both cheeks, Maggie stared all around. A four-piece jazz band was whipping up a storm on the small stage. Behind them, two identical curved staircases dramatically swept up to the balcony level, where people leaned over to survey the party below.

Everyone had the self-assurance that only wealth could bring. A certainty that they'd found their place in life. *How lovely it must be*, thought Maggie, *to be so sure of anything.*

Stella touched her arm and pointed to a small, round table to one side. They sat, and a tray of champagne with two glasses immediately appeared. The waiter popped the cork and filled them up.

'Here's to us,' Stella said, raising her glass.

'And to winning that Oscar,' said Maggie.

Stella beamed. 'It's really lifted my spirits,' she said, 'the fact the studio put me forward in the first place. I mean I know they *should*, but I was worried. What's that saying? Out of sight, out of mind.'

Maggie put her hand on Stella's.

'Don't be silly,' she said. 'How could they forget you? You're their biggest star.'

'Well, I *was*,' said Stella, sipping her champagne, 'until the divorce came through, then everyone turned against me. Such a lonely time – almost as awful as that sanatorium.'

Maggie stared at her. 'You were in a *sanatorium*?' she asked, shocked.

'For months. But that's another story for another time,' said Stella, waving her hand to dismiss it.

There was loud laughter at the next table, and Maggie turned to see someone she recognised.

'Is that…' She leaned in towards Stella. 'Is that Humphrey Bogart and Lauren Bacall?' She gasped.

Stella nodded. 'Don't stare, darling. It's a sure way to show you don't belong.'

Maggie grinned and turned to see which other famous faces she could spot. A thrill went through her as she saw a member of the Royal Family in the corner, chatting to a woman in a feathered, low-cut dress. Quite unexpectedly, a soreness blossomed in Maggie's chest. The very person she wanted to tell about all this, was no longer there. A familiar prickle of loneliness settled over her.

'Are you listening?' asked Stella.

'Sorry – what was that?'

'I said, do you think I stand a chance of winning? The Academy Award?'

Maggie looked at her and felt a sad fondness. Was there ever a moment Stella wasn't both self-obsessed and deeply insecure?

'I'm sure you stand an excellent chance,' she replied, draining her champagne. 'The studio would never have put you forward if they thought otherwise.'

'Well,' said Stella, taking a long drag of her cigarette. 'They do say success is the best revenge, and it would certainly stick one in the eye to Max, wouldn't it?'

Maggie didn't say anything.

'What is it?' asked Stella. 'You look like you were about to say something then thought better of it.'

Maggie shook her head.

'Go on,' said Stella. 'We said we'd always be honest with each other, remember? You don't think I can win, is that it?'

Maggie opened her bag and took a cigarette out. 'It's not

that at all,' she said. 'It's just… well…' She lit her cigarette. 'You do talk about Max an awful lot.'

Stella shifted in her seat. 'Well, we were married for many years. He was a big part of my life. It's hard to let go when you've been with someone for so long, however they treat you.'

Maggie nodded. 'I know.'

'You wake up, he's there. You go to bed, he's there. Then he's not. If you were married, you'd understand.'

For a moment, Maggie considered ignoring the comment, but her heart wouldn't let her deny his existence.

'I have been. Married. But I'm not anymore.'

'Really? Oh, well…' said Stella. 'I didn't know. Well, as a divorcée you must understand. It's a whole new life to get used to, isn't it?'

Applause erupted as the band finished their number, then the drummer beat out a new rhythm, the trumpet joined in and then the double bass. The fast tempo pulsed through the Café de P, and more people began to push towards the dance floor in anticipation.

'Let's dance,' said Maggie, grabbing Stella's hand.

'Oh, I don't—'

'Come on, Stella. It's a huge achievement to be nominated. This is your night. Let's celebrate properly.'

'You're right.' Stella dropped her cigarette in the ashtray and jumped up. 'Lead the way, darling!'

They started on the edges of the parquet dance floor and gradually nudged their way through, till they were at its very centre. They swayed their satin hips and raised their jewelled arms and laughed. And for a short while, Maggie felt happy. All the other dancers were in couples, but here she was with Stella Hope, just the two of them moving to the music and forgetting everything that was wrong in this world.

As the music escalated and the crowd thickened, Maggie began to wilt. She was sure her make-up had started to melt, but everything she needed for a quick fix-up was in her bag at the table. On her left, a woman was sweating profusely, her hair stuck to her face, one strap of her dress down as she threw herself around. On Maggie's right stood a jacketless man, his white shirt sticking to his back. Even Stella looked worse for wear – something Maggie rarely saw. Oh well. If ever there was a time to look dishevelled, this was it.

'What a wonderful crowd!' shouted Stella. '*This* is where I feel at home. You know, Max and I used to have the best parties in Hollywood.'

Maggie nodded. She'd heard all about Hollywood parties. They were infamous.

'Once he brought an *elephant* in,' said Stella loudly. 'Can you believe it?'

Maggie laughed. 'What a ridiculous idea,' she yelled back. 'Why would he do that?'

Stella shrugged. 'I suppose because he could.'

After half an hour of pushing and shoving to the music, Maggie motioned that she needed a drink. Stella followed her out of the crowd and back towards the table, but before sitting down again, she grabbed her bag and they fixed their faces in the ladies.

Once back at the table, Maggie drank a long, cold glass of water before pouring herself and Stella another coupe of champagne.

'Well, well, well – if it isn't my favourite leading lady!'

Fredrick Stanley pulled up a chair and joined their table.

'I don't recall inviting you to join us,' said Stella.

'This is London, sweetheart,' he said, leaning towards her. 'It's not an invitation-only affair.'

'What do you want?' asked Maggie.

'You're her keeper now, are you?' asked Frederick. 'If you must know, I came to apologise. For the other day.'

'For groping me?' asked Stella. Her jaw was fixed tight, and Maggie could see she was fuming.

'Yes, I mean,' he continued, 'I didn't think you'd take it the way you did.'

'You thought I'd enjoy it, did you?' asked Stella.

'I don't usually get many complaints,' he said with a smile. He seemed to be waiting for a response, but neither of them spoke.

'Anyway, I'd like to make it up you,' he said. 'To show there are no hard feelings, and all that. How about joining me for supper? There are some lovely little tables upstairs. Just the two of us.' He looked pointedly at Maggie.

There was a pause, then Stella said frostily, 'I can't think of anything I'd like to do less.'

'You can go now,' said Maggie.

Frederick looked between the two women. 'Oh, I see,' he said. 'Is there something else going on here? Is it a special friendship? What do the gossip rags call it? "Gal pals".'

Stella shook her head. 'You just can't believe a woman would turn you down, can you?' she asked. 'So, the only answer must be I'm not attracted to men, is that it?'

'Well, you're not, are you?' he said. 'That's why you went mad when I touched you.'

Stella bristled, and Maggie could sense something good was coming his way.

'You're right, Frederick,' said Stella. 'I'm not attracted to you. But that's not because I prefer women. It's because I don't consider you a man. You're a pathetic creep and you give decent men a bad name.'

Frederick's face crumpled with hate. He leaned towards her, his fists on the table, and Maggie thought he might thump her, but even Fredrick wouldn't do that. Not in public, anyway.

'Now, are you leaving?' asked Stella. 'Or shall I ask Maggie to send for the maître d'?'

'You're a bitch,' he said. 'No wonder Hollywood didn't want you.'

Stella didn't miss a beat. 'Have you ever used the secret staircase here, Frederick?' she asked. 'It's for the very famous, so I imagine not. But sometimes, if a customer proves a nuisance, he's ushered out. Would you like to see?'

He stood up, knocking the chair over, and stormed off.

Maggie put her hands together.

'Bravo!' she said, applauding Stella. 'You were spectacular.'

An hour later, arm in arm, Maggie and Stella wandered through the streets of Soho. Stella had agreed to walk the short distance to her flat rather than get a taxi, but first, Maggie wanted to take her somewhere.

'I can't believe you've never been to Bar Italia,' Maggie said, pushing open the door.

'Well, I've walked past,' said Stella, 'but never been inside.'

Despite the late hour, the small espresso bar was buzzing. There were two lads hanging on to their helmets – presumably the Vespas outside belonged to them – a few couples on dates and friends who'd obviously been somewhere fancy for the evening and had come straight here in all their finery. Everyone looked a little worse for wear, but in that happy, rumpled way after an excellent night out.

'Here,' said Maggie, finding two stools at the very end. They pulled themselves up onto them and ordered a couple of espressos. Stella looked around in awe.

'We're not overdressed?' she asked, clutching her fur, smoothing the skirt of her gown.

'Not at all,' said Maggie. 'Nobody here cares. That's why I love it.'

Tiny cups of lethal coffee arrived immediately, each on its own small metal tray alongside a glass of water.

Stella sipped at her espresso.

'Well, what do you think?' asked Maggie. 'You took me to your favourite Soho spot, and this is mine.'

Stella smiled, surveying the café. 'I think it's wonderful,' she said. 'Are you a regular?'

Maggie nodded. 'If I'm in town, I always pop in. I can sit by myself here without being bothered. Pubs aren't so easy.'

There was a friendly silence between them for a while. Stella offered Maggie a cigarette, took one for herself, and they both lit up.

'What happened?' asked Stella, blowing smoke out. 'Between you and your husband, if you don't mind me asking? Are you still friendly?'

Maggie froze, her hand halfway to her mouth.

'You don't have to say if you'd rather not,' said Stella, tapping her ciggie into her saucer. 'It's just, I didn't realise you were divorced too.'

Maggie inhaled and kept the smoke in.

'I was just thinking, earlier at the Café de P,' Stella continued, 'how you and me, we're similar: two ambitious single women, on our own, making our way.'

Maggie exhaled.

'I'm not divorced,' she said. 'I'm widowed.' She'd never said the words out loud before.

Stella jolted.

'Maggie, darling,' she said. 'I'm so sorry. What happened?'

Staring into the black dregs of her cup, Maggie willed herself not to cry. Not here. She didn't want to make a fool of herself. And not tonight. It had been such fun.

'Was he ill?' whispered Stella.

Maggie nodded. 'Long and drawn out. I'm sorry – I can't talk about it. I never have. I lost my mind for a while.'

'Oh, darling,' said Stella, stroking her arm. 'I didn't mean to pry.'

'That's alright,' said Maggie. 'You weren't to know.'

But sometimes, she wanted to say, I still wake immersed in the horror of it all. Those months of agony, watching the fear turn to anger in his eyes, as he knew how this would end. And now I might lose everything all over again.

CHAPTER TWENTY-EIGHT

'Did you enjoy the Flamingo Club last night?' called out Stella, from the bathroom. She popped her head into the living room, where Maggie was still half-asleep on her sofa.

'Is that where we were?' asked Maggie, as she leaned on her elbows to sit up. 'My head feels shocking. I should have gone home after Bar Italia. Then I wouldn't have missed the last bus.'

'Nonsense, we were celebrating,' said Stella, slipping on her jacket. She looked at herself in the full-length mirror and smiled at what she saw, then she checked her face in the light. Lovely.

'You know,' said Maggie, touching her forehead with the back of her hand, 'I think I'm coming down with something.'

Stella gave her a sympathetic smile.

'I think you might be hungover.' She went to the kitchen, fetched a glass of water and handed it to her.

'How come you're so perky?' asked Maggie. 'And you're all dressed and made up, too. I'm barely alive.'

Stella smiled. 'I only ever drink champagne,' she said. 'Never mix. You learn that if you attend enough Hollywood parties. Here.' She went to the bathroom and returned with a bottle of aspirin, and Maggie took two.

'I'll get out of your way soon,' Maggie said, swinging her legs off the sofa and sitting on the edge.

Stella waved her hand. 'Nonsense, you stay right there. I'll make us breakfast.'

'Really?'

She nodded. 'Yes, a Greek breakfast! Bread, grilled olives and strong coffee. That's what you need.'

'Oh, I don't think I can eat—' began Maggie.

'You'll love it,' said Stella. 'I just have to run over to my baker on Brewer Street first.'

Stella watched as Maggie tried to lie down on the sofa, using her arm as a pillow.

'But it's Sunday, isn't it?' Maggie mumbled. 'Everything's shut.'

'Not for me.' Stella winked. 'George is Cypriot, and it turns out he's a fan. Recognised me weeks ago and saves me a loaf every week.' She smiled as she remembered how lovely it was to be made a fuss over. The man had even invited her to join him and his wife for a Greek coffee. Of course she'd politely declined, but it was the thought that counted. 'I pick it up from his house and he won't even take any money, can you believe it?'

Maggie closed her eyes.

'I won't be long, maybe fifteen minutes?' said Stella. 'But he loves to chat, so who knows?'

She left the apartment and click-clacked down the stairs, out of the building and into the fresh Sunday morning.

Although she'd hated leaving Hollywood, she did have a soft spot for Soho. She'd heard so many Greek voices since she'd been here and it always made her smile. Hollywood was full of immigrants, too, but the Greek Cypriots and Italians and West Indians and Maltese here didn't all seem to want something from her. In Hollywood, everyone was constantly hustling, pitching for work, making connections, shooting for stardom.

At George's, she insisted, as usual, that she pay for the bread, and he responded, as usual, that he'd consider it an insult, and it was his pleasure to give it to her for nothing. He also added some halloumi cheese and fresh tomatoes to the bag. Along with the olives she had at home, this would be a feast.

As she walked back towards Dean Street, she thought about last night and how much she'd enjoyed drinking and dancing with Maggie. She'd been great fun, and it had been ages – years perhaps? – since Stella had had a good girlfriend to share things with. She'd always loved women's company but had found it difficult to make friends once fame had struck. You never knew what people's motives were, did you? And rather than risk being exploited or having her intimate life story sold to the papers by a so-called friend, like some stars had, it seemed simpler these days to keep oneself to oneself. She pictured the two blackmail letters that were locked in her desk. Someone in Hollywood *was* trying to exploit her, but she wasn't going to just roll over. They had a fight on their hands. They'd underestimated her, and as her *yiayia* used to say, you should never underestimate a small Cypriot woman.

Just before she reached her apartment block, the doorman spotted her and opened the door to the lobby.

'Thank you, Samuel,' she said, as she walked in, swinging her bag.

She stopped at the bottom step to adjust the strap on her sandal. It had been rubbing the back of her foot, threatening to cause a blister. She slipped off her shoes and held them in one hand, her bag of food in the other, as she climbed the stairs to her flat.

As she reached her floor, she stood for a moment in the hallway and picked up her foot behind her, twisting to see if her heel had blistered.

Maggie's voice floated from the apartment. Who was she talking to? Who did she have in there?

Stella took the key from her bag and was about to let herself in when something made her stop. Instead, she put her ear against the door.

'I'm working on it,' Maggie said. 'I'm trying to get as much information as possible.'

Stella's blood ran cold. Information about what?

There was a long pause. Was she on the phone?

'Yes,' said Maggie, 'that's right. I'm working for her now. Yes, Stella Hope.'

A tightness pulled at Stella's chest.

'No,' said Maggie. 'I've found out nothing yet. You can't ring me here. She doesn't know. Send me a telegram. At Ealing Village.'

Stella's neck was freezing cold now and her mouth trembled.

'Yes, I'll call you again in a few days. I'm surprised you were there. I was expecting your answering service.'

Pause.

'What is it in LA? Two in the morning?'

Pause.

'Alright. I'll do that.'

Stella heard her put the phone down.

Maggie. It had been Maggie all along. She knew someone in Los Angeles who'd got hold of the photos, and the two of them were working together to blackmail her. Stella swallowed hard. *Think, think*. She could go in and confront her, tell her the game was up, that she'd lose her job, be reported to the police. But what would stop her from calling this person in LA and getting the pictures to the papers? No. She needed to be smart, needed time to think. She had to secure the photos first. And in the meantime, she needed her out of her apartment.

She opened the door and Maggie jumped.

'Stella!' Maggie quickly moved away from the phone. 'That didn't take long. Where are your shoes?'

Stella looked down and realised she'd left her sandals in the hallway.

'I didn't say you could use my phone,' said Stella, 'but I just heard you ring off.'

Maggie's face dropped.

'Now I don't know who you were calling,' Stella continued, 'and why it was so urgent that it couldn't wait, but I don't like dishonesty. I've told you that before.'

Maggie moved towards her. 'I'm so sorry,' she began. 'I—'

'Stop,' said Stella, cutting her off. She knew whatever came out of Maggie's mouth next would be a lie. 'You should go. I'm tired, you're hungover, and I'm getting a headache, after all. My appetite's completely gone.'

'Oh, of course,' said Maggie, gathering her bag and putting on her shoes. 'I'm sorry – I was just calling a friend in Clapham. We were meeting for drinks later, but I wanted to cancel.'

Stella stared at her. 'Clapham,' she said.

'Yes.'

She'd let Stan know. He could deal with it.

'Well, whatever the reason,' Stella said coldly, 'it's my phone and not for your use.'

Maggie looked sheepish. 'I... I should have asked, of course I should,' she admitted. 'Sorry.'

Stella didn't say 'that's alright' – she simply stared.

'I'll just get my bag,' said Maggie, trying to smooth out her cheap dress at the same time. She'd slept in it and it was terribly wrinkled.

'Thanks again for letting me wear your pearls,' said Maggie. She'd returned them as soon as they'd come back last night. 'And the gloves. Are you sure you don't want those back?'

'Yes, I may as well,' said Stella, reaching out her hand. Last night she'd said Maggie could keep them, but why should she?

'Oh, alright,' said Maggie, opening her bag and passing them to her. 'I'll see you on set tomorrow, I suppose. Thank you for a lovely evening last night.'

She leaned in to give Stella a kiss on the cheek, but she pulled away.

'Close the door gently, would you,' said Stella, turning her back. 'This headache's getting worse.'

I have made a friend called Nancy. She must be around fifty and has the round, angelic face of a silent-movie star. She's been here so long she doesn't remember arriving.

'But that's probably the ECT,' she says casually, as she shuffles a deck of cards. We're sitting in the day hall, playing gin rummy.

'The E... what?'

'You know – the shock treatment. Electroconvulsive therapy. I was a huge pain in the butt – or so they tell me – so Faulkner gave me ten sessions.' She shrugs. 'I can't remember much of what happened before that.'

I sit open-mouthed and she laughs at my expression. How could it be that she's had something so savage done to her and yet here she is, sitting opposite me, dealing cards? I have no idea.

'So that's another reason not to be a pain in the butt,' she says.

'But will you get your memory back?' I ask.

'Maybe, maybe not. Everyone's different. I've lost years

of my life, then I'll remember a fragment, but it just doesn't fit.'

Nancy is the only person I can have a conversation with here. She doesn't scream and cry out like the others, but she does see things that are not there.

I look over my shoulder. 'Have you ever thought of getting out?' I ask.

She frowns and stares at me over her cards.

'You've never thought about it?' I whisper, incredulous. 'You don't want to be free? Get your life back?'

She shakes her head. 'I'm broken,' she says. 'I'm safer here.'

She asks me my story and I tell her what I know. The studio, the blood, the man crying over me as he injects me.

'The rest will come,' she says. 'It might all rush back at you when you're least expecting.' Then she pauses. 'You might not like it.'

'No, I want to know,' I say. 'To understand why I'm here.'

'Understanding won't get you out,' she says. 'Only Faulkner can do that.' Then she looks at the empty chair next to her. 'You're right, sweetheart,' she says to nobody.

They took Nancy's baby from her years ago, and since then, she sees the same little girl everywhere: at the foot of her bed each night, next to her at lunchtime. And if she's having a bad day, the girl comes to stroke her arm.

'I know it's not really her,' she admits, 'but, you know, it could be. If I left this place, I might not see her again.'

We play cards for a while, then two nurses arrive with our medication and watch as we knock back the pills, swigging them down with the stale orange juice that's handed out in tiny paper cups.

Once they've left, I tell Nancy how much I hate taking the tablets. They numb my brain and let the shadows in. I've tried not swallowing, and it's easy enough to tuck them up next to my gums, but where can I put them when I take them out of my mouth? These tunics have no pockets, and they watch us like hawks.

'Cissy likes extra,' Nancy says quietly, as she shuffles the cards again. 'She wants to forget everything. She'll take yours if you like?'

Cissy is the elderly lady who screams awake most mornings. When we finish our game, Nancy introduces me, and Cissy nods and holds out her hand.

'Not yet,' admonishes Nancy, turning to make sure a nurse hasn't seen.

This is good. This is very good. If Cissy takes my tablets, I'll be able to think straight.

I'll be able to plan my escape. It's just a matter of time.

CHAPTER TWENTY-NINE

Hollywood, Los Angeles
March 23, 1954 (two days before the Oscars)

It had been over a week since Ginny's love affair with Max had shattered so spectacularly. Today was the last day of shooting on *Double Trouble* and, along with Cynthia, she was waiting to see if Carrillo was happy with the final scene before they got changed. He was watching the dailies in the viewing room with Gary Stanning and one of the producers.

'I've loved this job,' said Ginny to Cynthia, as she kicked off her pointed shoes and slumped into a chair.

In fact, it had been a lifesaver. The gruelling schedule had taken her mind off her misery – until she got home of course, when she'd cry into the early hours. But because work had been so demanding, her tears had eventually stopped. She was determined not to throw away this chance. She had to get noticed in this film, and nobody was going to get in her way, especially not Max Whitman.

'I've had the best time, too,' replied Cynthia, standing over her. 'I just know it's going to be great for both of us. Think of it, Ginny – nothing will be the same again. Us and Gary Stanning! There's already a buzz. Even people on other sets are talking about it, and someone said they saw Max Whitman watching today.'

Ginny's heart jumped but she said nothing.

'And,' Cynthia continued, 'it's got box office hit written all over it. Nathaniel told me—'

'Who's Nathaniel?'

'One of the scriptwriters – straggly hair, looks like he hasn't seen daylight in a year?'

Ginny nodded.

Cynthia leaned down to half-whisper, 'Well, Nathaniel told me – in confidence – that he's been asked to work up an idea for the next one. Same characters and actors, different crime.'

'Really?' asked Ginny. 'Oh, that would be perfect!'

'It's a rumour, mind, but you never know,' said Cynthia. She stood up straight again and stretched, arms over her head. 'What have you got coming up tomorrow? I'm having a fitting for some comedy over on 2A.'

'Nothing yet,' said Ginny.

Anyone on a contract always knew what their next job was, as soon as the previous one ended, often before. There was rarely a break, as the studio liked to get their money's worth.

'Do you think that means they don't need me?' she asked.

'What do you mean not need you?' asked Cynthia.

'I mean,' said Ginny, 'perhaps they have nothing for me. I always know what I have coming up.'

'No,' said Cynthia. 'That would mean you're suspended. I'm sure they need you somewhere, especially after this film. I mean, you've done a great job, everyone's loved working with you, you've been prepared and never been late.'

Ginny leaned down and massaged her feet.

'I can't afford to live here without a job,' said Ginny. 'And I can't afford to go home, either.'

If she was out of work, she'd be out of pay, too. Waiting in limbo in Schwab's, hoping to be offered something at any minute but unable to work anywhere else, because of her contract. An unease filled her chest and her mind spiralled. How would she pay her rent? Would she have to rely on a new boyfriend to foot the bills? Everything came at such a price.

'Hey,' said Cynthia, grabbing her arm to make her look at her. 'Don't worry. If nothing comes up, I can help you.'

'You haven't got enough money yourself,' said Ginny. 'How will you do that?'

Cynthia shrugged. 'What's the worst that could happen?' she said. 'You lose your apartment. My couch is reasonably comfortable. And you hardly eat anything so there'd be no food bills.'

Ginny smiled. 'Can I make a confession?' she asked.

'Ooh, sounds serious.'

'I didn't like you when I first met you,' she said. 'I found you annoying.'

Cynthia burst out laughing. 'Charming!'

Ginny laughed too. 'But, well, now I want to thank you for being such a good friend.' She got up and hugged her. 'I was wrong about you. I have a habit of being wrong about people.'

'What's brought on all this soppiness?' Cynthia asked, frowning. 'I thought you Brits were all cold and emotionless. Look, I'm sure you'll get something – you wait. When we get back, there'll be a note in your pigeonhole and you'll be up at the crack of dawn again.'

Just then, Gary Stanning walked towards them. He'd kept his distance during filming, spending any downtime with his head in books, or doing complicated stretching exercises in the corner with his movement teacher. But now he was beaming.

'We did it!' he shouted, giving a little skip as he loosened his tie and whipped off his costume trench coat. 'You girls were great, really great. It looks fantastic.'

'You really think so, Mr Stanning?' asked Ginny.

'I really do,' he replied. 'That final scene was perfection. The way you play off each other, you've done yourselves proud.'

'You were pretty good too,' said Cynthia. 'But you knew that, right, Gary?' She winked at him.

There was a moment's pause, during which Ginny thought he would reprimand Cynthia for her familiarity. But then he roared laughing.

'Champagne at Chasen's on Beverly Boulevard,' he announced. 'Everyone's invited. I've presumptuously reserved all the booths.'

A few hours later, a little light-headed, Ginny walked back to her apartment. Cynthia had left Chasen's long ago with one of the prop boys. As she entered the lobby, Ginny checked her pigeonhole, and there it was, an envelope with the Star Studios logo in the top left-hand corner. The relief engulfed her and she let out a happy sigh.

Wandering upstairs, she heard giggling and music coming from Cynthia's room. Smiling to herself, she wondered how long it would be before she felt carefree enough to invite someone home. Spontaneous enough to turn the radio on and dance with a man's arms around her. At ease enough to let him repeatedly kiss her, as they leaned against each other till the early hours.

She opened the door to her apartment, kicked off her shoes and dropped her bag on the table. Oh well, at least she had work. She just hoped whatever was in this envelope was better than the films she'd been given before *Double Trouble*. She ripped it open and pulled out a single sheet of paper. On it was typed:

```
Attn of: Virginia Rose (Ginny Watkins)
From: Stan Fisher on behalf of Star
Studios

Date: March 23, 1954


This is to notify you that as of close of
business today, your contract with Star
Studios is terminated. Your services are
no longer required.
```

CHAPTER THIRTY

The night of the Oscars
Thursday, March 25, 1954

Ginny leaned on the sticky counter at the All-Nite Bar, sipping her gin and tonic, and stared up at the television screen in the corner. A crowd stood behind her, watching the Academy Awards. This was the second year it had been televised, and the atmosphere was one of high anticipation. Everyone gazed at the small screen, watching the stars as they stepped out of their limousines into a frenzy of flashing lightbulbs. The women had jewels caressing their necks, threaded through their hair, and furs around their shoulders. The men were resplendent in their pristine dinner suits. Ginny sat in silence as the people around her commented on everything: what they thought of the women's outfits, whether they liked an actor's last film, what they reckoned their chances were of winning tonight. It was all fair game.

Well, the night is full of stars, ladies and gentlemen, said the TV presenter, *and they've certainly all come out tonight. This is every movie fan's dream.*

Ginny watched the beautiful people parade across the screen.

I can see Elizabeth Taylor in her stunning strapless gown. And look, there's Marlon Brando, wearing that tuxedo with as much panache as he does a leather jacket. And there's Ol' Blue Eyes, Frank Sinatra, who's also nominated this evening.

Then the camera swung to a petite woman whose delighted face was framed by a dark, gamine crop, her fringe perfectly emphasising her liquid doe eyes.

And look, the adorable Miss Audrey Hepburn is here, too. Just twenty-four years old, ladies and gentlemen and nominated for Best Actress in Roman Holiday.

Swirling the ice in her glass, Ginny took a swig. She looked down at the bar. Audrey Hepburn brought back that magical night, watching *Roman Holiday* with Max. She pictured climbing that spiral metal staircase and reaching those two cinema seats in the heavens, next to the projector room. She saw it all. There he was now, lifting the armrest between them. She felt the thrill again as he pulled her close. The two of them tucked away from everyone's view, in a secret velvet-dark corner as the impossible romance flickered on screen and off. She'd never been happier. Eating fries in the back of his car, licking salt off her fingers, kissing him afterwards for hours, so much so that her lips felt bruised the next day. And the promises, of course, as they lay twisted in bed. A different Max. A different Ginny, too.

The presenter continued. *And here's the ladies' favourite, the ever-elegant Max Whitman.* Her head shot up and she was dazzled by his brilliance. He radiated pure joy.

And on his arm – could it be? Yes, it's his lovely new co-star, the delectable Diana di Lorenzo. We haven't seen Stella Hope here yet, but the night is young.

As the ceremony progressed, people came in off the street and the bar got even busier. Ginny stayed at her stool, spellbound like everyone else. She wanted to look away, to get up and leave, but felt compelled to drink it all in. With each award, the chatter got louder and so did the cheers and protests.

Finally, it was the Best Actor category and Ginny stared as each nominee's face froze in anticipation. Max was the only one who appeared nonchalant, whispering something in Diana di Lorenzo's ear. But he didn't fool Ginny – he wanted this more than anything.

There was a pause as the names were read out. *Not him, please*, she thought. *Anyone but him.*

'And the winner is Max Whitman!'

The bar erupted in cheers while Ginny seethed. Why did those who had the most in this world always receive more? Max beamed with elation, then kissed his co-star on the cheek before walking to the stage. He jogged up the stairs with the energy of a man half his age and accepted the gold statue graciously.

'Well,' he began, then shook his head as if this had been a huge surprise. The auditorium roared its approval. He put out his hands to quieten the crowd. After thanking a list of people, he placed his hand over his heart.

'I'm so overwhelmed,' he said. 'I doubt I deserve it, but I'll be forever grateful. What an honour to be part of this wonderful town. And to be recognised like this – it's truly a dream come true.'

The audience rushed to its feet for a standing ovation.

So, he finally had the status he'd craved for years. He had

an Oscar. What could possibly top this, wondered Ginny? She was sure he'd soon be hankering after a second.

And yet, he'd still felt the need to make sure her future was hopeless. He'd had her contract cancelled – she was sure he was behind it – but why? Out of spite? Or jealousy, because her new film looked set to be a big success? And perhaps he was incensed that she'd had the audacity to do it without his explicit 'approval'? She knew that now her contract was terminated it would be practically impossible to find work elsewhere. If a big star like Max fell out with a studio, others would still want him and he could go elsewhere. But someone of Ginny's status? Not a chance.

She took a long slug of her drink. Well, she wouldn't stand for it. She had to do something to fix it. She was no longer allowed on the Star Studios lot, and he wasn't taking her calls at the Sunset (she couldn't even get past reception, having tried twice). She'd even called Ida, in the hope of reasoning with Stan, but the messages she left were never returned.

She drained her glass. The gin gave her a reckless confidence, a notion that she could perhaps change all this; her anger gave her the determination to try.

'Want another?' asked the barman.

'Better not,' she said, and threw some dollars on the bar and pushed her way out. There was only one thing for it. There was a post-Oscars party tonight at Gerry Sherman's, with all the nominees and winners invited. Max would be there, and she had to get in.

Of course she wasn't invited, but she *had* to speak to him and make him – beg him to, if that's what it took – restore her contract. It was the least he could do after dropping her the way he had. If he had the power to rip apart her future so easily, he could also put it back together again. She just had to make him see sense, make him understand. Perhaps his win tonight would put him in a generous mood?

All she knew was that she couldn't return to England, and now she couldn't work in Hollywood, either. How would she live? What would she have to do to survive? Max *had* to listen to her. She'd make sure of it.

CHAPTER THIRTY-ONE

Back at her apartment, Ginny started getting ready for the party. She took off her T-shirt and pedal pushers and pulled on her black satin cocktail dress – the one Max loved – and silver heels. She brushed out and restyled her hair, then carefully reapplied her make-up; she had to look like any other partygoer.

At around midnight, when she knew the celebration would be in full swing, she called for a taxi. She'd originally asked the driver to drop her at the bottom of the hill to the Sherman Mansion – her plan was to sneak up on foot. But then, at the last minute, she changed her mind. It was such a long path to walk up. Might she lose her nerve and turn back? So she asked him to take her as close to the gates as he could, without driving in. Taxis often dropped people outside. If she behaved like every other guest, nobody would challenge her. After the first hour or so, invitations were never checked, and the only people turned away were those causing trouble. She'd brazen it out. Hollywood was full of fakes – another one would make no difference.

As the taxi approached the monstrous gates, she heard laughter and shouts, then in the half-light, she saw the blurry shapes of guests who had spilled onto the lawn.

'Okay, this'll do,' she said to the cab driver, and handed him some notes.

Getting out, she took a deep breath and walked through. The spotlights lit up a number of scenes before her, as partygoers dashed in and out of their beams like actors crossing a flickering screen. There were two overturned chairs near the gravel pathway, and an ice bucket had disgorged its contents across the lawn, the cubes glistening as they melted in the heat of the night. A man with his jacket off and shirt undone walked in front of her, forcing her to stop abruptly. A barefoot woman followed him, trailing a gold satin wrap and holding her slingbacks over one shoulder.

One of the Greek statues on the lawn had a fur stole draped over its outstretched arm. In the shadows she could make out a half-naked couple pressed up against the marble Athena, grinding into each other with a ferocity that made her look away.

The blazing torches that surrounded the mansion, which had seemed so elegant last time she was here, tonight crackled with mad glee. She dashed up the stairs and stood at the entrance to the grand hallway.

What state would Max be in? Would he even be sober, let alone agree to talk to her? She felt surprisingly clear-headed. A large man, arms folded, watched as guests walked in and out. He wasn't Cynthia's cousin, Tony. He stared at her. She lifted her chin.

'Hello, darling,' she called out, in an affected drawl.

He gave her a nod and in she went.

She snatched up a glass of champagne from a passing waiter as a prop and surveyed her surroundings. Utter mayhem. The grating rasp of music spilling from the podium was feverish, with the trumpeter and drummer going their own way, regardless of what the other was doing. In the corner, behind them, a man bent over a piano, sweating and jangling the same handful of notes over and over, trancelike. Dancers cavorted on the parquet flooring, arms everywhere, necks twisting this way and that, possessed by the cacophony of sound. This wasn't just drunkenness and high spirits… it was something else. A frenzied intensity, a film running so fast it was about to burn out in front of her eyes.

A startled man lurched towards her and she scooted away just before he threw up on the floor. With her hand over her mouth, she quickly moved away in case there was an encore coming.

'Hello again.'

She turned and saw a tall blond man next to her.

'Remember me? From the nightclub? You were with your friend. You smoked my cigarette.'

'Oh,' said Ginny. 'Yes. I remember. Hello.'

'How about we have a dance?' he said, leaning in towards her.

His breath smelled of whisky and she could see from his eyes that he was gone. He'd seemed so alluring when she'd first come upon him; now he was tawdry, his glamour nothing but a cheap veneer. Heavily, he placed his hand on her shoulder as if the movement had been a huge effort for him, but she shrugged it off quickly and he lost his balance and stumbled back.

'Sorry, I'm with someone,' she said.

Turning on her heels, she hurried up the steps to the balcony so she could lose herself in the crowd. He'd never manage the stairs.

A woman in a gold lamé catsuit was leaning over the bannister like a ragdoll, possibly sleeping, her arms hanging down towards the dance floor. The place was heaving. Everywhere she turned, there were partygoers propping up the bar, at the armchairs by the tiny round tables, sprawled on the couches that were dotted at intervals. How would she ever find him? Ginny tried to look at the faces of everyone around her, then leaned over the bannister, gazing onto the scene below. He had to be somewhere, but where could she even begin to hunt him down in this madness?

Suddenly, a drumroll sounded, followed by the clash of cymbals and cheers, as a spectacle unfolded below. Ginny stared as a beautiful black horse, with a white-feathered headdress encrusted in diamonds, was pulled across the dance floor by a man in a checked shirt and fringed cowboy chaps. In his other hand, the man had a rope lasso that he was twirling in the air. Sitting high on the horse's back was a woman who looked about twenty, dressed in a tiny, checked bikini with a Stetson on her head. Her frozen smile said she would rather be anywhere else in the world.

Close behind, a dozen or so other cowgirls followed, all dressed identically, all looking nervous and out of their depth. Ginny recognised a couple of them as actresses from her block or girls who hung around Schwab's. Girls forced to make ends meet by any means. Girls like her now.

The woman on horseback dismounted, and in a moment, the group of cowgirls was swamped by men and ushered as one up the stairs and towards the corridor, where private rooms led off in all directions.

Ginny felt her stomach lurch. She'd heard stories about this. You signed up for seven dollars and a hot meal, thinking all you had to do was sing and dance for the night, but also aware there was a risk it could become something else. The girls were brought in on a bus, where they got changed and had to deposit all their belongings. Once in, it was impossible to leave. How long before it came to that for her?

She lit a cigarette and watched and waited. There was no sign of Max, but he had to be here – he'd just won an Oscar. He was the man of the moment, and it wasn't in his nature to miss an opportunity to be celebrated by his peers.

Had he arrived early and left? Unlikely. After a while, she had to accept that the only place he could be was in one of the private rooms that ran off the corridor. Just then, a door opened and Stan walked out, striding towards her.

She ducked away and he went straight past and down the stairs. She was *sure* Max was here now. If Stan saw her, he'd have her thrown out, but if she could get to Max first, she could... appeal to his better nature? If he had one.

She wandered down the corridor towards the ladies. Someone had spilt champagne over the beautiful red carpet, and it was still trickling out of the bottle. A glass ashtray was smashed in the corner and a couple of handbags had been dropped nearby, their contents everywhere. Outside the lavatory, a half-eaten plate of shrimp was discarded on the floor. The rich were savages, she thought. They just walked through life, doing as they pleased, causing chaos and never having to tidy up their mess.

In the bathroom, she fixed her face in front of the mirror and let cold water trickle over her wrists to cool her. She looked for something to wipe her hands on. Several white hand towels were strewn on the table and some had fallen to the floor, dirty footprints over them. She shook her hands dry, smoothed her hair down and walked out. She'd have a quick look in the rooms, to see if she could find him.

She'd start on one side of the corridor and work her way down. All the doors were closed, and she tried to ignore thoughts of what might lie behind them. She put her hand on the first ornate brass door handle and pulled it down. Locked. She glanced around, then quickly put her ear to the door; a woman was sobbing inside and a man was shushing her. Should she knock? Make sure she was alright? But then what?

No, she had to find him.

As she tried the next door, it unexpectedly opened. Inside, two women were passed out on a couch, a fur covering one, the other naked. At their feet on the carpeted floor, a man sat cross-legged in a bathrobe, playing solitaire. He glanced up, looked down again and carried on. Ginny closed the door and moved on.

A few more doors were locked and then she came upon one that was ajar. She pushed it a little and there was Max, shirt off, his face slicked with sweat. She gasped at the chaos inside. The room was in disarray: a jumble of bedsheets on the floor, half-eaten food strewn over them, and he was sitting on a Persian rug, legs stretched out. He squinted up, then laughed when he realised it was her.

'Ginny, Ginny! Join the party!'

He had an intense, feverish look about him. An empty

vodka bottle lay by his side, along with an ice bucket with an upturned bottle of champagne. At his feet sat one of the cowgirls, shivering. It was Sandy, the girl who lived upstairs in Ginny's apartment block.

'Are you okay?' Ginny asked her.

She shook her head.

There was an antique Japanese rosewood table in front of them both and, balanced precariously on the edge, was a silver dish. Much of the cocaine that had been on the plate was now on the floor and across the table's intricate, ancient carvings. Standing at the other end of the table was Max's Oscar.

'Max,' said Ginny, closing the door. 'Max, can Sandy leave? I want to talk to you.' She knew the chances of a coherent discussion were low, but she had to try.

He let out a maniacal laugh. 'You always want to talk, Ginny.'

She walked towards Sandy and reached down for her arm, but Max knocked her hand away.

'No!' he said, flailing around.

In his hand was a gun, and she jumped back.

'Max, what are you doing with that?'

'It's Oscars night, Ginny,' he said, laughing. Then he waved it around. 'Lots of crazy fans out there.'

'Please, please put it down,' she said. 'It's hot – aren't you hot? Let's all get out of this room, shall we?'

'No – I'm staying here with her,' he said, pointing the gun at Sandy. 'She's mine.' He grabbed Sandy's arm and pulled her close. 'We were having fun, weren't we, Sandy? We've had some joy. *Don't tell anyone.*' He giggled like a child.

The party outside had erupted into a cacophony of shouts

and music, and Ginny could hear people running up and down the corridor, calling out to friends over the relentless beat. But in that room, just for a moment, everything was still.

Sandy was crying now.

'Oh, shut up, Shandy,' Max said. 'Sandy Shandy.' Then he started laughing again.

'Please,' said Ginny. 'Let her go and give me the gun.'

He dropped Sandy's arm, and she immediately shifted away, but he held the gun in both hands now, spinning the barrel around, squinting at it with one eye. 'Why do you always spoil everything?' he said to Ginny. 'Can't you see we're playing a game?'

A cold sweat covered her entire body, and her eyes darted to the door. Could she run outside and find Stan? If she left, what would he do to Sandy? She had to get that gun off him.

The girl was hugging her knees now, rocking back and forth, pressing her lips together. Max scrambled onto the couch, but even if Ginny made a grab for the gun, she'd still have to get past him to get out of the room.

'Max,' said Ginny, crouching down near him. He looked at her with real tenderness in his eyes. 'That's not loaded, is it?' she asked.

He smiled. 'Don't be stupid,' he said.

She let out a sigh of relief.

'There's no fun in that,' he slurred.

Ginny looked at him, then at the gun. 'What do you mean?' she asked.

'It's empty,' he said, spinning the barrel again then stopping it suddenly. 'Look.' Then he started laughing again. 'Except… for this beauty.' He tipped the open barrel towards his hand and a single bullet fell into his palm.

'Max!'

He quickly inserted it back into the barrel and spun it again.

'Heard of Russian roulette? Bet you can't find it!'

He pointed the gun at Ginny's face and her stomach dropped.

'Max, don't be stupid!' She'd tried to keep it light-hearted, but it had come out like a demand. 'Max, you're drunk and… and wired and… come on, please.'

He pulled the trigger and she screamed.

Nothing came out.

'Bang,' he said, in fits of laughter. Then he pointed it at Sandy's head and fired again. Sandy wailed.

Again, nothing happened, and he fell about laughing.

Ginny reached her hand out and saw it trembling violently. The room fell silent and all that existed was her, Max and the gun.

'Max, please,' she said, trying to keep the fear out of her voice. 'Come on – give it to me.'

'You want it?' he asked. He spun the barrel, pointed it at her again and pulled the trigger.

Nothing, and she fell to the floor in relief and started crying too.

She wanted to grab Sandy and rush for the door, but he'd try again. She knew he would. This was a game to him, but she felt sure there was only one way it could end.

'Oh, I forgot myself!' he said. He put the gun to his temple. He grinned. 'Bang bang.'

'Max, no!'

He clicked it again. Nothing.

'Ooh, that was lucky.' He laughed. 'Is there anything in here?' He opened the barrel and peered inside. 'Yep, still there.' He spun it again and again, faster and faster.

For a split second, there was just silence. The crying, the party outside, the music. All of it had melted away. Peace. But she knew it was momentary.

He gave one of his crazy laughs, the ones that she used to love. But now he sounded demented, and hell was at the door.

He pointed the gun and pulled the trigger one more time.

The noise was deafening. And the world filled with blood.

Someone screamed and suddenly the door swung open and slammed shut again. Stan was there.

'Jesus Christ, Max!' he gasped. He brought his hand to his mouth as he took in the scene before him: two women covered in blood, one cradling the other's head, or what was left of it. 'What have you done?'

'I think he's killed her,' she cried. Her arms red, right up to the elbow. 'He's gone m-mad and k-killed her.'

'Sssh... calm down, sweetheart,' Stan said, in a soothing voice. 'It's okay, I'm here.'

'Call an ambulance! The police!'

He leaned over, picked up the gun with a handkerchief and slipped it into his pocket.

'Max, come with me,' Stan instructed. Max stood. 'And bring that.' He pointed to the Oscar.

Stunned, Max did as he was told, clutching it to his chest.

'Listen to me, sweetheart,' said Stan, his voice gentle again as he turned away from Max. 'I'm going for help, but you need to stay with her and keep calm, alright?'

'Yes, alright.'

'I'm going to lock the door so nobody else comes in, okay?' he continued. She nodded. 'Good girl. Remember, stay calm. Help is on its way.'

He led Max by the arm, and just before he was pushed out of the room, Max turned and glanced at what he'd done, eyes wide in disbelief.

Then the door closed behind them and the key turned in the lock.

Radio KGFJ Los Angeles: special news bulletin

It's 3.30 on the morning of Friday, March 26th and we are interrupting our usual music programme to bring you this special news report, from our Hollywood correspondent, Sam Heckly. We're going live to Sam now.

Thank you, John. I'm here high up in the Hollywood Hills with some truly shocking news. There has been a catastrophic automobile accident involving Academy Award-winner Max Whitman and his beautiful soon-to-be ex-wife, screen legend Stella Hope. Yes, they were in the same car, despite being mid-divorce. We do know they are both alive – I repeat they are alive – but looking at the scene, I can only imagine that their injuries are serious.

A witness, who didn't want to give his name, says he heard the crash, then by the time he got to the scene, he saw Mr Whitman running back to the car to rescue his wife, not realising she'd already managed to clamber out. And, according to our witness, this is all despite him having sustained terrible injuries.

It seems Mr Whitman, who was at the wheel of his wife's red Chevrolet Corvette, skidded out of control and hit a tree head on. No other vehicles were involved.

Earlier last night, Max Whitman had won a Best Actor Academy Award and the couple were celebrating with several friends at a glitzy, showbiz party held at the mansion of friend and producer Gerry Sherman.

Police, who are at the scene now, are asking that fans stay home. The couple have already been rushed to hospital.

That's all we have for now, but we'll bring you updates when we get them. It's certainly a sad day for moviegoers everywhere.

This beautiful, talented husband and wife duo are in our thoughts and prayers.

Get well soon, Max and Stella, from everyone at KGFJ Radio Los Angeles.

CHAPTER THIRTY-TWO

Soho, London
August 1954

Stella lay in the bath crying. Could Maggie really have been responsible for those blackmail letters? Why else would she have been calling LA in secret from her flat? After asking her to leave, Stella had filled up the tub, let her clothes drop wherever they fell and immersed herself in the warm water. The suds from her Estée Lauder Youth-Dew bath oil spilled over the side as she sobbed. Careful not to rub at her eyes, she allowed herself the indulgence of a good ten minutes of weeping.

How could her one and only friend in London betray her? Presumably because she wasn't her friend at all. It was clear now that Maggie had got close to her to get to her money. Stella closed her eyes and took a deep breath in and out. Had there been signs she should have picked up on? Her story on the day they'd met had sounded so plausible, and even when Johnny told her it wasn't entirely true, Stella hadn't really minded. She hated lies, so why had she let it go so easily, she wondered? Maggie had been very convincing, but she knew the real reason was because Maggie had proclaimed she was such a big fan. Stella's ego had got the better of her and she'd lapped it up. Maggie was clever, she'd give her that.

She stood up, unplugged the bath and rinsed off. The water here was never hot enough. What had happened in her life where she, Stella Hope, couldn't even get a decent hot bath?

Taking a thick white towel, she wrapped herself and stepped onto the cool lino floor. She dried off as she considered whether she'd ever felt uneasy about Maggie. Missed a warning sign, perhaps? No, nothing. She'd liked her so much and had been desperate to believe her. She sighed. Maggie was also a wonderful make-up artist – one of the best Stella had ever had – and that was all gone now. And then there'd been the chats, how Maggie had listened to her worries, but that had all been part of the show.

'Christalla Petrakis,' she said out loud, 'you are far too trusting.'

She dropped the towel to the floor, smoothed on her Desert Flower body lotion and pulled on her robe. She had a choice: she could either lament all day on the sofa, drinking and smoking till she was ill, or she could get dressed and get out of the apartment. She pictured both options, as if they were roles she'd been offered, weighing up which she'd prefer. It was strange how in moments of real crisis she felt like she was watching herself on a screen. The car crash had been the same, as if it had happened to someone else, a character in a film.

Pulling out the stool, she sat at her dressing table and stared at the mirror. Her eyes were pink and puffy, but surely, today of all days, she could skip the brutal ice bath? She leaned in and examined herself again. Well, just because her friend had betrayed her, that was no reason to let standards slip. A quick five minutes of dipping her face in iced water would work wonders, then some cold cream, followed by a light make-up.

Once she was ready, she pulled on a pair of fitted black cambric trousers and a white linen shirt. Maggie had suggested she should wear more youthful clothes like this, and she had to admit they suited her.

She picked up her sandals from the hallway and swapped them for a pair of espadrilles. She'd wander through Soho and see where her mood took her. She needed air, she needed light. Because right now life seemed dark.

If you can't trust your best girlfriend – your only girlfriend – then what kind of a world was it anymore? It felt as if everything had become a little more dangerous. She didn't have the protection of the studio – or Max, come to think of it. But she did still have Hollywood. She had so much more in her, could reinvent herself, win back her fans and gain even more if given half a chance. She wouldn't stand by and watch everything fade out, like the end of a predictable movie. She stood at Cambridge Circus, waiting to cross. The road was empty but the lights told her she should wait. She dashed across regardless.

She was Stella Hope. She did what she wanted. And she was going back to Hollywood. She just had to find a way.

CHAPTER THIRTY-THREE

Ealing, London
August 1954

Maggie hurried alongside Walpole Park and headed for Ealing Studios. She'd overslept and would probably be fined. All day yesterday, she'd thought about Stella. Along with the remnants of her terrible hangover, it had been an awful Sunday.

As she darted around the back of the building, towards the staff gate, she pictured the fury in Stella's eyes when she'd caught her using her phone. She hadn't yelled or sworn – she was far too classy for that. It was worse. She'd frozen Maggie out.

Could Stella have heard what she was saying? No, if she'd heard that Maggie was on the phone to Los Angeles, she'd have asked questions. Stella was simply cross because Maggie had used her phone without permission. She'd told her before that she hated dishonesty, and this was the second time she'd caught her out.

Maggie walked in, found her card and put it under the machine for a time stamp. She'd just made it with a minute to spare.

Her stomach churned at the thought of facing Stella this morning. She was wondering how she could make it up to her, when she noticed Johnny standing in her place.

'Oh... hello,' said Maggie. 'Shall I take over?'

Stella was lying back in the chair, eyes closed, while Johnny was smoothing on cream.

'No need,' said Johnny, pulling a face towards Stella and widening his eyes. 'Stella's asked for me today, and it just so happens I'm free.'

Stella didn't move or say anything as Johnny continued rubbing cold cream into her cheeks a little too vigorously.

'For the whole day?' asked Maggie.

'That's right,' he replied and shrugged.

Maggie waited a moment, to see if Stella would comment, but nothing.

'Well, alright,' said Maggie. 'I'll see if anyone else needs me.' She walked away and looked back over her shoulder. Stella hadn't acknowledged her once.

After helping on another set for a few hours, Maggie walked over to the kitchen that was behind the canteen, as she usually did, to collect their lunches.

'Just for Miss Stella today,' said Rita, who was carrying a huge shepherd's pie from the oven to the counter.

'Sorry, what?' she asked.

'Miss Stella,' said Rita, thumping down the food, 'she said to just make a salad for her. Johnny collected it a minute ago. Said you were eating in the canteen now? I mean, I can do one for you if you want?'

Maggie felt the colour rise in her cheeks.

'No thanks, Rita. That's alright.'

She walked out, grabbed a tray from the canteen and joined the long queue. Did this mean she was no longer Stella's assistant? What about the extra money she was getting? She needed it more than ever now, as she'd be faced with a bill from Brodsky if he found something.

A couple of people spoke to her, and she responded with a smile and a few polite words, but inside she was falling apart. If her friendship with Stella was over, that would be the end of everything. She'd have nowhere to turn and she'd never get any answers.

She inched up the line and eventually took a plate of something stodgy, a cold drink and cutlery, and searched for somewhere to sit. The canteen was always crowded and lively with flirting and chatting. She used to love it here, but today it was the last place she wanted to be.

'Maggie! Over here!'

She looked behind her, and there was Tom, the cameraman, shifting up to make space. A couple of other men were at the table, but they all nudged along. She stalled, then walked towards him.

'Hello, Tom.'

She set her tray on the table and slid onto the bench opposite him.

'To what do we owe this pleasure?' he asked, doffing an imaginary cap.

She didn't respond to his joke and he hesitated.

'Well, whatever the reason,' he said, 'it's nice to see you, Maggie.' He scooped some shepherd's pie onto his fork, then said quickly, 'Do you fancy coming to the Red Lion with me one night? Just a drink.'

There's nothing she would have liked more than to shrug off her fears and spend a few hours in his sunny company. But she just didn't have the energy for conversation.

'Sorry, Tom – not really. Maybe another time?'

'Of course, no problem.' He shoved the food in his mouth, chewed and swallowed down hard. 'It's an open invitation. We'll do it one day maybe, eh? When the stars align! Anyway, how have you been?'

'Oh, I'm alright,' she said. 'Do you mind, Tom? I've got a splitting headache and not in the mood for a chat. I don't mean to be rude.'

'Of course.'

He smiled but she could see he was hurt. He stared down into his plate and continued to eat quickly. They sat in silence while he polished off his lunch and she pushed hers around the plate.

She speared a chip, ate it, then realised she wasn't hungry. Glancing to her right, she noticed a couple of the soundmen quickly look away. To her left, Jessie from wardrobe was sitting in the corner. They'd been friendly for a while, had gone to the pictures once or twice, but Maggie had dropped her when Stella had come on the scene, the way she'd dropped everything in her life.

Jessie noticed her, gave a little wave and mouthed, *You alright?* Maggie nodded and smiled.

Tom stood and picked up his tray.

'You hanging around for this afternoon?' he asked.

'Sorry?'

'The shoot with Stella Hope. They've put her on that new film, *My Forever Love*, with Frederick Stanley. Everyone says they're both furious.'

'What? No, I had no idea,' said Maggie.

'They only got the script this morning. I guess the bosses knew they'd kick up a fuss.'

'But they can't do that, can they?' asked Maggie. 'If they both object?'

'Apparently, they can,' said Tom. 'Orders from above. I'm on camera one. You're doing her make-up right?'

'No, Johnny's doing her all day. I don't have anything on this afternoon.'

'Well, you still might want to stay,' said Tom. 'I know you're friendly with her and I've got a feeling it's going to turn nasty.'

Poor Stella.

'Everyone needs a pal, now and then,' he said, as he walked away.

CHAPTER THIRTY-FOUR

'Sorry, everyone,' said Stella, 'can we go again?'

It was the third time she'd fluffed her lines and Robbie, the director, let out a huge sigh and walked away.

'There's no point getting cross, darling,' she called out to his back. 'Perhaps next time a bit more notice?'

Frederick grinned at her. 'No problem for me,' he said, loud enough for everyone to hear. 'Word-perfect every time.'

He'd been irritating her all afternoon, but she was determined not to show it. She was a consummate professional, everyone always said so, and she refused to lower herself to his level. But she was embarrassed to keep making mistakes, especially with so many people watching on set. What she needed was Maggie to run through the script with her, but she'd be damned if she was going to ask for her now.

She'd just have to get on with it.

'Action!' called the director.

Stella set her shoulders back, gathered all her determination and told herself this was it – she'd get it right this time.

Halfway through, she had the sensation of watching herself from above and thought she might stumble, but then the words came, she delivered them perfectly and finished with a flourish.

'Cut!' shouted Robbie.

Frederick gave her a round of sarcastic applause.

They had a few moments to rest, but then had to quickly move on to the next scene, to make up for lost time.

'Last looks!' called Robbie.

Johnny rushed on, fixed Stella's make-up and smoothed down her hair.

This was the scene she was dreading. The kiss. *My Forever Love* was a wartime tale, and she played Elizabeth to Frederick's Henry. They were sweethearts, and Henry was about to leave to fight the Germans.

He'd just droned on about always loving her and how he'd never forget her, then grabbed her tightly in a clinch. The camera went over his shoulder and closed in on her face. Their lips met in a passionate three-second kiss: those were the rules – no longer. As always, no 'excessive or lustful' kissing would be allowed.

One second. Two seconds. She was about to pull away when she felt his tongue push into her mouth. She bit down hard.

'Ow!' he screamed, jolting away.

The set erupted.

'Cut, cut, what the hell just happened?' shouted Robbie.

'She bit me! The bitch bit me!' cried Frederick.

He put his hand to his mouth then held it out and showed a small speck of blood.

'Look!'

Stella stormed towards Robbie, and a hush fell as everyone leaned forward to hear what she'd say.

'He put his tongue in my mouth,' she said, close to tears. 'He's disgusting. You *never* do that in a kiss scene. Everyone knows that. *Everyone.*'

A couple of onlookers nodded, and a woman repeated, 'Disgusting'.

'Stella, dear,' started Robbie, his hand on her arm. 'I think maybe you're overreacting. Perhaps Frederick here just got a bit carried away, swept away in the moment. I'm sure he'd like to apologise – wouldn't you, Freddie?'

Frederick was still nursing his tongue and said nothing. She poked Robbie's shoulder with her finger.

'Don't you *dare* tell me what just happened.' Poke. 'I *know* what happened. It was my mouth.' She glanced at Frederick with hate. 'He didn't get carried away, he did it on purpose. The way he rubbed his hands on my legs last week, the way he touches all the women around here.'

There were a few murmurs behind her, and she willed her voice not to shake.

'What kind of a director are you, letting this behaviour continue?' she asked. 'Do you think so little of the women on your set that this means nothing to you?'

Everyone stood completely still as they waited to hear Robbie's response.

'Now, listen here, Stella Hope,' said Robbie. 'You may have come from Hollywood, but in Ealing you're just like everyone else. He made a mistake, he's sorry. He'll come and apologise before the day's through, and we'll reshoot, okay? Let's not make this bigger than it is.'

'I'm not working with him,' said Stella. 'It's your choice.

Get a different male lead or I'm walking. You'll have to replace me.'

'But you're on contract,' said Robbie.

'So sue me. You decide who you want to lose.' She turned on her heels and left.

The problem with dramatic exits, is that you needed somewhere to go. You couldn't wander around indecisively if you'd just stormed out.

Stella took up a sharpish pace along St Mary's Road, still in her costume of a tight forties skirt suit, pointed shoes and full make-up. She'd thought to grab her handbag, but that was all. Of course, she should have got changed first, or at the very least asked the doorman to call a black cab to take her home. She peered down the road, but there were no cabs to be seen.

Then she saw the white façade of the Red Lion pub up ahead. She'd been there before, with Maggie. They were used to film people there – everyone at Ealing Studios called it Stage Six because they frequented it so often – and nobody would bat an eye at her get-up.

Walking in, she congratulated herself on finding the perfect spot to cool off before returning in half an hour or so to get changed and go home. It was late afternoon now, and it would be a while before the evening crowd descended. The pub was empty apart from a few stalwarts propping up the bar.

She bought herself a gin and tonic and found a quiet corner. She'd just sat down when Frederick Stanley squeezed in beside her.

'What on earth?' she gasped, trying to shift away but unable to. She was pushed right against the wall. 'Did you follow me?'

His face was sweating and the make-up he still wore had caked into the creases under his eyes.

'Listen, Stella, I'm sorry, okay? You have to come back. I'll lose my job.'

She tried to use her elbows to make space, unsuccessfully.

'I don't have to do anything of the sort,' she said. 'Now move. You're squashing me.'

'You have to,' he said.

She pushed the table a little to create distance, and her drink sloshed over the glass.

'You got away with it once,' she said, 'when you groped me under my skirt.' She could feel her leg trembling slightly but couldn't let him see. 'You're not getting away with it again.'

She glanced around for a back door but saw nothing. A wave of claustrophobia swept over her. To even get out from behind the table, would require him to move. Where was the barman? This quiet corner now felt like a trap.

'Come on, Stella,' said Frederick, smiling.

He put his hand on the back of her neck then let it slowly trace a path around the front of her body, between her breasts and into her lap. A rage rose in her, and she tried to bat his hand away, but he grasped her leg now, pressing down hard.

'Hello!' she called out. 'Hello, somebody!' There was no response.

'Look at you,' said Frederick, pressing hard now. 'You

play the big star in front of everyone, but you're just a frightened little girl, aren't you?'

'Stop it,' she said. Her legs were trembling.

'You're shaking,' he said, rubbing his hand along her thigh. 'There's nothing to be scared of. We can be friends, you know.'

'Leave me alone,' she said, her voice tight. 'Just leave me alone. What have I ever done to you?'

'You've done nothing, Stella, but if you'd like to, I've got lots of ideas. Come on now, come back to the studio, tell them it's all a big misunderstanding and we'll be friends again. Then I'll leave you alone. I promise.'

'And what will you do if she doesn't?'

Stella turned and there was Maggie, holding a pint and staring at them. She slowly walked towards their table.

'No, go on,' continued Maggie. 'Tell me, Mr Stanley. What's the plan if she doesn't do what you want? Will you keep touching her the way you are now?'

'What?' said Frederick, pulling his hand away.

'Will you follow her home?' she asked.

'Of course not!' he said, his voice louder now.

'Maybe you'll force yourself on her?' asked Maggie. 'Like you did with Sally in wardrobe? Then try and get her fired? Do you really think they'd choose you over Stella Hope?'

A smile spread on Stella's face. She couldn't believe the way Maggie was speaking to him. No fear at all.

'How dare you,' he said, standing up now. 'I'm not an animal. And anyway, Sally lied about everything. I did nothing of the sort.'

'There were witnesses,' said Maggie, 'but they were too

scared to speak up. Who knows? Maybe now they wouldn't take much convincing. You don't have many friends, you know.'

He turned to leave then looked back at Stella.

'Are you coming?' he asked. 'To tell Robbie it's all okay with us?'

Stella shook her head.

'Please, Stella. He said he'll take me off the film if you don't, and God knows what they'll give me next.'

Stella stared at him coldly while opening her handbag. She kept her eyes on his as she took out a Piccadilly and lit it. Then she blew smoke in his direction.

'No,' she said.

'Bitch,' he said, as he walked away from the table.

Maggie stepped into his path and deliberately held her beer out. He pushed past and it spilled over his trousers. Jumping back, he gave her a filthy look.

'Oops,' said Maggie.

The door slammed as he left.

CHAPTER THIRTY-FIVE

Minutes later, after washing her hands, Maggie returned to Stella's table, thinking she'd have disappeared, but she was still sitting there and had bought her a fresh pint.

'Sit,' said Stella, pushing the pint towards her. 'How did you know where to come?'

Maggie pulled up a chair.

'I saw him leave just after you,' she said. 'I was worried, so I followed him. I don't know why. I just had a bad feeling.'

'Well,' said Stella, 'that drink is my way of thanking you. Your intuition was right. My intuition about *you*, however, was completely wrong. You've lied from the start. Drink up, then go. I want nothing else to do with you.'

Maggie's mouth trembled, and she knew once she started crying she might not stop.

'Stella, let me explain,' she said. 'There's something I have to talk to you about.'

'I know what you're mixed up in,' said Stella, 'and you won't get away with it.' She took a drag of her cigarette.

'You saw a lonely, rich woman and decided to target me from the outset.'

'What do you mean?'

'Don't bother denying it. I know you're involved in this whole blackmail affair.'

'No, that's not true!'

'Yes, it is. I heard you on the phone to Los Angeles. You've never been a true friend to me,' Stella continued, in a furious hushed tone, 'because it's always been about the money. It all makes sense now: telling me not to go to the police, advising me that perhaps I should pay the ransom! So it could all go in your pocket. That's the truth, isn't it, Maggie? How could you?'

Maggie burst out crying.

'Oh please, spare me the theatrics,' said Stella.

'Can I say something?' said Maggie, trying to keep her breathing under control. 'Would you let me explain?'

She rummaged in her bag for a handkerchief but couldn't find one, so used her fingertips instead. Her breath was ragged and all the heartache she'd kept to herself for months poured out. Putting her head down on the table, she quietly sobbed.

'Control yourself,' said Stella coldly. 'Where did you get the pictures of me? Who were you calling in LA? Is it that photographer? How do you know him? Or has he sold them on?'

Lifting her head, Maggie tried to say something, but Stella slapped the table, making her jump.

'Are you even a fan?' she asked, in a furious whisper, as if that would be the worst lie of all. 'I can't believe anything you've told me. The sob story about being a widow, none of it. I'd report you to the police right now if I wasn't so worried about the scandal.'

She ground her cigarette in the metal ashtray with force, making it spin, and immediately lit another.

'Can I speak?' asked Maggie. 'Yes, I've lied to you and it looks bad, I understand. But it's not—'

'Ha!' laughed Stella, scornfully. 'You've lied. There! You said it and yet you still—'

Maggie grabbed her arm. 'Stella, shut up – *please*.'

Stella pulled her arm away, but it had stopped her in her tracks.

'Five minutes,' said Maggie. 'Give me five minutes without any interruptions.'

After taking a long drag, Stella nodded. She held her elbow in one hand and her cigarette up near her face, a picture of disdain.

Maggie opened her bag, took out her Woodbines and lit up. She took a deep breath and began.

'I was calling LA from your apartment,' she said, 'because my phone is in the corridor at home, and I can't afford a call to the States anyway. I'm stony broke. Got debts, too. Last time I did it from the studios at night, but it's too risky.'

Stella shifted in her seat but didn't speak.

Too many details, Maggie realised, but she had to tell it right. She had to make her believe her story, because this time it was the truth.

'But this isn't about the letters you've been getting,' continued Maggie. 'It's not about blackmail or money. I was calling a private investigator in Hollywood, Jim Brodsky. He advertises in one of your movie magazines.'

Maggie took a puff of her cigarette.

'You see,' she said, 'I'm trying to find my daughter, and I think you can help. Her name is Ginny.'

CHAPTER THIRTY-SIX

Stella frowned and shook her head.

'Why would I know your daughter?' she asked.

'You probably don't,' said Maggie, 'but Max does. She's an actress, at Star Studios, and… well, they were having an affair. A relationship. She told me, but I'd been sworn to secrecy.'

Stella's face dropped, then she quickly recovered herself and swallowed hard, knocking back her gin.

'I'm sorry,' said Maggie, 'but it had been going on for a few months.'

Stella gave a tight smile. 'It's alright,' she said. 'She wouldn't be the first. Carry on.'

Maggie had imagined this moment for months now, and here she was, telling Stella everything. Her mouth felt dry and she took a small sip of her beer. She put her hands on top of the table and twisted them as she spoke.

'I think Ginny was with Max the night she disappeared,' she said. 'She'd write me these wonderful letters full of her news, but over time they became less frequent, and then suddenly they just stopped. No explanation, nothing. She wouldn't do that unless something was wrong.'

She flicked the ash from her cigarette into the ashtray.

'I tried to get in touch with her,' she said. 'I called her apartment block several times, using the phone at home, but the bills were astronomical and now I'm in debt. I was frantic, then I heard that the great Stella Hope, Max's ex, was coming here on loan. It felt like a sign. If I could get close to you, perhaps I could find out what had happened to Ginny.'

'How do you know anything's happened to her?' asked Stella. 'I mean, she may have gone on a trip, or met a new beau or even signed with a new studio? Grown women don't tell their mothers everything, you know.'

Maggie shook her head. 'She left all her clothes, everything. Even her suitcase.'

'How do you know?'

'After a month or so, I managed to get hold of one of her friends when I called. A girl called Cynthia. She said she'd been wondering about Ginny too, and had asked the landlady to unlock her apartment. Her things were all there, but she'd just vanished. The last Cynthia had seen of her was the night of the Oscars. On her way to some wild party at a mansion up in the hills.'

'Gerry Sherman's?' asked Stella. 'The night of the crash?'

Maggie nodded. 'Yes, Sherman. That's the name. I knew you were there that night, too. The crash was all over the papers.'

'So you think she was at the Oscars party?' asked Stella.

'I'm sure of it.' Maggie paused. 'And if she was there,

Max would have seen her, don't you think? Even if they didn't go to the party together. I mean, I think they were still involved. He might know something. Someone has to know where she is.'

Her heart was thumping hard. Hearing the worry in her own voice made it all the worse.

'What's happened to her, Stella? It's... it's as if she's disappeared off the face of the earth. I've sent letters to the studio, even tried calling them once, but nothing. Nobody knows and nobody seems to care – apart from me and Cynthia. It's as if Ginny never existed.'

'How long has she been missing now?' Stella asked, as she started counting on her fingers. 'The Academies are end of March so... April, May—'

'Over four months,' said Maggie. 'And every single night I've gone to bed desperate for news, and each morning I wake, thinking that today might be the day I find her. I don't know what to do. I was hoping you might be able to help me, but now I realise that's ridiculous. I mean, did you see anything that night? I have a photo of her, here.' She took a crumpled picture from her bag. 'This is her at Regent's Park. We had a day out before she left.'

Maggie watched as Stella peered closely at the girl in the photo. Ginny had worn that red and white floral dress that day, the one she loved. Her shoulder-length dark hair was blowing slightly in the summer breeze and she was laughing.

'She looks just like you,' said Stella.

Maggie let out a sob and Stella moved next to her and put her arm around her.

'I'm so sorry about all the lying,' gasped Maggie.

'Shh… come on now. Get yourself together. But I don't know why you didn't tell me about her from the outset instead of sneaking around.'

'I just didn't know how to,' said Maggie. 'And before I knew it, I'd lied. And then it felt more and more difficult. I always meant to tell you, I did. I also wasn't sure how you'd take it, about Ginny and Max.'

'What do you mean?' asked Stella.

'Well, I don't know if you're still in love with him.'

'Trust me, darling,' said Stella, opening her handbag, 'the only person in love with Max is Max. That ship sailed long ago.'

She passed her a handkerchief and Maggie dried her eyes.

'I'm sorry about her, I truly am,' said Stella, passing the photo back. 'But I don't remember seeing her there that night. It was a while ago now – and a huge party, so many people, crazy things going on. I mean, even if I had spoken to her, I doubt I'd remember. There's a lot I don't remember about that night.'

'Of course,' said Maggie. 'The accident.'

'Some of it comes back to me,' said Stella. 'The other day I woke and remembered exactly what a friend had been wearing and a conversation we'd had. But most of it…' She shook her head. 'I think I've blocked it out.'

'Is there anyone you can ask about Ginny?' said Maggie. 'Can you call Max perhaps? Ask him what happened to her? He'd know, surely? Or perhaps anyone else who was there?'

The door banged and Stella looked around. A crowd of men she recognised from the studios had just walked in.

'Max doesn't talk to me anymore,' she said. 'I was kidding

myself that things could be amicable between us. He's never forgiven me for going ahead with the divorce. He says I'm to blame for'—she motioned to her face—'all his injuries, though I have to say the surgeons did a very good job on him.'

'But he was the one driving,' said Maggie.

'Yes, but he came back for me,' Stella pointed out. 'He thought I was in the car and ended up cutting his face even more. I'd already got out, and... well, there you have it. Max Whitman: hero. Stella Hope: villain. I doubt he'd even take my call.'

'But who else was there that night? Someone might have noticed her, might know where she is?' asked Maggie.

Stella opened her mouth to say something, but then stopped herself.

'What?' asked Maggie.

She shook her head.

'Please,' said Maggie, 'just tell me.'

'These kinds of parties,' Stella began, in a quieter voice, 'there's a lot of drink, platefuls of joy...'

'Joy?'

'Cocaine,' she said. 'And anything else you want. All kind of things go on there.'

Maggie's heart started to race. 'What kind of things?'

Stella looked down at the table, took a deep breath, then after a moment looked straight at her.

'Darling,' she said, 'they're full of people with too much money taking advantage of people who have nothing and are desperate to get ahead.'

Maggie shook her head, not understanding.

Stella finally said, 'They bring girls in. Pay them a

pittance and then pass them around. Nobody complains because, well, the police are in on it. They pay off the cops and supply girls for their annual ball, so everyone benefits. Unless you're one of the girls.'

It took a couple of seconds for Maggie to take it all in, then an image of Ginny flashed into her head. Her hand flew to her mouth and she rushed to the ladies. Kneeling in front of the toilet bowl, she retched.

Is this what had happened to Ginny? Had she been used this way? Had she been desperate enough to fall so far? Maggie retched again. Had someone promised her the world if she'd do exactly as he said?

She retched a third time, and felt her hair being held back. Stella was behind her, rubbing her back as she sobbed. What had happened to her little girl? Where was she? Had they hurt her? She'd lost her husband years ago and now she'd lost her daughter, too.

She was anchorless.

In the taxi, on the way back to her Soho apartment, Stella talked through her idea with Maggie. An hour later, after she'd made them both a quick coffee, Stella placed a few calls then began to pack. Maggie sat on the bed, legs bent, hugging her knees as she watched, stunned. She was still incredulous.

'But are you *sure*, Stella?' she asked. 'I mean *absolutely* sure?'

'Of course, I'm sure,' said Stella, folding a silk Hèrmes scarf and placing it inside her suitcase. 'How else do you expect us to find Ginny if we don't go back to Hollywood?'

'But—I mean—I have no money or anything,' said Maggie.

'You're my assistant,' said Stella, with a wave of her hand. 'Don't worry about that. I'm assuming you'll come and work for me again?'

'Well, of course,' said Maggie.

'Good, because that way we can help each other. You see,' she continued, taking some shoes from the bottom of the wardrobe, 'I have to find out who's blackmailing me, and my chances of doing that here are zero. The letters are coming from LA, Ginny was last seen in LA – it makes sense for us both to go.'

Maggie nodded, contemplating it all.

'But your contract?' she asked. 'You're just walking out? You know Ealing will call Star Studios as soon as they realise you've left?'

Stella stopped what she was doing and gave an exaggerated shrug. 'I'm taking a well-earned break,' she said, in a haughty voice. 'Let them sue me. After the way they treated me yesterday, they're lucky I don't bring charges against *them*.'

Maggie's chest tightened with gratitude. 'I don't know how to thank you,' she said, in a quiet voice.

Stella gave her a smile then glanced at her watch. 'You can thank me by packing quickly,' she said. 'We'll get a cab to yours then head off.'

Maggie watched as Stella expertly rifled through her large jewellery box, pulling out each tray in turn, and wrapping every item. First was an ink-black jet necklace, and then a stunning starburst emerald brooch. As she emptied the box, she pulled out the final tray and took out a small gun.

'Stella! What on earth—'

'Oh, it's not loaded,' said Stella, admiring the mother-of-pearl handle. 'Max gave me it years ago. He even paid for lessons.'

'And you brought it *here*?' Maggie asked. 'You can't just carry guns around in England. There are rules.'

'Oops!' laughed Stella. 'I didn't think of that.' She wrapped it in a scarf and dropped it inside her suitcase. 'Lucky for me I never get searched,' she said, with a wink. 'Movie stars never do.'

Maggie shook her head and smiled, then after a few moments asked, 'Do you really think we'll find her?'

Stella didn't reply.

Maggie wasn't sure if she'd heard and was about to ask again, when Stella looked at her and said, 'We're going to do everything we can.'

MATILDA MAYHEW'S CONFIDENTIAL

September 3, 1954

HOPE RETURNS TO HOLLYWOOD

Well, we didn't see this one coming! The diva is back!

Last night, Oscar-nominated screen goddess Stella Hope returned to Los Angeles, after walking out on her contract at Ealing Studios in London. Rumour has it, she's fallen out with several lead actors and directors at the studio.

Stella's assistant and stylist, an Englishwoman called Maggie Watkins, who has accompanied her from London, dismissed rumours of bad blood. 'Miss Hope has been working very hard,' she insists, 'and is taking a well-deserved break to visit friends in Hollywood.'

Would one of those friends be her ex, Academy Award-winner Max Whitman? Could she be seeking a reconciliation? There's nothing we'd like better than to see these two screen legends reunite.

Here's hoping!

Till next time, movie lovers.

Your friend,

Matilda

CHAPTER THIRTY-SEVEN

Private bungalow number 4,
Beverly Hills Hotel, Los Angeles
September 1954

Maggie stood in front of the mirror in Stella's suite, put a little Three Flowers Brilliantine on her fingertips and ran it through her hair to try and tame the frizz. This Californian weather was playing havoc with her waves, and it seemed, in her hurry, she'd also brought all the wrong clothes.

'You'll suffocate in that,' said Stella, emerging from her bedroom and pointing at Maggie's slacks and long-sleeved shirt.

'I thought it would be chilly,' replied Maggie, tugging at her top. 'It's September, after all.'

'It's always warm in LA,' said Stella. 'Here, hold on...' She walked to her dressing room, and Maggie followed. Spread before her was a treasure trove of wonderful clothes: rail upon rail of day dresses, evening dresses, casual wear, shoes paired up on shelves, handbags above them, and a long line of couture at the far end, all encased in protective bags.

'You kept all this here while you were in London?' asked Maggie. She couldn't believe how much there was.

'I always keep this bungalow. They give me a very good rate. This is the only place I have now, since Max and I parted ways. The ranch is up for sale, but until we get rid of it, it seems I'm homeless.'

Maggie smiled to herself. Hardly homeless: a luxurious bungalow with access straight from the street, for privacy, but with all the amenities of one of LA's most exclusive hotels. It was quite a place. The hotel itself was painted a striking peachy pink with contrasting pistachio green and set in acres of landscaped gardens.

'Of course, there's the farm in Cyprus,' said Stella, 'and it will probably come to me in the end, but that's a whole other life.'

She rifled through the rails.

'Here we are!' she said triumphantly, taking a fitted white shirt from a hanger. It had fashionable capped sleeves and a V-neck.

'It's far too small for me, what with my chest. Try it on.'

Maggie took off her own shirt and slipped it on. It fit perfectly.

'Thanks, Stella.'

'Wonderful,' said Stella. 'I'll call Saks over on Wilshire and see if they can open early for us one day. We can get you a couple of pieces to tide you over. What you're wearing is fine for seeing Mr Brodsky today.'

Maggie shook her head. 'It's okay, I can just wash this out and wear it. I don't have the money for new clothes.'

'Nonsense, darling,' said Stella. 'You're in Hollywood now. You must look the part.'

'But Stella—'

'No buts,' she said. 'You're here as my assistant, so I'll

take care of the cost. How are we going to be taken seriously if you're feeling out of sorts?'

Maggie felt her throat tighten and turned away. She walked to the mirror near the door.

'I appreciate it,' she said. 'I really do.'

She took the lipstick from her pocket, applied it and allowed herself a small smile.

They were going to find her girl.

On the cab ride to Jim Brodsky's office, Maggie stared out of the window. So this was Hollywood, the place Ginny had come to. Where she'd hoped her dreams would come true. Maggie had never seen palm trees before, and the cars here were all ridiculously long. And advertisements – so many of them wherever she looked: Pepsi-Cola, Texaco petrol, Kodak film. Relentless sunshine beating down all the time.

She couldn't quite believe she was here; it had happened so quickly. It had been a mad, spontaneous decision to leave London but of course, with the kind of wealth that Stella had, she could do whatever she liked.

This was Maggie's first time sharing a living space with a famous actress. In fact, her first time on a plane. It was sheer luck that she even had a passport. She'd been asked to go to Paris last year, as Johnny's assistant, but the film had fallen through at the last minute when wardrobe realised the lead actress was hiding a four-month pregnancy.

'What's he like, this Brodsky?' asked Stella.

Maggie shrugged. 'I've spoken to him a few times. He seems nice enough. Bit gruff, but sympathetic. He was shocked when I rang to say I was here.'

'I bet he was. You didn't say anything about the letters, did you?'

'No, of course not,' said Maggie.

'Good. I need to have a dig around for myself first, then I'll decide if I'm going to hire anyone.'

'In fact,' said Maggie, 'I didn't say you'd be coming with me today. I mean, he knows we're friends, and that you paid my fare. But I wasn't sure if you'd want to come along today, or even be publicly involved, you know, with my trying to find her.'

Stella squeezed her hand. 'Of course I do.'

Maggie nodded, then after a few moments she said, 'Ginny's a good person. I want you to know that. Max told her the two of you were through. Otherwise, she never would have—'

'Listen, darling,' Stella interrupted. 'I don't blame her. He's a beautiful man and an excellent liar. It's a dangerous combination. I imagine he got her the contract and promised her the world – he did that with a few of them.'

'You're being very understanding,' said Maggie.

Stella shrugged. 'I decided years ago I wouldn't let him hurt me anymore. You know, we'd only been married one week when he started fooling around?'

Maggie frowned. 'That's awful.'

'I had a breakdown thanks to him,' said Stella, staring out of the window. 'Ended up in some godawful place that I thought I'd never get out of.'

'The sanatorium?' asked Maggie. 'You mentioned it at the Café de Paris.'

'Well, Stan hushed it all up,' said Stella. 'Told the press I was exhausted. By the time I returned, I had to accept that

I'd married a cheater. Divorce just wasn't an option then – we were already Hollywood's Golden Couple.'

She turned back to Maggie. 'So I told myself I'd stop loving him,' she continued, 'and focus on my work instead. And creating this.' She gestured to herself.

'Well,' said Maggie. 'You did a wonderful job.'

Brodsky was tall and thin with an attractive face and impeccable taste in suits. Not at all what Maggie had expected. Maybe she'd watched too many movies, but she'd pictured a down-and-out thuggish type with body odour. He was, however, elegance personified. His steel-grey suit was tailor-made, and on his tie was an exquisite silver tie pin.

'This is my friend, Miss Stella Hope,' said Maggie.

He kept his composure, but his face flushed pink at the sight of her. Stella had obviously noticed too, because she bestowed on him one of her full-wattage movie-star smiles.

'An honour,' he said. 'Please, have a seat.' He pulled a chair out for Stella before she could get to it herself, then one for Maggie. 'May I offer you a drink?'

They both refused, so he took the worn leather chair behind the desk.

'So what have you found out, Mr Brodsky?' asked Stella, taking charge straight away. 'Any idea what might have happened to Ginny?'

'Not yet,' he replied. 'But the good news is there's no sign she was admitted to hospital that night or in the days that followed the party. And thankfully, no deaths that match.'

'Deaths?' asked Maggie.

He nodded. 'It's something we always have to check in the case of a missing person. According to the police,' he continued, flicking through his notepad, 'there were five deaths reported on the night of March twenty-fifth right through to midnight of the twenty-sixth: an elderly gentleman from natural causes; a middle-aged woman with her father, in a gas explosion over on Catalina Street; a young suicide who's been ID'd; and the fifth was a woman around Ginny's age, but who had been seriously ill for a while and died in hospital. She was buried by the county because nobody claimed her.'

'How awful,' said Stella.

'Are you...' Maggie swallowed. 'Are you sure it wasn't her? The unclaimed one?'

'I'm certain,' he said. 'I have the photo of Ginny that you posted.' He pulled it out from a folder. It was the same one that Maggie carried around.

'Perhaps she looks different now? I'm sure she said something about the studio changing her hair,' said Maggie. 'I can't believe I don't even know what my daughter looks like anymore.'

He leaned in and gave her a gentle smile. 'It wasn't her, Maggie,' he said. 'The deceased appeared to be of Hispanic or Latino heritage, with a large birthmark, here.' He pointed to his neck.

Maggie felt relieved then fleetingly wondered if this other woman's mother was looking for her, too.

'So what now?' asked Stella. 'Have you been in touch with her friend? The one Maggie spoke to in the apartment?'

'Yes, I visited Miss Cynthia Clark a couple of days ago. Didn't tell me much,' he said. 'She was quite mistrustful. Not that I blame her, as she doesn't know me. But I got the feeling there's more there.'

'In what way?' asked Maggie.

'I don't know,' he said, tapping his fingers on his notepad. 'I felt she was holding out on me. Something she wanted to say but didn't. And there's this landlady, an elderly woman who by all accounts rules the apartment block.' He flicked back through his notepad. 'Mrs Ackerman. But she wasn't answering her door. You're seeing Cynthia tomorrow, is that right?'

'Yes,' said Maggie. 'Maybe she'll tell me more. In her letters, Ginny said she was her closest friend.'

He nodded. 'Ask her about Ginny's work too, and any arguments she may have had. Any insight into the days leading up to that night could be useful. Her... her relationships too. Let me know what you find.'

Stella raised an eyebrow and there was a silence.

'It's very kind of you, Mr Brodsky,' she began, with a smile, 'but you don't need to be discreet on my account. Maggie's told me that my ex-husband was in a relationship with Ginny.'

He touched his tie pin, as if checking it was still there. 'Well, I wasn't sure how much you knew, Miss Hope. I didn't want to offend.'

'Not at all.' Stella put her hand to her hair and pushed it back slightly.

Brodsky gave a small cough. 'I'm a huge fan, by the way.'

Stella's face lit up. 'Well, thank you.'

Maggie glanced at her then at Brodsky. Were they really

flirting, here, now? If she wasn't so indebted to them both, she'd be annoyed.

'And I appreciate your discretion,' continued Stella. 'Obviously, I'd rather Max's philandering stayed private, but our priority of course is to find Ginny. And, well, if people *do* find out what a cheating bum he is in the process, then...' She gave a nonchalant shrug. 'So be it.'

Maggie had to smile, despite herself. She couldn't help but admire Stella's grit.

'Perhaps you can help, too, Miss Hope,' said Brodsky. 'With your connections, could you ask a few discreet questions among your Hollywood friends? See if anyone remembers that night, remembers seeing her at the party? Who she left with? I understand you were there too?'

'I was,' said Stella, 'though my memory of the evening is patchy.'

'Of course, the accident,' he said. 'I'm so pleased you escaped unhurt.'

Maggie gave Brodsky a sidelong glance, and he quickly looked away and started shuffling some papers.

Stella turned to Maggie. 'I've just had a marvellous idea,' she said. 'Let's drop in on a brunch party one weekend, what do you say? They're always well-attended, and we can ask a few questions. More civilised than an evening party and much more likely to get us somewhere.'

Maggie felt flustered at the thought. She didn't know how to behave at these glitzy events, let alone what to wear or say.

'Can I advise some caution as well?' said Brodsky. 'Just go gently with the questions.'

'What do you mean?' asked Maggie.

'Well, there's no sign of her – she's been missing a while. She may have gone off by herself somewhere. Sometimes people don't want to be found. But if that's not the case, someone may have gone out of their way to hide what has happened.'

Maggie felt a heavy, familiar dread in her stomach. 'You mean like Jean Spangler?' she asked.

'Jean who?' said Stella.

'An actress who disappeared,' said Brodsky, 'about five years ago now.'

'She was in a film with Kirk Douglas,' said Maggie, 'they'd just wrapped, and then she vanished. They found her handbag in Griffith Park – but no sign of her.'

'I don't remember that,' said Stella. 'Did they ever find her?'

'No,' said Brodsky. 'She had a note in her bag with the name "Kirk" on it, something about going to see a doctor and how she couldn't wait. At first, he said he didn't know who she was, then he said he remembered her but he'd been in Palm Springs at the time.'

'Do you think Ginny was pregnant?' asked Maggie. 'Has someone hidden her away till the baby is born? Or forced her to have a termination?'

Brodsky shook his head. 'I don't know, and I don't want to worry you even more,' he said, 'but the movie industry is full of corruption. I'm sure Miss Hope would agree?'

Stella nodded.

'The studios bribe the police,' he continued, 'so the police are willing to turn a blind eye if asked. Reports go missing, evidence disappears, witnesses change their minds or move house. Everyone has something on everyone else. That's Hollywood.'

Maggie closed her eyes.

'Well, that all sounds pretty hopeless,' she said, her voice breaking. 'Is there any chance she's okay, do you think?'

Stella squeezed one hand and Brodsky reached out and squeezed the other.

'We're going to assume she is, until we know she isn't,' he said. 'I just want you to know what we're up against, that's all.'

CHAPTER THIRTY-EIGHT

The following day, Maggie arrived early at Ralph's Diner. On the phone, Cynthia had asked if they could meet there rather than at the apartment. Maggie had been disappointed, as she'd wanted to see where Ginny lived, but she'd agreed, nonetheless.

She slid into a corner booth, ordered a black coffee and waited. Stella wasn't with her today, as she had a busy schedule. Maggie had heard her talking to Brodsky on the phone about the blackmail letters and making a plan to see him. And last night a call came in from Star Studios, and Stella had spent a good ten minutes arguing with the person on the other end. It sounded like she was being hauled in to be reprimanded for leaving Ealing Studios, but after hanging up, she didn't mention it. She'd tell her in due course if she wanted to.

Maggie stirred her coffee and took a sip. She could never repay Stella for bringing her here to find Ginny, but she had to admit, it was also good to get away for a while. They spent most of their time in taxis, but whenever they were on the street, Stella turned heads: fans stopped her for autographs, others asked about Max, someone had even tried to kiss her yesterday, but Maggie had elbowed them away. It was clear Stella needed a security person of sorts, someone to walk around with, but when Maggie had mentioned it, she'd waved away the thought. In the past, Stella had only frequented exclusive places, where everyone was famous to a certain degree and nobody would dream of approaching her. Now, however, she was out there with everyone else.

The bell on the door rang and Maggie looked up to see a young woman walking towards her, dark curls bouncing.

'Maggie?' she asked. 'I'm Cynthia.'

She held out her hand and Maggie stood and shook it with both of hers.

'Thank you for seeing me,' Maggie said. 'I'm worried sick. This is so unlike her.'

Cynthia nodded and slid into the booth opposite her. 'Me too.'

She ordered a coffee.

'So tell me,' began Maggie, 'was there anything about Ginny that was different in the days before she disappeared? Did she say anything or do anything unusual?'

'Not really,' said Cynthia, sipping her coffee. 'Like I said on the phone, if anything, everything had been going great for her. For both of us. We'd been in a film together with Gary Stanning, can you believe that?'

Maggie smiled, although she had no idea who that was.

'It comes out soon,' said Cynthia. 'It could have been a big break for the two of us. They were thinking of making a sequel, but now it looks like it will just be a one-off.'

'Well, I hope it's still successful,' Maggie said. 'So things were going well?'

'Yes, I mean Ginny's a talent. Everyone says so. She can do comedy, drama, and she picks up accents like that.' Cynthia clicked her fingers. 'Also, she has that look – sort of girl next door, but put her in a lovely gown with some make-up and she's a knockout. And once they did her eyebrows and fixed her teeth—'

'What?'

'Her teeth – the gap,' said Cynthia, pointing to Maggie's own tiny gap.

Maggie ran her tongue over it. 'They got rid of it?'

Cynthia nodded. 'And dyed her hair as well. Almost white – pillow-case white. Well, that's what Marilyn calls it.'

Maggie stared at her.

'Monroe?' said Cynthia. 'It's the same shade.'

'Yes, yes, I know who you mean. Ginny's a brunette – well, light brown. I can't imagine her as a blonde.'

'I know, but it looks wonderful now. It's what they always do,' said Cynthia, 'when they see something in you. My hair was down here,' she motioned to her backside, 'and now look at it.' She flicked her wavy bob.

Maggie didn't comment.

'Sorry, I'm gabbling,' said Cynthia. 'I do that when I'm nervous. I don't know what else to tell you. You know they changed her name, right?'

'Yes,' said Maggie. 'She told me in one of her letters – Virginia Rose. Do you think she *definitely* went to that party, the night of the Oscars?'

'Yes,' Cynthia replied. 'I saw her on her way out all dressed up, and I asked where she was off to. I remember being surprised she was going by herself to a party like that, at the Sherman's. I didn't know she'd been invited and normally we'd take each other, but I thought that maybe…' She hesitated and shook her head.

'Maybe what, Cynthia?'

'Well, I mean, I don't know for sure, but I thought maybe she was meeting someone. Her boyfriend. She's quite secretive.'

Maggie finished her coffee and the waitress came and instantly refilled it. Once she'd walked away, Maggie asked, 'Who was he – is he? Her boyfriend?'

She knew, of course, but wanted to see if Cynthia did.

Cynthia shrugged. 'Like I said, secretive. I asked her once if she was seeing someone and she denied it. But she definitely was, because she'd go out late sometimes and not come back till the next day.'

Maggie nodded.

'Oh,' said Cynthia. 'I'm not a snoop. It's just that it's a small building and you notice things like that. You hear people coming back. And even if I didn't hear her, Mrs Ackerman always complained the next day.'

'The landlady?'

'Yes. Her mind went years ago, but her hearing is perfect! And there were the nice clothes and flowers and things.' Then Cynthia leaned forward and said in a hushed tone, 'And they'd arrive with these cards in stiff white envelopes. I saw one once – it had a Sunset Tower crest in the corner – but then she whipped it away. I assumed it was someone who was married, maybe a studio exec or something. She didn't say anything to you?'

'No,' said Maggie. 'Could I ask you a favour? Can I

come and see her apartment? I just want to see where she lived.'

'Well,' said Cynthia, unsure, 'there's someone else living there now. Another girl. But we can see if she's in. It's not far, just the next block up.'

Minutes later, they were standing outside apartment 2c, 220 Laurel Avenue. Cynthia knocked and they waited. As she raised her hand to knock again, the door swung open and woman in a dressing gown opened up.

'Oh, pardon me,' she said, pulling her gown closed.

'Hey Hildy, this is Maggie,' said Cynthia. 'She's Ginny's mum. You know the girl who had the apartment before you?'

'Oh, hello,' said Hildy, frowning. 'I got this place fair and square. I can't leave now.'

'No, it's okay,' said Maggie. 'It's just... It's just that Ginny's gone missing. I haven't heard from her for months now. I've come all the way from London to try and find out what's happened to her.'

'Well, I'm sorry to hear that,' said Hildy. 'Cynthia did mention that she'd just upped and left, but that's all before my time. I never met her so I can't help you.'

'Hey!'

Maggie turned to see a small woman in a patterned silk robe shuffling towards her. She was dragging a broom, and with it a pile of dust and sweepings.

'What's all this commotion? Who are you?' she asked, pointing at Maggie with the broom. Lilac shadow was smeared across her eyelids, and her grey curls were clipped back with a shiny red bow that had once been a Christmas decoration.

'Mrs Ackerman,' said Cynthia. 'It's alright, she's with me. This is Maggie. Ginny's mother. You know Ginny from 2c? Who's gone missing?'

'But *she's* the girl in 2c,' said Mrs Ackerman, pointing at Hildy.

'Well *now* she is but... oh, never mind,' said Cynthia.

'All this toing and froing,' said Mrs Ackerman. 'I'm sick of it. You can't stay overnight you know. Not unless you pay rent.'

'Oh, I'm not,' said Maggie. 'I just wanted to have a quick look around Ginny's room.' Mrs Ackerman turned away, muttering as she carried on sweeping. Then Maggie said, 'If that's okay with you, Hildy. Just to see where she lived.'

'Well, I suppose you can come in,' Hildy said, 'but her stuff is gone. This is all mine.'

Maggie and Cynthia stepped into the small apartment. A tiny kitchen, a single bedroom and no bathroom. Presumably they all shared one somewhere along the corridor.

'What happened to her belongings?' Maggie asked. She turned to Cynthia. 'I thought her suitcase was still here?'

Cynthia shrugged. 'It was, when I got Mrs Ackerman to open up,' she replied, 'but everything must have been cleared out afterwards.'

'There was nothing when I came,' said Hildy. 'Well, some cosmetics I threw out, a pair of old shoes under the bed, but that's it. I didn't think any of it was important. You see, I hadn't even met Cynthia yet, so I had no idea Ginny had vanished. Most of the things that were left, I took to the thrift store. Sorry, I didn't know you'd come for them.'

'It's not your fault,' said Maggie.

'There's a drawer of stuff in the kitchen that I haven't

cleared out yet,' said Hildy. 'Nothing much, but you're welcome to look.'

Hildy beckoned her through and Maggie followed, then watched as she pointed to a drawer.

'Take a look,' said Hildy. 'It's just junk, I think.'

Maggie pulled it open. Inside was a pair of scissors, a ball of string, a pill bottle, a few pencils, a notepad, an old lipstick and some gift ribbon.

She picked up the pad and flicked through it to see if anything had been written on it. Nothing. She turned it over but there was nothing on the card backing either. Then she remembered something she'd seen in a movie once, and held it up to see if there was an impression of an address or a note. Again, nothing. Maggie pushed her hand into the drawer to check if something had got caught and peered inside.

'Do you mind if I pull it out?' she asked.

Hildy shook her head.

She grabbed both sides and tugged. There was nothing in the drawer – neither trapped behind nor shoved down the side. How could this be all that was left of Ginny? It was as if she'd never been here.

Maggie picked up a brown bottle and shook it, rattling some tablets inside.

'What's this?' she asked Cynthia. 'Was she ill?'

Cynthia peered at the bottle. 'They're pinks – to help us unwind. Sleeping tablets. We carry the blues with us – they're uppers. Lots of girls take them.'

'Whatever for?'

'It's just the way it is,' said Cynthia. 'It's hard work, especially when you're doing classes in the mornings and learning lines. They help you get through the day, but then you need something to sleep.'

Maggie stared at the name, Virginia Rose, that had been handwritten on the label, along with that of the prescribing doctor.

'Who's Dr M. Summers?' she asked.

'He works for the studio,' Cynthia said. 'Never actually met him, but he seems nice enough. He calls with some questions, about your medical history, that sort of thing, then the tablets are delivered.'

Maggie nodded. 'Hildy, do you mind if I take these?' she asked. 'I mean, you're not using them, are you?'

'That's fine,' said Hildy, patting her dressing gown pocket. 'I've got my own right here. Look, I've been meaning to throw out all that stuff from the drawer. Do you want it?'

Maggie realised that she did and nodded. After rummaging in the kitchen cupboard, Hildy returned with a large paper bag and emptied the drawer into it.

Maggie scrunched the top of the bag, said her goodbyes to Cynthia and Hildy and started down the stairs.

'She'd come in all hours, you know,' said Mrs Ackerman, who was polishing the bannister with ferocity. 'The girl in 2c. They all do.'

'Did she ever say anything to you?' Maggie asked. 'Anything at all? Where she was going, who she was meeting?'

Mrs Ackerman flinched. 'Who did you say you were again?'

'I'm her mother. Please.'

Mrs Ackerman looked her up and down then motioned with her head towards an apartment at the end of the corridor. Maggie followed her.

'This is my place,' she said. Then, in a whisper, 'Let's talk in here. I've done a top-to-toe sweep of it. There are no listening devices and we can't be seen.'

Maggie's heart sank. The old woman was obviously unwell. Could she be trusted to remember anything?

She entered the dark apartment. Shawls had been pinned to the windows and even an old air brick at the top of the wall had been taped over. Several pretty stained-glass table lamps stood at intervals on the floor and high up on shelves. They were all switched on, throwing rainbow patches on the walls and ceiling. Piles of *Photoplay* magazines teetered in the corners.

Mrs Ackerman shooed a cat off the sunken, battered couch so they could sit, then noticed Maggie staring at the opposite wall. Covering the entire space were dozens of chrome-framed black-and-white movie stills and publicity shots of a beautiful young actress.

'Recognise her?' Mrs Ackerman asked, then fluttered her eyelashes.

Maggie looked at the photos then back again at the woman before her and at the photos again. It was *her*.

'Before the talkies,' Mrs Ackerman said. 'You ever heard of Ruby Devoré?' She waited but Maggie gave a small shake of her head. 'Well before your time, but that's who I was. I'm not her anymore of course. I don't know where she went.' She laughed. 'Everyone loses themselves here. Just like your girl.'

Maggie's throat tensed; this was just too awful. Mrs Ackerman sat, so she did too.

'So,' Maggie said, 'do you remember the night of the Oscars?'

'I listened to it on the wireless,' Mrs Ackerman said, pointing to a huge contraption on the sideboard. 'I can tell you who won any category. Test me if you like.'

Maggie frowned.

'Mrs Ackerman, my daughter – the girl in 2c. She went missing on that night. She left for a party and then just disappeared. Do you remember the last time you saw her?'

Mrs Ackerman glanced at her, then said, 'She came back in the early hours. He swore at me. I asked what he meant bringing her back so drunk, and he called me a name I won't repeat and told me to mind my own business.'

'Who said this?' A wet shiver ran down Maggie's back. 'It was definitely that night? You're sure she came back?'

'I don't know his name,' said Mrs Ackerman. 'Big man, had his coat wrapped around her. She could barely stand.'

Max? But he'd had a crash that night so it couldn't be him. Unless he brought her back then returned to the party?

'Had you seen this man before?' she asked. 'Is he famous? A movie star?'

Mrs Ackerman laughed. 'He was no movie star.'

'Then what happened?' she asked.

'He took her inside. I told him he couldn't stay. It's a female-only building. But he slammed the door in my face. They left a few minutes later.'

'*They?*'

'There were two of them, I think. Or maybe one. I don't know, it was late.'

'And did you see her leave with him? Them? Did you see her again?'

Mrs Ackerman smiled sadly and shook her head.

'No. I didn't,' she said. 'That was the last time. Then I heard the girls talking in the corridor, saying she'd gone.'

She reached out and squeezed Maggie's hand.

'I'm sorry,' she said. Then – as if this had been just an everyday kind of conversation – her voice brightened, and she asked, 'Are you English?'

Maggie nodded.

'I've always loved the accent. I met Cary Grant once, you know. Lovely manners, though a bit of a ladies' man. I have some Earl Grey tea somewhere.'

She got up and Maggie could hear her rummaging in the cupboard next door.

'Don't worry,' she called from the kitchen, 'I boil the water three times. To make sure it's safe. The government puts all sorts in it, so you have to be vigilant. They sprinkle it in the air too. That's why the windows are protected.'

Maggie looked down and saw she was still clutching the paper bag with Ginny's belongings. Had Ginny come back from the party that night? Who had brought her home? Could Mrs Ackerman be trusted to remember anything straight?

She opened the bag and stared at the remnants of her daughter's life. This was it. All she had left of Ginny was here in her hands.

That, and a muddled story from a woman who thought the government was poisoning her.

CHAPTER THIRTY-NINE

Stella sat on the leather couch in the reception at Star Studios, tapping her handbag impatiently. So far, Stan Fisher had kept her waiting fifteen minutes.

'Are you sure I can't get you anything?' asked Ida, with an embarrassed smile.

Stella shook her head. 'No, thank you, Ida. I'm fine.' She had a good mind to get up and walk out.

At that moment, Ida's line buzzed and she pressed the button.

'Send her in,' said Stan's voice.

Stella rose, put her shoulders back and marched into his office. Stan rose and walked around his huge desk, bending down to give her a kiss on the cheek. She lifted her face for him but didn't return the greeting.

'You ask Ida to call me, drag me here to see you, then you keep me waiting fifteen minutes?' she asked frostily. 'What kept you? Was your bookie placing bets on whether I'd show?'

'Don't start, Stella,' he said. 'If anyone should be angry

here it's me. Now sit yourself down and tell me calmly what happened. Why did you walk out? Ida says when she spoke to you yesterday you were very upset.'

She chose the club chair, not the sofa next to him, and opened her handbag for her Piccadillys.

He lit her, lit a cigar for himself, and leaned back, arms stretched out along the back of the couch.

'I know that you didn't want to go to London,' he said, a cloud of thick smoke rising above him, 'but you can't just walk out on your contract. You know that. Not without repercussions. So explain to me, without yelling, why you're back in Hollywood.'

She puffed her cigarette and held it out in her hand.

'The movies there are small,' she said disdainfully, 'the roles are pedestrian and the actors, well – the male lead was an absolute wolf.' Another puff. 'Less experienced actresses may have to endure that kind of behaviour, but I don't.' She tapped her ash away. 'I do not turn up to work to be molested. Is that plain enough for you?'

'Oh, come on. It can't have been that bad,' he said. 'Did you speak to the director?'

She leaned forward.

'Of course I did, Stan. I'm not some young starlet that doesn't know how it works. But he didn't want to know. And it wasn't the first time it had happened.'

'Well,' he said, 'I'm sure there was a solution that didn't involve breaking contract, bringing the shoot to a halt and flying thousands of miles.'

'Perhaps,' she said, taking another puff, 'but I also want to get to the bottom of these blackmail letters, so I thought a break would be good. The idea that someone has these photos is awful. But now I'm here, together we can stop him.'

Stan got up, went to the sideboard and poured himself a whisky. He didn't bother asking if she wanted one. He kept his back to her.

'You're on a contract, Stella. That's all there is to it. Technically, we can sue you.' He turned to see her reaction.

She shrugged.

'You can try,' she said, 'but I doubt you'll want the terrible publicity.'

'Warner Brothers sued Bette Davis and won in court,' he said.

'True,' she said, 'but the public was on her side – she got much better roles afterwards and they had to increase her salary. So I'd say she won in the end. Anyway, you don't want to sue me, Stan. Can you imagine the headlines? *Studio Turns on their Biggest Star.*'

He let out a sigh and ran a hand through his thick, grey hair. He'd aged since she'd last seen him.

'Look, Stan,' she said, her voice gentler now. 'Being sent to London felt like punishment. I mean the place is fine, but nobody knows who I am over there. But here, in Los Angeles, I'm a two-time Academy Award nominee. I may even win this time. People *adore* me here. Why would you send me away when my fans are here?'

'We did what was best for the studio, Stella, and for your career.'

'What was best for Max, you mean.'

He stood over her now.

'We value you, we really do,' he began, 'but – how can I put this, Stella, without it sounding like a threat?'

She raised her eyebrows. 'Oh, go ahead, darling. I'm a big girl now. I don't scare easy.'

'Well, you have one year left with Star Studios,' he said, sipping his whisky. 'Which means you're still ours.'

She had a sudden urge to throw a chair at his head.

'And *while* you're ours,' he continued, 'we get to say where you go and what you do. It's not up for negotiation. It's the law. You know that.'

He walked back to the couch and sat, staring at her. His kindly uncle façade had well and truly slipped away.

She took a drag of her cigarette. 'I'm not anyone's, Stan. Remember that. I belong to myself.'

'You know what I mean,' he said.

'Look,' she said, doing her very best to sound reasonable, 'we're not the first movie couple to fall out. I don't see why you had to make such a drama of the whole thing.'

'It was a business decision,' he said, 'nothing more. Ealing called and asked for you. Things between you and Max were getting worse by the day, the press were turning on you after the accident, and I thought it would stretch you, be a good move. Expand your fan base.'

She hated lies, but knew she shouldn't make an enemy of him. She needed him, after all.

'We could call this a suspension,' he said, 'and I'd add the time you've taken onto the end of your contract. That's what I *should* do. But I'll tell you what – let's just call it a week's break. I won't even add it on.'

'You make it sound as if you're doing me a favour, Stan,' she said. 'But you know suspensions can't be added to the end of contracts anymore. They passed a law about ten years ago, or didn't you hear? Olivia made sure of that.'

Stella had long admired Oscar-winner Olivia de Havilland, who'd contested the practice in court and won – but some studios still bent the rules, extending contracts if they could get away with it.

'Anyway, a week might not be enough,' she continued. 'I have some business to attend to.'

He sat forward. 'Are you meeting with other studios?' he asked. 'Because you know that's not allowed.'

'No, of course not. I'm talking about the blackmail letters. We need to find out who's sending them and put a stop to the whole thing. I'm not paying him, Stan, but I can't risk the photos getting into the papers.'

'Ah, yes, the letters,' he said, rubbing his forehead.

'What?'

He held his hands out in a giant shrug.

'I've looked, Stella. That address you gave me? For the photographer? I personally went myself, but it was years ago. He's not there and nobody's heard of him.'

'But why didn't you tell me?'

'I tried calling you in London, but you'd upped and left. And that fan? The one who was harassing you and Max? Not a trace of him, either.'

'So what do we do now?' she asked.

'Well, I don't think there's much we *can* do,' he said. 'We can ignore whoever it is, of course, but if he goes to the papers…'

'Can't you pay off the gossip press? A pre-emptive strike?' she asked. 'Do it now, and tell them if they get any French photos of any of your stars they can't print them?'

He shook his head. 'Those kinds of gossip rags aren't in my pocket anymore. They just don't take bribes the way they used to – they sell too many copies.'

'What do you mean?' She felt sick. 'You can pay *anyone* off, surely? You're Stan Fisher.'

'I'm afraid not. The appetite for this kind of scandal is huge now. You know how the public loves a Hollywood star who's fallen from grace.'

'But Stan, this is all I have. I have no family here, and no husband anymore. My work is everything to me. If there's a scandal, my reputation will be ruined. I'll never get cast in another film, let alone win an Academy.'

'Or...'

'Or what?'

'Well, you said the letters were coming from LA, right?'

She nodded. 'They had a Hollywood postmark.'

'So he'll know you're in town – everyone's heard you're back. When he sends you another letter, you pay him. In exchange for all the photos, of course. We make sure we get all of them this time. Then, of course, we'll catch him too. If we can.'

'*If we can?*' she asked, her heart thumping fast. 'Listen to yourself! *Pay him?* You *might* catch him? That's no solution at all.'

She stood up, threw her cigarette onto his expensive parquet floor and killed it with her shoe.

'You've abandoned me, haven't you?' she said. 'You don't care what happens.'

He rolled his eyes.

'What did I do to you, Stan, apart from make you hundreds of thousands of dollars?' She walked to the door.

'Stella, you're hysterical,' he said. 'Calm down and come back when you're ready to talk sense. I'm offering to help you here, but you're just not listening. Of course, we'll go after him.'

She turned back, furious. Was he just placating her now, like a child? She would *not* cry in front of him.

'Look,' Stan continued, 'when he tells you where to drop off the money, you call me straight away, okay? We'll get the photos, your money *and* we'll get him.'

'You promise me?' she said. 'You swear on your life that you'll do that?'

'I promise.' He put his huge hand over his heart. 'You must know we care about you, Stella,' he said gently. 'Why would we put you forward for an Oscar if we didn't? You're Stella Hope. The studio would be nothing without you.'

She gave him a tight smile and was about to leave it at that, but just couldn't help herself.

'You've taken it down,' she said.

'Sorry?'

'My picture.' She pointed to the three posters hanging on the wall. 'I used to be there, right in the middle.'

Another actress graced her position now. A younger face, a starlet she didn't recognise but soon would, no doubt. Eyes full of sparkle and optimism. As Stella left the building, she felt a pang of guilt. She realised she hadn't asked him about Ginny.

*T*here are fleas on the ward and they need to cut our hair and wash us down. The screaming has not stopped for over an hour now as each woman is dragged to the tub room, one by one. I watch them return, scarecrows, hair hacked haphazardly short. There are a few women who have had their heads completely shaved, with nicks on their scalps bleeding. I touch my hair, which is at my shoulders now. It's brittle, and I haven't seen a mirror since being here. It'll grow back, I tell myself, pretending not to care. Even if someone here knew me, I doubt they'd recognise me now. Every woman returns with red eyes, and some have stories to tell of the medicated soap they make them use.

'They're letting the men in the room,' shouts one woman, as she runs around the day room, being chased by two nurses. 'Orderlies shouldn't be allowed in! It's disgraceful!' She's tackled to the floor and her yells are muffled.

Nancy clutches at her blanket when they come for her.

'But my daughter won't recognise me,' she shouts, as they

drag her away. Much later, she returns, her head shaved and her mouth swollen.

I run to her bedside.

'What happened?' I ask. 'Did they hurt you?' She shakes her head and won't speak.

'Hey, Hollywood!'

I turn and see an orderly leaning in the doorway. It's Karl – he's worse than the rest, and they're all bad.

'Your audience awaits,' he says, and bows, giving a sarcastic swoop of his arm.

My feet won't move, so he walks towards me as everyone watches. Another orderly joins him and they each grab an arm and pull me through.

It's just hair, it's just hair, I repeat to myself. It will grow back. They throw me into the tub room.

A nurse approaches wearing a rubber apron and gloves and the men stand and watch. She pushes me down into a chair and begins to hack at my hair with huge scissors. I close my eyes and think about the styles I've teased my hair into over the years. A French bob, a chignon, curls and fringes and plaits and ponytails. I think about the styles I'll try when I get out of here. I can hear the bite of the shears near my ear, destroying everything I am. I feel the whisper of hair as it falls onto my shoulders and into my lap. I have lovely hair. Everyone says so. I had lovely hair. I will again, won't I?

'Take everything off,' says the nurse. 'We're burning it all.'

I strip, pretending nobody is watching. Pretending the two orderlies are not nudging each other.

'Get under the shower,' she says, handing me some pink

liquid. 'Wash everything – your hair, your face. Down below, too.'

Karl sniggers.

'Especially down below,' he says. 'You Hollywood types are disgusting.'

I turn my back and lather up as instructed. A hose is sprayed at me and I don't look to see who is doing it, I just keep scrubbing and washing. The quicker this is over the better. I scrub at my hair, and the antiseptic stench hits my nostrils, stinging my face and burning my eyes. Karl says something, but I pretend I don't hear him.

'I said, do you need some help?' he shouts. The hose is turned off.

'That's enough water,' says the nurse. 'Here.' She throws me a towel. 'Your clothes are there.' She points to a corner where a new tunic is folded.

'Come on, Hollywood,' Karl says. 'Let me help you there.'

He takes a step towards me. A rage rises in me and I scream in his face like a wild woman.

He bursts out laughing. I scream again – my voice is all I have left.

'So she really is crazy,' the other one says.

'I'm not fussy,' says Karl. 'I've never had an actress before.'

'For heaven's sake, you two,' says the nurse. 'We've got a whole ward to get through.'

They both shrug.

'No problem,' Karl says. 'I'll just take a rain check.'

I'm still wet but I dress quickly. My arms are red and I hug myself, shaking. As I'm pulled and pushed back to my bed, I think of Peg – what is her surname? I can't remember.

I never met her. She died years ago, but her story is well-known among actresses, and so she is now, too. She came to Hollywood chasing fame, like all of us. But if success doesn't claim us, failure will.

Peg climbed to the top of the 'H' of the Hollywood sign and threw herself off.

I lie strapped in my bed, and I feel so close to Peg tonight.

CHAPTER FORTY

Private bungalow number 4,
Beverly Hills Hotel, Los Angeles

For two days now, Maggie had been mulling over the events at Ginny's apartment. She'd called Brodsky and filled him in on everything: Ginny's new look, the pills she'd found in her kitchen drawer and, of course, what Mrs Ackerman had said about Ginny returning drunk in the early hours. He said he was digging around, promised her he'd be in touch, and until then she was to sit tight. But she'd been sitting tight for months now.

Earlier today, Brodsky had called for Stella. He just happened to be passing and had invited her to join him for an impromptu coffee. She hadn't returned for hours and, rather than get cross, Maggie had been glad to have the bungalow to herself.

Now, lying on the sofa as Stella finished in the bathroom, Maggie checked the time. It was nine in the evening, and she lit a cigarette as she waited. She yearned for a quick bath, and to slip into her pyjamas and escape to bed. Rather than feeling closer to discovering what had happened to Ginny, she now felt more confused.

She took a long drag of her cigarette, flicked the ash into the saucer on the floor and exhaled. Perhaps they'd have a breakthrough tomorrow.

'And the worst part about it,' said Stella, exiting the bathroom in a cloud of steam, 'is they don't seem to care.'

'What? Sorry, who doesn't?'

'The *studio*,' said Stella. 'My visit the other day.' She pulled her silk kimono tight around her waist. 'The photos? Stan said he'd *try* and help me find the culprit.' She walked over to the huge mirror, put her fingertips to her cheeks and stretched the skin back. 'I swear I've aged in the past week.'

The phone rang and they looked at each other quizzically before Maggie picked it up. It was Brodsky.

'Too late?' he asked.

'Not at all – what is it? Have you found something?'

Stella mouthed, *Who is it?*

'Brodsky,' Maggie said.

'It could be something, it could be nothing,' he continued. Maggie's mouth went dry. 'I'm in the Polo Lounge.'

'Give me five minutes,' she said, replacing the receiver.

'He's here?' said Stella. '*Now?*'

Maggie nodded. 'In the lounge. He says he's got something.'

In a matter of moments, they'd both made themselves presentable, and Stella had even put on some lipstick. Maggie noticed her fluffing up her hair a little as they took the two steps down into the hotel's lush garden. Stella clasped her hand and they walked the couple of minutes on the path that led to the lobby.

'You must think I'm selfish,' she said. 'I'm sorry, darling.' She looked contrite. 'There's me complaining about the studio and you're going through all this. *And* I stupidly forgot to ask Stan about Ginny.'

Maggie gave a tight smile. 'That's okay – let's see what Brodsky has to say, shall we?'

'Just remember.'

'What?'

'You're stronger than you think,' said Stella. 'We both are. Always keep that in mind.'

Maggie nodded. Was she preparing her for bad news? Had Brodsky told her something over coffee? They pushed through the glass double doors that led to the lobby, then turned right into the Polo Lounge. It was mostly empty except for a woman with a peek-a-boo hairstyle that fell over one eye, just like the film star Veronica Lake. She looked twenty at most and was sitting next to man in a suit with his tie at half-mast. He could have been her father, but probably wasn't.

Brodsky got up and waved from a dark green corner booth. He had a club soda in front of him.

'What can I get you?' he asked.

'Nothing,' said Maggie, not waiting for Stella to answer. They both sat down. 'Please just tell me what you've found.'

'Okay.' He leaned in and they both did the same. He took a quick swig, then put a manila folder on the table between them. 'I got copies of all the newspapers from the day after the car crash. Of course everyone reported it, as you can imagine. These are the interesting ones.'

Maggie stared as he laid out the broadsheet, the *Los Angeles Examiner,* on the table in front of them, alongside the tabloid *Los Angeles Mirror*. On each front page was a photo of Stella's car, smashed around a tree, debris everywhere.

Maggie had seen the pictures before, in the papers back home, but looking at them now made her realise how close Stella had come to being killed. Both newspapers had also printed beautiful, soft-focus publicity photos of Stella and Max, cheek-to-cheek. The *Mirror* also ran a photo of Max in his pristine dinner suit hours earlier that evening, kissing his Oscar.

'Sorry if this brings it all back,' said Brodsky to Stella.

'Not at all,' she said, lighting up. 'It feels like a lifetime ago.'

'So what has this got to do with Ginny?' asked Maggie.

'Look,' he said, and turned the page of the *Mirror*. There was an in-depth article about Max and Stella's respective careers, as well as a picture of the huge wrought-iron gates outside Gerry Sherman's mansion, which stood open as partygoers walked through.

The caption read:

The scene before tragedy struck: Max Whitman and Stella Hope were attending a party at the Sherman Mansion in the Hollywood Hills.

The photo had been taken from outside the gates, but a few revellers could be seen on the lawn. A couple of trombonists were sitting on the steps, smoking during their break, and a group of women dressed as cowgirls were adjusting their Stetsons and chatting.

'There,' he said, pointing to a woman in profile, entering the gates. 'Is that Ginny? You said her hair is white-blonde now. That's what made me look twice.'

Maggie peered. The woman's hair shone bright as a star. She was the only guest by herself and was wearing a chic black cocktail dress with silver heels. It was a grainy photo, but the height and size were right. She peered at her face.

'It could be... I think it is. But I just don't know,' she said, her voice thick with distress. 'How can I not tell? Are there... are there any photos of her inside?'

'Once the party heats up,' said Stella, 'the photographers have to leave. Nobody wants to be snapped when things really get going, so they just hang around outside.'

'Maggie!'

They all turned towards the entrance to see Cynthia standing there, a small parcel in her hands.

'I was coming to give you this,' she said, walking over. Then her eyes widened as she saw who was also at the table.

'Cynthia,' said Maggie, 'this is my good friend Stella Hope. You've met Mr Brodsky, I think?'

Cynthia nodded, lost for words for a moment, then regained her composure. 'Miss Hope,' she said, holding out her hand. 'I love your work.'

Stella shook her hand and smiled. 'That's very kind.'

'Sit down,' said Brodsky. 'Maybe you can help?'

He showed her the newspapers and the photograph.

'Could that be Ginny?' he asked, pointing to the woman.

'That's her,' said Cynthia with no hesitation. 'Those are my shoes. We're always borrowing each other's clothes.'

'You're certain?' Brodsky asked.

'One hundred per cent.'

'Well, that proves she got there,' he said.

'The question is, did she get back? Mrs Ackerman says she saw her coming back drunk,' said Maggie. 'But who knows?'

'I wouldn't go by anything she says,' said Cynthia. 'She's not well. She has these episodes.'

Maggie shook her head, not understanding.

'Ranting,' said Cynthia, 'banging doors late at night, saying the government is coming to take us in our sleep, that kind of thing. I mean she's harmless but'—she pointed to her head and made a twisting motion—'she's not all there.'

'I think Cynthia's right,' said Brodsky. 'Let's just keep an open mind for now.'

Stella pulled the newspaper towards her and stared at the car-crash photo.

'This is for you,' said Cynthia, handing Maggie the parcel she'd been holding. 'It's a cashmere sweater that Ginny let me borrow. I've had it a while. I thought you might like it.'

Maggie took the parcel and opened it. Inside was a beautiful lilac short-sleeved top with a swirling heart embroidered just below the left shoulder, and the initials VR.

'Looks expensive,' said Maggie, stroking it. 'VR?'

'Her new name, Virginia Rose,' said Cynthia. 'I think it was a gift. She made me promise to look after it. We joked when I wore it that perhaps the initials stood for Very Rich.'

Stella shifted in her seat and glanced at Maggie.

'They embroider them to order,' Stella said. 'I have one with my initials, too.'

Cynthia glanced at the newspaper. 'Oh, look!' she said, pointing at the women dressed as cowgirls. 'There's poor Sandy.'

There was a moment's silence.

'Who?' asked Brodsky.

'Sandy, from our building,' said Cynthia. 'That must be the last picture of her. Can you *believe* that she shot herself?'

Maggie looked at Stella and they both looked at Brodsky.

'Hold on,' said Brodsky, 'she went to the same party as Ginny and she killed herself afterwards?'

'Yes, though I don't know when she died exactly,' said Cynthia. 'It was dreadful. You see, nobody realised what she'd done until, well...'

'What?' asked Maggie.

'Well, the studio was trying to get hold of her, then there was this smell. Coming from her apartment. Eventually the cops went in and found her, along with a suicide note. They think she'd been there a day or so.'

Maggie made a whimpering sound and Stella immediately put her arm around her.

'I'm sorry,' said Cynthia, almost in tears. 'I didn't mean to upset you, I wouldn't have said anything if I'd known. It's just seeing her in the photo was a shock.'

'What does this place do to women?' choked out Maggie.

'Let me get this straight,' said Brodsky. 'So... Ginny goes missing, and this girl Sandy takes her own life. And they were both at the same party? On the night of the Oscars at the Sherman Mansion?'

Cynthia nodded.

'Is that what you call a coincidence?' asked Stella.

'It's what I call unlikely,' said Brodsky, flicking through his notebook.

They watched him as he started looking for something.

'Ah, here we go,' he said, pointing at his own handwriting. 'On the night of the party, March twenty-fifth to midnight the following day, five people died in the LA area: an elderly man from natural causes, a father and daughter in a gas explosion, an unidentified woman of Hispanic origin, who'd been ill, and a young suicide by gunshot – a woman called Alexandra Hughes.'

'That's her,' said Cynthia. 'Alexandra Hughes. She used the name Sandy, and the studio preferred it. Said Alexandra was too high class for her image.'

'So what do we do now?' asked Stella. 'The two things must be connected?'

'Possibly,' said Brodsky. 'Did anyone see Sandy after the party?'

Cynthia shook her head. 'When the police were called, when they found her, we were all talking about it. Some of the girls in the block had been to the party – they were in a dance troupe with her – but nobody remembers seeing her later that night.'

'Was she friends with Ginny?' asked Maggie.

'They were friendly,' said Cynthia, 'but not especially close.'

'It's all connected to the party, isn't it?' said Maggie to Brodsky. 'It has to be. Something happened that night.'

'I don't know,' he said, 'but if that's the last time either of them was seen, then perhaps.'

'These parties,' said Stella, blowing smoke above their heads. 'They're notorious.'

'What do you remember of that night?' Brodsky asked her. 'I know you had concussion but is there anything unusual you recall?'

'Not really,' she replied, 'but then I barely made it through the gates. I was in two minds about going at all, and I ended up arriving very late. I was still in the car, and I'd just pulled the brakes on ready to hand the keys to the valet, when Max rushed out saying there'd been a tip-off.'

Everyone was listening intently.

'He said the police were about to raid the place for drugs,' she continued. 'You know, the way they do once a year to prove they're not really corrupt.'

'Then what happened?' asked Brodsky.

'Max was in a terrible state, obviously drunk, almost certainly high. But Stan was with him, the studio's Executive Manager. He insisted we get out of there fast. I didn't have a chance to think. Max shoved me across the seat and drove off. He wouldn't let me drive. Of course, he crashed into a tree within seconds, just where the road bends.'

Brodsky frowned, nodding. Nobody spoke, then finally after a few moments Stella said, 'Well? What is it? That's what happened.'

He rubbed his face.

'I've already checked the records for that night,' he said. 'I went through everything. There was no drugs raid planned. No tip-off reported. Whatever his reason was for leaving in a hurry, that wasn't it. Max lied.'

CHAPTER FORTY-ONE

Hollywood Hill Club,
N Sycamore Avenue, Los Angeles

When Stella had said they were attending a brunch party that weekend, Maggie had imagined some swish hotel or bar, not this. She stared up at the stunning, intricately carved Japanese castle that stood on the brow of the hill. She'd never seen anything like it. Steadily, she followed Stella up the winding stairs, holding on to the handrail.

'Isn't it magnificent?' said Stella. 'Welcome to the Hollywood Hill Club.'

'What *is* this place?' Maggie asked, as she gazed down on the stunning landscape. They were high above Hollywood Boulevard and seemed a million miles from the bustle of the city.

'It used to be called the 400 Club, and before that the Yamashiro, which means Mountain Palace. But, what with Pearl Harbour, they dropped the Japanese name. Come on, you'll love it inside. It has a fishpond, and gardens, too.'

As they walked towards the main house, Maggie could hear the distant buzz of voices and confident laughter. These weren't her people. Was anyone here really going to be able to help them? Shouldn't she be out there looking for her daughter?

She looked down at the new fitted white cocktail dress that Stella had insisted on buying for her, and even though she knew she looked the part, she felt an imposter. Stella herself was resplendent in a cherry-red dress with a sweetheart neck that showed just enough flesh.

'Look, I know it's nerve-wracking, darling,' said Stella, taking Maggie's arm, 'but the guests here will be the same crowd that were at the Oscars party. We might get lucky. Someone might remember something.'

'We *are* expected, aren't we?' Maggie asked nervously. 'I mean, we *were* invited, right?'

'Not exactly,' said Stella, as they entered the house.

Maggie grabbed her arm. 'We're gatecrashing?'

'They wouldn't dare turn us away,' said Stella. 'Come on, shoulders back, head up.'

She plucked two coupe glasses filled with champagne from a passing waiter and handed one to Maggie.

'Drink,' she said.

Maggie sipped and tried not to stare at her surroundings as they wandered through. The walls were made from gold silk panels and decorated with paintings of Japanese women in traditional costume, sitting on the ground, or bathing or talking. Above her, the ceiling was also gold, with delicate paintings of flowers strewn everywhere. The furniture, which was carved from beautiful dark wood, consisted of the occasional chair or small table dotted throughout. They appeared to be hundreds of years old and definitely not for using.

'Through here,' said Stella, and they walked into a spacious cocktail lounge, which had windows along one side. 'This is the Skyview,' she said, 'for obvious reasons.'

It was spectacular. They were looking out across the beautiful landscape, high above the Hollywood Hills that were brushed with autumnal russets and golds. But nobody was taking any notice of the view. Dozens of guests were chatting and drinking and laughing and ignoring what lay beyond their little world. There were faces Maggie recognised from magazines and the movie screen, and at any other time she'd have been excited to see them. But that all seemed irrelevant now. Did someone here really know what had happened to Ginny?

As they walked through the crowd, there were a few cries of surprise at Stella's presence. She said her hellos, kissed a couple of cheeks but carried on moving.

'We heard you were back, darling, but couldn't believe it!' called one woman in a feather boa.

'Didn't like London?' asked a sweaty man, slurring his words.

'Stella!' exclaimed an older woman, a cluster of pearls at her throat. 'You *must* come for lunch! So much to catch up on.'

Keeping her arm linked through Maggie's, Stella nodded and smiled and moved like water through the crowd, not allowing anyone to trap her in conversation.

'Ah,' she said to Maggie. 'There he is.'

Max Whitman stood in a corner, a large tumbler of whisky in his hand. He looked at Stella in shock.

'Darling,' said Stella, approaching. 'You're looking well, all things considered.'

He put his hand up to his left cheek, where his cheekbone had undergone surgery. Maggie tried not to stare. His face looked remarkable. Yes, he'd aged, but the surgeons had done an impressive job. If anything, he had a more distinguished, haunted look now than the way she remembered him from his movies.

'What the hell are you doing here?' he asked. 'Didn't they ship you off to London?'

'They did,' said Stella, 'but you know I just couldn't stay away.' She gave him a cold smile. 'Can I introduce my friend, Maggie?'

Maggie put her hand out, and after a moment's hesitation, Max took it and shook it with reluctance. He looked at her warily – did he see Ginny in her?

'What do you want, Stella?' he asked. 'Who even invited you?' He glanced behind his shoulder, as if searching for someone who could throw them out.

'Charming,' said Stella. She took a sip of her champagne, then said, 'I invited myself. I'm here because I wanted to ask you about Ginny.'

He flinched, his face reddening. 'What? Who?'

'Ginny,' repeated Stella. 'The young actress you were having an affair with just before the crash.'

'I... I don't know what you're talking about.'

Maggie opened her bag and took out the photo, showing it to him.

'She's my daughter,' she said. 'I don't know where she is. I'm going out of my mind with worry. Please Mr Whitman, if you know anything?'

He shook his head, not touching the picture, barely glancing at it.

'Why would I know anything about your daughter?' he asked.

There was a pause and Maggie said, 'Because she told me she was having an affair with you. And she was coming to see you the night she disappeared. She's blonde now – you must know—'

'Look,' he interrupted, stepping back a little. 'I can't help you, okay? I don't know her. I wasn't in a relationship with her, and I doubt we've even met. There are all sorts of crazy fans out there.'

Maggie put the photo back in her bag.

'My daughter isn't a fantasist, Mr Whitman,' she said. 'I know you were close, more than friends. I can't believe you don't know anything...'

He knocked back his whisky. 'I can't help you.' He started to walk away.

'Max?' said Stella.

He turned. 'What?'

'You really should be a bit more imaginative when it comes to gifts, you know.'

'*What?*'

'The cashmere sweater? With the double heart? I expect every ingenue in Hollywood has one by now.'

He stormed off, and Maggie felt a familiar cloak of anxiety drop over her shoulders.

'Why would he lie?' she asked Stella. 'Why would he pretend he doesn't know her?'

'Because,' Stella replied, 'we're on to something.'

For the next hour or so, Maggie followed Stella as she

pulled friends to one side and showed them Ginny's picture. Had they been to the party? Did they know her? Did they remember her from that night? A couple said she looked familiar, but they discovered nothing new that was helpful.

The party had moved to the garden, and they were about to go outdoors too when they heard a man's voice.

'Well, it can't possibly be the divine Miss Stella Hope? Surely not!'

Stella turned and a smile spread across her face.

'Monty!' she shouted.

'Now why would London let you go?' asked the man, kissing her on each cheek. 'Are they mad?'

She laughed and Maggie watched as Stella revelled in the glory.

'This is my good friend, Maggie,' said Stella. 'This,' she said to Maggie, 'is Monty Summers.'

Maggie shook his hand and then realised where she'd heard the name before.

'*Dr* Summers?' she asked. 'The studio doctor?'

'That's right,' he said, with a bemused smile. 'Are you an actress, too?'

'No, but my daughter is.' She opened her bag and began fumbling inside. 'Look,' she said, showing him the photo, 'that's her, though she looks different now. She's gone missing – have you seen her?'

Confusion swept over his face. 'I'm sorry, but she doesn't look familiar.'

'I'm not explaining myself properly,' Maggie blundered on, 'but she came to you. For the uppers and downers all the girls take? But now, you see, she's been missing for months.

I'm frantic. Was she ill when you saw her? Or perhaps she was pregnant and wanted to hide away till the baby was born? I just don't know what to think. I—'

Stella put her hand on Maggie's shoulder.

'Take a breath, Maggie,' she said. 'Just take a breath. It's okay.'

Maggie tried to inhale deeply but it caught in her chest, and when she spoke, her voice was shaky. 'We came here to find out what happened, but nobody seems to know, and I just – look.' She pulled out the pill bottle from her bag. 'This was one of the few things that was left.' She pointed to the name. 'Virginia Rose – that's her. Ginny.'

Dr Summers didn't say anything, but all the colour seeped from his face and he tugged at his tie.

'Monty, are you alright?' asked Stella.

He bent over, hands on knees, letting the blood rush to his head.

'Monty?' asked Stella. 'What's the matter? Can I help?'

His breaths came out fast and he stayed like that, bent over, for a few more seconds before getting up slowly.

'Forgive me,' he said, mopping the sweat from his face with a handkerchief. 'I haven't been well lately, and I sometimes get light-headed.'

Maggie grabbed his arm. 'You can tell me anything,' she said. 'Did she have a termination? Perhaps you helped? I wouldn't blame you for anything. I'll keep your name out of it.'

He moved, making her hand fall away.

'I'm sorry I can't help you,' he said. He looked like he was about to cry. 'I need to go. I'm not well at all.'

He pushed past them and quickly left the room.

Panic rose in Maggie's chest. 'He's lying,' she said. 'He knows something. Max, too.'

Stella stared after him, not speaking.

'Why won't they tell us what happened?' Maggie asked. 'Was it so terrible? What are they covering up?' Stella didn't respond, but looked shocked. 'Stella? What is it?'

'I've just remembered something,' she said. 'Watching him rush off like that.'

'Who? Monty?'

Stella nodded and pulled her to one side.

Maggie nudged her. 'Well?'

'On the night of the party, they took Max first in the ambulance,' she began. 'He was in such a bad way. I had to wait for a second ambulance, so they wrapped me in a blanket and I sat on the ground and waited.'

Maggie nodded. 'And?'

'He was there – Monty. He came just after the accident. Someone must have called him.'

'So?'

'He wasn't there for me,' said Stella. 'He didn't even see me. But I remember him now, running right past me. I remember thinking, *Why's he going that way?*'

'Which way?' asked Maggie.

'Away from the crash. He was running up the stairs,' she said. 'Into the house. Something must have happened in the house.'

CHAPTER FORTY-TWO

East Whittier, Southern California

A few days later, Maggie sat in the small, modest home of Sophia Hughes. It had taken her an hour to get to this place of lush orange groves and new developments, and the taxi was waiting outside to take her back once she was done. Brodsky had called in some favours, found Mrs Hughes' phone number and, after Maggie had called there'd been an agonising wait. But finally Sophia had called back and had agreed to see her.

Maggie glanced at the framed photo on the table next to her, of the young blonde with a heart-shaped face and an impish smile.

'Is that her?' she asked. 'Is that Sandy?'

Sophia nodded, taking a coffee cup from a tray and handing it to her. Then she picked up the photo.

'She was such a sweet kid – kind, funny, talented,' she said, stroking the photo. 'But I suppose every mother thinks their child is special.'

Maggie sipped her coffee then took the picture from Sophia. Sandy looked like a girl on the brink of something wonderful. 'I do appreciate you seeing me,' Maggie said, returning the photo to the table. 'And I'm sorry to bring this all back. I know it can't be easy.'

'It's alright,' said Sophia. 'I was just shocked to get the call. I like to talk about her. Nobody wants to anymore. They all rally around at the start, but then a few months later the visits stop. One of my neighbours crossed the street today so she wouldn't have to face me.'

'That's just awful,' said Maggie.

Sophia shrugged, offered her a cigarette and then a light. 'It's nice to have company,' she said. 'Ask me what you want.'

'Well, to start,' began Maggie, 'do you know if Sandy was good friends with Ginny? If they mixed with the same crowd? I know they were at the same party the last time Ginny was seen.'

Sophia shook her head. 'I don't know,' she said, 'but she was friendly with lots of girls. Loved it in Hollywood. She'd just got a contract, you know. Said her dream was about to come true.' She took a drag of her cigarette. 'I suppose if you're doing that kind of job, you've got to believe everything could change in a moment.'

Maggie nodded. 'Ginny has that optimism, too,' she said. 'Such self-belief. Even though she knows it's cut-throat.'

Sophia let out a gentle sigh and looked off to the side of the room. Then she turned to Maggie.

'Can I ask *you* something?' she said.

'Of course,' replied Maggie.

'If you were planning on killing yourself, how would you do it?'

Maggie's cup clattered in her saucer. 'I... er... I don't know. I've never considered it.'

'Just think about it for a moment,' Sophia said. 'If you wanted to end it all, what would you do?'

'Well,' said Maggie, blowing smoke to one side, 'sleeping pills, I suppose. Maybe alcohol too. That's what you hear people do. I think it's meant to be the easiest way. I imagine you just fall asleep and don't know anything about it.'

'Yes, sleeping pills and alcohol,' repeated Sophia. She picked up her spoon and stirred her coffee noisily before taking a sip. 'Me too. But I take it you heard how my little girl died?' she asked.

Maggie swallowed hard. 'She shot herself,' she said, her voice flat. She heard it had been in the head. 'I can't imagine how awful that was for you.'

Sophia put down her cup and stared at her hands in her lap. There was a long pause while she picked at her fingernails, but Maggie didn't want to say anything. She sensed she was building up to something, so she let the silence fill the room.

Finally, Sophia leaned forward, her eyes full of pain, and whispered fiercely, 'It doesn't make sense.' Despair was etched deep in her face. 'Nothing fits anymore.'

For a moment, Maggie assumed she meant that her own life no longer made sense without her daughter, but then Sophia said, with fervour, 'Her death. The way she died.' Her lips pursed. 'I don't buy it.'

Maggie felt a heavy, dreadful sensation seep into her stomach as she asked, 'What... what do you mean?'

'She hated guns,' said Sophia. 'Didn't even know how to use one.'

'Did they find one in her apartment?' she asked.

'Right next to her,' said Sophia.

'Well, perhaps she'd learned to use one?' said Maggie, but before she'd even finished speaking, Sophia was shaking her head.

'No – not my girl.' She took another tiny sip of her coffee. 'She'd *never* own a gun.' She rubbed away a tear and stared into her cup.

Maggie's instinct was to get up and put her arm around her, but something about the woman's demeanour told her that wasn't what she wanted. Sophia seemed to be barely holding together the threads of her life – one show of affection and she'd unravel. Maggie felt a pang of guilt for putting her through all this, but she had to find Ginny.

'So...' Maggie began, shifting in her chair, 'what do *you* think happened?'

Sophia gave a small laugh. 'Well, that depends what day of the week you ask me.'

Maggie smiled in recognition. She felt the same about Ginny, her mind constantly changing.

'You know those carousels?' Sophia continued. 'At the fun fair? Well, that's what it's like in my head, her death going round and round all day. Except it never stops.'

Maggie nodded. Ginny was always with her; various terrible scenarios about her disappearance would reel through her head too, like a film she was forced to watch.

'The only thing I know for sure,' said Sophia, 'is that my daughter would never be so desperate that she'd do *that*.'

Taking a long drag, Maggie swallowed the smoke before speaking.

'Hollywood, though,' she broached. 'It does things to you – to women, in particular. All these young girls hungry for fame, and all these men in positions of power.'

'You're right,' said Sophia. 'And she told me she'd had to do some jobs she hated, just to keep going. She had a contract, but the studio hadn't given her any parts yet, so she had no money. And, well...' She glanced around at her own modest surroundings, then touched the collar of her dress, trying to flatten it down. 'I couldn't exactly help her out there.'

Maggie sipped her coffee.

'I came up with all kinds of crazy explanations,' said Sophia, with a smirk. 'At one point, I even convinced myself she owed money to gangsters and they'd killed her because she couldn't pay up.' She shook her head, putting down her cup. 'But suicide? For a start, there was no blood in her apartment.'

'Really?' asked Maggie. Surely a gunshot wound would mean lots of blood?

'Strange, isn't it?' said Sophia. 'On the day of her funeral, I dropped by her place, just to see it for myself. I thanked the landlady for doing a deep clean, expecting her to give me a bill. But she said there'd been no bloodstains, nothing. Just the smell. How can Sandy have shot herself in the head and not left a trace?'

Maggie frowned. 'Did anyone hear anything? A gunshot?'

'Nobody's come forward,' said Sophia.

'Did you tell the police what you've just told me?' asked Maggie. 'That nothing makes sense?'

Sophia let out a bitter laugh. 'Of course! This one officer wrote it all down in his notebook and it came to a big fat nothing. But look at me.' She gesticulated to her surroundings. 'I live miles away and can't afford detectives and lawyers. I had to let it go.'

Maggie's throat tensed but she was determined not to cry. Whatever happened in this unpredictable, terrifying world, it seemed it was always women who paid the price.

'You know, I didn't even get to see her before the funeral,' said Sophia, tapping her cigarette in the ashtray, 'although I think that was for the best. By the time I found out, the studio had already taken care of it all. The cops said I would barely have recognised her anyway, what with the mess and...' She pointed at her face. 'Thank God for small mercies. That's not how I want to remember her.'

She pulled at a chain around her neck. 'This is hers – they let me have it,' she said, smiling. Maggie leaned in to see an oval-shaped locket hanging from it.

'That's pretty,' she said.

'I gave it to her when she was sixteen,' said Sophia. 'She always wore it. Never took it off.' She opened it into two halves but the slots for photos were empty. 'I promised her I'd get some pictures of the two of us for inside, but I never did.'

She started to cry, and Maggie opened her handbag, took out a handkerchief and handed it to her. Then she sat next to her and put her arm around her.

'I'd like to take her some flowers,' Maggie said. 'If that's alright. Where is she buried? Is it the small churchyard I passed on the way, by the stream?'

'Oh no,' said Sophia, dabbing at her eyes. 'She's three buses away – I've only made the journey once myself. The studio got her a fancy plot downtown. They insisted on paying for it.'

A cold sweat licked the back of Maggie's neck, and she dropped her arm.

'But why?' she asked. 'I mean, Sandy wasn't even really working for them yet.'

'I asked the same question,' said Sophia. 'They insisted it was already done. Within hours of me getting the news, some accountant was on my doorstep, saying the arrangements had been made. Star Studios were footing the bill.'

'What else did he say?' Maggie asked.

'That they wanted to give her a good send off, and give me some money, too,' replied Sophia, with a smirk. 'But like you say, she wasn't a star – she'd done nothing yet.'

'Who was it? The man who turned up?'

Sophia shrugged. 'Just a man in a suit – nondescript. Running an errand for someone else, I think. Seemed to get worried when I said I didn't want the money.'

Maggie leaned forward. 'Then what happened?' she asked.

'Well, he literally wouldn't leave. He sat on my porch for two hours, and finally I accepted. The police were going to do nothing, said there was no case, so…' Her voice faded now and she glanced at the photo. 'I hope she'll forgive me. They send me a cheque every month, too. For my living expenses, they say. I wish I could send it back, but I can't work and I'm by myself.'

Star Studios was buying her silence. Maggie was certain of it, and Sophia knew it, too.

'Please don't think badly of me,' she said, as if she could read Maggie's mind.

'Oh no, I don't,' Maggie protested. 'I can't imagine how hard it's been.'

'And that out there.' Sophia pointed to the side window. 'That's from them, too. Arrived a few days ago.'

Maggie got up to look. She pulled back the curtain and there, in the harsh Californian daylight, sat a shiny black Cadillac. A fat cockroach basking in the scorching sun.

'Ridiculous,' said Sophia, tugging at her dress collar. 'I don't drive. I told the man who towed it here that I've got no use for it. Said he was just following orders and I should sell it.'

Maggie sat back on the couch. 'I heard she left a note,' she said. 'Would you mind telling me what she wrote?'

'Just the one line,' said Sophia. '*Sorry – I can't do this anymore.*'

Maggie nodded.

'That's when I knew,' said Sophia, 'that this whole thing was a pack of lies.'

There was a pause and finally Maggie asked, 'How?'

'She signed the note *Sandy*,' said Sophia. 'She never used that name in letters to me, always just put an *A* on the end, for Alexandra. It was as if she was sending me a sign.'

Maggie waited.

'She hadn't done this to herself,' said Sophia, 'someone had done it to her.'

CHAPTER FORTY-THREE

The journey back to the Beverly Hills Hotel would take over an hour, but Maggie couldn't wait that long. She had to speak to Stella straight away, to tell her what Sophia had said. She asked the taxi driver to pull in at a local drug store and wait for her while she telephoned. The main reception put her through to Stella's bungalow, and Maggie heard it ring several times but Stella didn't pick up. So she searched her address book for Brodsky's number. He answered straight away.

'We need to go back to Ginny's apartment,' she said. 'Can you come? It's important.'

'What is it?' he asked. 'What did Sandy's mum tell you?' She could hear the excitement in his voice.

'She says nothing about her death adds up – but there's something else.'

They arranged to meet in Ralph's Diner first, and as they sat in a booth she sipped her black coffee and recounted the conversation and what she suspected. He frowned as he listened and didn't touch his cup. By the time she'd finished, colour had risen in his cheeks.

'You realise this is a very serious accusation,' he said. 'We can't say anything – to anyone – until we have proof.'

'I know,' she replied. 'I'm telling Stella, though. If I'm right, it changes everything.'

'Okay. Shall we go? Are you ready?'

She nodded.

He threw a couple of dollars on the table to pay the bill and they walked towards Ginny's flat on Laurel Avenue. Once there, they made their way to Mrs Ackerman's apartment on the ground floor.

Maggie knocked on the door and they waited, looking at each other. *Please*, thought Maggie. *Please, let her be home.*

'Go away!' yelled a voice from inside. 'I don't need what you're selling.'

'Mrs Ackerman?' called Maggie. 'Mrs Ackerman, it's me, Maggie. I came to see you the other day about Ginny. My daughter who's missing. You made me tea?'

'The Englishwoman?' she called.

'Yes. Can I just speak to you for a minute, please? It's important.'

There was silence, then eventually two bolts scraped across the door and two locks clanked open, one at the top, the other at the bottom. The door creaked a fraction, to reveal a sliver of Mrs Ackerman standing in the shadows.

'Who's he?' she asked. 'Men aren't allowed, you know. No sleeping over is allowed.'

'He's just a friend, Mrs Ackerman. He's helping me find Ginny.'

The woman let the door open a touch more and adjusted

today's bow, which was a shiny green, embedded firmly on the nest of hair on her crown. She peered at Brodsky with fascination and then opened the door fully as he removed his hat.

'How do you do?' he said, holding his trilby to his chest and dipping his head slightly.

Mrs Ackerman offered her hand, and without missing a beat, he gave it a delicate kiss. She giggled.

'You flirt!' she admonished.

'Mrs Ackerman,' said Maggie, 'do you remember we were talking last week about Ginny? You said you saw her come home, with a man?'

'That's right,' she said, pushing the bow further into her hair. 'He was very rude. Foul language.' She smiled at Brodsky. 'I like men with manners. Like you.'

He acknowledged the compliment with a nod.

'You said he brought her home drunk,' continued Maggie, 'and then a short while later he left?'

'I warned him,' said Mrs Ackerman. 'This is a female-only building. I expect I scared him off.'

'Can you show us where that happened?' Maggie asked. 'Where they were when he swore at you?'

'Are you from the government?' she asked Brodsky. 'Because I know they have some good-looking ones now, to trick us.'

'I'm not, ma'am,' he said. 'I can assure you. I'm just a concerned friend.'

She looked him up and down.

'Alright then,' she said. 'Wait a moment.' She closed the door, and they could hear her rummaging inside.

Finally, she emerged wrapped in a silver-grey crocheted

shawl, keys in hand. She locked the door top and bottom, gave the handle a good shake to make sure it was secure, then shuffled along the corridor. Maggie and Brodsky followed her up the stairs.

'Up and down, up and down,' she said. 'These stairs will kill me one day.'

There was a piece of newspaper in a corner on the landing and she bent over it, and for a moment, it seemed she might topple. But she swiped it up, shoved it in the pocket of her housecoat and continued. They passed the first floor where she stopped for a breath, then they approached the second – Ginny's floor – and Maggie and Brodsky both looked at each other. But Mrs Ackerman kept walking. On the third floor, she stopped and wandered down the corridor, then looked over her shoulder.

'Don't dawdle,' she said, as she made her way to a door at the end.

She stood outside it and pointed.

'Here,' she said. 'This is where they were. I remember sitting there.' She pointed to a rickety chair in the corner that had a ripped seat. 'I sat and waited for him to leave.'

Maggie swallowed hard and looked at Brodsky. She put her hand out and touched the wooden door, and the number on it: 3c.

'Ginny lived in 2c,' she said to Mrs Ackerman. 'I thought you said it was the girl in 2c you saw late that night?'

'No, it was definitely this room,' she said. 'She came back drunk, then a day or two later... well. They found her. It took days to get that smell out of the room. I'm very sorry for your loss.'

Maggie turned to Brodsky.

'This is *Sandy's* room. They were bringing *Sandy* back.'

'Look, I don't know her name,' said Mrs Ackerman, 'but it was the girl who killed herself. She was out cold when he brought her back, all wrapped up in his coat. Had a hat on like a cowboy. Couldn't even stand – he had to carry her in.'

'You know, Mrs Ackerman,' began Brodsky.

'Please, call me Ruby,' she said.

'Ruby, you've been so helpful.'

She smiled.

'But just one last question,' he said. 'Are you sure it was definitely this room – 3c? It's very important. Are you certain you saw them here and not going into the room downstairs?'

'Yes, I'm certain,' she said, affronted. 'It's the only floor that has a chair. I was sweeping up and told him I'd wait for him to leave. He didn't like that. But that's what I did. I sat there till he left.'

Maggie could hear the blood thumping in her ears.

'Now I have a busy schedule today,' said Mrs Ackerman, as she started to wander off, 'so if you'll excuse me.'

Maggie sank into the chair and Brodsky knelt beside her.

'No blood in the room,' she said quietly.

'And nobody heard a gunshot,' he replied.

'Poor Sandy,' she said. 'She wasn't drunk that night, was she? When they brought her back?'

'I don't think so.'

'She was already dead.'

'Stay here,' said Brodsky, jumping up. 'I'm going to check all the other floors for chairs.'

A few minutes later he returned, out of breath. Maggie was still sitting, her head in her hands.

'She's right,' he said. 'No chairs on any other floor. This is where she sat that night – outside Sandy's room. Even so, she's not the most reliable witness.'

'That party,' Maggie said. 'Everything leads back to that party. Both Ginny and Sandy went.'

'One ends up dead,' he replied, 'and the other goes missing. But if something did happen there, we still need a witness.'

Maggie looked at him.

'There is someone who knows,' she said. 'Someone who was there that night.'

*T*he lights click on and Cissy screams into the early morning.

'The men are here!' bellows someone, and then the howls begin. In seconds, the ward fills with the sound of roaring women.

'What's happening?' I shout to Nancy. I press onto my elbows and try to sit up, but the straps pull me back down.

'They're taking her,' yells Nancy. 'The orderlies are taking Cissy.'

I strain my neck to see, and my heart lurches as I watch Karl approaching. First, the top of his head, then his face as he walks closer, his torso, and finally he's standing there next to my bed.

'You're in big trouble, Hollywood,' he says, his eyes full of excitement as he unbuckles my straps. 'She didn't even take the tablets. She saved them all. Gave you up so quickly.'

I kick out, but in seconds someone has grabbed my legs. Karl puts a hand around my throat and bends down to my face, and I can smell tobacco and sour milk. I twist my *head, but his other hand pulls it back and he drops a wet kiss on my lips.*

'You're going for some therapy,' he says. 'Good luck, doll.'

Suddenly I'm standing and being dragged away. Voices erupt behind me.

'Where are they taking her?'

'Bring her back!'

In moments, I'm in the tub room and stripped of my nightdress.

The canvas covering has been removed from one of the baths, and the men lift me inside, naked, while a nurse stands and watches. I try to climb out, but I'm buckled down in moments. The orderlies laugh as they pull the canvas tight over the tub, trapping me inside, and fitting it tight around my neck so that only my head protrudes.

I know what happens here. At least it's not shock treatment, I tell myself. I can cope with this. It's not electricity in my brain. That would be much worse. This is just water. I'll be alright.

I screw shut my eyes as freezing cold water is pumped into the bath. The gasps catch in my throat and shivers race through me, like ice-snakes under my skin. They twist up me and around me and over me and inside me and invade me completely, covering the flesh on my legs then my hips, then my waist. And now the water is at my chest, and my breasts are so cold. And now at my neck and the snakes sink their frozen fangs into my shoulders and I give myself up. I'm conquered.

The water circles my neck and licks at my ear lobes, where it stops. I swallow hard to battle the claustrophobia that makes me nauseous. I've heard tales of people kept here for hours, sometimes days. To steady nerves, they say, but it's severe punishment, of course. The bite of the cold is excruciating. I steady my breath. I will pretend I'm not here.

Think of something good. Something happy. There must be something happy that has happened in your life. Picture it now. I search and search. I think of late nights and early mornings, dressing up, laughing on a staircase, holding my contract for the very first time. Waiting for that big break. But the picture disintegrates rapidly. There is nothing now.

I drown in the pain.

CHAPTER FORTY-FOUR

It was nine in the morning on the following day, and the sun was already burning through the sparse September clouds. Maggie, Stella and Brodsky were in the car on their way to see Dr Summers. Stella was in the passenger seat, next to Brodsky, and Maggie leaned forward between them.

'How will you get him to talk?' she asked Stella. 'You saw what he was like at the party – he practically fainted when I asked him about Ginny.'

'I don't know,' she replied, 'but I've known him for years. If anyone can, I can.' She turned to look at Brodsky. 'Jim, you should wait outside. I think you'll make him skittish.'

'You'll be careful?' he said, patting her hand.

Maggie caught the tender look he gave Stella as he took his eyes off the road. He had it bad. It had been clear from the day these two met that they were attracted to each other, but she'd been so preoccupied she'd missed how close they'd become.

'Don't worry,' said Stella, 'Monty's harmless. I think I'll get more out of him without you there.'

Brodsky nodded.

'Here it is,' said Stella, pointing to a smart white building across the road. Brodsky pulled up and they got out. 'You'll stay here?'

'Of course,' he said. And he leaned back in his seat and pulled out a newspaper. 'Just remember – if he won't talk, make him think you know more than you do.'

They got out and Stella put her fingertips to her lips, kissed them, then gave him a wave. A few moments later, they were in the elevator going up to Dr Summers' apartment.

'You're sure he's not at the studio today?' asked Maggie.

'His secretary said he was home.' Stella stood in front of Maggie and took her by the shoulders. 'Take a breath,' she said. 'It's going to be alright.'

Maggie did as she was told, but still felt jittery. If she was right about the doctor, he held the key to finding Ginny. They reached the second floor and she followed Stella as she walked purposefully towards a heavy mahogany door. On the wall next to it was a discreet silver plaque that read:

DR MONTGOMERY SUMMERS
BY APPOINTMENT ONLY

Stella pointed at the small peephole in the middle of the door, so Maggie stood out of view with her back to the wall. Stella knocked and there was the sound of something falling inside, as if someone had been startled. Then there was rustling and quiet cursing as footsteps approached.

The door stayed shut. He was obviously looking through the peephole.

'Monty?' called Stella. 'I really need to see you. I'm

not at all well...' Silence. 'Look, I know I don't have an appointment, darling,' said Stella, 'but please. It's urgent.'

After a few moments, the door opened slowly.

'What's the matter?' said a concerned voice. 'I'm busy, can you come back?'

Stella quickly put her foot over the threshold. Then she reached out and pulled Maggie towards her and they both slipped in.

'What? Hold on!'

They shut the door behind them. Dr Summers stood there aghast.

'Monty, you remember Maggie, don't you?' said Stella briskly. 'Her daughter Ginny is missing. We need some answers. About the night of that party.'

'Look, I can't tell you anything,' he said. 'I... I don't know anything. Please.'

On the floor behind him were piles of cardboard boxes, and by the wall stood a suitcase. Card folders had spewed their contents at his feet, across the polished parquet floor. He bent down and started shuffling everything together.

'Are you leaving?' Maggie asked.

He didn't reply, but it was clear he was. He piled file upon file, but his hands were shaking now, and the folders slid away from him again. He cursed and started scooping up everything once more.

'Monty, stop,' said Stella, crouching down as he scrabbled furiously. 'Stop!' She put her hand on his shoulder. 'Let's have a drink, shall we? You got any scotch?'

They both got up and Maggie pulled all the papers together into a pile and put them on a side table, then followed them both into the living room. A mirrored cocktail bar ran down one side, and a low antique cherry-wood table sat in the middle. A luxurious L-shaped couch in a delicate eggshell blue fabric had a cream blanket thrown over one arm. His taste was impeccable, the atmosphere one of serenity and wealth – he, on the other hand, was a wreck. His face was sweaty, and he tugged at his shirt collar, undoing two buttons and loosening his tie.

Maggie sat and watched as he sank into a cream suede chair opposite her. He wouldn't look at her, but stared down at his hands instead, twisting his fingers this way and that. Stella busied herself at the bar, returning with three tumblers full of scotch over ice. She held out the silver tray and he snatched one up, downed half of it, took a deep gulp of air then drank the rest. The women looked at each other.

Maggie had so much she wanted to ask him about the night of the party, but they'd agreed Stella should take the lead.

Calmly opening her bag, Stella took out her cigarettes and offered them around. She lit hers and Maggie's, but Monty shook his head.

'So, Monty,' Stella began, 'shall we stop pretending?' She blew smoke towards him.

He looked up, his face full of worry.

'It's clear you know something,' she continued. 'I know you were there at the Sherman's that night, the last time Ginny was seen. I saw you rushing to the house.'

He frowned, as if trying to recall seeing her.

'I was sitting outside,' she explained, 'waiting for the

ambulance. You ran right past me – didn't even see me in your hurry.' She took another puff. 'We've known each other, how long? Twenty years? You never go to those parties. You loathe them. Why were you called to the house that night?'

'Nothing,' he blurted, not making sense. 'It was nothing. I... I don't know.'

Maggie glanced at her.

'Look, darling,' Stella continued, tapping her cigarette in an ashtray, 'I know you, you're a decent man in a town where there aren't many. And I really like you, I always have. But just look at her.' She nodded towards Maggie and he turned to her for the first time. 'This woman hasn't slept for months because she's worried sick about her daughter. She needs to know what happened.'

He shook his head.

Stella let out a sigh. 'Alright, let me put it this way,' she said. 'A friend of mine is sitting across the road in his white Pontiac. Take a look if you want,' she said, pointing to the window. 'He happens to be a private detective. If you don't start talking, he'll have the police here in minutes. I'm sure there are many illegal prescriptions and misdemeanours they can pull you up on.' She paused. 'If you want to play it that way, and I really don't.'

He let out a jagged breath, as if breathing itself was a challenge now, and walked to the bar. Pouring himself another drink, he took a swig and left the glass on the bar as he sat back down, elbows on knees, head in hands.

'Dr Summers,' said Maggie. 'Monty? Please. We know a girl died that night – Sandy Hughes. We think it happened at the party because she was definitely there, and so was

Ginny. What did you see? Is Ginny mixed up in it, too? Did you see either of them?'

'I had nothing to do with that,' he said, looking up. 'With Sandy.' He rubbed his eyes.

'What happened to her?' asked Stella. 'And Ginny?'

He hesitated.

'Is she alive?' asked Maggie. 'Is Ginny alive?'

He nodded, and a tidal wave of relief swept through her.

'Whatever you saw or did,' said Maggie, 'you can do a good thing now by telling us what happened. Where is she?'

He shook his head. 'Some things can never be made right. The things they've made me do…'

Maggie shot Stella a glance but neither said anything.

'You know,' said Monty, 'I barely recognise myself sometimes.' He put a hand to his forehead and rubbed, as if trying to erase his existence. 'When you asked about Ginny at the brunch party the other day, I knew it was all about to blow up in my face.'

'And that's why you're leaving,' said Stella.

'I'll tell you where she is,' he said, 'but you must promise to give me time to get out of town. They don't know I'm going.'

'Who doesn't?' asked Stella.

'The studio. I… I just can't do this anymore. If they know I'm going, they'll stop me.'

Stella frowned. 'Surely you can do what you want?'

He let out a scornful laugh. 'You'd think so, wouldn't you? I have a train ticket for eight o'clock tonight. A friend's sending everything on after. Once I stop turning up for appointments, they'll realise, but by then I'll be long gone.'

'Help us find her,' said Maggie, 'and we'll let you go.'

'Alright,' he said. And he took a deep breath, gave a small cough, and then told them everything he'd seen and done.

CHAPTER FORTY-FIVE

The Oscars Party
What happened at the Sherman Mansion
Friday, March 26, 1954

The door is unlocked, a large man pushes him into the room, and he stumbles on something. There's a Stetson at his feet. A key turns and the latch clicks behind him, and the man grabs his arm and steers him to the centre of the room.

A woman lies there, a terrible sight. Half of her head blown away. Blood and gore everywhere. The rest of her is drained of colour, as if she's made of wax. He's crying now, hysterical at the sight. He won't have anything to do with this. He won't be involved in murder.

The man slaps his cheek to calm him down. Tells him it was an accident, a stupid drunken game gone wrong.

'Get a hold of yourself, Monty,' he says, in his ear. 'It's not her you're here for. It's the other one.'

Next to the body is another woman, her clothes heavy with blood. Her arms stained to the elbow, as if wearing long red gloves. She's hysterical, sobbing.

The large man whispers instructions in his ear, so he kneels and opens his doctor's bag.

'Please stop,' he says to her, the tears taking hold of him again. 'Let me help you calm down.'

He takes a syringe from inside, fills it so he can release her from this horror for a while, and takes one arm. She stares at him, eyes wide, and realises what he's about to do. 'No!'

She pulls away, but the big man kneels too, and holds her down. Together they keep her still, and he injects her.

'I'm sorry,' he says, 'I'm so sorry, I'm sorry.' And he's crying over her.

In seconds, she's silent.

'That's it, Ginny,' says the big man. 'That's it – you can sleep now.'

Then the big man turns and tells him what to do next. He refuses. There are rules to follow, court orders needed. He's never done it this way before, though he knows others who have. No, he won't do it, he can't. But then he's reminded what will happen if he doesn't, and he tells himself he has no choice.

So finally, he takes the form he's handed, fills it in and signs it. Then he wipes his face and tumbles further into hell.

CHAPTER FORTY-SIX

Hollywood, Los Angeles
September 1954

'You had her *committed*?' Maggie asked.

She stared in horror at Monty. He wouldn't look at her. Hands clasped tight in her lap, she pressed down hard to stop her urge to hit him. Stella came and sat next to her and put her arm around her shoulders.

A thick silence filled the room. His face was grey, his eyes empty, as if telling his part in this nightmare had sapped his very life force.

Finally, he gave a small nod.

'To an asylum?' she asked, appalled. 'How could you? Where is she?'

'It's… it's an hour away. You have to believe me,' he said, 'I've never done anything like this before. They made me. They threatened me. I didn't have a choice.'

'Of course you did!' shouted Maggie.

'No,' he said. 'No, I didn't. I've never had a choice about any of it. They… they said they'd have me arrested for…' He turned to Stella. 'You understand, don't you? You know I'm homosexual, right?'

'Darling,' she said, 'half of Hollywood is queer. What's that got to do with it?'

'But you know what happens if I get reported? They'd say I was soliciting for sex – they'd pay a fake witness – and I'd never survive in prison.' He ran his hand through his hair. 'They've held this over me for years – made me do things I hate – doling out drugs to the talent, wrecking their bodies, finding doctors for terminations, sometimes for women who don't want them, and...'

'And committing women to asylums,' said Maggie.

'This once. Yes. Committing a woman to an asylum.'

'You could have refused,' she said.

'Refused?' he replied, with a smirk. 'Have you met Stan Fisher?'

Stella dropped her arm from Maggie's shoulder.

'Stan?' she repeated, baffled.

'Yes, Stan. Friendly, helpful Stan,' said Monty. 'The best actor in town. Cross him and good luck to you. He knows every gangster in LA.'

'Stan is blackmailing you?' Stella asked. She gave a small laugh then frowned, as if entertaining the thought was just too ridiculous.

Monty nodded.

'Since when?' asked Maggie.

'For years. He's known about my preferences since I started at Star Studios. Used it against me from day one. And now with this Lavender Scare – kicking queers out of office, ruining us financially – well, he's really turned the pressure on.'

Maggie had read about the witch hunt: dozens of people

in prominent positions being hounded out of their jobs because of their sexuality.

'No,' said Stella, shaking her head. 'Not Stan – he wouldn't.'

'Shocking, eh?' said Monty. 'Because he's such a nice guy, right?'

Maggie's mind started whirring.

'Are you saying he made you commit Ginny?' she asked. 'And that he faked Sandy's suicide?'

'Who else?' said Monty. 'He'll do anything to protect his stars, everyone knows that. And it's Max Whitman we're talking about here. That's who he's protecting – that's who shot Sandy.'

Stella fell back onto the cushions, eyes wide in shock, as if she'd been shot herself.

'Wait – what?'

'Max – that's who killed Sandy,' Monty replied. 'Well, that's what I heard. Some stupid game with a gun that went wrong. And Ginny saw it all. That's why she had to be kept quiet.'

Maggie turned to face Stella. It was her turn to give some comfort now, and she took her friend's hand.

'That must be why he rushed out of the party,' Maggie said to her. 'And practically killed you both driving away.'

'Max?' repeated Stella. 'A murderer?'

'Accidentally, but yes,' said Monty. 'Cocaine, champagne – you know how scary and wild those parties can get. And once he'd fired that shot, there was only one thing for it – a cover up.'

'You bloody idiot, Max,' muttered Stella to herself.

Maggie was aghast, but Monty's story had the ring of truth about it. If these people would do anything to become famous, imagine what they'd do to cling on to that fame. Just when she thought she'd seen the dark underbelly of Hollywood, it twisted and turned like a depraved beast, revealing a more terrible side.

'So,' began Maggie, 'are you saying that Stan Fisher blackmailed you to make you part of this cover up? To save Max's skin?'

'No,' interrupted Stella. 'I agree Max is stupid enough to get into a terrible situation – to shoot a girl and accidentally kill her. I've seen him drunk and out of control. But Stan wouldn't do this. He wouldn't sacrifice Ginny's life like this – lock her up to shut her up? It's just too cruel. He'd have found another way.'

'You're overestimating his morals,' said Monty.

Stella shook her head. 'Putting Ginny in an asylum? I mean, what was the plan? That she'd be locked away for the rest of her life?'

'Look, I'll prove it,' said Monty, and jumping up, he walked to a desk in the corner. Stella and Maggie looked at each other. Opening the drawer, he pulled something out.

'He sends me cash from the studio every month,' he said, waving an envelope, 'in the post, so he doesn't leave a paper trail. Then I have to pay West Hills – where Ginny's kept – from a separate account. I've not made this month's payment. He'll find out soon enough.'

Stella stood and put out her hand.

'Let me see,' she said, taking the envelope.

It was open and the notes were spilling from the top.

Maggie knew what she was thinking. She rose and stood next to her.

'Turn it over,' Maggie said.

Stella did. On the other side was printed Monty's name and address. The writing was in a familiar heavy hand, in blue pencil.

Stella threw the envelope to the floor.

'I'm going to kill him,' she said.

CHAPTER FORTY-SEVEN

Stella was hissing with anger.

'And you're sure it's the same handwriting as your blackmail letters?' asked Brodsky.

They were all in his car, driving back to the Beverly Hills Hotel. She sat up front with him, Monty in the back with Maggie. They'd just filled Brodsky in on what they'd discovered about Stan.

'I'm certain it's him,' Stella replied. 'Same blue pencil, same heavy handwriting as the ransom note. How could he do this? I've trusted him for years.'

Monty hadn't been surprised when she'd told him moments ago that they shared the same blackmailer.

'It's a town full of secrets,' he said, 'and Stan knows all of them.'

'So he's playing both sides,' said Brodsky. 'Covering up everything for his stars, keeping them squeaky clean for the public, but then blackmailing them when it suits him.'

'But I don't understand,' said Maggie. 'He goes to such

lengths to fix everything. Why then threaten the very people he's meant to be protecting? Why do this to Stella?'

'He's broke,' said Monty.

'How can he be?' asked Maggie. 'He's got one of the biggest jobs in Hollywood.'

'He likes the horses,' said Monty, 'but he stopped winning a while ago. And he has three ex-wives.'

They turned a corner.

'I'll drop you at the hotel first,' said Brodsky to Stella. 'Whatever you do, don't speak to Stan. Don't let on that you know it's him. Get some rest while we go and get Ginny from the asylum, then I'll come back and we can deal with it. Together.'

She nodded but said nothing.

'Will they really let her out?' asked Maggie. 'They won't try and stop us?'

'I signed the papers,' said Monty. 'I'm her doctor, so if I turn up and say she has to be released they have to discharge her. But Stella, promise me you won't let Stan know she's out till I'm on that train? Remember – 8 p.m.'

'I'll wait till then,' said Stella. 'But then I'm going to let him have it.'

'*Not* by yourself,' said Brodsky.

'Okay, okay, just drop me off here,' she said, irritated at being told what to do. Brodsky pulled up outside the private entrance to Stella's bungalow, and she got out before they could continue haranguing her, skipping the goodbyes. Of course she should wait before confronting Stan. It was the smart thing to do.

As she took her key from her handbag, a man in an

immaculate burgundy uniform with gold stripes on the cuffs tipped his hat at her.

'Good afternoon, Miss Hope,' he said.

'Hello, Donald,' she replied.

'You've had a delivery – I wasn't sure when you'd return, so I've slipped it under your door.'

'Thank you, Donald.'

She opened up and saw the large brown manila envelope by her feet. A whisper of dread swept over her and she delayed picking it up till she'd lit a cigarette.

Then she kicked it over with the toe of her shoe and saw her name in the familiar handwriting. She picked it up, took the silver letter opener from the bureau in the corner, then sat on the arm of the sofa, put the cigarette in her mouth and sliced open the flap.

She blew the smoke out, put the cigarette in the ashtray and steeled herself. He'd never sent a large envelope before, and in the split second before she dipped her hand inside, she knew what she'd find.

Pulling it out, she saw a large black-and-white printed photograph of herself, naked, lying on a sofa, her head facing the camera. The expression on her young face was one of resignation. Stella swallowed hard and turned the photo over.

Printed in the same despicable blue pencil were the instructions:

TIME TO PAY UP
$50,000
9 P.M. TONIGHT, LOCKER 7

Underneath the message was a key, firmly stuck to the back of the photo. From it hung a label with the address for the Pacific Greyhound bus depot at 6th and Los Angeles Street.

She didn't bother peeling it off, but dropped it all on the sofa, stood and walked to the bathroom.

So he thought it was that easy, did he? A time, a place and she'd just hand it over. No questions asked, no information on how she'd get the photos back. Nothing. She pictured her pretty gun with the mother-of-pearl handle that Max had given her all those years ago. It was wrapped in a silk scarf on the top shelf of her wardrobe. She had an urge to grab it and go to Stan right now, demand the photos and deal with this situation once and for all.

Instead, she ran a bath, sprinkled in some Estée Lauder Youth-Dew bath oil and poured her second scotch of the day. She balanced the tumbler on the edge of the bath as she undressed and slid into the warm, comforting water. As she lay there thinking, sipping her drink, she told herself that Brodsky was right. She should bide her time, wait for them all to return with Ginny, before confronting Stan.

But when had she ever done what she was told?

*Y*esterday was Matron's birthday and the orderlies showed a film for her. Max Whitman's face, huge, on a screen made from a grubby sheet. As I watched the movie unfold, my own story started to come together.

And now my life comes to me in fragments: the Oscars party, Max drunk and manic, the noise as the gun went off, my arms soaked in her blood. A man leaning over me, crying as he takes my arm. Someone next to him, telling him what to do. Who was he? I close my eyes to try and see him, but all I envisage is her face moments before he killed her, the disbelief in her eyes. Then nothing.

And now I'm almost me again. If I could just find that final piece. The one that shows who put me here, that lets me see the whole picture. I twirl a lock of hair around my finger as I think.

Dr Faulkner is the key. I ask if I can speak to him, but Matron refuses. I need to show him I'm mended, explain that I don't belong. Nancy says there are only two ways to see the doctor: you have to be very ill or pregnant. (Women *often get pregnant here and are punished for it. The orderlies never are.)*

So I need to make myself ill. I search the day room for something to eat, something to make me sick. But they're careful and don't allow us crayons or pencils or anything poisonous. Then I remember. Cigarettes! We barter them all day. I whisper my plan to Nancy, and she says she will help.

I crumble one and pretend to cough, swallowing the dry tobacco as I put my hand to my mouth. Nancy has water ready to help it go down. My stomach heaves but I continue. Nancy gives me hers. I do the same.

A few minutes later I feel a sweat on my back and nausea creeps up my stomach to my throat. I stand and wave my hands at the nurses.

'She's ill,' says Nancy. 'She needs help.'

The nurses arrive in a pair.

'You look terrible,' says the nice one who leaves my buckles loose. She puts her hand on my forehead.

'I feel awful.'

'Is it the fever, do you think?' she asks the other nurse.

They start discussing what to do, and I put my hands out to stop them talking, and they pause. Then I bend over and am violently sick on the floor, splattering their white shoes.

'I'm sorry, I'm sorry,' I groan, and the nice nurse pulls a face and I really am sorry it's her. She's the only one who's shown any kindness.

The other women near me groan.

'Oh god, take her through!' shouts one of them.

I lurch and am sick again. Within moments, I'm in a side room, lying on a bed, with a sick pan near my head.

An orderly tries to buckle my cuffs to the bed, but the nice nurse stops him.

'You can't do that,' she says, 'she'll choke. I'll get the doctor. You keep guard.'

So he stands at the door, and I close my eyes, exhausted. Later, I feel a hand on my wrist and I wake to see Dr Faulkner taking my pulse. He motions for me to sit up and puts a stethoscope to my chest – here, here, and there. Then he takes my blood pressure, shines a small torch into my eyes and asks me to open my mouth.

'Your vitals are stable,' he says. 'Did you eat something unusual?'

'No doctor,' I say. 'I just eat what I'm given. The porridge had a sour taste today, but I'm always hungry, so I just got it down.'

He nods.

'I see.'

He looks at me askance. Does he know?

'I remember everything,' I say in a whisper.

'Good, good,' he responds absentmindedly.

'I know what happened – the night they brought me here.'

He winds up his stethoscope. A look of annoyance flickers across his face.

'You're tired,' he says. 'You need to go back to the ward.'

I grab his hand and the orderly steps forward.

'Listen to me,' I say. 'A girl was killed. I saw it all. Call the police.'

He pauses.

'You're delirious,' Faulkner says.

'No – he killed her. He shot her in the head. I saw it.'

'You're dehydrated,' he says. 'It's the vomiting. You're hallucinating. I'll tell the nurses to give you more water.'

'You have to believe me,' I shout, but he turns to walk to the door.

I lurch off the bed and throw my arms around his waist, sinking my face into his white coat.

'It's true!' I shout, into his back. 'He killed her. I saw him do it.'

In a blink, the orderly has peeled me off and hurled me aside with such force that I cry out. My arms ache but I scramble up and throw myself at the doctor again. I get nowhere close. My wrist cuffs are buckled to the bed, then my ankles. I wince and the orderly pulls the buckles tighter.

'Tell Matron to get her to the first floor,' Faulkner says to the orderly. 'We'll give her a course of ECT. They're busy today but should be able to fit her in after the others.'

Then he turns to me and says, 'The electricity will calm you. You'll feel better.'

What have I done? I've just found myself, and now I will be lost again.

CHAPTER FORTY-EIGHT

West Hills Psychiatric Institute, Los Angeles

Maggie and Monty pushed through a pair of creaking wooden doors and stood in the cavernous belly of the asylum's lobby. Maggie stared around the dilapidated room. The West Hills Psychiatric Institute was a dump. Wooden beams, bleached with age, ran up the walls and across the sagging ceiling, ancient bones of a huge beast. A lazy metal fan whipped the warm air above her head. She felt light-headed, and she grabbed Monty's arm to steady herself. Brodsky had parked just inside the gates and was waiting for them.

She wished Stella had come. She always felt stronger with her around. But by the time she'd thought to ask Stella along, they'd dropped her off at the hotel. And anyway, Stella had been devastated when she realised it had been Stan blackmailing her.

Maggie looked up. Here she stood in this monstrous building, and somewhere deep inside these walls, they had her daughter.

The journey had taken an hour or so in Brodsky's car, but for Maggie, it had been six terrible months.

'She's definitely here, isn't she?' she asked Monty.

He nodded. She leaned on the splintered ledge in front of the nurses' station and took a deep breath.

'It'll be alright,' he said, patting her hand but not sounding at all convinced himself.

'What a place,' she said. 'If this is the reception, imagine what the rest of it is like – the rooms you can't see.'

A door opened and a young man walked into the office behind the partition.

'Can I help you?' he asked.

He wore a tired grey-white shirt and his tie hung a little low. It was one of those fake ties, and there was a piece of loose black elastic that stretched around the back of his neck. A scratched name tag said he was Jack.

'Yes,' said Maggie. 'I've come to collect my daughter. Ginny Watkins. Or Virginia Rose. You might have her under that.'

Monty pulled his credentials from his pocket and showed them to him.

'I'm her doctor and I had her committed in the early hours of March twenty-sixth this year. I'm here to sign the relevant documents to have her released.'

The young man stared at them both and pulled an incredulous face.

'You're mistaken,' he said, his voice high now. 'There are no releases today. I'd know about it. They always tell me because I'm in charge of the book. See.' He showed them a big ledger that was open in front of him. 'Nothing here.'

Maggie's heart quickened.

'You won't have it written down,' said Monty, 'but as her physician I'm telling you that she is to be released. Please go and get your superior, Jack.'

Jack didn't speak.

'Now?' Monty said.

He shrugged. 'I can go but it won't make a difference.'

Jack left his post and disappeared out of the room.

'What does he mean?' asked Maggie. 'They can't keep her in here, can they? If you tell them to let her go, they have to, right?'

Monty frowned. 'Just one step at a time,' he said. 'Let's see what he says.'

Maggie's gut said this was not a good start. 'But what if he refuses,' she said. 'I mean, what if—'

'Look,' said Monty urgently, 'you have to stay calm, okay?'

'Calm?' Maggie spat. 'What the hell are you talking about, Monty? I can't stay calm. They have Ginny and I want her back.'

'I know, I know,' he said, tugging at his collar. 'I'll do my best, alright? There's no reason they wouldn't let her out, I'm sure of it.'

She took a few deep breaths, but it was no good. The panic had engulfed her. She was starting to sweat and her mind was racing. It had come down to this, this very moment. It was all going to end here, right now, one way or the other. What if they didn't let Ginny out? What if they said she wasn't here at all?

The office door slammed again and Maggie watched

through the smudged glass as Jack returned. He held his head high, as if he'd unearthed some confidence from somewhere.

'Dr Faulkner says you need an appointment to see him and he's very busy,' he reported. 'He's asked me to ask you to phone his secretary, make an appointment and come back another day.'

'No,' said Maggie, and she put her hand on the glass partition and slid it open.

'Excuse me, madam,' Jack said. 'You're not allowed—'

She reached in and grabbed him by the collar and pulled him towards her. His eyes widened in fear as he spluttered.

'Maggie,' shouted Monty. 'Maggie, stop. You'll choke him!'

She loosened her grip a little, grabbed more of his shirt then pulled him closer towards her.

'Jack,' she said firmly, 'you tell Dr Faulkner we're going nowhere. He comes out now or I'll have the police here in minutes. We have a private detective waiting outside.'

She flung him back and he almost fell over as he scrambled to get out of the room. Monty stared at her, astonished.

'What?' she barked.

He shook his head. 'Nothing.'

A couple of minutes later, the door opened, and a bald, whiskery man entered the lobby.

'What's going on here?' he demanded. 'You've assaulted my staff, madam.'

'Jack's alright,' said Maggie. 'Aren't you, Jack? No harm done.'

'I... I don't want any trouble,' said the lad.

'Well, neither do we,' said Monty. He passed his card to Faulkner. 'I'm Dr Summers. We met about six months ago, when I admitted one of your patients. We need to talk.'

Faulkner hesitated but then said, 'You need an appointment, but as you're so insistent.' He gave Maggie a filthy look. 'Come this way.'

They walked through the office and down a white tiled corridor that stank of disinfectant and misery. Finally, he showed them into a dark room at the very end.

'Sit, sit,' he said. 'You have five minutes.'

My throat is sore from screaming. I'm on the first floor and I'm on my back, being wheeled along the corridor. I watch the ceiling lights slide over me as the buckles gnaw at my wrists and ankles.

I come to a stop and the orderly looks down on me.

'Hey, Hollywood. Stop thrashing around,' he says. 'You're going to have to wait a while, and you're making it worse.' Then he laughs. 'Lots of lunatics before you today.'

He places his hand on my forehead and strokes it.

'You'll feel better after the electricity, you'll see,' he says. 'You'll be all calm in there.' And he taps my temple.

I thrash some more, but he walks away.

CHAPTER FORTY-NINE

Maggie noticed Monty pull back his shoulders, as if steeling himself.

'I signed the papers to commit a woman called Ginny Watkins six months ago,' he said. 'As did you. I'm here to sign the documents to have her released. This is her mother, and she'll be taken into her care.'

The doctor scoffed.

'I know the patient you're talking about, but that's not how it works,' he said. 'You know that. There's been no correspondence about this, no meetings to discuss her progress. We have procedures for a reason. We need to ascertain that she's safe to release. There's a process to follow.'

Neither of them spoke.

'You can't just come and take her,' he said.

'Of course we can,' said Maggie. 'She shouldn't be here, and I want her back. She's coming with me. Today.'

'Madam—' started Dr Faulkner.

'Mr Summers here is her doctor,' she interrupted. 'He

says she's to be released and he'll sign the papers. That's all there is to it.'

'But I'm also her doctor, and we both need to sign papers, and I don't agree,' said Faulkner. 'She's not ready to be released.'

Monty moved his chair closer and leaned across the desk.

'Look,' he said. 'She was brought here under false pretences, as you well know, so you can let her out whenever you want. Don't pretend there are procedures when everything about this has been corrupt from the very start. You're getting paid a fair amount each month to keep her here, much more than you should. How do I know? Because I'm the one making the payments. But that money is stopping now, so you'll gain nothing by keeping her here.'

The doctor's eyes darted from Monty to Maggie and back again, but he didn't say anything.

'Doctor,' said Maggie, 'I'm sure there are many illegal activities going on under this roof. I don't know if Jack mentioned it, but we have a private detective outside, just by your gates. He'd be happy to escort you to the local precinct and see what they make of all this.'

'These so-called papers you talk about,' said Monty, 'you and I know it's just a formality – a front. There was no court order from a judge when Ginny was committed, so you can release her if you want. Nobody is checking up because she's not in the system. It's not the first time you've locked up a Hollywood woman without cause, I'm sure. Or any woman for that matter.'

'I have no idea what you're talking about,' said Dr Faulkner, lining up the notepad and pen on his desk.

'Oh, come on,' Monty said, laughing scornfully. 'That

poor actress, Frances Farmer, thrown in an asylum for eight years – for nothing more than drink-driving and being a foul-mouthed pain?'

'That wasn't here,' said Faulkner. 'I had nothing to do with that.'

'But I bet you've done similar over and over again,' said Monty. 'We love a badly behaved woman in Hollywood, don't we? But only in the movies, not in real life.'

Maggie pictured the women who weren't famous who'd been locked away, and the ones who weren't missed by anyone. This place must be full of them. Loud women, pregnant women, women who were simply inconvenient. Women like Ginny, who'd witnessed something they shouldn't have. Lock them up. Shut them up.

Dr Faulkner got up and walked to the window, staring at the trees outside.

'I'll let her go, but make it worth my while,' he said, not looking at them.

'With pleasure,' said Maggie. 'I'll have you arrested for attempted bribery, if you like. How's that for a start?'

He turned round in a fury.

'But *this* so-called doctor here,' he said, pointing to Monty, 'has done everything I have. Why aren't you threatening him?'

'Believe me she has,' said Monty. 'But I'm getting out of it. I've been in hell for years. You, however, don't seem to think what you're doing is wrong.'

'Release her now,' said Maggie, 'and we won't report you. We won't mention the extra money you were getting and we'll say you had no idea what was going on. But do it again,' she continued, 'put another woman away without good reason and all of this will come tumbling down on your head. We have someone watching you.'

Of course, they didn't, but would he risk calling their bluff? Faulkner didn't move for a few moments then, exasperated, he pulled a form from his drawer and pushed it towards Monty.

'Fill in her name and yours and sign it,' he said, irritated, 'then you can have her.'

Maggie burst out crying. Monty quickly scribbled the details and pushed the paper back.

Then Faulkner said, 'She's on the first floor, in the middle of treatment. So you'll have to wait.'

'Treatment?' Maggie got up, knocking the chair over. 'What treatment?'

'ECT,' he said. 'Electroconvulsive therapy. We had several sessions planned, but at least she'll benefit from the first one.'

'But she doesn't need treatment,' shouted Maggie.

Faulkner looked up at the clock on the wall.

'Too late,' he said. 'They took her up twenty minutes ago.'

I have been lifted onto a table. It's cold and hard and there are two orderlies at my feet, a nurse at my head. I glance to one side and see a metal box with dials on it. Then I feel something cold and thick being smeared onto my temples. I try to twist away but can hardly move.

'Will you stop fighting?' says the nurse. 'It won't hurt you, it's just the gel, that's all. So the electricity doesn't burn your skin.'

She shoves something hard into my mouth, between my teeth. It tastes of rubber and I spit it out. She does it again, clamping my chin with her hand this time.

'Take it,' she says, 'you don't want to bite your tongue in half, do you?'

I bite down with all the hate I have inside me.

CHAPTER FIFTY

Maggie and Monty charged out of Faulkner's office and raced down the corridor. Suddenly they were in the lobby again.

'ECT!' shouted Monty. 'Jack! Where is it?'

Jack peered from his cubicle and pointed to the staircase.

'First floor,' he said, dazed, 'but—'

They didn't wait to hear the rest. Maggie's heart thumped loud and mad as she flew up the stairs, two at a time. She stopped dead at the top and Monty crashed into her.

'Where is it? Where is it?' she said, looking frantically in all directions. She had to be in time, please. She couldn't fail Ginny now – not at the last hurdle.

'This way!' Monty shouted, pointing to a sign at the far end. She ran alongside him and together they slammed into a set of double doors and continued hurtling along the slippery corridor. At the very end was another set of double doors. Above it, a flashing red lamp.

That's it, keep going, thought Maggie. *She is just on the other side of that door. Ginny's waiting for you.*

But the doors felt so far away and she wanted to collapse and cry at the injustice of it all. After all these months of waiting, she couldn't possibly lose her now. *Please, let her be alright. Let Ginny be alright.* She bolted towards the flashing red light, which now she could see declared: *DO NOT ENTER.*

She held out both hands and pushed through the old wooden swing doors.

*S*omething padded is placed at my temples, the orderlies tug at my wrists and ankles to make sure the buckles are tight, and the nurse asks everyone: 'Ready?'

I'm sobbing and choking. The blood is roaring in my ears.

'Ready,' comes the reply.

She turns the dial. Nothing happens.

'Damn connection,' she says. 'Let's go again – everyone ready?'

'Ready,' comes the response.

Again nothing.

'It's the wire at the back,' says one of the orderlies. 'It happened last week. You can hear it buzz when it's working. Let me take a look.'

He walks behind my head and his knees crack as he crouches down. I can hear the tinkle of metal and screws.

'There,' he says eventually, dusting his trousers off, 'that should do it. Give it another try.'

I'm biting down hard, waiting to be destroyed, when a

storm of voices whips through me. Everyone is shouting, and the confusion is terrifying, so I bite even harder.

A man is yelling about papers and prosecuting everyone in the room.

Suddenly, there's a loud click, a hush falls and the machine next to my head buzzes to life. The world is heavy with hesitation, and I'm teetering on a precipice, unsure which way I'll fall.

A hand pulls the electrodes from my temples and takes the rubber stopper from my mouth. Someone loosens my buckles, and I'm free.

It's then that I hear it. A terrible sound. A blood-curdling scream.

'It's not her!' shouts a woman. 'It's not her!'

CHAPTER FIFTY-ONE

'Where's Ginny?' screamed Maggie. 'It's not her! Where is she?'

Monty pulled her away and leaned over the girl on the table.

'That's Ginny,' he said. 'It's her, the girl at the party. The one I brought here.'

A rush of terror swept through Maggie as she looked at the girl one more time.

'No – that's not my daughter!'

She stared into the girl's eyes as they stared back at her in confusion. Then Maggie saw something there she recognised. It was a face she'd seen just days ago, in a framed photo. This was the girl who they'd said was dead. The one who they'd said had shot herself.

'I told them I wasn't Ginny,' said the girl. 'That they'd mixed us up. But they kept telling me I was. But Ginny's gone.'

Maggie's blood froze as her brain frantically tried to

understand. Her heart knew before her head what this meant, and in that moment, it split wide open.

She fell to her knees and howled.

CHAPTER FIFTY-TWO

Private bungalow number 4,
Beverly Hills Hotel, Los Angeles

Stella had just smoothed on her Desert Flower body lotion when the phone rang. It was Brodsky.

'Did they find her?' she asked excitedly. 'Did they get Ginny?'

There was a silence, then in a gentle voice, he told her what had happened.

'What do you *mean* it wasn't her?' she asked. 'Monty took her there himself. He said she was there.'

'The girl he had committed wasn't Ginny,' he said. 'Stan had told him it was, but he lied.'

'But I don't understand,' said Stella. 'Maybe she was under Virginia Rose – did you ask?'

'Stella?'

'Yes?' she said, her voice full of apprehension.

'The girl under Ginny's name – it was Sandy,' he said. 'It had always been Sandy.'

There was a pause while this information sunk in. Stella's hand covered her mouth.

'No,' she cried. 'Does that mean...' Her tears were choking her now. 'Does that mean that the girl who died, who Max shot...'

Brodsky sighed. 'I'm sorry,' he said. 'It was Ginny who died that night. Sandy saw everything.'

Stella's heart lurched. 'Poor, poor Maggie – my god, how will she bear it?'

'I know,' said Brodsky. 'It's the worst news possible.'

'Oh, Jim,' she cried, 'I need to go to her – I'll come straight away. Where is she? I'll call a cab right now.'

'Look Stella, you'll only upset yourself even more,' he said with concern. 'And she won't know you're there. She's at the local hospital – a proper medical hospital – heavily sedated. They're keeping her overnight. Monty got Sandy released – she's there, too.'

'But darling, I'm her friend,' Stella admonished. 'I can't just sit here while she's going through hell.'

However lovely some men were, they just didn't understand, did they? This bond between women.

'I have to do something useful,' she said. 'I have to do something *now*.'

'Tomorrow,' he said firmly. 'Let's pick her up together.'

'I don't get it,' said Stella. 'Why would Stan do such a thing?'

'No idea,' said Brodsky. 'But we'll get to the bottom of it, I promise. In the meantime, stay put. Maggie will need you when she comes back.'

Stella didn't respond.

'Look, I'd better go now,' Brodsky continued. 'I'm here with one of my old buddies at the precinct, trying to build a case against Max and Stan. Sandy's in no state for much, but once she's better, it will all hinge on her. There's lots to do.'

He rang off and Stella sat on the edge of the bath trying to take it all in. Her eyes scanned the room and stopped at the sofa, where she'd discarded the latest ransom demand scrawled on the back of the large nude photo of herself.

Stan Fisher had a lot to answer for.

She considered her options and realised there were really only two: do nothing or do something.

She went to her dressing table and applied a light base, dusted her face with powder and pencilled her eyebrows, brushing out the line with a soft toothbrush she kept for this purpose, the way Maggie had shown her. Then she applied mascara and lipstick, and carefully slipped on her navy and white Dior belted day dress. Finally, she tied a white headscarf over her head and stared at herself in the mirror.

Being famous meant she'd rarely had to do much for herself. If there was a problem, she'd wait and someone else would solve it. Well, today was different. She was sick of waiting for others to make everything alright.

'Christalla Petrakis,' she said out loud, 'today you're taking care of business yourself.'

She opened her wardrobe and felt along the top shelf, where she found the scarf. She unwrapped her gun, loaded it and dropped it into her handbag. She donned her Gucci sunglasses and walked out.

Then she got a cab to Stan Fisher's house.

CHAPTER FIFTY-THREE

The Fisher Mansion, Los Feliz, Los Angeles

Stan lived thirty minutes away in an ostentatious mansion in the exclusive hillside neighbourhood of Los Feliz. Stella had visited a handful of times, in the early days. She remembered loving the champagne brunches and raucous parties, and being impressed by the estate, too. But that had been a lifetime ago.

Today was a different story. She got out of the cab and stared up at the flaking terracotta stucco walls. The two palm trees on either side of the gates were parched yellow, and the uniformed security man who usually suffered for hours in his guard box was absent. The gate was ajar, so she slipped inside and quickly walked up the dusty drive. The purple Mexican petunia, which had once carpeted a huge area, had withered, and weeds had choked the life from the scarlet frangipani.

She glanced to one side, where Stan's sports cars used to line up, shiny and ready for adventure. Today, there was just one car: a dusty old blue Lincoln Capri.

Steadying her breath, she opened her bag and checked

the contents. She had no idea what she was about to do but felt compelled to confront him. Standing in front of the huge oak doors, she pressed the bell and heard a mournful chime deep in the belly of the house. Then a heavy tread of footsteps approached and the door swung open.

There stood Stan, in his paisley silk dressing gown, hair sticking up on one side and a cigar in one hand.

'Stella? What the—'

She dived under his arm and straight into the hall, getting as far as the living room door before he caught up.

'Hey!' He grabbed her arm and turned her around, but she kicked him hard in the shin and he let go as he yelped in shock.

She ran into the living room and started pulling the leather-bound books off his shelves, the magazines from his monstrous coffee table, throwing papers on his desk to the floor, looking in drawers.

'Stella?' he shouted. 'Stella! What the hell are you doing?'

He stood on the threshold, watching her as she quickly surveyed the room. She started at the other end, searching under and behind anything that wasn't fixed – cushions, chairs, even in a briefcase that was slung on the sofa.

'Where are they?' she said. Her eyes darted all over the room. Under the rug? She flipped it over. No. Under the sofa? She pushed it to one side – nothing but dust balls. 'Where are the photos?'

'What?' he began.

She spun round, a wild look in her eyes. 'Don't you *dare* pretend you don't know what I'm talking about,' she spat, her Greek accent in full flow now. 'The photos of me. The French photos you've been using to blackmail me.'

He opened his mouth to speak, but then didn't.

'Hand them over, Stan,' she demanded. She started kicking all the papers that she'd thrown to the floor. 'I know it's you blackmailing me, and I know about all your sordid crimes. Give me the photos or I'll get you locked up for so long you'll never see daylight again.'

He walked towards her and stood inches away, breathing hard. She raised her chin to face him square on. Could she fight him off? Not a chance.

'Let me give you some advice,' he said, his voice deep and flat. 'Don't ever threaten me.'

'And why's that, darling?' She was working hard to keep her tone steady. 'Will you have me killed?'

He turned away and sat heavily in an armchair.

'Stella, go home,' he said. 'I'm expecting visitors and they're not the sociable kind.'

She sat down opposite him, still clutching her bag.

'After all these years, you betray me,' she said. 'You're a snake, Stan. You kept the photos and had them all along, waiting to cash in one day. Hit on hard times, have you?'

He rubbed his face. 'If I told you what I owed,' he said, shaking his head. 'And to who. It would make your toes curl. And there are three ex-wives…'

'Poor Stan,' she said sarcastically, 'and gambling debts, too. And I'm sure none of it's your fault, right? Why blackmail *me*, Stan? What have I done except make you rich?'

His face hardened. 'Why *not* you?' he said. 'You're not so special, Stella. I've got something on everyone. It was simply your turn.'

How many others, apart from herself and Monty, had he blackmailed over the years?

'Admittedly, you weren't my first choice,' he said, 'because I actually like you. I mean, I haven't used them for all this time, have I?' A shadow crossed his face. 'But I owe a *lot*.'

'If you needed money for a debt—'

'It's not just a debt, it's the *mob* – don't you understand?'

'Well, you could have asked,' she said.

He laughed and looked to one side, as if sharing the joke with someone else in the room.

'Oh, you'd love that,' he said. 'Me coming cap in hand to the great Stella Hope.'

'And blackmail's better?' she asked. 'Where's your shame? Your loyalty?'

'Hey,' he said, leaning forward, 'I've done more than enough for you over the years. I've spent my *life* protecting you – in fact, all the talent at the studio. Things you know about, and things you don't. You don't know the half of what I've done to look after you.'

She stared at him and considered not showing all her cards just yet, but couldn't help herself.

'And Max,' she said. 'I know what you did to cover up for Max, that night at the Oscars party.'

He shifted in his seat. 'I... I don't know what you're talking about.'

'He shot that poor girl, and you got him out of there quick as anything. Pretending it was a drugs raid – pushing him into my car.'

Stan stared at her, frowning. She could see his brain whirring, trying to figure out how she knew.

'She's out, by the way,' Stella said. 'The girl you put in the asylum.'

His face fell.

'Surprise!' she said.

'What...? How...?' She could see it dawn on him. 'Monty,' he said.

'Don't bother going after him. I put him on a plane this morning, so he's long gone.' *He'll be at the train station now*, she thought, *and out of California by nightfall.*

Stan looked at the cigar he'd been holding this whole time. It had gone out, so he relit it and puffed.

'Well, someone's been busy,' he said. 'But what's all this to you, Stella? What do you stand to gain? Why do you even care?'

She felt the anger build inside her.

'I care,' she began, spitting out the words with fury, 'because Maggie, my dear friend, has been searching for her daughter for months. And today she discovered that Ginny died at that party, in the most horrific of ways.'

Stan puffed at his cigar and looked away.

'But that's not all, darling, is it?' she continued. 'You covered it up and didn't even allow her the dignity of a proper funeral, with a gravestone with her own name on it. *That's* why I care, Stan. Because unlike you, I have a heart.'

He sighed, then said in quiet voice, 'You'd better go now.'

'Why did you do it?' she asked. 'Why did you swap them over? The two girls?'

'I'm not saying anything else. Get out.'

'I mean I understand you getting Max out of the room, but why pretend it was Sandy who died?'

'Look,' he said, leaning forward, a bear about to pounce,

'I don't want to hurt you, Stella, but if you carry on, I can't—'

She was sick of it all, sick of him and his lies, the threats. A rage soared inside her. In a flash, she'd opened her bag and was pointing the gun at him.

'Stella, what the hell!'

'Talk,' she shouted. 'Why did you do it?'

'For God's sake, Stella – you're not going to shoot. Just put it—'

She pointed the gun to one side and pulled the trigger. A vase on the sideboard exploded. The noise shocked her. She hadn't fired it since she'd had lessons, all those years ago, and she suddenly remembered the thrill of it.

'Jesus Christ, Stella! Stop it, right now.'

'Tell me why you did it,' she said.

'Stop being stupid, just—'

She shot at the wall behind his head and a picture crashed down.

He turned and stared, aghast.

Her hand was shaking so much now that she had to clasp the gun with both hands, her handbag still swinging from her wrist. A surge of adrenalin made her feel anything was possible. She could shoot him, God, she really could.

'Talk,' she said, 'or the next one's for you.'

He put out both hands as if to calm her but stared at the gun as he spoke.

'It was just a cover up, alright?' he said. 'Plain and simple. Some photographer had been following Max, got pictures of him kissing Ginny and was desperate to publish them. Then Max goes and shoots her at the party. Can you imagine if that had got out? Max kills his secret girlfriend? Even as a "suicide" it would look bad. It would have destroyed his career. I had to move quickly.'

'So fast that Sandy's mother didn't even see the body.'

He shrugged. 'I gave her some jewellery her daughter had been wearing, a cheap necklace. And who wants to see their kid with a gunshot wound to the head? That was some mess to clean up. Anyway, her mother wouldn't have recognised her.'

Stella laughed, incredulous. 'Of course not! Because it wasn't her kid! It was Ginny. And you locked up Sandy because she's expendable, too? To protect the mighty Max's reputation?'

'I was doing my job,' said Stan, as if he'd had no choice in the matter. 'I had to – he's my biggest star.'

'Oh, I see – Max's reputation matters, but mine you're willing to sacrifice to pay off a debt.'

'I was desperate, and I thought you'd pay up straight away,' he said. 'I have to admit, you surprised me when you didn't.'

Her arms were aching now, and she moved a little in her seat. He got up slowly and she kept the gun pointed at him as he wandered around the room while he spoke.

'Look, Stella, who are the police going to believe? Me or a two-bit actress who's just come out of an asylum? And anyway, you know I've got most of the police department in my pocket. Let's just make this situation work for both of us, okay? Give me the $50,000 and I'll give you the photos. I don't have them here, but I'll bring them to you.'

She would never believe another word he said, but she let him carry on talking.

'And to show there's no hard feelings,' he continued, 'I'll

speak to someone upstairs and get them to let you off your contract. How about it? I'll make sure you can go to any studio and do any work you want. But you have to drop this Sandy/Ginny affair – just let it go. I can get some money to your friend Maggie, too, if that helps – something every month. I'm sorry about Ginny, she was a nice kid, but what happened has happened.'

Stella shook her head. 'That's a woman's life you're talking about,' she said.

'Don't be ridiculous, Stella,' he said, impatiently now. 'You probably didn't even know her, and she was sleeping with Max. What happened at the Sherman Mansion has got nothing to do with you. Look, it's just a tragic situation best forgotten.'

'So let me get this straight,' she said. 'I say nothing to anyone and *still* pay off your debt?' she asked.

He laughed. 'Who'd believe it, but you're actually my last chance. Do you want me to beg? With your fifty thousand I can make the amount I need. Without it, I don't know what they'll do.'

'And if I refuse?'

'By the weekend, every gossip rag in Hollywood will have you naked on their front page.'

Stella shrugged. 'Hmmm… I think your price is too high. Let you and Max get away with everything – as you always have – and all for the sake of hushing up a scandal. I think I'd sooner be ridiculed than let you get away with this.'

A flash of anger crossed his face, and he suddenly lurched towards her.

Without hesitation, she pulled the trigger. His scream was full of fury, as he clutched his arm. The bullet had entered just below his shoulder and blood was now oozing out from between his fingers.

'You shot me!' he shouted, blood filling his hand now. 'You bitch! You shot me!' He bent over gasping, in shock.

A thrill swept right through her, as she now held the gun steadily in her hand. He was dancing on the spot, yelling in pain. Imagine finishing him off! How wonderful would that feel? She could save the world from Stan Fisher once and for all, and all the other terrible deeds he had yet to commit.

He was still clutching his arm as she dropped the gun in her bag and dashed from the room. His screams filled the corridor as he lumbered behind her, but she was too quick for him.

Within moments, she was on the street, adjusting her headscarf and hailing a cab that had just turned the corner. She got in, put on her Guccis and sped off into the early evening sunset.

THE
LOS ANGELES
EXAMINER

September 18, 1954

CRIME REPORT:
MURDER OF STAR STUDIOS'
MOVIE MOGUL

Late last night, the body of Star Studios' Executive Manager, Stan Fisher, aged 54, was found by his housekeeper in his Los Feliz mansion. He'd been shot four times – three in the chest and once in the arm.

A statement from the Los Angeles Police Department says the investigation is ongoing, but as yet there are no known suspects. Rumours that Mr Fisher owed large sums of money to an organised crime syndicate have not been confirmed.

When asked to comment, Ida Kellner, of Star Studios and secretary to the deceased, said: 'I knew Stan Fisher for twenty-five years. He worked hard and was always on time. That's the best I can say.'

Mr Fisher leaves three ex-wives, none of whom were available for comment.

MATILDA MAYHEW'S
CONFIDENTIAL

September 24, 1954

PICTURE EXCLUSIVE!
STELLA HOPE AS YOU'VE NEVER SEEN HER BEFORE!
SCREEN GODDESS REVEALS BLACKMAIL ORDEAL

'I'm not ashamed of my past,' she says, in a heartfelt interview about nude photos.

Oscar-nominated screen goddess, Stella Hope, discusses her hush-hush past in a bid to beat her blackmailers.

Today, Miss Hope and I shared a delicious mimosa in the Polo Lounge of the Beverly Hills Hotel, as she confided that when she arrived in Hollywood as an ambitious nineteen-year-old starlet, she faced some very difficult decisions.

'I was penniless and the rent was due,' she said. 'Like any young Hollywood hopeful, I was desperate to make a name for myself. So I decided to do whatever it took to survive. I agreed to pose for some French photos, as they're called – wearing nothing but my smile. I was naïve and I took the photographer at his word when he assured me that my face would be obscured. He paid me fifty dollars and it helped me keep heart and soul together for the next few weeks.'

And just six months later, young Stella was paired with Max Whitman, becoming the hottest couple both on and off screen for several years.

'As soon as I was spotted by Star Studios,' she recalls, 'I was assured that these photographs would be found and destroyed. But just a few months ago, I discovered that someone had taken possession of them and was trying to blackmail me. I received several threatening letters, demanding a large amount of money. If I refused, they said they would release these images to the world.'

But in a remarkably plucky move, steely Stella has refused to pay up, and instead is calling checkmate on her blackmailer. She's released this naked photo of herself, along with this interview, to beat the blackmailer at his own game.

Asked if she'd name her blackmailer, Miss Hope said: 'No. His name won't cross my lips again. All I will say is that Star Studios have neglected their duties, and if they'd like to sue me for breaking my contract, they are welcome to try.'

Stella assures us she has no plans to turn her back on Hollywood. In fact, she has an exciting new project coming up that she will announce very soon.

When asked if she'd like to pass on a message to her fans, she said: 'While you may be shocked to see this photograph – and any others that may be published – I implore you to look at this girl's face and see the fear and determination there. And if you've ever loved any of my movies or bought a magazine because I was on the cover, then I hope you can find it in your heart to show some love to this younger Stella, too. Because she's still part of me. She's the girl who just wanted to make movies, and sprinkle a little stardust into people's lives.'

Till next time, movie lovers.
Your friend,

Matilda

CHAPTER FIFTY-FOUR

Private bungalow number 5,
Beverly Hills Hotel, Los Angeles
November 1954

Maggie stood in front of the mirror inspecting her face. It had been eight weeks since she'd discovered that Ginny had died, and this was her first social engagement. Well, it was just a lunch with Stella, but still. It was the first time she was stepping out and *not* attending to some business or other connected to Ginny's death, such as another interview with the police, with Brodsky by her side, or a visit to the funeral parlour to arrange a new headstone. Today she was doing something just for herself.

She took her Max Factor Clear Red from her pocket and slicked it on her lips. She'd already applied a little mascara and some rouge, and she almost looked like her normal self. The weeks spent indoors had taken their toll, but her skin was finally returning to its rosy hue. She was staying in the bungalow next door to Stella's, which Stella had insisted on renting for her, so Maggie could have some privacy in her grief when she wanted, and company when she didn't. What would she have done without Stella these past few weeks? Together, they'd talked late into the night, Maggie telling her about Ginny as a child, the films she'd made in London and her dreams of Hollywood.

They'd shared several late-night whiskies, and Maggie had also recounted the events of that traumatic day at the psychiatric hospital several times, the day she'd discovered that Sandy had survived and Ginny had not.

Stella hadn't just provided good company, she'd also showered her with impromptu gifts: a luxurious cashmere throw, a new nail polish she'd liked the look of, relaxing massages in Maggie's room. She even suggested they go on a girls' weekend away if Maggie felt like it, wherever she fancied.

But there was only one thing Maggie truly wanted; she needed a certain favour from Stella. It was a very specific act of kindness, and after discussing it with her, Stella had happily agreed.

Rubbing some Three Flowers Brilliantine on her fingertips, Maggie swept back her hair with her hands, then looked at herself. She was thinner, the line between her brows a little deeper, but at least now the mirror reflected someone she recognised. During those first few weeks, her grief-filled days had left her so distraught that it felt as if a madness had descended like a storm and claimed her. But slowly she was beginning to rebuild her life from the wreckage.

She knew that the way to survive was to think of the good in Ginny's life and the promise in her own future. The way Ginny had died would always be with her, but she couldn't allow it to determine the rest of her years. She had to believe that the days ahead of her could eventually hold happy, carefree moments, in honour of her daughter if not for herself.

Stan Fisher was already dead, but the case against Max was ongoing. She needed strength for that. She needed hope. Whether he'd be arrested and go to trial was uncertain, and there was, of course, the unshakeable fear that, with his money and connections, he'd sidestep any punishment at all. She knew it was a fact of life that men like Max Whitman rarely paid the price for their crimes.

The phone rang. It was reception telling her that Miss Stella Hope had just returned from her shopping trip and was waiting for her in the Polo Lounge.

Stella was immaculate in an understated Givenchy cream linen dress.

'Darling,' she said, rising from a corner booth to give Maggie a kiss on each cheek. After a quick glance at the menus, they ordered a dry martini and a cobb salad each. 'So how are you today?' she asked, peering at her with concern.

Maggie smiled. 'Better, thank you. I feel like I'm finding myself again. I've dreaded contact with people during the past few weeks, but I've been looking forward to this.'

'Well, that's excellent news,' said Stella, beaming. 'Now, what about the nightmares?' she asked, raising an eyebrow. 'Are you sleeping at all?'

Maggie nodded. 'Actually, I am,' she said. 'It took a while to really accept that she's gone, and sometimes I still replay it all in my mind, that terrible evening. The way it might have all happened.'

Tears sprung to Stella's eyes and she quickly blinked them back before putting one hand on Maggie's arm. 'Try not to torture yourself,' she said.

'I'm okay,' said Maggie, patting Stella's hand. 'Thankfully, it's not as bad as it was – I just can't see the scene as clearly anymore.'

'Well, that's a good thing,' said Stella.

There was a pause between them, then Maggie spoke. 'Anyway, let's talk about happier things, shall we? What have I missed?'

So they made easy chit-chat for a while, Stella filling her in on the latest Hollywood gossip as they sipped their drinks.

'Isn't this lovely?' said Stella, when their salads were placed before them. 'Two girlfriends having lunch and a good gossip. It's wonderful to have you back, Maggie. I know it's a long road ahead, but don't forget – you're stronger than you think.'

'Thank you,' said Maggie, spearing a piece of lettuce. 'I don't know if I've ever thanked you properly, in fact. For bringing me here, helping me look for Ginny, taking care of me.'

Stella gave her hand a quick squeeze. 'I wish none of it had happened, but I'm glad I was able to help.'

They sat in comfortable silence for a moment then Maggie grinned and asked, 'Sooo... how's Mr Jim Brodsky? Still conducting his investigations?'

Colour rose in Stella's face.

'Stella Hope, are you actually blushing?' said Maggie, laughing. 'What's happened? Are you two an item now?'

'Yes, well – let's just say the preliminary investigations have led to some interesting developments,' said Stella.

'I'm going to need details,' said Maggie. 'Witness statements, evidence...'

'Oh, I couldn't possibly,' said Stella, pretending to look shocked. 'Well, not until we've had a few more drinks, at least. But seriously, he's good for me. He keeps making plans, mapping our future. I think this one might stick.'

Maggie took a sip of her martini. 'I'm so pleased for you,' she said.

Stella sat back and looked at her friend. 'And what about you? What of your future?' she asked.

'Oh, heavens,' said Maggie. Fleetingly she thought of Tom, the cameraman who was keen on her back at Ealing Studios. 'I'm a wreck right now – I'm not ready for a relationship. Maybe one day, but not for a while.'

'No, I didn't mean a man,' said Stella. 'Your future, your career. You have such a talent, Maggie. Have you thought any more about my proposal? Opening a make-up academy here? I'd happily back you.'

Maggie sliced into her avocado and said, 'It's what I've always wanted, but I just don't know if I can stay in Hollywood. Ginny came here so full of hope, and who knows if Max will ever be punished for killing her? I mean, if I stay, am I going to think about her the whole time?'

Stella opened her bag and took out the *Los Angeles Examiner*.

'I was going to show you this later,' she said, unfolding the newspaper. It happened a few days ago but has only just made the paper.'

'What is it?' asked Maggie.

'Something that might help you decide.'

Stella moved her plate and lay the paper on the table. She pointed to a photo of Max and the headline beneath it.

ACADEMY-WINNER MAX WHITMAN
TAKES OWN LIFE

Maggie gasped and felt the heat rise in her face.
'Go on, read it,' said Stella.
Maggie traced the words with her finger.

Academy Award winner, Mr Max Whitman, aged 46, was found in the Penthouse Suite of the Sunset Tower Hotel on Saturday, 6 November, having died from an apparent barbiturate overdose. Mr Whitman was under investigation for the murder of actress Ginny Watkins (Virginia Rose) earlier this year, and police say his arrest was imminent. He left no note.

Once one of the highest-grossing movie stars in Hollywood, Mr Whitman made his name on the screen as the sweet-talking gentleman cowboy, though he'd been attempting more serious roles of late. However, with the recent accusations, his contract had been terminated and the actor who'd once been half of Hollywood's Golden Couple, with ex-wife Stella Hope, hadn't been seen in public for weeks.

Miss Hope was unavailable for comment.

When Maggie had finished, she looked up at Stella, searching her face for a reaction.
'It's alright,' said Stella. 'You can be pleased. I don't mind.'
'I... I don't know what to say,' said Maggie.
'What is there to say?' said Stella, lighting a cigarette. 'He killed Ginny.' She took a drag of her cigarette. 'He

was bound to go to trial, and even if he wasn't convicted, his career was over.' She glanced around the room then turned her attention back to the newspaper. 'This was his easy route out.'

'Are you alright?' asked Maggie.

Stella nodded and tapped her cigarette in the ashtray. 'I fell out of love with him years ago. And I have Jim now.' She smiled. 'So that helps, too. You know, Max and I were only ever really happy for a few weeks – at the start.'

'Still,' said Maggie, smoothing the paper with her hand. 'He was your husband. I wouldn't blame you for feeling sad, or grieving for him.'

'I'm honestly fine,' said Stella, and she really looked like she was. 'I lost him long ago.' She motioned to the waiter for two more martinis and they appeared almost immediately.

'You know,' Stella continued, 'there was only one moment when I doubted my decision to leave him. When I wondered if I should have stayed.'

'Really?' said Maggie, leaning forward. 'When was that?'

'The night Ginny died, the night of the car crash. Remember how he rushed back to the car to save me? But I'd already got out?'

'Yes,' said Maggie, 'and he was so badly injured, and you were blamed.'

'Exactly,' said Stella. 'We'd already talked about divorce by then, and I did stop and think to myself later that he must really love me. I mean, what kind of mad devotion sends a man running back to a burning car for his wife? Or his soon-to-be *ex*-wife, when he's already injured? I felt terrible about it, and everyone called him a hero.'

'Well, you wouldn't be human if you didn't feel guilty,' said Maggie. 'It was such a selfless act on his part.'

There was a pause, then Stella took a long drag of her cigarette and raised an eyebrow.

'What's that look for?' asked Maggie, smiling.

'Well,' Stella replied, 'it turns out Max Whitman might not be quite the hero we think.'

'What do you mean?' said Maggie.

'I remembered it months later, but I never told anyone. It came to me clear as day,' said Stella. Then she pressed her lips together, to try to stop laughing.

'Go on,' said Maggie.

'After the crash,' Stella continued, trying to keep a straight face, 'he wasn't coming back to the car for me at all.'

Maggie shook her head, not understanding.

'Darling,' Stella said, 'he was coming back for his Oscar.'

Maggie gasped. It was just too awful – but hilarious, too. Diners nearby turned and stared as Stella's laughter rang out loud.

Maggie burst into laughter too, the first time in months.

'A huge star with an even bigger ego!' cried Stella. Then, in a quieter voice, 'And, yes, I know I'm one to talk.'

EPILOGUE

The evening of the Oscars ceremony
Five months later
Wednesday, March 30, 1955

*T*his is Matilda Mayhew reporting live from the 27th Academy Awards, at the RKO Pantages Theatre, Hollywood, for NBC.

Tonight is Hollywood's most important night, and it certainly hasn't disappointed if your name is Stella Hope.

In a well-deserved win, our favourite screen goddess has just claimed Best Actress for her performance in Queen of Desire. Tonight, she was stunning in a gold Dior evening gown, as she stepped out with her dashing new fiancé, Jim Brodsky. Accompanying them was Maggie Watkins, Stella's good friend and make-up artist, and young newcomer, Cynthia Clark, who is starring with Stella in her next production.

We all love a good comeback story, and Stella's is one of the best. In the footsteps of Marilyn Monroe and Marlon Brando, she's just launched Hope Productions, her own company where she's a free agent to work with whoever she chooses. And it's not just directors, writers and actors *queuing around the block for her. She has a new generation of younger fans, too, who've joined those she's had for years. It seems Stella can do no wrong. This Oscar is her second award this month. Just a couple of weeks ago, she travelled to London to receive a prestigious BAFTA for Best Foreign Actress in the Ealing Studios'* film, A Heart Like No Other. *What a class act!*

Maggie looked out of the stretch limousine window as they left the Oscars ceremony and watched the Hollywood streets glide past. It wasn't for everyone, this town, but she'd grown fond of it and had decided to stay. Somehow, she felt closer to Ginny here too, and when she thought of her now, she smiled.

Sitting next to her was Cynthia, who'd been caught up in the whirlwind excitement of the evening. She was a joy to be around and had been giving them all a running commentary on which stars she'd spotted and what they were wearing (along with her scores out of ten).

On the row behind, Stella and Brodsky were chatting quietly in the corner. He was holding her hand as they discussed plans for the next day. In Stella's other hand was her Academy Award. She sparkled when she was close to him, and it was clear they were blissfully happy. Maggie had noticed that many of Stella's insecurities seemed to have gently fallen away too, especially now she had created such a buzz around Hope Productions and was in high demand. In the space of a few months, she'd surrounded herself with actors, directors, crew and writers as passionate as she was about this new future. *Well,* thought Maggie, *that's what comes from being an icon of Stella's stature – you inspire deep devotion.*

As she nestled back in her seat, Maggie thought of her own future here. In just one week, she was opening the doors to her hair and make-up academy, Maggie's Place. She was thrilled to be sharing her years of experience, and helping young female make-up artists take their first steps in the industry.

Maggie smiled and leaned her head on the window. She thought of the favour she'd asked of Stella months ago – a meeting with Max. Stella had come up with some story to see him, then taken Maggie up to his room and left.

He had looked terrible, and she was glad. Face puffy, sweaty, unshaven. She thought he might call security, but instead, he'd stood by the sofa staring at her, as if he'd seen a ghost. She didn't say much, just asked if he was looking forward to the trial. And how he thought he'd fare in prison, assuming he didn't get the gas chamber. The fear etched deep in his face as she spoke.

Then she took the bottle of pink pills from her bag, unscrewed the lid and emptied them into a pile on the table, next to his whisky. For him, an escape from humiliation and shame. Not that he deserved it. For her, of course, something much more important: justice for Ginny. Dropping the empty bottle in her bag, she left. He hadn't said a word.

She stared out of the window now and as the car took a bend, the Hollywood sign appeared on the horizon. She let out a gentle, satisfied sigh.

Everyone's right about this place, she thought. *If you want something bad enough, there's always a way.*

AUTHOR'S NOTE

Contains spoilers

A *Beautiful Way to Die* is inspired by the true crime cases that Hollywood has swept under the carpet. From the 1920s to the mid-1950s, when the studios were all-powerful, they often had 'fixers' at their head, men who – like Stan Fisher – were employed to make crimes disappear. They were willing to do anything to save their actors' reputations. To a lesser extent, fixers still exist today.

Famous fixers of the time are now Hollywood folklore, and include MGM's Eddie Mannix and Howard Strickling, and Twentieth Century Fox's Harry Brand. Ex-cop and private investigator Fred Otash was also a fixer, sometimes working both sides, as well as for scandal magazine *Confidential*. These men have often been depicted in films and books, either as themselves or as thinly veiled characters such as in *Hail, Caesar!*, *Chinatown*, *Hollywoodland* and *LA Confidential*.

Here's some detail on the true stories mentioned in the book, that show the darker side of Hollywood.

Kirk Douglas and Jean Spangler

After appearing in a film with Kirk Douglas in 1949, Jean Spangler, a bit-part actress, went missing. Two days later, her bag was found in Griffith Park, with a note inside. It read: *Kirk, can't wait any longer. Going to Dr Scott. It will work best this way while mother away.* Soon after, Kirk Douglas called the police to say that he wasn't the Kirk in the note, and that he'd never met Jean (despite having just worked with her). He later said that he did know her, but they weren't friends (and he was in Palm Springs at the time of her disappearance). The police didn't investigate it further. Theories include that she may have been pregnant and had undergone a termination that went wrong. Jean was never found.

Peg Entwhistle

Hollywood is full of actors and actresses who never make it. Peg Entwhistle was a young starlet who was in just one film before taking her own life. She climbed to the top of the 'H' on the Hollywood sign and in desperation threw herself off. She was just twenty-four.

Frances Farmer

This promising actress, who'd already achieved a degree of fame, was sent to a brutal asylum for eight years. Her mother committed her, pointing out erratic behaviour, heavy drinking and a hate of authority as justification. But Frances wasn't insane, she was just badly behaved. Her lurid life story, *Will There Really Be a Morning?*, which was published posthumously and recounts the shocking treatment she received in the asylum, has since been discredited as her ghostwriter's attempt to clear her own debts. That's not to say that Frances *didn't* experience horrors while locked up. Remarkably, when she left the asylum, she made a minor comeback on television.

Patricia Douglas

It was common practice for girls to be shipped into Hollywood parties – as Sandy is in this book. For a few dollars and the promise of a hot meal, they'd sing, dance and provide entertainment. But sometimes 'entertainment' would also mean sex. Patricia Douglas, a dancer, was just seventeen when she decided to take the studio to court after being raped at an MGM party. Although the crime hit the front pages, a studio smear campaign followed. The district attorney was friends with the head of MGM and dropped the case. Patricia didn't work in Hollywood again. *Girl 27* is a documentary by David Stenn about what happened.

The casting couch

A Beautiful Way to Die is also set against the backdrop of the 'casting couch' of 1950s Hollywood and London. This phrase – which often refers to exploitative behaviour in the acting profession – is used to describe someone with less power being forced to perform sexual favours for someone senior, in order to advance their career. The practice was rife in the 1950s, a time when powerful men could demand what they wanted from desperate women. If the women didn't comply, they'd be labelled 'difficult', work would dry up and their careers were often ruined. Fast forward seventy odd years – in 2017, we saw Harvey Weinstein's crimes hit the front pages, telling of how he wrecked dozens of actresses' lives and careers. You have to ask, what has changed?

Other facts in the book

Here's where I've taken a liberty with the facts for the sake of the story.

By the mid-late 1950s, some actors had started pulling away from the studios, not wanting to sign contracts, and setting up their own companies. Like Stella Hope, actors such as Marilyn Monroe and Marlon Brando were branching out with their own production companies, but in reality, a few years later than stated in this book.

Audrey Hepburn actually received her Academy Award in New York, not LA, as the Oscars that year was televised from both cities. Also, the gap between being nominated for an Oscar and the Awards ceremony is much shorter today than mentioned here. *Roman Holiday* was released in September 1953, not January 1954, when Max and Ginny watch it. It's thought that the Skyview bar was given its name in the early 1960s not 1950s, but the spectacular view was the same.

The layout of Ealing Studios is fiction, though the meeting room with the round table did exist, as did the canteen where much flirting took place. Today, Ealing Village is still a beautiful estate of art-deco flats, boasting a pool, clubhouse and tennis courts.

If you want an insight into life as an actress back then, read these – the most entertaining books I came upon during research: *Miss D and Me: Life with the Invincible Bette Davis* by Kathryn Sermak, *Ava Gardner: The Secret Conversations* by Peter Evans and Ava Gardner, and *Behind the Shoulder Pads: Tales I Tell My Friends* by Joan Collins.

And, yes, I wrote a book set in Hollywood so I could watch lots of films. Here are the ones I particularly loved. *The Snake Pit* (Olivia de Havilland is sent to an asylum – that's all you need to know), *The Sweet Smell of Success* (Tony Curtis and Burt Lancaster on power and corruption with such a sharp, bleak script – it's wonderful), *Hollywoodland* (Eddie Mannix and the cover up around Superman actor George Reeves' death), *All About Eve* (Bette Davis as an older actress stressing out about her protégée's scheming ways). And, of course, *Sunset Boulevard*, the ultimate movie about movies, about a star trying to make a comeback. Go watch them all.

ACKNOWLEDGEMENTS

My first thanks go to Charlotte Levin, whose tireless support and constant badgering kept me on deadline. Without our writing sprints I'd still be on chapter one. Her plot thoughts were also invaluable. Also to my writing group friends, Kate Wheeler, Marianne Holmes and Liz Ottosson for their cheerleading over the years and willingness to talk character and plot so readily.

My agent, Abi Fellows, is a remarkable person and I feel lucky to have her on my side. Thanks for everything, Abi, and to all at DHH Literary Agency. And a huge thank you to my super-talented editor, Peyton Stableford, who immediately saw the darkness at the heart of this book (and helped me make it even more twisted). Along with my Publicity Manager, the wonderful Polly Grice, they're an absolute joy to work with. And to the rest of the Head of Zeus team for their support: Jo Liddiard, Andrew Knowles and Zoe Giles in marketing; Karen Dobbs, Vicki Eddison and Dan Groenewald in sales; and Simon Michele and Jessie Price for creating the cover. And to everyone else at Head of Zeus and Bloomsbury who worked on this book.

A couple of credits where due: Lisa Marks for her help in locating a good map of old Hollywood. All the places mentioned existed (some still do), apart from Ralph's, the All-Nite Bar and the cinema on Melrose Avenue, which are fiction. April Brooks Clemmer (@aprilshollywood) for her excellent zoom talk on early Hollywood estates, with wonderful detail on Yamashiro, the Japanese palace high in the Hollywood hills (now a restaurant I'm determined to visit). Make-up artist Erin Parsons (@erinparsonsmakeup) whose social media is packed with tales of vintage make-up and movie-star beauty tricks.

Thank you to my writing pals in the CoT group, who make me laugh on a weekly basis, on our Friday zooms (better than therapy). To the Curtis Brown Creative gang of 2015. And to my constant good friends – I'm grateful to be surrounded by excellent women: Nicole Carmichael, Helen Gent, Rosalind Lowe, Alison Lusuardi, Vicky Mayer and Sat Wilks. Extra-special thanks to two extra-special people: my cousin, Anna Kioufi, who's always there for me, especially when the drama hits, and Andrew, whose willingness to talk about my book *yet again* over dinner is never taken for granted. And finally, my lovely sons, Ryan and Aaron, and their amazing women, Andrea, Melanie and the mighty Mia, who this book is dedicated to. I can't wait to see what you do in this world.

READING GROUP
QUESTIONS

Contains spoilers

1. Why do you think Ginny is so drawn to Max Whitman? What does he represent?

   a. How much is Ginny a victim of events and at what point could things have taken a different turn? Is she naïve or an optimist? What would you have done in her position?

   b. Is Ginny really in love with Max? And is he in love with her?

2. Why do you think Stella is so ready to trust Maggie? What does she represent?

3. Think about all the main players: Ginny, Stella, Maggie, Max and Stan. What did you think of them all at the start of the book and how did those feelings change? Which character undergoes the biggest change, and how?

4. Monty Summers, the doctor at the heart of Ginny's disappearance, says he has 'no choice' to do what he does. Do you agree?

5. The precarious nature of chasing fame is referred

to several times in this book. Despite the hardship and danger faced by young starlets, why do Ginny and Cynthia and Sandy continue in their quest? What's at stake if they succeed – or fail?

6.   This story is inspired by true Hollywood crimes and scandals. How does this real-life element affect the way you feel about the book?

7.   What are the similarities and differences between this story and the stories of Harvey Weinstein and the MeToo movement?

8.   Compare the experiences of Stella and Max after their divorce. How do they differ and what does this say about Hollywood?

9.   Monty says that Hollywood loves badly behaved women, but only on the screen. How do you feel about the celebrities you admire? Would you forgive them for anything?

ABOUT THE AUTHOR

ELENI KYRIACOU is an award-winning editor and journalist. Her writing has appeared in the *Guardian*, the *Observer*, *Grazia*, and *Red*, among others. She's the daughter of Greek Cypriot immigrant parents, and her most recent novel, *The Unspeakable Acts of Zina Pavlou*, was selected as a BBC *Between the Covers* book club pick.

Follow her on
@EleniKWriter and www.elenikwriter.com.